CW01346282

The Revels Plays COMPANION LIBRARY

SARAH DUSTAGHEER, PETER KIRWAN, DAVID MCINNIS and LUCY MUNRO
general editors

SUSAN BROCK, SUSAN CERASANO, PETER CORBIN, PAUL EDMONDSON,
E. A. J. HONIGMANN, GRACE IOPPOLO, J. R. MULRYNE and
ROBERT SMALLWOOD
former editors

For over fifty years *The Revels Plays* has provided for students of early modern English drama carefully edited texts of major and lesser-known plays of the period. *The Revels Plays Companion Library* aims to complement and expand upon the work of *The Revels Plays* through pioneering new research into the background, context, and afterlives of these plays and their authors.

The *Companion Library* aims to publish work that will enable students of early modern drama to examine the achievements of dramatists from a broader perspective, while supporting the work of editors through the development of contextual knowledge and new theoretical frameworks. The series includes volumes of a variety of kinds, from new editions of important primary documents to critical monographs and edited collections on authors and topics pertinent to *The Revels Plays*. Together, the two series offer a foundational base for new scholarship on early modern drama.

To buy or to find out more about the books currently available in this series, please go to: https://manchesteruniversitypress.co.uk/series/revels-plays-companion-library/

Thomas Nashe and literary performance

Manchester University Press

THE REVELS PLAYS COMPANION LIBRARY

Thomas Nashe and literary performance

Edited by Chloe Kathleen Preedy and Rachel Willie

MANCHESTER UNIVERSITY PRESS

Copyright © Manchester University Press 2024

While copyright in the volume as a whole is vested in Manchester University Press, copyright in individual chapters belongs to their respective authors, and no chapter may be reproduced wholly or in part without the express permission in writing of both author and publisher.

Published by Manchester University Press
Oxford Road, Manchester, M13 9PL

www.manchesteruniversitypress.co.uk

British Library Cataloguing-in-Publication Data
A catalogue record for this book is available from the British Library

ISBN 978 1 5261 4946 6 hardback

First published 2024

The publisher has no responsibility for the persistence or accuracy of URLs for any external or third-party internet websites referred to in this book, and does not guarantee that any content on such websites is, or will remain, accurate or appropriate.

Typeset
by New Best-set Typesetters Ltd

CONTENTS

LIST OF FIGURES — page vi
GENERAL EDITORS' PREFACE — vii
NOTES ON CONTRIBUTORS — viii
A NOTE ON DATING AND SPELLING — xi
ACKNOWLEDGEMENTS — xii
ABBREVIATIONS — xiv

INTRODUCTION: WHY NASHE? WHY NOW? – Chloe Kathleen Preedy and Rachel Willie — 1

1 'FRISKING ... ALOFT': THE PNEUMATIC SPIRITS OF THOMAS NASHE'S 'PAPER STAGE' – Chloe Kathleen Preedy — 23

2 A FLOOD IN A FURROW: NASHE, NEWS, AND MONSTROUS TOPICALITY – Kirsty Rolfe — 43

3 TEXTUAL SUPERFICIALITY AND SURFACE READING IN NASHE'S PROSE – Douglas Clark — 67

4 'WHEN PRINTS ARE SET ON WORK, WITH GREENS & NASHES': NASHE'S 'POPULARITY' REVISITED – Lena Liapi — 88

5 THOMAS NASHE AND HIS TERRORS OF THE AFTERLIFE – Chris Salamone — 107

6 THOMAS NASHE AND THE VIRTUAL COMMUNITY OF ENGLISH WRITERS – Kate De Rycker — 127

7 THOMAS NASHE BEYOND THE GRAVE – Rachel Willie — 147

AFTERWORD – Jennifer Richards — 169

BIBLIOGRAPHY — 178
INDEX — 201

LIST OF FIGURES

4.1 Comparative extents of works by Nashe, Greene, and sermon-writers *page* 93
7.1 *Mar-Martine* title page. From *Mar-Martine*. London: [s.n.], 1589 149

GENERAL EDITORS' PREFACE

Since the late 1950s the series known as The Revels Plays has provided for students of the English Renaissance drama carefully edited texts of the major Elizabethan and Jacobean plays. The series includes some of the best-known drama of the period and has continued to expand, both within its original field and, to a lesser extent, beyond it, to include some important plays from the earlier Tudor and from the Restoration periods. The Revels Plays Companion Library is intended to further this expansion and to allow for new developments.

The series includes volumes of a variety of kinds. Through monographs and collections of essays, the series presents new critical interpretations of the literary and performance culture of the period. Other volumes provide a fuller context for the plays of the period by offering new collections of documentary evidence on Elizabethan theatrical conditions and on the performance of plays during that period and later. A third aim of the series is to support the overall Revels enterprise through the publication of editions of masques, pageants and the non-dramatic work of Elizabethan and Jacobean playwrights, as well as small collections of plays by a single author or grouped by theme, edited in accordance with the principles of textual modernisation of The Revels Plays. Taken as a whole, The Revels Plays Companion Library supplements and extends the work of the overall Revels enterprise.

SARAH DUSTAGHEER
PETER KIRWAN
DAVID MCINNIS
LUCY MUNRO

NOTES ON CONTRIBUTORS

Douglas Clark is a Researcher at the University of Galway. His work has recently appeared in the journals *Renaissance Drama*, *Studies in Philology*, and *Women's Writing*. His first book, *The Will in English Renaissance Drama*, will be published by Cambridge University Press. In summer 2024, he will be a residential research fellow at the Folger Shakespeare Library.

Kate De Rycker is a lecturer in Renaissance literature at Newcastle University. She is an associate editor of the *Works of Thomas Nashe* (Oxford University Press, forthcoming) for which she is editing *The Terrors of the Night*, and a general editor of *The Oxford Handbook of Thomas Nashe* (Oxford University Press, forthcoming). She has published on Nashe and his engagement with the Italian controversialist Pietro Aretino in *English Literary Renaissance* and on the English reception of Aretino as a writer of urban experience in *Renaissance Studies*, a special issue on 'Aretino's Cityscapes' which she co-edited with William T. Rossiter. Her research interests are in early modern print culture, the growth of professional authorship, and precarity in both the early modern and contemporary period.

Lena Liapi is an Honorary Research Fellow in Early Modern History at Keele University. Her research focuses on cultures of communication, print, and the cultural history of crime in early modern England. She has published a monograph titled *Roguery in Print: Crime and Culture in Early Modern London* (Boydell & Brewer, 2019), as well as articles and chapters on news, crime, and the public sphere. She is currently working on a new project, 'News in Conflict: Cultures of Communication in England and France, 1688–1720'.

Chloe Preedy is an Associate Professor in Early Modern Drama at the University of Exeter. She is the author of *Marlowe's Literary Scepticism:*

NOTES ON CONTRIBUTORS   ix

Politic Religion and Post-Reformation Polemic (Bloomsbury, 2013), which won the Roma Gill Prize in 2015; and of *Representing Aerial Environments on the Early Modern Stage: Theatres of the Air, 1576–1609* (Oxford University Press, 2023), which she wrote while leading the AHRC-funded project *Atmospheric Theatre: Open-Air Performance and the Environment* (2018–21). Her co-produced Arden Early Modern Drama edition of Christopher Marlowe's *The Jew of Malta* was published in 2022 and she recently co-edited a special issue 'On Air' for the journal *Performance Research*.

Jennifer Richards, FBA, FEA, is the English (2001) Professor, University of Cambridge. She was previously the Joseph Cowen Chair of English Literature at Newcastle University until 2023. She is the author of several books, most recently *Voices and Books in the English Renaissance: A New History of Reading* (Oxford University Press, 2019), which won the European Society for the Study of English (ESSE) biennial award for Literatures in the English Language (2020). She is a general editor of the *Works of Thomas Nashe* (Oxford University Press, forthcoming), and the lead of the AHRC-funded *Thomas Nashe Project*. She is co-leading a new collaboration funded by the Leverhulme Trust with literary scholars, musicologists, software engineers, and bio-environmental scientists: *Bee-ing Human*.

Kirsty Rolfe is University Lecturer in English Literature at Leiden University. She is currently an associate editor on the Thomas Nashe project, for which she is editing Thomas Nashe's *The Anatomie of Absurditie* as part of the *Works of Thomas Nashe* (Oxford University Press, forthcoming). She has an ongoing interest in the theory and practice of scholarly editing, in particular how it relates to gender and precarity, and is currently working on an article about editing early modern anti-woman texts from a feminist perspective. In addition her research focuses on international networks of textual transmission and Protestant confessional sympathy in the first half of the seventeenth century. She has published articles on plague and on military news reports, and is currently working on a book about news, providence, and emotion in the Thirty Years War.

Christopher Salamone is a Supernumerary Fellow in English at Mansfield College, University of Oxford. His research explores the representation and rhetorical function of ghosts in early modern literature and textual afterlives more generally. Recent publications in this area include '"Las sir! I'm no Ghost": The Misprision of Spectral Presence in Caroline Drama' in *Arrêt sur scène* (2022) and '"I Am Not Here": Staging the (Un)Dead and the Thresholds of Theatrical Performance', in *Dramatic Apparitions and Theatrical Ghosts*, ed. Anne C. Hall and Alan Nadel (Bloomsbury, 2023). Forthcoming publications include an essay on Nashe's seventeenth-century textual hauntings for *The Oxford Handbook of Thomas Nashe*, ed. Andrew Hadfield, Jennifer Richards and Kate De Rycker (Oxford University Press, 2025). His interest in textual afterlives extends to Shakespeare's reception and mediation in the eighteenth century, the subject of his forthcoming first monograph, *Shakespeare and the Eighteenth-Century Miscellany* (Taylor & Francis, 2024), as well as an article in *Eighteenth-Century Life* (2017), exploring the fragmentation of Shakespeare's works across eighteenth-century poetic miscellanies.

Rachel Willie is Reader in Early Modern Literary Studies at Liverpool John Moores University. Her monograph *Staging the Revolution: Drama, Reinvention and History 1647–72* (Manchester University Press, 2015) was shortlisted for the University English Early Career Book Prize 2016. With Kevin Killeen and Helen Smith, she has co-edited *The Oxford Handbook of the Bible in Early Modern England, c. 1520–1700* (Oxford University Press, 2015; winner of the Roland H. Bainton Prize in Reference Works 2016), with Gábor Gelléri, *Travel and Conflict in the Early Modern World* (Routledge, 2020), and, with Emma Depledge, a special issue of *Huntington Library Quarterly* on 'Performance and the Paper Stage' (2022). From 2019 to 2021, she was Principal Investigator on the AHRC-funded research network *Soundscapes in the Early Modern World*.

A NOTE ON DATING AND SPELLING

In accordance with current scholarly practice we have silently amended the calendar year to begin on 1 January and not 25 March as was the custom in seventeenth-century England. Days of the year refer to Julian calendar dating as this was the calendar used in England at the time; England did not subscribe to the Gregorian calendar that was (and is) used by many of its continental neighbours until the eighteenth century. In presenting quotations we have retained original spelling and punctuation but normalised j/i and u/v, in line with current scholarly practice. In referencing early printed books, the first citation in the notes to each chapter gives the full entry in original spelling and all further citations adopt the standardised title the work is known under today. Short Title Catalogue numbers have generally been included only in the bibliography: the exception to this rule is where more than one edition of the same text is discussed.

ACKNOWLEDGEMENTS

This collection had its genesis in a conversation in York in 2011. At this time a shared interest in the works of Thomas Nashe led Tamsin Badcoe, Chloe Preedy, Lena Liapi, and Rachel Willie (who had previously studied together at the University of York) to submit a proposal for a joint panel on 'Nashe's Public Travels: Past, Present and Future' to the organisers of the 2012 Reading Conference in Early Modern Studies. The proposal was accepted and Michelle O'Callaghan was kind enough to chair the resulting panel session. After preparing our research papers and discussing Nashe with other conference attenders, many of whom shared our view that Nashe's writings were underrepresented within literary criticism at that time, our initial interest grew into plans for an edited volume on Nashe that eventually developed into the current volume. Since 2012 there has been something of a resurgence of interest in Nashe's works, as discussed in our introduction. We have very much enjoyed witnessing that revival, and relished the opportunity to collate a volume that will complement and extend the exciting research, teaching, and editorial developments that have reshaped Nashe studies over the last decade, and which will bring Nashe's works to new readers and continue to promote fresh insights into his texts in the years to come.

The current volume is the product of significant collaboration between both the listed contributors, to whom we are immediately indebted, and various Nashe experts who kindly shared their insights into and experiences of working with these texts. Tamsin remained a supportive and insightful source of advice and informal editorial input throughout, as together we found the balance between our ambitions for the planned volume and our other responsibilities, while Lena developed her conference paper into a foundational chapter for the proposed collection. As our plans developed, we were fortunate to gather a wonderful group of contributors, whose work you will find represented in the current volume. Other academic colleagues were generous in sharing their thoughts on Nashe with us along the way, including Joseph Black. Jennifer Richards was not only an incisive and enthusiastic commentator as we sketched our initial proposal but also kindly agreed to contribute the afterword to this collection. Of course no academic book can reach print without the generous support of many people and institutions. In addition to those named above we have benefited from the expert assistance and advice of the Huntington Library's digital research team and of various colleagues within our departments when preparing this volume. The Research Institute for Literature and Cultural History at Liverpool John Moores University generously funded the employment of a research intern to undertake the indexing for this volume, and we are grateful to them for this assistance and to Philippa Earle for her excellent work in preparing the index. Finally, special thanks are due to Matthew Frost at Manchester University Press, who took an interest in our initial proposal and has been a brilliant source of advice and support throughout. It has been a pleasure to work with Matthew and the other members of MUP's publishing team, and we are delighted to have this opportunity to thank Matthew for his good humour and for everything that he has done for the field of early modern studies during his time at MUP.

ABBREVIATIONS

ELH   *English Literary History*
ELR   *English Literary Renaissance*
EMLS   *Early Modern Literary Studies*
MLQ   *Modern Language Quarterly*
ODNB *Oxford Dictionary of National Biography* (Oxford: Oxford University Press, 2022). https://www.oxforddnb.com/
OED   *Oxford English Dictionary Online* (Oxford: Oxford University Press, 2019). https://www.oed.com
PMLA *Publication of the Modern Languages Association of America*
SEL   *Studies in English Literature, 1500–1900*
STC   *A Short-Title Catalogue of Books Printed in England, Scotland, & Ireland and of English Books Printed. Abroad 1475–1640*. 2nd edition. First compiled by A. W. Pollard and G. R. Redgrave, and revised and enlarged by W. A. Jackson, F. S. Ferguson, and K. F. Panzer (London: London Bibliographical Society, 1976–91)
Wing *A Short-Title Catalogue of Books Printed in England, Scotland, Ireland, Wales, and British America, and of English Books Printed in Other Countries, 1641–1700*. Compiled by Donald Wing. 2nd edition. Revised and enlarged. 4 vols (New York, 1972–98)
YES   *Yearbook of English Studies*

INTRODUCTION: WHY NASHE? WHY NOW?

Chloe Kathleen Preedy and Rachel Willie

As he flees captivity with his lover Diamante, the English protagonist of Thomas Nashe's *The Unfortunate Traveller* (1594) 'couragiously rob[s]' the Italian courtesan who tormented them.[1] Jack Wilton's mock-heroic framing of their revenge indirectly interrogates both imperial Rome's legacy and the cultural values promoted by early modern humanist authorities, as the fictional page muses that antiquarians 'mistooke' the ancient proverb '*Dimicandum est pro aris & focis*: for it should have been *pro auro & fama*: not for altares and fires we must contend, but for gold and fame'.[2] This revisionist message complements earlier passages in *The Unfortunate Traveller* that interrogate the relationship between print publication and Pietro Aretino's 'corrupted fame', complicating his creator Nashe's existing commitment to a 'penniless' public persona through an intersecting emphasis on the implications for one's posthumous reputation.[3] As Kate De Rycker has demonstrated, such issues preoccupied Nashe through his writing career, but his concerns were exacerbated by his ongoing rivalry with the Cambridge scholar Gabriel Harvey.[4] By 1592 Nashe was denouncing Harvey as 'a forestaller of the market of fame', characterising his latest textual salvo against Harvey as a martial action that would be presided over by a new patron deity: 'Saint Fame for mee, and thus I runne upon him'.[5] The implied inter-reliance of transactional and reputational success signals that, despite the canonising address and mock-chivalric imagery, Nashe's Saint Fame can – as Matthew Steggle argues – be best understood as a periphrasis for 'public opinion', with the 'public' in question comprised of those who consume Nashe's printed works and those who will remember him after his death.[6]

Associations between fame and opinion were already present within the classical iconography of *fama*, or Rumour.[7] However, the contemporary implications of Nashe's appeal to 'the market of fame' were not missed by his Elizabethan detractors.[8] Harvey's response, *Pierce's Supererogation* (1593), stretched Nashe's brief allusion into a heavy-handed threat by implying that his own present work was merely '*A Preparative to certaine larger Discourses, intituled* Nashes s. fame':

> Rest you quiet; and I will not onely not struggle with you for a tytle; but offer here to renounce the whole advantage of a late inquisition, upon a clamorous denunciation of S. Fame herselfe: who presumed she might be as bould to play the blab with you, as you were to play the sloven with her.[9]

There is no evidence that the advertised sequel was ever published, despite Harvey's claims to have '*Nashes S. Fame*' already 'finished in writing, and ... almost dispatched in Print'.[10] Yet Harvey's various allusions suggest a mock-encomium in the style of Desiderius Erasmus's *Praise of Folly* (1511) or François Rabelais's *Gargantua and Pantagruel* (1532–64): Nashe's 'Idoll', whom Harvey compares mockingly to Sir Gargantua, is for instance envisaged placing a 'wispen garland over her powting Croscloth' and 'riding in the ducking-chariot of her Triumphe' into a textual combat that will leave her 'utterly undone'.[11] Harvey's depiction of a Saint Fame who controls Nashe as her 'blacke *Sanctus*' seeks to exploit his Protestant readers' presumed antagonism towards anything that might suggest Catholic sympathies, as well as inherited classical and medieval anxieties (often expressed in similarly gendered and misogynistic terms) about the fine line between good and bad *fama*.[12] Harvey also spares a moment to target Nashe's transactional approach to the 'market of fame', accusing 'Tom Drumme' of being as 'Penniles a person of any reckoning, as he is a man of notorious fame': that is, of criminal notoriety.[13] Such sustained mockery apparently struck a nerve, with the Respondent of Nashe's *Have With You to Saffron Walden* (1596) promising that 'if I doo not (in requitall of S. Fame) ensaint and canonize him for the famousest Paliard and Senior Penaquila, that hath breathed since the raigne of S. Tor, let all the droppings of my pen bee seazed upon by the Queenes Takers for Tarre'.[14]

For all Nashe's belligerence, his anxiety about his posthumous reception seems prophetic in hindsight. Nashe's reputation has on the whole fared better than Harvey's, but he and his works spent many years consigned to the ranks of the so-called 'minor' Elizabethans.[15] Even his great nineteenth-century editor Alexander B. Grosart observed deprecatingly that 'as one turns back upon the now completed Works, one feels that the Man is too shadowy ... and the Writings too hasty and unsubstantive, for anything like elaborate criticism or estimate'.[16] Meanwhile, C. S. Lewis's assessment that 'if asked what Nashe "says" we should' ('[i]n a certain sense of the verb') 'have to reply, Nothing', has long troubled Nashe scholars.[17] In recent decades, however, the many qualities of Nashe's writings – including their allusiveness and resistance to narrow definitions of literary 'substance' – have increasingly been championed. By the end of the twentieth century important studies by Jonathan Crewe and Lorna Hutson had started to elevate Nashe's reputation, as the rise of New Historicism, New Materialism, and Poststructuralism displaced the more restrictive "Golden Age" narratives once favoured by critics such as Lewis.[18] By the start of the twenty-first, as Steve Mentz observes in *The Age of Thomas Nashe* (2013), Nashe was finding favour among readers interested in 'print culture and the history of the book; histories of sexuality and pornography; urban culture; the changing nature of patronage, including theatrical patronage; polemic and "cheap print"; religious controversy; and evolving definitions of authorship and even "literature" as such'.[19] Such themes remain central to Nashe's critical reception, with recent studies comprehending Elizabethan proto-imperialism and violence against the body, attitudes towards employment and public activity, Nashe's involvement with early modern theatrical culture, and religious and medical responses to the ever-present threat of plague.[20] Moreover, while Nashe's works continue to be regarded as 'difficult to teach', there is reason to hope that his presence on early modern literature courses will become more secure in the decades to come, especially since the challenge of teaching Nashe without access to affordable, up-to-date editions will be somewhat mitigated by Joseph Black, Andrew Hadfield, Jennifer Richards, and Cathy Shrank's planned six-volume critical edition of Nashe's works.[21] Indeed there is much in Nashe's work that, despite his many historically specific allusions, might also resonate suggestively in our media-conscious present, including Nashe's concern for his public image and reception, attention to the mostly unregulated dissemination of self-perpetuating discourse within a commercial sphere, and satirical takes on prevalent social and cultural expectations.

NEWS, PERFORMANCE, AND THE MARKETPLACE OF PRINT

In the 1970s J. B. Steane could confidently comment on Nashe's status as a minor Elizabethan writer who deserved greater recognition than he is given as a 'formidable controversialist' and a 'lively ... Elizabethan journalist'.[22] Fifty years on, our understanding of what constitutes 'minor' and 'controversialist' and even 'Elizabethan journalist' feels less secure. While Crewe, Hutson, Mentz, and others unpicked the assumption that Nashe was a minor poet to rehabilitate him to the point that Andrew Hadfield and Jennifer Richards can assert 'Nashe not only shaped English literature as we understand it today but also expanded its range and possibilities', other scholars were turning their attention to news, cheap print, and popular culture.[23] Taking 1588, 1642, and 1688 as snapshots, Joad Raymond illustrates how the kinds of news that was sold at a bookseller in St Paul's Churchyard would look very different at each of these points in history. In 1588 the focus would primarily be on news from continental Europe. News turned to domestic politics in the mid-seventeenth century, when tensions between king and Parliament escalated, leading to civil war, regicide, a brief republic before the restoration of the monarchy and then the so-called 'glorious revolution' to replace the monarch with his daughter and son-in-law/nephew. During Nashe's early years, and before 1580, printed domestic news was rare and much of the printed news was in the form of ballads.[24] As the seventeenth century progressed, printed news circulation became more common and with the outbreak of civil war a number of mercurial pamphlets emerged. But news circulation and identifying what was newsworthy led to anxieties about what kinds of information ought to circulate in the commonwealth; this anxiety was something which, as Kirsty Rolfe notes in Chapter 2 below, Nashe would tap into as these new forms of news circulation began to emerge in the sixteenth century.[25] News and its circulation fed into wider discourses about who had the right of access to news as models for literary patronage began to fracture.

Following the dissolution of the monasteries in the late 1530s, Graham Parry argues, literary patronage was primarily in the gift of the nobility. An author might receive a small sum of money from the printers for producing the text but their main source of income would be from a generous, stingy or erratic patron. As the Elizabethan period progressed, more and more writers attempted to make a living by the pen and patronage consequently became more fragmented and diffuse.[26] Nashe may have received £5 for dedicating *Christ's Tears over Jerusalem* (1593) to Elizabeth Carey, but at other times he bitterly bemoaned the lack of financial return that could be gained from writing.[27] Playwrights could expect to receive from an acting company between £5 and £8 for a play and 40s for contributing to or revising a play.[28] Conversely, pamphlets were neither lucrative nor well-esteemed. Yet many writers wrote pamphlets and many of these writers were also concerned with an English literary culture where they celebrated and derided their contemporaries in print. The 'private Epistle of the Author to the Printer, Wherein his full meaning and purpose (in publishing this Booke) is set foorth', which prefaces Nashe's *Pierce Pennniless His Supplication to the Devil* (1592), is framed as a private letter yet is intended for public consumption.[29] It comprises much of the literary conventions of the reluctant author distressed by the unintended publication of a work. Privacy is underscored by the insistence that the letter is a private epistle yet its publication means it ventures forth into the public realm.[30] The defence of the work also underscores its place within the public sphere:

INTRODUCTION 5

Faith I am verie sorrie (Sir) I am thus unawares betrayed to infamie. You write to me my booke is hasting to the second impression: he that hath once broke the Ice of impudence, neede not care how deepe he wade in discredit ... If it have found any friends, so it is, you knowe very wel that it was abroad a fortnight ere I knewe of it, & uncorrected and unfinished, it hath offred it selfe to the open scorne of the world.[31]

The opening to the epistle is worth lingering on because of how it positions Nashe's work in the world. It initially appears as the formulaic deprecating approach to printing and publication that is a feature of such letters to the printer. However, the tone is more forceful and characteristic of the hectoring and railing style for which Nashe became well known. The apology is not directed outward to the reading public that will receive the imperfect copy but instead focuses inward to the aggrieved subject. The impudent printer circulated Nashe's work before he could correct the copy and the unfinished book has made Nashe the subject of infamy. Performative disdain permeates the preface, as it does the text where the impoverished writer Pierce Penniless laments his lack of fortune. The metatextual concern with print culture also embraces literary patronage as the writer/patron Sir Philip Sidney is mourned and lesser scholars are judged unfit to inherit his crown. But Nashe is not only focused upon print production, circulation, and patronage; his distressed print persona also intersperses railing against vice with defences of poetry and plays. What emerges is a rich, part-fabricated, literary community that embraces print culture, theatrical culture, and celebrated writers and actors.

Of course Nashe is primarily known as a 'proser', but Jennifer Richards has recently drawn attention to the performability and 'live moments' of Nashe's prose style.[32] In so doing Richards does not negate Nashe's literary qualities and nor does she conflate the very specific stylistic subtleties of printed prose and dramatic performance. Instead Richards invites us to think more critically about the relationship between print and voice. The tonal registers adopted by Nashe highlight the importance of breath and the need to regulate the voice, whether in reading aloud, or in projecting an actor's part, or in singing. In Chapter 1 below Choe Preedy analyses the 'pneumatic substance' of Nashe's work, underscoring how breath is fundamental to the material production of Nashe's 'new stile'.[33] Yet it was this new style – the 'straunge fancies' and 'monstrous newfanglednesse' – that Harvey most vociferously decried.[34]

In this battle of the university wits Harvey perhaps came off least well, but both writers presented a literary persona to the reading public and both writers were also intensely concerned with what form English should take as a literary language. 'Like Nashe', Samuel Fallon writes, 'Harvey was interested in regulating the disorderly, often disreputable literary productions of English print writers'.[35] While this dispute between Nashe and Harvey is thus firmly embedded within literary production, it might have had its origins in topical religio-political disputes. John Lyly hinted that someone in the Harvey circle was behind the Marprelate pamphlets – six pamphlets printed between October 1588 and September 1589 that attacked episcopal worship, the Elizabethan Church Settlement, and the Archbishop of Canterbury, John Whitgift (1530–1604, Archbishop of Canterbury from 1583). Although the Marprelate controversy was, as Jason Scott-Warren notes, where Nashe 'cut his teeth' as a professional writer, Lyly and Harvey also wrote pamphlets in support of the bishops.[36] The aspersion that Harvey had a connection to the Martinists thus hit a nerve and Gabriel Harvey's brother, Richard, struck back with *A Theological Discourse of the Lamb of God and His Enemies* (1590). Here Richard Harvey attacked Lyly and condemned Nashe for his criticism of prominent writers in the preface to Robert Greene's *Menaphon* (1589). Nashe retaliated by criticising *Lamb of God* in *Pierce Penniless* and in the same year Greene ridiculed the Harveys in his *Quip for an Upstart Courtier* (1592). Gabriel Harvey then focused his ire on Greene, with a 'cameo' condemnation of Nashe in *Four Letters* (1592). By the time *Four Letters* was printed, Greene had died and it was left to Nashe to respond, which he did in *Strange News* (1592), at which Gabriel Harvey fired back *Pierce's Supererogation*. Nashe attempted to call a ceasefire with his 1593 preface to *Christ's Tears*, but Harvey rejected (or was oblivious to) the attempt at a truce and went on the attack with *A New Letter of Notable Contents* (1593); Nashe responded by retracting his overture through revising the preface to *Christ's Tears* (1594). After a break of two years, Nashe then printed his extended response, *Have With You to Saffron Walden* (1596), to which the addressee of *Have With You*, a Cambridge barber named 'Richard Lichfield', supposedly retorted through printing *The Trimming of Thomas Nashe* (1597). Eventually the dispute came to an end when Archbishop Whitgift and Richard Bancroft (1544–1610), Bishop of London, ordered the destruction of a list of books, which included those by Nashe and Harvey, and decreed that no further editions be printed.[37]

What becomes abundantly clear from this brief chronology of the Nashe–Harvey dispute is the rapidity of the production of text.[38] Nashe's apology in the preface to *Christ's Tears* did not reach Harvey until after *Pierce's Supererogation* and *New Letter* had been received by Harvey's printer, John Wolfe. Some have suspected that Wolfe, keen to cash in on the quarrel, might have engineered the situation to mean that Harvey did not have the opportunity to retract.[39] This draws attention not only to the mechanics of the virtual communities created in ink but also to the role of the printing press in the marketplace of print. On the one hand the Nashe–Harvey dispute was a petty squabble between writers who perceived themselves to be on opposing sides in a quarrel over literary aesthetics, but on the other hand the argument asks us to interrogate what literary style embodies in vernacular languages in the late sixteenth century. These forms of writing would continue to impact and inflect print production, and also illustrated an anxiety over how writing would be received and consumed after the death of the author. As Rachel Willie notes in Chapter 7 below, during the climactic years that flanked the outbreak of civil war in 1642, John Taylor the Water Poet imagined the ghost of Thomas Nashe offering a spectral commentary on contemporary anxieties in church and state.[40] Through his association with the Marprelate controversy, Nashe's literary persona continues to be invoked as an arbiter into the seventeenth century. Yet it was less as a literary author that Nashe's spirt was summoned and more as a literary dramatist: perhaps Harvey's most famous assault on Nashe was to liken Pierce Penniless to Richard Tarlton, an Elizabethan clown famous for, among other things, his abilities as a caustic extemporiser.[41] In dismissing Nashe's abilities as an author Harvey denies that Nashe's writings form part of a textual community; through being disassociated from the page, Nashe's extemporising words have greater affinity with verbal utterances on the stage. Nashe's prose style is thus presented as nebulous, sitting at the hinterland of the stage and page and operating within a live textual environment that is fully anchored to neither the page nor to the stage.

NASHE THE DRAMATIST

Harvey's dismissive characterisation of Nashe's style exploited associations that Nashe had already hinted at. The latter's most familiar print persona, the 'distressed Orator Pierce Penilesse', connects textual prodigality to urban leisure activities that include not only dancing, dicing, and drinking, but also playgoing.[42] This satirical spokesperson's report that the London-based 'vagrant Reveller' and 'unthrift' 'haunts Plaies' at once parodies the charges levelled against English commercial drama by its contemporary detractors and hints at Nashe's close involvement with the theatre.[43] The only surviving dramatic work that is credited solely to Nashe is *Summer's Last Will and Testament* (pub. 1600). This piece was probably written to entertain Archbishop Whitgift's Croydon-based guests while the commercial playhouses were closed due to plague in 1592, and is described by its clownish prologue as 'no Play neyther, but a shewe'.[44] Nashe may also have written entertainments for university performance, with one of his print adversaries naming him as the co-author of a controversial lost 'Show', *Terminus & Non Terminus*, that was performed at

St John's College in 1586–87.[45] Yet Nashe was at least equally familiar with the professional playing companies and their paying audiences. He is credited with a lost anti-Martinist play, *The May-Game of Martinism* (1589), which was apparently intended for performance by the Children of Paul's and at the Theatre, and was probably the 'yong Juvenall' who 'writ' an unidentified 'Comedie' with Robert Greene; this comedy might have been *George-a-Greene* or *A Knack to Know a Knave*, though the reference most likely indicates another lost piece.[46]

Collaboration appears to have been central to Nashe's dramatic practice. He co-authored the notoriously scandalous *Isle of Dogs* (1597) with Ben Jonson; is credited alongside Christopher Marlowe on the title page of the satiric children's drama *Dido, Queen of Carthage* (c. 1596–98); and is a likely candidate to have collaborated with Marlowe on *Doctor Faustus* (c. 1588).[47] There is also increasing scholarly agreement that Nashe co-wrote *1 Henry VI* (1592) with William Shakespeare and another playwright, probably contributing the first act of this drama. Moreover Nashe himself discusses his interrupted hopes of 'writing for the stage' in a summer 1596 letter to William Cotton, after London's theatres were closed by the plague and while the Chamberlain's/Lord Hunsdon's Men company was going through a period of upheaval.[48] Nashe's total theatrical output may well have been considerably higher than the eight plays he has been credited with to date; only around a sixth of the roughly three thousand works written by English playwrights between 1567 and 1642 survive today, and it is possible that the targeting of Nashe's satirical writings in the 'Bishops' Ban' of 1599 further reduced the odds of his playtexts surviving.[49] Even without access to more extant plays, interest in Nashe's dramatic output is on the rise. Indeed, the generic, formal, and dramaturgical diversity of the surviving works with which Nashe is most strongly associated today indicates his versatility as a playwright, further enriching our understanding of Elizabethan England's diverse, innovative, and frequently collaborative theatrical culture, as well as Nashe's related involvement in public performance of various kinds.[50]

Nashe's dramatic output has attracted growing attention in recent years, but his own interest in the theatre has long been recognised by critics. *Pierce Penniless* contains one of the period's best-known accounts of playgoing, as Nashe at once champions the civic and martial value of English drama and reflects on the affective force of theatrical experience.[51] In a section ostensibly concerned with the sin of sloth, Pierce characterises playgoing as the most acceptable urban pastime for 'men that are their owne masters (as Gentlemen of the Court, the Innes of the Courte,... Captaines and Souldiers'), being preferable to 'gameing, following of harlots, [or] drinking'.[52] Plays are said to usefully distract those 'certaine waste' 'men' who might otherwise 'make mutinies at home', while providing moral guidance to the apprentices and 'youth of the Cittie' by 'shew[ing] the ill successe of treason, the fall of hastie climbers, the wretched end of usurpers, the miserie of civill dissention, and how just God is evermore in punishing of murther'.[53] Moreover, although Pierce declines to 'handle this Theame otherwise than *obiter* [in passing]', Nashe's fictional spokesperson provides a telling illustration of his claim that plays can provide 'a sharper reproofe to these degenerate effeminate dayes of ours' than the 'worme-eaten bookes' of 'our English Chronicles', demanding:

> How would it have joyed brave Talbot (the terror of the French) to thinke that after he had lyne two hundred yeares in his Tombe, hee should triumphe againe on the Stage, and have his bones newe embalmed with the teares of ten thousand spectators at least (at severall times) who in the Tragedian that represents his person, imagine they behold him fresh bleeding.[54]

The specific reference to representing Talbot, the English hero who features so prominently in the first part of *1 Henry VI*, suggests that Nashe is indulging his fondness for self-citation within a work that was probably published in the same year that the collaborative English history debuted onstage. The present-tense nature of the described experience, which stresses 'Talbot''s 'fresh bleeding' wounds and the flowing 'teares' of the playgoers, is also notable; Nashe's defence of dramatic performance stresses theatre's liveness, as furthered by Pierce's subsequent boast that '[n]ot Roscius nor Æsope those admyred tragedians that have lived ever since before Christ was borne, could ever performe more in action, than famous Ned Allen'.[55] In this sense there is a suggestive continuity between the theatrical qualities that Nashe celebrates and the performative techniques that he utilises in his prose works, whereby moments of immediacy and supposed improvisation are imbued with affective force.

Nashe is most often celebrated today for the linguistic and stylistic innovativeness of his prose writing. As Lena Liapi puts it in her contribution to this collection, his most lasting legacy was, and is, that the name 'Nashe' 'became synonymous with his style'.[56] Yet Nashe's dramatic works would have been noteworthy too for their visual and non-verbal acoustic effects. The fictional Pierce's references to 'behold[ing]' 'spectators' hints that Nashe was more interested than some of his contemporaries in dramatic spectacle, and several of the plays he is associated with contain cues for striking stage effects.[57] In the first act of *1 Henry VI*, for instance, actions including '*the funeral of King Henry the Fifth*', '*hurly-burly*' scuffles between rival English factions, a duel between the French Dauphin Charles and '*Joan*' (better known as Joan of Arc), and military combat between French and English forces complement the play's dialogue allusions to 'undaunted' martial honour and calls for the fictional 'English nobility' to '[a]wake, awake ... Let not sloth dim your honours new begot'.[58] The intensifying threats to English glory that emerge in the opening act are epitomised by the 'witch' Joan, who fights 'clad in armour' amid an analogically evoked 'smoke' and 'noisome stench' that would probably have been a lingering material presence after the previous scene's gunpowder-powered effects (1.5.21, 1.5.3, 1.5.23–4). Existing cultural and theatrical conventions associating sulphur-emitting gunpowder weapons and stage storms with the devil indicate that these devices, which include the violently destructive firing of a 'piece of ordnance' by French gunners and a storm that *'thunders and lightens'* 'in the heavens' (1.4.15, 1.4.96 SD, 1.4.97), could themselves have complemented Talbot's charge that Joan 'serv'st' the devil (1.5.7). Indeed, Chris Salamone demonstrates the extent and depth of Nashe's textual fascination with demonic apparitions and spectres in Chapter 5 below, although the specific episode from *1 Henry VI* in which Joan conjures *'Fiends'* onstage is usually attributed to Nashe and Shakespeare's unidentified co-author rather than Nashe himself (5.2.28 SD).[59]

Nashe displays a comparable interest in visual and nonverbal effects in *Summer's Last Will and Testament*. As the dying Lord of Summer summons his 'officers' in turn 'to count' for 'the wealth I gave them to dispose', each reportedly enters to the accompaniment of music, dancing, or both.[60] Vertumnus's entrance was perhaps the most visually arresting, with the stage directions in Walter Burre's edition describing a *'trayne'* of *'singing'* attendants dressed in *'suites of greene mosse, representing short grasse'*; a *'morris daunce'* featuring *'the Hobby horse'*, which Paul Whitfield White suggests may have been performed by a touring troupe; and a comic sequel of '*3. Clownes, & 3. maids, singing ... [and] daunsing*'.[61] The episode may even have echoed a similar sequence in Nashe's lost play *The May-Game of Martinism*, which Martin Wiggins and Catherine Richardson consider featured 'pageantry, masquing, and a morris dance of Martinists'.[62] Those watching *Summer's Last Will* three years later would next have witnessed the characer of Solstitium entering *'like an aged Hermit, carrying a payre of ballances, with an houre-glasse in eyther of them'*, and accompanied *'by a number of shepherds, playing upon Recorders'*; a *'verie richly attir'de'* Sol, preceded by *'a noyse of Musicians'*; Orion and his fellow hunters *'hallowing, and blowing their hornes'*; Harvest singing *'with a sythe on his neck'*; and, in another potentially memorable sequence, *'Bacchus riding upon an Asse trapt in Ivie, himselfe drest in Vine leaves, and a garland of grapes on his head'*.[63] This emphasis on spectacle and acoustic effects complements Nashe's ongoing thematic defence of 'high dayes and solemne festivals', which associates a love of entertainment and elaborate display with unstinting hospitality.[64] Conversely Christmas's miserly insistence that 'the god of hospitality' 'is now growne out of fashion' is anticipated by the character's entrance, with Nashe's text suggesting that he and his 'raging' brother Back-winter 'com'st not as the rest, / Accompanied with some musique, or some song'.[65] At the same time, as White argues, the lavish appearance of the other characters (and, by implication, of the show itself) is itself subjected to indirect scrutiny: the claims made by Christmas convey a pointed and potentially risky critique of those landlords who 'feede the poore twelve dayes, & let them starve all the yeare after', or 'like the Sybarites, do nothing all one yeare, but bid ghestes against the next'.[66]

It is virtually certain that the lost *Isle of Dogs* engaged in a more extended and provocative satire of Elizabethan attitudes, and perhaps of individuals. Contemporaries described Jonson and Nashe's play as 'lewd', 'seditious', and 'slanderous', prompting an investigation by the Privy Council: Jonson and two of the play's actors were imprisoned in the Marshalsea for several months, while Nashe fled to Yarmouth to escape arrest.[67] Reflecting on this experience in *Lenten Stuff* (1599), Nashe laments the 'straunge turning of the Ile of Dogs, from a commedie to a tragedie', and later denounces those 'of the worser sort' who 'use mens writings like bruite beasts, to make them draw which way they list'.[68] As Douglas Clark argues in Chapter 3 below, however, Nashe's sustained preoccupation with the dangers of misinterpretation often goes hand in hand with prompts for future readers to decipher his work's meaning.[69] The same is true of dramatic texts such as *Summer's Last Will and Testament*, in which Will Summers's asides to the assembled audience members apparently invited them to consider whether 'it [is] pride that is shadowed' by the personation of Sol, the 'two-leg'd Sunne, that never came neerer heaven, then Dubbers hill'; or whether Whitgift's 'court' will agree with this clown of 'small learning' about the 'reason' behind Back-winter's 'rayling part' in the staged entertainment.[70]

Such strategic public disclaimers about the 'meaning' of Nashe's works indirectly acknowledge the extent to which their author engages in potentially provocative social commentary, including within the context of commercial or occasional dramatic performance. In the case of *Summer's Last Will and Testament*, for instance, White argues that the potential to identify the dying Lord of Summer with Nashe's patron Whitgift 'would have been unmistakable', since 'Whitgift, the lord of Croydon manor, would have been seated throughout the performance on a dais in the upper part of the hall, staring ahead at the playing space where Summer is enthroned'.[71] Moreover this entertainment reportedly featured many of the same strategies that Nashe employs in his prose writings to create a sense of immediacy and connection between the fictional narrative and those consuming his work. The self-consciously improvisational style that Nashe adopts in *Pierce Penniless* or *Lenten Stuff* is for instance apparent in the stage direction that calls for the actor playing the clown Will Summers to enter with '*his fooles coate but halfe on, comming out*', as well as in the speech that follows:

> I am a Goose or a Ghost at least; for what with turmoyle of getting my fooles apparell, and care of being perfit, I am sure I have not yet supt to night. Will Summers Ghost I should be, come to present you with Summers last will, and Testament ... God forgive me, I did not see my Lord before. Ile set a good face on it, as though what I had talkt idly all this while, were my part.[72]

The same prologue displays Nashe's characteristically self-conscious performance of authorship, first playing on the affinity between the entertainment's title and Will Summers's own name, and then launching into a tongue-in-cheek critique of its author: 'the Idiot our Playmaker ... [who] like a Foppe & an Asse, must be making himselfe a publike laughing stock, & have no thanke for his labor'.[73] The fictional Summers continues in this vein throughout the show that follows, addressing and interacting with the real-life audience members, the actors, and the fictional characters in ways that punctuate the layers of theatrical performance and stress the porous relationship between them.

Will Summers's ongoing complaints about the length and quality of the performance in which he plays a part presumably enhanced the show's comedic impact. The character's interjections could have also strategically managed the responses of Nashe's real-life playgoers, prompting them to distance themselves from criticisms made by that 'great foole Toy': that is, the actor playing Summers.[74] The technique recalls Nashe's extensive reliance on bracketed asides and rhetorical questions within his prose works, with Summers for instance demanding in closing of the audience: 'How is't? how is't? you that be of the graver sort, do you thinke these youths worthy of a Plaudite for praying for the Queene, and singing of the Letany?'[75]

Within the live context of performance these interjections additionally draw attention to the physical presence of the players. Whereas Summers's report that these 'poore fellowes' 'have bestowed great labour in sowing leaves, and grasse, and strawe, and mosse upon cast suites' playfully mocks the earlier emphasis on display, the prologue's initial charge that the 'Actors ... cleare your throats, blowe your noses, and wype your mouthes e're you enter, that you may take no occasion to spit or to cough' onstage, may have gained a more charged significance within an entertainment performed at a time when a real-life plague epidemic was raging through the nearby city of London.[76] Nashe's dramatic dialogue further couples this 'plague [that] raignes in most places in this latter end of summer' with the danger posed by 'Back-winter or an after winter', casting them as consecutive environmental threats to human health in a manner that might well have concerned Whitgift and his household, especially given the high incidence of severe storms and ruined harvests that Elizabethan England suffered during the 1590s.[77] Moreover, while the risk of a severe winter is deferred within the fictional context through Summers's intervention, the latter's closing bequest of 'my withered flowers, and herbes, / Unto dead corses, for to decke them with' still implies that the plague might threaten the lives of those taking refuge at Croydon.[78] This ominous inference is reinforced by the show's scripted songs, which offer a moving reminder of death's imminence; the repeated line of the penultimate song, 'Lord have mercy on us', echoes the liturgical phrase that was marked on the doors of plague-infected households.[79] Such unsettling tonal shifts between comedy and tragedy are reminiscent of Nashe's practice in prose works such as *The Unfortunate Traveller* and *Christ's Tears over Jerusalem*, as well as his emphasis on drama's affective force within *Pierce Penniless*. In consequence it is unsurprising that, when the fictional, dying Summer confesses that 'thy song hath moved mee', even the clownish Summers (whose status as the 'Ghost' of Henry VIII's real-life fool further hints at death's shadowy presence) agrees, perhaps punningly: 'Lord have mercy on us, how lamentable 'tis'.[80]

INTERPRETING NASHE'S TEXTUAL PERFORMANCES

If the threat of the plague 'haunts' Nashe's 1592 entertainment, it is this textual and stylistic ghosting that defines his wider literary output.[81] As the pieces in this volume illustrate, Nashe's writing is remarkable for both its variety and its allusiveness, as Nashe weaves each new work he produces from the web of his earlier publications in a consciously playful and rejuvenating cycle of publicly performed and self-promotional literary production. In addition the seven chapters in this volume move beyond locating Nashe within the immediacy of 1590s London to demonstrate that Nashe's writing draws from past textual acts and informs future writings in ways that are indebted to the stage and create novel kinds of literary performance. The thematically arranged chapters that follow thus address Nashe's use of the past, his engagement with the Elizabethan present, and his textual legacy.

In his prose works Nashe consistently and self-consciously identifies his writing as 'light', in contrast to the reputedly 'heavy' style of rivals such as Gabriel Harvey. Beginning with a discussion of Nashe's preface to Thomas Newman's 1591 edition of *Astrophel and Stella*, in '"Frisking ... Aloft": The Pneumatic Spirits of Thomas Nashe's "Paper Stage"', Chloe Preedy illustrates how Nashe invoked Mercury – the trickster god of travellers and scholars – to foreground his consciously mercurial prose. What emerges is a discussion of the alchemical quality of Nashe's prose style, in which a literary output that is shown to be 'environmentally embodied' is then disseminated through pneumatic exchanges.[82] Attending to breath, Preedy demonstrates how Nashe implicitly cultivates textual permeability as his writing traverses the typographical boundaries of the printed page.

Nashe's authorial self-representation as a messenger is further complicated by his print denunciations of uncritical news-reading; his mercurial style lays him open to charges of monstrosity, even as he criticises others for their paper monsters. In 'A flood in a furrow: Nashe, news, and monstrous topicality', Kirsty Rolfe begins by outlining late sixteenth-century news culture before focusing on *The Anatomy of Absurdity* (1589) and a 'prodigy' pamphlet entitled *Strange News out of Calabria Prognosticated in the Year 1586, Upon the Year 87*, a collection of prophecies printed in 1587 and attributed to the fictional prophet John Doleta. *The Anatomy of Absurdity* was Nashe's first stand-alone work to reach print and contains a stinging criticism of credulous readers who are taken in by 'news'.[83] Through understanding Nashe's use of early modern stereotypes about news, Rolfe contends, we gain greater insights into the Nashe–Harvey quarrel and how both writers invoked the performability of the page to defend their authorial persona and attack the persona of their textual enemy.

Douglas Clark's chapter, 'Textual superficiality and surface reading in Nashe's prose', complements Rolfe's attention to mercurial permeability and the wider conditions of publication by interrogating the self-conscious materiality of Nashe's own work. Clark considers Nashe's attention to the materiality of his printed texts in light of authorial concerns about the future misconstruction of his works. Focusing on *The Anatomy of Absurdity* and *Lenten Stuff*, Clark considers how the distorted surfaces of 'waste' texts, formal features such as prefaces, and the marketing of literary texts as appetising commodities acquire significance within Nashe's publications.[84] Acknowledging that Nashe's internal commentaries on literary style and reception are often contradictory and even contested, he argues that Nashe deploys his own form of 'surface reading' to defend his texts from superficial interpretation, in a manner that is at once wary of and indebted to a 'surface logic' that privileges outward appearances over inner substance.[85] In the process Clark demonstrates how an increased attentiveness to questions of form and materiality can shed new light on the early modern production, consumption, and reception of printed texts, especially when it comes to the cultural significance that surface reading possessed.

The fraught relationship between 'popular' culture and Nashe's self-representations is directly addressed in '"When prints are set on work, with Greens & Nashes": Nashe's "popularity" revisited', as Lena Liapi reassesses Nashe's reputation as a 'popular' writer or 'hack'.[86] Responding to earlier studies that considered Nashe's writings within the context of the Martin Marprelate controversy, she argues that Nashe's supposedly popular prose works do not necessarily invite a wide readership, since Nashe resisted conventional title-page marketing strategies, deployed literary terms and techniques that restrict the likely audience for his published texts, and authored critical commentaries that seek to distinguish his own writing from that of less educated or articulate contemporaries. At the same time Liapi demonstrates that Nashe uses populist strategies to establish 'a brand name which was not only well known but also employed throughout the early modern period to connote a biting writing style': that is, Nashe was 'popular' in the sense that he and his writings possessed widespread cultural visibility.[87] The role that personal and stylistic notoriety played in Nashe's literary reception importantly qualifies our understanding of what 'print popularity' might mean in the early modern English context, while enriching our appreciation of Nashe's own print performances as a satirist and controversialist.

Chris Salamone revisits the nature of Nashe's authorial legacy, analysing Nashe's articulated ambivalence about the promises and pitfalls of literary remains. Where much recent criticism on Nashe's works remains attuned to his corporeal style and interest in bodily metaphors, Salamone's 'Thomas Nashe and his terrors of the afterlife' instead considers the Elizabethan author's interest in, and rhetorical use of, the insubstantial world of spirits. Noting that '[s]pectres haunt his work thematically and formally', Salamone argues that Nashe's fleshless apparitions often function as a means to figure authorial presence and posthumous reputation.[88] From the detailed commentaries on the spirit world that feature in *Pierce Penniless* and *The Terrors of the Night* (1594) to the spectral presence of dramatic 'ghosts' such as Will Summers and Talbot or the necromantic spirits that attend Cornelius Agrippa in *The Unfortunate Traveller*, Salamone demonstrates how Nashe's fictional spirits prompt readers to confront the relationship not only between the living and the dead but also between the author, the printed text, and that text's readers. Indeed, for Salamone, that imagined future readership extends far beyond the temporal span of Nashe's own lifetime, allowing the Elizabethan author to articulate a conception of the afterlife to come that registers his texts' power to bestow a posthumous existence in which he will remain a 'ghostly absent-presence', haunting their readers as he is haunted by dead colleagues and enemies.[89]

A similar interest in uncanny hauntings informs both Nashe's textual representation of contemporary authors and his own resurrection as a literary celebrity after his death, as Kate De Rycker demonstrates. In 'Thomas Nashe and the virtual community of English writers', De Rycker draws from Derridean theories of textual haunting to illuminate how ghostly visitations were transforming the trope of the literary influence of dead authors into the formation of a virtual community which bridged the divide between living and recently dead English authors. De Rycker explores how Nashe and his fellow professional writers created this virtual community to lay claim to literary respectability, despite their often marginal social status. Nashe not only wrote about the uncanny ability of writing to give an authorial presence to contemporary literary figures but was himself resurrected as a literary celebrity after his death by others, most forcefully in the Cambridge *Parnassus* plays (*c.* 1598–1601) in which Nashe appears both as a character (Ingenioso) and as a name in a literary anthology: *Belvedere* (1600), which itself helped to codify contemporary English literature and helped to give marginalised writers a performative space on the page and the University stage.

Finally, Rachel Willie turns to the ghostly legacy of Nashe's textual forms. In 'Thomas Nashe beyond the grave' Willie examines how later writers, especially John Taylor the Water Poet, appropriated Nashe's personae as a means of engaging with civil war discourse. By tracing such posthumous representations, she additionally considers how Nashe, as a figure finally divorced from his own creations, was utilised as a means of responding to and reanimating political debates. What emerges is the lack of control authors have over their persona and performability post-mortem and how satire, often construed as highly topical, can be repurposed for different political contexts. The past Elizabethan Marprelate controversy collides with later Stuart controversies over Laudian reforms in church governance and the figure of Nashe is invoked as objective commentator, even as the textual utterances lack Nashe's performability.

In an afterword Jennifer Richards unites the different strands explored in this volume, reflecting on the implications for a present-day critical appreciation of and engagement with Nashe and his works. Collectively each chapter's shared focus on Nashe questions early modern conceptions of authorship and textual transmission, and invites us to reconsider the relationship between the performances that take place within the printed page and the staged theatrical performances whose past realisation is encoded within the surviving playtexts of this period. As an author whose

INTRODUCTION 17

prose texts at once reflect a fascination with their material substance and engage with more intangible themes of movement, voice, and legacy, Nashe's version of the printed 'paper stage' invites us to recognise the affinity between such pulped-wood products and the timber-framed platforms of the early modern theatre.[90] Indeed, as we have seen, contemporaries such as Gabriel Harvey both registered and, in Harvey's case, repudiated a perceived liminality in Nashe's published texts that prospectively complicated distinctions between comic author and clown; pamphleteer and player; the print author and their public personae. While we are not suggesting that the experience of reading Nashe's printed texts is interchangeable with that of attending a live theatre performance, the preoccupation that these works display with performativity, lively motion, and ghostly afterlives nonetheless mitigates arbitrary or overly rigid categories of early modern literary production. On the one hand, Nashe's interest in and involvement with the sixteenth-century theatre has left its traces not only in the small sample of surviving dramatic texts to which he most likely contributed but also within his prose works. On the other hand, these prose works are themselves testament to Nashe's fluid conception of literary qualities that might traditionally have been seen as the preserve of live theatre, in so far as he gives prominence to experiences of breathlessness, forgetfulness, immediate dialogic exchange, and haunting presence. Thus, if the volume that follows is one in which most of our contributors consider Nashe's works and his legacy with an eye to their material composition and circulation as print texts, it is also one that asks how we might understand the importance of performativity for a prose author and playwright whose extant dramatic oeuvre is likely a shadow of his original output, and whose approach to prose composition arguably circumvents and surpasses later generic expectations. From this perspective Nashe is above all an author who *plays* at (and with) authorship, and whose published works frequently present themselves, and were received as, performances upon the 'paper stage' of the print market.[91]

NOTES

1 Thomas Nashe, *The vnfortunate traueller* (London, 1594), sig. N4r.
2 Nashe, *Unfortunate Traveller*, sig. N4r. As R. B. McKerrow notes, Erasmus for instance refers to the Latin formula 'To fight as though for hearth and altar' as a traditional phrase while discussing the proverb '*Dignum propter quod vadimonium deseratur* / Worth breaking bail for' in his *Adages* (I.viii.18). Desiderius Erasmus, *Collected Works of Erasmus: Adages: Ivi1 to Ix100, Volume 32*, trans. and ed. R. A. B. Mynors (Toronto: University of Toronto Press, 1989), pp. 134–5; Thomas Nashe, *The Vnfortunate Traueller*, in *The Works of Thomas Nashe*, ed. R. B. McKerrow, 2nd edn, rev. F. P. Wilson, 5 vols (Oxford: Blackwell, 1958), II.292 nn. 10–11.

3   Kate De Rycker, 'Commodifying the Author: The Mediation of Aretino's Fame in the Harvey-Nashe Pamphlet War', *ELR*, 49.2 (2019), 145–71 (p. 155). See also Chris Salamone, Chapter 5 below. Nashe's 'penniless' persona is most fully developed in *Pierce Penilesse*, which was published two years before *The Unfortunate Traveller*.
4   De Rycker, 'Commodifying', pp. 145–71.
5   Thomas Nashe, 'To the Gentlemen Readers', in Thomas Nashe, *Strange newes, of the intercepting certaine letters* (London, 1592), sigs B2r and B3r.
6   Matthew Steggle, 'Gabriel Harvey, the Sidney Circle, and the Excellent Gentlewoman', *Sidney Circle Journal*, 22 (2004), 115–29 (p. 126).
7   See for example Philip Hardie, *Rumour and Renown: Representations of Fama in Western Literature* (Cambridge: Cambridge University Press, 2011), esp. pp. 78–177.
8   Nashe, 'To the Gentlemen', *Strange News*, sig. B2r.
9   Gabriel Harvey, *Pierces supererogation or A new prayse of the old asse* (London, 1593), sigs A2r and F3r.
10 Harvey, *Pierce's Supererogation*, sig. **IV. No entry for this work appears in the Stationers' Register for the relevant years, so it is possible that Harvey's supposed text is a fiction invented to pressure Nashe, although it may also have been abandoned or lost, perhaps as a result of the 1599 Bishops' Ban targeting Nashe's and Harvey's satirical writings.
11 Harvey, *Pierce's Supererogation*, sigs V2r and T2r.
12 Harvey, *Pierce's Supererogation*, sig. V1v. On the continuing dual association of fame with rumour and reputation, which early modern writers inherited in part from classical and medieval authors, see Keith M. Botelho, *Renaissance Earwitnesses: Rumor and Early Modern Masculinity* (Basingstoke: Palgrave Macmillan, 2009).
13 Nashe, 'To the Gentlemen', *Strange News*, sig. B2r; Harvey, *Pierce's Supererogation*, sigs V2r and D1r.
14 Thomas Nashe, *Haue vvith you to Saffron-vvalden. Or, Gabriell Harueys hunt is vp* (London, 1596), sig. H4v.
15 J. B. Steane, 'Introduction', in Thomas Nashe, *'The Unfortunate Traveller' and Other Works*, ed. J. B. Steane (London: Penguin, 1972), pp. 13–44 (p. 13).
16 Alexander B. Grosart, 'Memorial-Introduction – Biographical', in *The Complete Works of Thomas Nashe*, 6 vols. (n.p.: Huth Library, 1883), I.xi–lxxi (xiii, vii).
17 C. S. Lewis, *English Literature in the Sixteenth Century, Excluding Drama* (Oxford: Oxford University Press, 1954), p. 416.
18 Jonathan Crewe, *Unredeemed Rhetoric: Thomas Nashe and the Scandal of Authorship* (Baltimore: Johns Hopkins University Press, 1982); Lorna Hutson, *Thomas Nashe in Context* (Oxford: Oxford University Press, 1989). The importance of the transition from 'Golden Age' narratives for Nashe's reception is discussed by Steve Mentz in 'Introduction: The Age of Thomas Nashe', in *The Age of Thomas Nashe: Text, Bodies and Trespasses of Authorship in Early Modern England*, ed. Stephen Guy-Bray, Joan Pong Linton, and Steve Mentz (London: Routledge, 2016), pp. 1–8 (pp. 1–2). Other major twentieth-century studies of Nashe include G. R. Hibbard's *Thomas Nashe: A Critical Introduction* (London: Routledge and Kegan Paul, 1962) and Charles Nicholl's *A Cup of News: The Life of Thomas Nashe* (London: Routledge and Kegan Paul, 1984).
19 Mentz, 'Introduction', pp. 1–2.
20 See for example Andrew Hadfield, 'Spenser, Raleigh, Harvey, and Nashe on Empire', *English*, 68 (2019), 143–61; Tamsin Theresa Badcoe, '"As Many Ciphers without an I": Self-Reflexive Violence in the Work of Thomas Nashe', *Modern Philology*, 111 (2014), 384–407; P. B. Roberts, 'Underemployed Elizabethans: Gabriel Harvey

INTRODUCTION

and Thomas Nashe in the *Parnassus* Plays', *Early Theatre*, 21 (2018), 49–70; Laurie Ellinghausen, *Labor and Writing in Early Modern England, 1567–1667* (Aldershot: Ashgate, 2008), pp. 37–62; Maurice Hunt, 'Thomas Nashe, *The Vnfortvnate Traveller*, and *Love's Labour's Lost*', *SEL*, 54 (2014), 297–315; Per Sivefors, 'Prayer and Authorship in Thomas Nashe's *Christs Teares over Jerusalem*', *English*, 65 (2016), 267–79; and Beatrice Groves, 'Laughter in the Time of Plague: A Context for the Unstable Style of Nashe's *Christ's Tears over Jerusalem*', *Studies in Philology*, 108 (2011), 238–60.

21 Stephen Guy-Bray and Joan Pong Linton, 'Postscript – Nashe Untrimmed: The Way We Teach Him Today', in *The Age of Thomas Nashe*, ed. Guy-Bray, Pong Linton, and Mentz, pp. 160–82 (pp. 170 and 175); Jennifer Richards and Andrew Hadfield, 'The Edition', *The Thomas Nashe Project* (Newcastle: Newcastle University, 2020). https://research.ncl.ac.uk/thethomasnasheproject/theedition/ (accessed 17 January 2024).

22 Steane, 'Introduction', p. 13.

23 Andrew Hadfield and Jennifer Richards, 'Thomas Nashe: A Dominant Literary Voice in Elizabethan England', *Shakespeare and Beyond* blog, Folger Shakespeare Library. https://shakespeareandbeyond.folger.edu/2017/09/26/thomas-nashe-elizabethan-england/ (accessed 17 January 2024).

24 See, for example, Jenni Hyde, *Singing the News: Ballads in Mid-Tudor England* (London: Routledge, 2018).

25 Kirsty Rolfe, Chapter 2 below.

26 Graham Parry, 'Literary Patronage', in *The Cambridge History of Early Modern English Literature*, ed. David Loewenstein and Janel Mueller (Cambridge: Cambridge University Press, 2002), pp. 117–40.

27 Joad Raymond, *Pamphlets and Pamphleteering in Early Modern Britain* (Cambridge: Cambridge University Press, 2003), p. 58; Parry, 'Literary Patronage', p. 127. In this volume Kate De Rycker notes Nashe rarely served as a writer residing in aristocratic household for long (Chapter 6 below).

28 Raymond, *Pamphlets and Pamphleteering*, p. 58.

29 Thomas Nashe, *Pierce Penilesse his supplication to the diuell* (London, 1592), sig. ¶1r.

30 'Publics' and 'Publicness' has garnered much critical attention over the last few decades, in part due to the 'Making Publics' project, which ran from 2005 to 2011 at McGill University and other reappraisals of the Habermasian conception of the public sphere, which influenced earlier studies such as Alexandra Halasz's *The Marketplace of Print: Pamphlets and the Public Sphere in Early Modern England* (Cambridge: Cambridge University Press, 1997). See, for example, *Making Publics in Early Modern Europe: People, Things, Forms of Knowledge*, ed. Bronwen Wilson and Paul Yachnin (Oxford and New York: Routledge, 2010), and *Making Space Public in Early Modern Europe: Performance, Geography, Privacy*, ed. Angela Vanhaelen and Joseph P. Ward (Oxford and New York: Routledge, 2013). For a discussion that takes Nashe's paper stage as a starting point for considering the printing of play pamphlets and publicness in the 1640s and 1650s see Rachel Willie, 'Viewing the Paper Stage: Civil War, Print, Theatre and the Public Sphere', in *Making Space Public in Early Modern Europe*, ed. Vanhaelen and Ward, pp. 54–75.

31 Nashe, *Pierce Penniless*, sig. A1r.

32 Jennifer Richards, *Voices and Books in the Renaissance: A New History of Reading* (Oxford: Oxford University Press, 2019), pp. 230–82.

33 Chloe Kathleen Preedy, Chapter 1 below, p. 29.

34 Gabriel Harvey, *Foure letters, and certaine sonnets* (London, 1592), sig. D2v. Here Harvey is decrying Greene, but 'his sworne brother, M. *Pierce Penni-lesse*' (sig. D3v) is also implicated in the criticism.

35 Samuel Fallon, *Paper Monsters: Persona and Literary Culture in Elizabethan England* (Philadelphia: University of Pennsylvania Press, 2019), p. 137.

36 Jason Scott-Warren, 'Nashe's Stuff', in *The Oxford Handbook of English Prose, 1500–1640*, ed. Andrew Hadfield (Oxford: Oxford University Press, 2013), pp. 204–18 (p. 206).

37 Jason Scott-Warren, 'Harvey, Gabriel (1552/3–1631), Scholar and Writer', *ODNB* (Oxford: Oxford University Press, 2016) (https://www.oxforddnb.com/view/10.1093/ref:odnb/9780198614128.001.0001/odnb-9780198614128-e-12517); see also Rebecca Hasler, '"Tossing and turning your booke upside downe": *The Trimming of Thomas Nashe*, Cambridge, and Scholarly Reading', *Renaissance Studies*, 33 (2019), 375–96, and Fallon, *Paper Monsters*, pp. 136–7. R. B. McKerrow also offers an invaluable overview of the dispute. See *The Works of Thomas Nashe*, ed. McKerrow, 2nd edn, rev. F. P. Wilson. 5 vols (Oxford: Basil Blackwell, 1958), V.65–110.

38 Fallon, *Paper Monsters*, p. 137 n. 45.

39 Fallon, *Paper Monsters*, p. 136; Georgia Brown, *Redefining Elizabethan Literature* (Cambridge: Cambridge University Press, 2004), p. 76.

40 Rachel Willie, Chapter 7 below.

41 For an extended discussion see Karen Kettnich, 'Nashe's Extemporal Vein and His Tarltonizing Wit', in *The Age of Thomas Nashe*, ed. Guy-Bray, Pong Linton and Mentz, pp. 99–114.

42 Nashe, *Pierce Penniless*, sig. A4v.

43 Nashe, *Pierce Penniless*, sig. F2r.

44 Thomas Nashe, *A pleasant comedie, called Summers last will and testament* (London, 1600), sig. B2r.

45 *British Drama 1533–1642: A Catalogue*, ed. Martin Wiggins with Catherine Richardson (Oxford: Oxford University Press, 2012), II.369; Richard Lichfield [?], *The trimming of Thomas Nashe Gentleman* (London, 1597), sig. G3r.

46 Robert Greene, *Greenes groats-vvorth of witte, bought with a million of repentance* (London, 1592), sig. F1r; *British Drama 1533–1642: A Catalogue*, ed. Wiggins with Richardson, II.482–3; *British Drama 1533–1642: A Catalogue*, ed. Martin Wiggins with Catherine Richardson (Oxford: Oxford University Press, 2013), III.110, III.193.

47 *British Drama 1533–1642: A Catalogue*, ed. Wiggins with Richardson, II.427. Wiggins and Richardson favour 1588 as the most likely first performance date for *Dido*, but many critics suggest the play was written a couple of years earlier.

48 *British Drama 1533–1642: A Catalogue*, ed. Wiggins with Richardson, II; Thomas Nashe, 'Letter to William Cotton', BL MS Cotton Julius C.III, fol. 280, qtd in Katherine Duncan-Jones, 'Thomas Nashe and William Cotton: Parallel Letters, Parallel Lives', *EMLS*, 19 (2016), 1–13 (p. 6). On Nashe's likely involvement with *1 Henry VI*, see also Gary Taylor, 'Shakespeare and Others: The Authorship of *Henry the Sixth, Part One*', *Medieval & Renaissance Drama in England*, 7 (1995), 145–205; and Brian Vickers, 'Thomas Kyd, Secret Sharer', *Times Literary Supplement*, 13 April 2008, pp. 13–15.

49 Arthur F. Kinney, 'John Lyly and the University Wits: George Peele, Robert Greene, Thomas Lodge and Thomas Nashe', in *The Cambridge Companion to Shakespeare and Contemporary Dramatists*, ed. Ton Hoenselaars (Cambridge: Cambridge University Press, 2012), pp. 1–18 (p. 14); David McInnis and Matthew Steggle, 'Introduction: Nothing Will Come of Nothing? Or, What Can We Learn from Plays That Don't

INTRODUCTION 21

Exist?', in *Lost Plays in Shakespeare's England*, ed. David McInnis and Matthew Steggle (Basingstoke: Palgrave Macmillan, 2014), pp. 1–16 (p. 1); De Rycker, 'Commodifying', p. 169. As Kate De Rycker points out, it is unclear how far this act of censorship led to the loss of *works* (as opposed to individual editions) by authors such as Nashe and Harvey.
50 Mentz, 'Introduction', p. 4.
51 See also Per Sivefors, '"Maymd soldiours or poore schollers": Warfare and Self-Referentiality in the Works of Thomas Nashe', *Cahiers Élisabéthains*, 95 (2018), 62–73, esp. pp. 64–5; Steven Mullaney, *The Reformation of Emotions in the Age of Shakespeare* (Chicago and London: University of Chicago Press, 2015), pp. 116–17.
52 Nashe, *Pierce Penniless*, sig. F3r.
53 Nashe, *Pierce Penniless*, sigs F3r–F3v.
54 Nashe, *Pierce Penniless*, sigs F3r–F3v.
55 Nashe, *Pierce Penniless*, sigs F3r and F4v.
56 Lena Liapi, Chapter 4 below, p. 97.
57 Nashe, *Pierce Penniless*, sig. F3r.
58 *King Henry VI, Part I*, ed. Edward Burns (London: Arden Shakespeare, 2001), 1.1.0, 1.2.103 SD, 1.3.56 SD, 1.1.127, and 1.1.78–9; edition hereafter cited parenthetically.
59 Salamone, Chapter 5 below. On contemporary associations between the devil and gunpowder weapons or stage storms see J. R. Hale, *Renaissance War Studies* (London: Hambledon Press, 1983), esp. pp. 394–7; Leslie Thomson, 'The Meaning of *Thunder and Lightning*: Stage Directions and Audience Expectations', *Early Theatre*, 2 (1999), 11–24.
60 Nashe, *Summer's*, sig. B3r.
61 Nashe, *Summer's*, sigs B3r–B4r; Paul Whitfield White, 'Archbishop Whitgift and the Plague in Thomas Nashe's *Summer's Last Will and Testament*', in *Religion and Drama in Early Modern England: The Performance of Religion on the Renaissance Stage*, ed. Jane Hwang Degenhardt and Elizabeth Williamson (Aldershot: Ashgate, 2011), pp. 139–52 (p. 146).
62 *British Drama 1533–1642: A Catalogue*, ed. Wiggins with Richardson, II.483.
63 Nashe, *Summer's*, sigs C2r, D1r, D3v, E2r, and E4v.
64 Nashe, *Summer's*, sig. H3v.
65 Nashe, *Summer's*, sigs H2r and H4v.
66 White, 'Archbishop Whitgift and the Plague', p. 147; Nashe, *Summer's*, sigs H2r–H2v.
67 *British Drama 1533–1642: A Catalogue*, ed. Wiggins with Richardson, III.407. The imprisoned actors were Robert Shaa and Gabriel Spencer.
68 Thomas Nashe, *Nashes Lenten stuffe* (London, 1599), sigs B1r and I4r–I4v.
69 Douglas Clark, Chapter 3 below.
70 Nashe, *Summer's*, sigs D3v and H4v.
71 White, 'Archbishop Whitgift and the Plague', p. 140.
72 Nashe, *Summer's*, sig. B1r.
73 Nashe, *Summer's*, sig. B1r.
74 Nashe, *Summer's*, sig. I2v.
75 Nashe, *Summer's*, sig. I1v.
76 Nashe, *Summer's*, sigs I1r and B2r; Kinney, 'John Lyly and the University Wits', pp. 14–15; White, 'Archbishop Whitgift and the Plague', pp. 140–2 and pp. 148–52.
77 Randall Martin, *Shakespeare and Ecology* (Oxford: Oxford University Press, 2015), pp. 10–11.
78 Nashe, *Summer's*, sig. H4v.
79 Nashe, *Summer's*, sig. H1v; White, 'Archbishop Whitgift and the Plague', p. 150.

80 Nashe, *Summer's*, sigs B1r and H2r.
81 Nashe, *Pierce Penniless*, sig. F2r.
82 Preedy, Chapter 1 below.
83 Rolfe, Chapter 2 below.
84 Clark, Chapter 3 below.
85 Clark, Chapter 3 below.
86 Liapi, Chapter 4 below.
87 Liapi, Chapter 4 below, p. 90.
88 Salamone, Chapter 5 below, p. 107.
89 Salamone, Chapter 5 below, p. 117.
90 Thomas Nashe, 'Somewhat to reade for them that list', in Philip Sidney, *Syr P.S. His Astrophel and Stella* (London, 1591), sig. A3r.
91 Nashe, 'Somewhat', sig. A3r.

I

'FRISKING … ALOFT': THE PNEUMATIC SPIRITS OF THOMAS NASHE'S 'PAPER STAGE'

Chloe Kathleen Preedy

In his preface to Thomas Newman's 1591 edition of Sir Philip Sidney's *Astrophel and Stella*, Thomas Nashe invokes the Graeco-Roman god Hermes, or Mercury: divine 'secretarie', patron of scholars, and legendary inventor of 'letters'.[1] Announcing that 'Apollo hath resigned his Ivory Harp unto Astrophel, & he like Mercury, must lull you a sleep with his musicke', Nashe implies that the recently deceased Sidney has surpassed both deities: 'thy divine Soule, carried on an Angels wings to heaven, is installed in Hermes place, sole prolocutor to the Gods'.[2] Yet the seemingly courtly, neoclassical compliment is complicated when Nashe adds that his 'heavie gated' preface cannot 'daunce trip and goe so lively … as other Sheepheards that have beene fooles in the Morris time'.[3] Nashe's mockery of the very pastoral mode that Sidney's *Arcadia* had enriched extends his prior allusion to the shepherd-god Mercury's parallel reputation as a thief and a trickster, hinting that to be 'lively' is at once 'foolish' and preferable to an excessively 'heavie' 'stile'.[4] Similarly, whereas Nashe's paean to 'Astrophel' ostensibly exploits Mercury's classical associations with rhetoric to distinguish Sidney's elevated literary output from the vain imitations of 'golden Asses', the preface's alchemically inflected allusions to this 'quicksilver' god simultaneously acknowledge the financial pressures that drive those who write for a living to 'breede' book after book.[5] Indeed Nashe's contention that *Astrophel and Stella* will purify the 'grosse fatty flames' of poor imitations such as Nicholas Breton's *A Bower of Delights* foregrounds the present edition's comparable emergence from manuscript exclusivity on to the 'paper stage' of print.[6] At a time when the metal quicksilver was the central catalyst in alchemical transformation and the laxative 'herbe called Mercurie' was prescribed by physicians as a remedy for 'choller, and melancholy' Nashe exploits the related potential of 'Mercury''s notorious volatility to advertise a 'lively' writing style that will purge stale and 'heavie' discourse.[7] Moreover that promise is aligned at least as much with Nashe's commercial output as it is with Sidney's verse collection. Indeed, in a characteristic rhetorical sleight, Nashe's overt mockery of those who 'goe the lighter away' and self-deprecating characterisation of his 'stile' as 'heavie gated' are in practice undercut by his informal tone, long-running sentences, digressive asides, and claim to here 'keepe pace with Gravesend barge'.[8]

Nashe returns to the idea of Mercury as the professional author's muse in *Have With You to Saffron Walden*, his 1596 riposte to Gabriel Harvey. Having first 'earnestly' commended himself to Apollo, Nashe appeals in particular to 'Joves ancient trustie Roger'.[9] This 'sprightly Mercury', whose subservience to Jove signals his affinity with poor, marginalized authors, comes 'frisking ... aloft' with 'wings for his moustachies, wings for his ey-brows, wings growing out of his chinne like a thorough haire, wings at his armes, like a fooles coat with four elbowes, wings for his riding bases, [and] wings at his heeles in stead of spurres'.[10] The comically exaggerated description, rolling subclauses, allusions to spurs and fool's coats, and quasi-theatrical direction to enter 'aloft' suggest an affinity between Nashe's Mercury and the 'Tarletonising' clowns of the Elizabethan stage: an effect reinforced by the author's plea that this jigging, 'frisking' deity 'inspire my pen with some of his nimblest Pomados [vaults] and Sommersets [somersaults]' 'since now I have more use of him than Alchumists'.[11] Implicitly responding to and subverting Harvey's 1593 attack on his frivolously 'frisking penne' and 'Mercuriall fingers', Nashe repurposes a figure he has previously identified with Sidney's neoclassical poetics to advertise the 'sprightly' qualities of his own commercially orientated writing.[12] Nashe even suggests that his light-fingered, light-footed Mercury is the 'true Prince of Wingan-decoy' (that is, the North American territory that Elizabethan colonisers commonly referred to as Virginia), in a punning, pointed rejoinder to the equally deceptive – but less immediately profitable – imperialist fantasies of authors such as Richard Hakluyt or the 'Mercuriall brested M. Harborne'.[13] Thus, during a period in which Mercury was often evoked in connection with linguistic order and rhetorical prowess, Nashe exploits the Graeco-Roman deity's co-existent reputation as an itinerant patron of alchemists, merchants, and thieves to foreground the idiosyncratic features of his light, consciously 'Mercuriall' prose.

Mercury's elemental associations with alchemical transformation and medicinal purgation are also significant in this regard. Scholars have long recognised Nashe's distinctive insistence on the wasteful nature of his commercial publications, with his co-option of Mercury in *Have With You* likewise suggesting both advertised profligacy and Nashe's apparent dissatisfaction with the dominant literary modes of humanism and neoclassicism.[14] The device further hints at how Nashe's commitment to an upwardly ascendant 'light' style is informed by and inflects his intensely humoral conception of the printed text as a nexus not only of typeset sheets but also of pneumatic forces that flow between author and readers within the imaginary environment of the 'paper stage'.[15] In *Thomas Nashe in Context* (1989) Lorna Hutson suggestively registers Nashe's 'highly physical' conception of cerebral energy, comparing Nashe's interest in 'vital liquids – tears, cider, blood' – to the conjunction of 'liquid assets' and discursive exchange in Ben Jonson's *Every Man In His Humour* (1598). These circulating fluids would have possessed considerable pneumatic significance for Nashe's humorally minded contemporaries, who held that 'the body was filled with moving currents of air in the bloodstream, [and] that the air taken within the body became part of the stuff of consciousness'.[16] The 'spiritual' aspects of Nashe's writings have also received more recent critical attention: Beatrice Groves has re-evaluated *Christ's Tears over Jerusalem* (1593) in light of psychophysical beliefs about the curative properties of laughter ('good spirits'), while Chris Salamone's analysis in Chapter 5 below offers a fascinating account of Nashe's demonological and spectral interests.[17] So too has the 'liveness' of Nashe's writing, with Jennifer Richards insightfully proposing that Nashe interrelates writing, reading, and speaking as he 'translates the effect of live theatre into prose'.[18] Indeed Nashe's 'exceptional sensitivity to the materiality of words' informs his ongoing emphasis on stylistic lightness and peripatetic narration.[19] As Harvey's attack on the 'light' and 'puffing' author hints, Nashe's early modern contemporaries were alert to – and sometimes disturbed by – his commitment to a consciously 'ayry' mode.[20] While many shared Nashe's distinctly materialist understanding of invention, verbal communication, and the respiratory processes that facilitated poetic consumption, detractors still regularly denounced Nashe and his works for flaunting their unduly 'fleeting incorporeall substaunce, circumscribed with no limits'.[21] When Nashe identifies his 'frisking' style with the propulsive powers of a comically extra-winged Mercury in *Have With You*, then, he indirectly acknowledges that publications such as *Pierce Penniless* (1592) might be aptly termed 'Paper-monster[s]' not only in recognition of their pulpy membranes and inky veins but also for their affinity with the insubstantial fictions that an adversarial Stephen Gosson decried in *The School of Abuse* (1579): mass-marketed 'windball[s]' that are 'puffed up' like puppets with 'browne paper', with 'tow', and – at least figuratively – with overblown discourse.[22]

BREATHING SPACE: NASHE'S PNEUMATIC PERFORMANCES

For Elizabethan authors such as Stephen Gosson and George Puttenham, comparing a text to an inflated paper monster signals spiritual and stylistic failure. In Nashe's work, on the other hand, the analogy complements an ongoing resistance to influential formulations of literary value.[23] Yet all three authors, like many of their contemporaries, share an understanding of literature as an environmentally embodied mode, which relies for its composition and consumption on a series of pneumatic exchanges.[24] Humoral authorities held that the cognitive and emotive exchanges that enabled the human mind to generate and respond to live and fictional impressions were dependent on the internal circulation of animal spirits (*pneuma psychikon*), which were refined from and fuelled by inspired air.[25] For Gosson and Puttenham the danger is that unpredictably spreading or swelling fictions might corrupt the body and soul into which their airy traces are received and digested; although Gosson stresses drama's contagious potential to attack unruly playgoing while Puttenham champions the poet's mastery of order and proportion, their fictional aetiologies demonstrate a common concern with what the French essayist Michel de Montaigne terms 'straggling' thoughts that 'wander' 'in the aire'.[26] In contrast, Nashe's writings connect the erratic progress of his literary fictions to the prospect of pneumatic interaction between reader and text, self-consciously performing the kind of imaginative disorder that authors such as Montaigne, Puttenham, and Sidney claimed marshalling one's 'idle' fantasies into prose or poetry would correct.[27] Nashe even introduces his own *Lenten Stuff* (1599) as the product of 'dishumored composing' by initially 'melancholly' 'spirites' and 'bemudded' 'intellectuall faculties', which must be 'rouze[d]' to the 'most outstretched ayry straine'.[28]

Nashe's attention to the pneumatically embodied impact of his writing complements the wider resistance to neoclassical poetics that critics such as Robert Weimann have discerned in his work.[29] Weimann's efforts to align Nashe's practice with the values of commercial Elizabethan drama also usefully highlights the extent to which Nashe's style is indebted to his knowledge of theatrical and performative conventions. As Jennifer Richards has recently demonstrated, Nashe regularly blurs the boundaries between page and stage, reproducing the experience of live performance in his prose works.[30] In particular, Nashe's textual allusions to imaginative production and transmission are typically expressed in terms that evoke the embodied pneumatic exchanges of the early modern playhouse. Important studies by Gina Bloom and Gail Kern Paster have shown that dramatists including William Shakespeare and Ben Jonson were conscious of how their visually and vocally realized fictions reached the assembled audience members during theatrical performances; Nashe, who co-wrote *The Isle of Dogs* (1597) with Jonson and collaborated with Shakespeare on *1 Henry VI*, would have been equally familiar with air's significance as a performative technology.[31] In addition to playfully depicting the challenges of dialogic exchange in his only surviving single-authored play,

Summer's Last Will and Testament (1592), Nashe often simulates a comparably pneumatic transmission process for and within his prose publications.[32] Thus, as his fictional counterparts declaim from their 'paper stage[s]', Nashe implies that even the printed voice is not so much '*em*bodied ... as it is temporarily attached, released, and exchanged' within and between the minds of authors, narrators, and readers, carried by the breath-fuelled spirits that enable cognitive, emotive, and sensory perception.[33]

Breath's significance as 'the physical substance that enables the actors to convey to audiences the language of the script' is especially evident in live theatre.[34] That prominence is due as much to limitations as to possibilities: for instance, as Gina Bloom points out, players might struggle to regulate their breathing during long speeches, or strain to project lines successfully on windy days.[35] Such interruptions to an idealised cycle of pneumatic exchange might impede an audience's access to the production, but they also testify to the immediacy, even exceptionality, of the theatrical experience. It is this effect that Nashe simulates within his prose narratives. *Have With You* is 'frame[d] ... in the nature of a Dialogue', while most of Nashe's published works contain instances in which an imagined reader is addressed: techniques that recall the dialogic exchanges of an English theatre wherein players might speak to members of the assembled audience as well as to each other; and at which the experiential continuity between the natural-lit stage and the 'auditorium', and between actors and audience members, was a defining characteristic of contemporary commercial performance.[36] Moreover, these implied exchanges often raise issues that are themselves suggestive of immediacy and shared presence. In *Pierce Penniless*, for instance, Nashe announces that readers must wait until his fictional speaker is 'at leasure to talke to thee', and extends this conceit by ventriloquising the anticipated criticisms of an impatient consumer: 'Whilst I am thus talking, me thinks I heare one say, What a fop is this he entitles his booke *A Supplication to the Divell,* and doth nothing but raile on ideots.'[37] Nashe's narrators often demonstrate even greater haste, 'running or galloping on journeys which have no certain points of origin or arrival', or, as in the preface to *Lenten Stuff,* 'already leaving' the textual present to 'correct the [printing-press] faults ... that escaped in my absence'.[38] In both the latter work and Nashe's earlier *Terrors of the Night* (1594) such implied motion is further accompanied by the breathlessness that might be expected to result in real life or on the stage. In *Terrors*, for instance, the narrator breaks an extended disquisition on false prophets with the admission that 'I have rid a false gallop these three or four pages: now I care not if I breathe mee, and walke soberly and demurely halfe a dozen turns, like a grave Citizen going about to take the ayre'.[39] Here Nashe's allusion to turning suggestively elides the narrative act of taking the air with the reader's anticipated turning through the pages of his text, characterising both as active, interrelated pneumatic processes.

Lenten Stuff extends the connection between imaginative perambulation and textual digestion that is hinted at in *Terrors*. Towards the start of this text, the narrator announces that he will lead his readers on 'a sound walke round about Yarmouth' 'to whet your appetites' for his history of the red herring.[40] Almost immediately the narrative loses the sense of ordered progression that such 'sound' action might seem to promise, launching into a digressive, 'unruly' history in which the convergence of words 'spoken to fore' and the 'forespoke' disrupts any linear chronology.[41] Similarly the architectural and geographical precision initially implied by Nashe's terminology of miles, yards, and feet is qualified by the passage's self-advertised status as a 'transcursive repetory'.[42] The resulting impression of an account 'raveling out' is exacerbated by the narrator's concluding farewell to those other, aborted chorographies that cost him such 'brainetossing', as the preceding passage becomes retrospectively haunted by the 'smothered', unassimilated 'dribblements' with which the narrator 'yet ... pants and labours'.[43] Inspired air and the cognitive spirits that breath enlivens are here expended prodigally in order to spare the ink and paper that Nashe so viscerally evokes in his texts. Indeed the narrator later admits that only a hasty 'posting' has prevented him from 'runne[ing] tenne quier of paper out of breath'.[44] Respiration's role in generating fictional matter is reiterated later in this work, as the narrator dismisses an extended attack on 'selfe-conceited misinterpreters' with the confession that 'my redde herring which was hot broyling on the coles, is waxt starke cold for want of blowing'.[45] Likewise the text's ending is heralded by the closing of the speaker's 'bagge of my winde': a conceit that simultaneously evokes the classical maritime trope of Aeolus's ship-driving breezes and the narrative shortness of breath that 'ascending' the 'lofty mountaine creast' of the herring's 'trophees' would supposedly induce.[46] Such concatenating pneumatic challenges might seem to presage an imminent failure akin to that suffered by *The Unfortunate Traveller*'s 'hard bound' rhetorical 'plodders', who 'gaspt and gapt for winde' as their imaginative faculties fill with 'stale', 'Grosse' fumes.[47] In the event, however, Nashe's 'friskin' Lenten narrator possesses 'wind' enough to continue, launching into yet another multi-clausal sentence whose projected geographical range expands to encompass four countries as well as the focal town of Yarmouth. As Douglas Clark observes in Chapter 3 below, that closing flourish intriguingly revives Nashe's opening statement that he is 'not yet one quarter emptied of my notes',[48] hinting at respiration's ongoing contribution to a process of atmospheric recycling and the human body's medically-celebrated ability to use 'otherwise useless and unprofitable expired air as the material for the voice'.[49] Thomas Judson and Valentine Simmes's 1599 edition even adds a parenthetical asterisk below the summative 'Herring for Yarmouth. / (`*`)': a typographical device sometimes used in place of an author's name, but perhaps here employed to create the illusion that the dialogue between narrator and reader might continue past the 'FINIS' of a quarto that has prominently advertised Nashe's authorial presence.[50]

Nashe's characterisation of reading as a challenging pneumatic process is neither unique nor inevitably radical. Stephen Gosson had noted the threat of being 'carried beyonde' one's 'reach' when considering theatrical 'abuses' that 'passe the degrees of the instrument' in his 1579 *School of Abuse*, while Nashe's *bête noire* Gabriel Harvey calls for a 'breathing pawse' after wandering 'out-of my accustomed way' in *Pierce's Supererogation* (1593).[51] As Harvey's parodic dig at 'Pierce's' wandering style suggests, however, what was striking is the way that Nashe applies such tropes. Whereas Nashe's polemical antagonists cite the unreliable movements of internal and external *pneuma* to argue for textual limits, Nashe identifies narratively simulated breathing with a lively discourse that seemingly 'overslip[s]' the boundaries of the printed page.[52] As figurative *pneuma* ebbs and flows through the lines of Nashe's prose works, the conceit complements Nashe's well-known valorisation of the 'extemporall' mode by simulating the flawed 'liveness' of vocal delivery; Nashe writes, in Richards's words, 'as if he is animating pen and paper with his breath'.[53] Such devices work with Nashe's carefully tailored rhetorical punctuation to suggest not only conversational intimacy between the narrator and his anticipated readers but also the kind of shared pneumatic experience that is more commonly associated with playgoing, hinting that Nashe here also seeks to textually replicate the communal emotional affects that he admires in drama.[54] Moreover, imbuing the imaginative space of the print text with aerial and ethereal matter enhances Nashe's self-presentation as a mobile observer whose marginalised, restless state paradoxically guarantees his authority by enabling him to speak without suspicion of self-interest or bias.[55] Thus, by conceptualising his print texts as sites of pneumatic exchange, Nashe establishes the airy foundations upon which he will advance his 'new wit', 'new stile', and 'new soule'.[56]

'*Vacuus viator*':[57] Nashe's light prose

As Nashe's promises of 'a new stile' hint, the Elizabethan author's attention to the pneumatic substance of his works is complemented by his writing's self-proclaimed lightness. For Nashe that term seemingly implies the narrator's capacity to traverse the horizontal and vertical axes of his environment with breath-taking speed. In *Pierce Penniless*, for instance, the eponymous narrator anticipates the many-winged Mercury of *Have With You* by asserting that he and his interlocutors possess 'the wings of choise words', in a boast that perhaps glances at the elevated but constrictive ambitions of neoclassical poetics as well as disparaging the flat prose of 'lay Chronigraphers'.[58] Pierce's related claim to be '*vacuus viator* [one who travels light]' is realised not only by his lack of financial substance but also through the proclaimed airiness of his textual genesis and habitation.[59] In this work's mock-'private' epistle, 'Tho. Nash.' claims that he will become an 'evil Angel' to 'haunt' his detractors 'world without end'.[60] Since many authorities held that devils and ghosts fashioned their earthly forms from 'darke and thick ayre', as Nashe's heavily derivative account of 'what the Divell is' later affirms, this metaphorical threat playfully implies that the prose author's 'voice' is at once disembodied and materially transmitted through the printed page and surrounding air.[61] Similarly, *Have With You* opens with the fictional Importuno (who represents Harvey) demanding of the respondent 'Tom', alias 'Piers Penniless': 'Where hast thou bin this long time; walking in Saint Faiths Church under ground, that wee never could see thee? Or hast thou tooke thee a Chamber in Cole-harbour, where they live in a continuall myst[?]'.[62] Characteristically blurring the boundaries between the text's environment and the reader's, Nashe here identifies the implied space between publications with hell and the London suburbs: both locations imaginatively traversed by Pierce. The specific invocation of 'myst', regarded as a 'midle' stage of vaporous exchange between the 'ayre' and the 'earth, or waters', is especially intriguing, in that it potentially recalls the comparably vaporous processes of textual composition and consumption.[63] Consiliadore's punning elaboration that 'we have mist you a great while, as well spiritually as corporally; that is, no lesse in the absence of your works than the want of your companie', further evokes this pneumatic context.[64] The print text is thus characterised as the marriage of a 'corporeal' frame – the bound paper pages – with the 'spiritual' substance of the fictional narrative, itself conceived (according to prevalent humoral theories) by the airy spirits of Nashe's brain.

In characterising his fictional counterparts as 'spiritual' presences within the space of the text, Nashe references mainstream humoral beliefs about how imaginative fictions were generated and received. However, his emphasis on the light airiness of his print works contrasts with the care that many authors took to avoid such charges, which often denoted a perceived dearth of spiritual or social substance. In *The Art of English Poesy* (1589), for instance, 'lightness' operates as a synonym for frivolity: Puttenham, having lamented that 'a light headed or phantasticall man' is often called 'a Poet' 'in disdayne', proceeds to warn his readers against those 'trifling' effects and 'toyes' that might make their compositions appear 'too light and triviall'.[65] Sidney, too, uses 'lightness' to suggest insignificance, arguing that 'the lightest reasons that may be will seem to weigh greatly if nothing be put in the counterbalance'.[66] Gabriel Harvey often exploited such associations between 'lyghtnes' and 'vanitie' or 'foly' in his attacks on Nashe, accusing his rival's works of being too frothy and frivolous.[67] To engage in 'meere Nashery' is, according to Harvey, to have 'no substance, but light feathers' and 'no transcendents, but lightest phantasies'; Harvey's 'vaine Nash' is accused of building narratives that, like 'Castels of vapours, or pillars of smoke', 'make a mighty showe in the Aier, and straight Vanish away'.[68] Moreover, this familiar charge is reiterated by the anonymous author of the *Trimming of Thomas Nashe* (1597), who likens Nashe's printed works to 'a bundell of strawe that beeing sett on fire consumes it selfe all in smoke', concluding that 'thou hast no true fire in thee, all smoother'.[69]

Whereas charges of lightness were anathema to authors who sought to assert their work's moral and social credentials, Nashe expresses little concern at this characterisation of his literary output. On the contrary, he embraces Harvey's would-be derogatory image of his 'frisking penne', invoking an equally 'frisking' Mercury to announce the responsive polemic *Have With You* and advertising *Lenten Stuff* as 'a light friskin of my witte'.[70] The latter text also extols the skill of a Yarmouth artificer who manufactures items of artificially little 'poise' (weight), while Nashe even likens his *Lenten Stuff* and the earlier *Terrors* to 'moate[s]' or 'wind bladder[s]' that get 'tost' 'in the ayre'.[71] These extreme examples are admittedly instances of self-conscious deprecation, but the reflexive criticism voiced by Nashe's narrators typically prioritises enhancing (rather than eliminating) textual lightness. The speaker of *Terrors* for instance worries that readers will not enjoy an overly 'lumbring' 'tale', while *Have With You*'s Respondent promises that his parodic biography of Gabriel Havey will be 'abridge[d]' lest 'my Book ... grow such a bouncer, that those which buy it must bee faine to hire a porter to carry it after them'.[72] As the latter example suggests, Nashe is especially critical of Harvey's 'Heavie', 'gor-bellied Volume[s]', playing on a contemporary tendency to express literary value or worth in terms of 'substance' by charging both the material text and his rival's style with being too bloatedly 'heavie' to sell.[73] Here Nashe's specific targets are the 'serious' folio volumes and the 'lumbring' 'Hexamiter verse' favoured by classicists such as Harvey and Richard Stanyhurst: arguing that hexameters are ill suited to 'this Clyme of ours', Nashe draws a vivid analogy between such 'wallowing' poetry and 'a man running upon quagmiers'.[74] Harvey's own efforts at 'that drunken staggering kinde of verse' are elsewhere likened to the heaving motions of 'a horse plunging through the myre'.[75] Moreover, Nashe implies that such restrictive heaviness might become contagious: thus the narrator of *Strange News* (1593) worries that to 'run hobling' through a step-by-step critique of Harvey's 'dogrell' is to 'infect my vaine with his imitation', in a suggestively humoral pun, and laments that 'my stile with treading in thy clammie steps is growne as heavie gated, as if it were bound ... with the irons at Newgate'.[76]

CLEARING THE AIR: FROM CAUSE TO CURE

Nashe's pedestrian and equestrian analogies recall the stylistic punning of earlier classical texts. For instance, Ovid's *Amores* famously begins with the mock-confession that '[w]hen in this workes first verse I trode aloft', love 'tooke one foote away', reducing his martial hexameters to the 'five feete' of 'amorous laies'.[77] At the same time Nashe's criticisms of the 'mud-born' Harvey's infectious errors extend his own case for 'light' over 'heavy' writing.[78] Nashe's comparisons between his rival's prose and the physically and pneumatically constrictive experience of trying to move through a bog, a quagmire, or in chains are especially intriguing. During a period in which prisons and marshes alike were feared as sources of the 'thicke, cloudy, moyst, and ill smelling vapours' said to carry epidemic disease, these analogies further Nashe's accusation that Harvey's writing chokes the 'vaine[s]' of his imagination and, by implication, of the text's readers, thereby impeding the effective circulation of the pneumatically fuelled spirits that powered cognitive and corporeal activity.[79] Indeed, Nashe explicitly connects the 'thickening' of the brain's humours with disordered and 'mishapen' thought in *Terrors*, arguing that 'our braine oppressed with melancholy' is akin to 'a standing puddle' or 'a clocke tyde downe with too heavie weighs or plummets'.[80] Since mobility-impeding bogginess and heaviness are faults that Nashe frequently attributes to Harvey's works, such claims complement Nashe's wider endorsement of his own light, 'friskin' style as a corrective to the melancholic contagion associated with more ostensibly 'substantial' works.[81]

Nashe's attention to the threat of imaginative contagion extends his ongoing interest in the pneumatic nature of the printed text. Early modern humoralists emphasised the interrelated vulnerability of the body, mind, and soul; and, just as external 'infection of the Aire' might threaten corporeal well-being, so corrupted internal *pneuma* was linked to mental and even spiritual disorder.[82] Contemporary attacks on imaginative literature frequently exploited such associations. Stephen Gosson for instance warns prospective playgoers that taking in commercial drama's 'wanton speeches' and spectacles will 'gaule the minde, where reason and vertue should rule the roste', while his fellow anti-theatricalist William Rankins elaborates that the 'infectious sight of playes' will transform 'the temple of our bodies' into 'a stage of stinking stuffe', 'manifold vices, &c spotted enormities'.[83] Nashe's detractors likewise attacked his prose works as foul, contagious emanations. Harvey's sweeping censure in *Pierces Supererogation* of a commercial print culture 'where nothing but flat, and ranke grosenesse blotteth the paper, infecteth the aier ... and annoyeth the world' positions Nashe as one of the 'pestilentest' offenders, alongside the 'king of the paper stage' Robert Greene.[84] Nashe's culpability was further expounded by the unidentified author of *Trimming*, who claims that Nashe's polluted 'breath' or *'anima'* – 'the forme by which thou art, what thou art, by which also thy senses woorke, which giveth use to all thy faculties and from which all thy actions proceede' – has initiated a spreading textual contagion: 'this breath stinketh and from this breath (as little rivers flowe from a fountaine) all thy woordes flowe foorth and the fountaine beeing corrupted (as you knowe) likewise all the lesser rivers needes must bee corrupted'.[85] Moreover, both Harvey and *Trimming*'s author analogically relate internal pneumatic contagion to external examples of atmospheric contagion. In particular, by suggesting that the 'quicksilver' 'Invention' of 'Penniles' and his ilk results in nothing but 'smoke' and 'smoother', these authors imply an overlap between the spiritual threat that Nashe's 'insubstantial' print works are said to represent, and the quintessentially urban and primarily corporeal danger posed by a rapid escalation in the number of domestic and industrial fires, and of their polluting emissions.[86]

Nashe comically replicates this charge in *Have With You*. Early in his text 'the Opponent' Importuno demands whether 'Tom' has come from 'a Chamber in Cole-harbour, where they live in a continuall myst, betwixt two Brew-houses'.[87] Rather than deny his authorial and textual affinity with the polluted environs of a rapidly-expanding city, Nashe's Respondent counters that it is paying readers who 'set Harvey and mee on fire one against another', whetting 'us on to consume our selves' in order 'to recreate and enkindle their decayed spirites'.[88] If Harvey's polemic is here credited as an incendiary spark, Nashe more often stresses the detrimental impact of his rival's heavy prose: *Strange News* offers a tongue-in-cheek prayer that Harvey's 'tedious', 'stinking' *Four Letters* 'not come abroad to corrupt the aire, & impostumate mens ears' with their punningly foul content;[89] while Harvey's recent anti-Nashe polemic is characterised in *Have With You* as the joint product of the 'dampe ... contagion' that fostered the 1593 plague and the stale, 'cloystred' air of an 'immured' Harvey's chamber.[90] Ultimately, as Lorna Hutson notes, Nashe's mock-biography presents *Pierces Supererogation* as 'nothing more than an infectious ...

hoard of [barren] rhetorical *exampla*'.[91] Furthermore Harvey's 'owne spirit of Bragganisme' is said to have 'infected' his text's dedicatees, Barnabe Barnes and Anthony Chute, in an extension of Pierce's prior contention that 'one bad pamphlet is enough to raise a damp that may poison a whole Tearme, or at the least a number of poore Clyents that have no money to prevent ill aire'.[92]

Whereas Harvey's 'slow', 'stinking' prose threatens to incubate the kind of 'grose mistempred vapors' that early modern authorities identified with the plague, Nashe presents his light, witty prose as a prospective cure.[93] Literature's corrective potential was a common theme for early modern authors. Groves has shown that Nashe himself explores laughter's potential as a plague remedy in *Christ's Tears*, having previously employed curative imagery in his prefaces to *Menaphon* (1589) and *Astrophel and Stella*: the first ironically urges 'Gentlemen' readers to 'phisicke their faculties of seeing & hearing' by exchanging the cloyingly 'odoriferous savours' of 'over-rackt rhetorique' for the implicitly excremental stink of 'wast paper', while the second announces that the poetic 'beames of his [Sidney's] spirite' will dissolve the 'fatty flames' of inferior prior publications.[94] *Have With You* is even more emphatically advertised as a corrective response to airborne contagion, with Nashe noting in the prefatory epistle that 'as Hippocrates preserved the Citie of Coos from a great plague or mortalitie (generally dispersed throughout Greece) by perswading them to kindle fires in publique places, whereby the aire might be purified', so his text will purge Harvey's *Supererogation* by 'enkindling' an 'everlasting fire' in the print sphere.[95] Indeed, since atmospheric purification and improved ventilation were often recommended by early modern physicians during times of plague, and the 'first and chiefest remedie' was 'to chaunge the place, [and] flie', Nashe's emphasis on the windy attributes and horizontal and vertical mobility possessed by his deliberately light writing acquires intriguing medical resonances.[96] Thus, in arguing that his explosively pneumatic print works might even revive the 'spirites' of those previously mired within Harvey's 'substantial' prose, Nashe hints that their ultimate effect on the consuming minds of his readers might not be dissimilar to that of the 'Northren winde[s]' or 'quicke Bonefires' that respectively disperse or consume 'the malignant vapours of the [pestilential] ayre'.[97]

CONCLUSION: NASHE'S PNEUMATIC TRAVELLERS

Few readers would deny that Nashe's writings are strikingly material, even by the standards of an Elizabethan culture that 'had difficulty in thinking of an immaterial substance'.[98] As Hutson points out, though, it is not only bodies and other solid items that Nashe conceives of as graspable resources;

his words, too, prove to be intractably, insistently material.[99] This effect stems in part from Nashe's proto-alchemical fascination with the imagination's potential to turn 'the abstract into the concrete, by turning intellectual resources into coins'.[100] Yet if commercial considerations inform Nashe's ongoing negotiation of the transactions that shape the brain's fantasies into fictional narratives, so too does his fascination with 'spirits': from demonic and spectral apparitions to the pneumatic matter that enables imaginative stimuli to be received, processed, and transmitted.[101] As Nashe evokes the nexus of pneumatic exchanges through which future readers will encounter and consume his published works, his 'copious', 'extemporall' style at once places pressure upon and augments the textual simulation of these breath-fuelled interactions, with the 'ever-inflationary rhetoric' that Nashe so relishes matched by the simulated near-breathlessness of his narrators.[102] Even as they seemingly hyperventilate to the point of dyspnoea, however, these speakers anticipate Shakespeare's quintessentially theatrical Cleopatra in their paradoxical ability to 'breathless, pour breath forth'.[103] In the process they acquire a unique ability to traverse the liminal spaces between the typographical 'crosse waie[s]' and 'Parenthesis' of the printed page; the narrative, its narrator(s), and its envisaged reader(s); the publication and its textual precursors, sequels, and refutations; or the fictionally evoked places of the earth and realms of the cosmos.[104] The consciously light nature of Nashe's writings implicitly endorses this textual permeability, as the advertised airiness of his authorial 'spirit' enables his speakers to wander erratically but freely through their 'transcursive' repertories.[105] Similarly, whereas many contemporary authors signal their work's literary substance by ascribing measurable limits to their texts and fictions, with Gabriel Harvey for instance promising that 'I know the le[n]gth, that is, the shortnes of mine owne foote', Nashe focuses on the explosively revitalising potential of a 'quicksilver' imagination.[106] That is not to say that Nashe never criticises emptily windy discourse. His *Anatomy of Absurdity* (1589) disparagingly likens 'Italinated' works to 'drummes, which beeing emptie with in, sound big without', while his fictional interlocutor Consiliadore condemns Harvey (that 'newe blowne' 'bubble') for coining 'gowtie' words that 'sound' as hollowly as the 'tenfold echoing rebound of a dubble Cannon in the aire'.[107] Even in such instances, though, inflated volume and insubstantiality are problematic in so far as airy textual matter is limited by or reverberates off a constricting boundary; in contrast, Nashe compares his own neologisms to a 'strong' 'winde', as if 'the extra breath that is required to enunciate them were itself a source of energy'.[108] The distinction, it seems, is between the thick accumulation of trapped words and the penetratingly windy discourse that might disperse this miasmic fug: with heavy prose said to 'stale' the spirits and induce mental contagion, the greatest risk for Nashe's speakers is not to be accused of lightness but rather to no longer 'blowe' as freely as 'the winde' from one 'Countie' or thought to the next.[109] Thus, like the many-winged Mercury of *Have With You*, the 'sprightly' narrators of Nashe's 'light' publications come 'frisking ... aloft' on to their 'paper stage[s]', stirring and clearing the imagined environments of his pneumatically immersive texts with their ceaseless, 'lively' motion.[110]

NOTES

I would like to thank Manchester University Press's anonymous peer reviewers, Douglas Clark, Lena Liapi, Chris Salamone, and Rachel Willie for their comments on an earlier draft of this chapter.

1 Thomas Nashe, *A pleasant comedie, called Summers last will and testament* (London, 1600), sig. F4v.
2 Thomas Nashe, 'Somewhat to reade for them that list', in Philip Sidney, *Syr P.S. His Astrophel and Stella* (London, 1591), sig. A3v. Cf. Ovid [Publius Ovidius Naso], *Metamorphoses*, trans. A. D. Melville, ed. E. J. Kenney (Oxford: Oxford University Press, 2008), I:669–723.
3 Nashe, 'Somewhat', sig. A4r.
4 On Mercury see for example Ovid, *Metamorphoses*, I.669–723 and II.676–710. Gavin Alexander discusses Sidney's reputation as the 'shepherd knight' in *Writing After Sidney: The Literary Response to Sir Philip Sidney, 1586–1640* (Oxford: Oxford University Press, 2006), esp. pp. 56–75. See for instance Edmund Spenser, *The Ruines of Time*, in *The Yale Edition of the Shorter Poems of Edmund Spenser*, ed. William A. Oram et al. (New Haven and London: Yale University Press, 1989), pp. 225–61. Spenser anticipates Nashe's conceit that Sidney has been carried to heaven by 'wing footed Mercurie' (l.666); his *Complaints* were entered into the Stationers' Register in December 1590 and probably circulated in manuscript before publication (Stewart Mottram, *Ruin and Reformation in Spenser, Shakespeare, and Marvell* (Oxford: Oxford University Press, 2019), pp. 72–4).
5 Nashe, 'Somewhat', sig. A4v.
6 Nashe, 'Somewhat', sig. A3r. On the relationship with Breton's *Bower of Delights* see Michelle O'Callaghan, *Crafting Poetry Anthologies in Renaissance England: Early Modern Cultures of Recreation* (Cambridge: Cambridge University Press, 2020), pp. 124–8.
7 Joseph A. Porter, *Shakespeare's Mercutio: His History and Drama* (Chapel Hill and London: University of North Carolina Press, 1988), pp. 35–7; William Bullein, *Bulleins bulwarke of defence* (London, 1579), sig. H3v; Nashe, 'Somewhat', sig. A4r. Quicksilver was additionally prescribed 'to heale the Pox' (Bullein, sig. M4r). See also Robert Burton, *The anatomy of melancholy* (Oxford, 1621), sig. Ff4r; Tanya Pollard, *Drugs and Theater in Early Modern England* (Oxford: Oxford University Press, 2005), p. 37.
8 Early modern authors apparently regarded barges as the fastest mode of domestic or urban transport, with dramatic characters who plan to travel 'with all speed' catching the Gravesend barge. See for example John Fletcher, *The Tamer Tamed*, ed. Lucy Munro (London: Methuen, 2010), 5.2.7. O'Callaghan suggests that Nashe's 'Gravesend barge' analogically denotes the commercial verse collection Nicholas Breton's *A Bower of Delights* (p. 126), additionally implying that Nashe's prose

'trip[s]' just as fast as the supposedly 'lighter' work. Cf. for example Thomas Nashe, 'To all Christian Readers', in Thomas Nashe, *Haue vvith you to Saffron-vvalden. Or, Gabriell Harueys hunt is vp* (London, 1596), sigs D1r–D1v;Thomas Nashe, *Strange newes, of the intercepting certaine letters* (London, 1592), sig. F3r.

9 Nashe, 'Christian', sigs D3r–D3v. Nashe (who studied at St John's College) probably uses 'roger' in the cant sense of an 'itinerant beggar pretending to be a poor scholar from Oxford or Cambridge' (OED, *n*1).

10 Nashe, 'Christian', sig. D3v.

11 Nashe, 'Christian', sig. D3v. See Karen Kettnich, 'Nashe's Extemporal Vein and His Tarlonizing Wit', in *The Age of Thomas Nashe: Texts, Bodies and Trespasses of Authorship in Early Modern England*, ed. Stephen Guy-Bray, Joan Pong Linton, and Steve Mentz (Farnham: Ashgate, 2013), pp. 99–114; also Gabriel Harvey, *Pierces supererogation or A new prayse of the old asse* (London, 1593), sig. T4r.

12 Harvey, *Pierces supererogation*, sigs C1r and D2r; Thomas Nashe, *The vnfortunate traueller* (London, 1594), sig. A2v.

13 Thomas Nashe, *Nashe's Lenten Stuff*, in *'The Unfortunate Traveller' and Other Works*, ed. J. B. Steane (London: Penguin, 1971), p. 397 n. 128; Thomas Nashe, *Nashes Lenten stuffe* (London, 1599), sig. D2v. Nashe's distrust of imperialism is discussed by Matthew Day, 'Hakluyt, Harvey, Nashe: The Material Text and Early Modern Nationalism', *Studies in Philology*, 104 (2007), 281–305; Andrew Hadfield, 'Lenten Stuffe: Thomas Nashe and the Fiction of Travel', *YES*, 41 (2011), 68–83.

14 See for example C. S. Lewis, *English Literature in the Sixteenth Century, Excluding Drama* (Oxford: Oxford University Press, 1944), p. 416; G. R. Hibbard, *Thomas Nashe: A Critical Introduction* (Cambridge, MA: Harvard University Press, 1962), p. 25; Jonathan V. Crewe, *Unredeemed Rhetoric: Thomas Nashe and the Scandal of Authorship* (Baltimore and London: Johns Hopkins University Press, 1982), p. 91; Lorna Hutson, *Thomas Nashe in Context* (Oxford: Oxford University Press, 1989), p. 123; Peter Holbrook, *Literature and Degree in Renaissance England: Nashe, Bourgeois Tragedy, Shakespeare* (Newark: University of Delaware Press, 1994), p. 35 and p. 56; Robert Weimann, *Authority and Representation in Early Modern Discourse*, ed. David Hillman (Baltimore and London: Johns Hopkins University Press, 1996), pp. 161–73; Georgia Brown, *Redefining Elizabethan Literature* (Cambridge: Cambridge University Press, 2004; 2009), pp. 53–61; Corey McEleney, 'Nashe's Vain Vein: Poetic Pleasure and the Limits of Utility', in *Age of Thomas Nashe*, ed. Guy-Bray, Linton, and Mentz, pp. 153–69; and David Landreth, 'Wit without Money in Nashe', in *Age of Thomas Nashe*, ed. Guy-Bray, Linton, and Mentz, pp. 135–52.

15 Nashe, 'Somewhat', sig. A3r.

16 Hutson, *Thomas Nashe in Context*, pp. 36 and 218, also pp. 80–2; Gail Kern Paster, *Humoring the Body: Emotions and the Shakespearean Stage* (Chicago and London: University of Chicago Press, 2004), p. 41.

17 Beatrice Groves, 'Laughter in the Time of Plague: A Context for the Unstable Style of Nashe's *Christ's Tears over Jerusalem*', *Studies in Philology*, 108 (2011), 238–60 (p. 239); Chris Salamone, Chapter 5 below.

18 Jennifer Richards, *Voices and Books in the English Renaissance: A New History of Reading* (Oxford: Oxford University Press, 2019), p. 248; also pp. 230–82.

19 Hutson, *Thomas Nashe in Context*, p. 4. See also Neil Rhodes, *Elizabethan Grotesque* (London: Routledge & Kegan Paul, 1980), p. 33; and Jason Scott-Warren, 'Nashe's Stuff', in *The Oxford Handbook of English Prose 1500–1640*, ed. Andrew Hadfield (Oxford: Oxford University Press, 2013), pp. 204–18 (p. 208).

20 Gabriel Harvey, *A nevv letter of notable contents* (London, 1593), sig. D1v; Nashe, *Lenten*, sig. D3v.
21 Richard Lichfield [?], *The trimming of Thomas Nashe Gentleman* (London, 1597), sig. B1v. This anonymous work is sometimes attributed to Gabriel Harvey. On pneumatic humoralism see for example Paster, *Humoring*; Gail Kern Paster, 'Becoming the Landscape: The Ecology of the Passions in the Legend of Temperance', in *Environment and Embodiment in Early Modern England*, ed. Mary Floyd-Wilson and Garrett A. Sullivan (Basingstoke: Palgrave Macmillan, 2007), pp. 137–52; Katherine A. Craik, '"The Material Point of Poesy": Reading, Writing and Sensation in Puttenham's *The Arte of English Poesie*', in *Environment and Embodiment*, ed. Floyd-Wilson and Sullivan, pp. 153–70; and Tanya Pollard, 'Spelling the Body', in *Environment and Embodiment*, ed. Floyd-Wilson and Sullivan, pp. 171–86.
22 Nashe, 'Christian', sig. D3v; Thomas Nashe, *Pierce Penilesse his supplication to the diuell* (London, 1592), sig. A3r; Stephen Gosson, *The schoole of abuse* (London, 1579), sig. A3v; George Puttenham, *The arte of English poesie* (London, 1589), sig. S2v. *Pierce Penniless* and *The School of Abuse* are the only currently searchable Elizabethan-era publications on *EEBO* to include the phrase 'paper monster', suggesting that Nashe may be echoing Gosson's specific terminology in a work that elsewhere rebuts antitheatrical discourse. Nashe uses the related term 'puppetplay' to criticise poorly written publications in his 1591 preface to *Astrophel and Stella* ('Somewhat', sig. A3r).
23 See for instance Hutson, *Thomas Nashe in Context*, p. 123, p. 143; McEleney, 'Nashe's Vain Vein', p. 154.
24 See Paster, *Humoring*, pp. 14–19; Craik, '"The Material Point"', pp. 154–64.
25 See John Sutton, *Philosophy and Memory Traces: Descartes to Connectionism* (Cambridge: Cambridge University Press, 1998), pp. 21–49.
26 Michel de Montaigne, *Essays*, trans. John Florio (London, 1613), sigs Ee4r and Kk2r. See for instance Gosson, *School*, sigs B6v–B7r; Puttenham, *Art*, sigs K1r–K1v; also Craik, '"The Material Point"', pp. 154–5.
27 Montaigne, *Essays*, sig. Kk2r. Cf. for instance Sidney's contrast between the 'wholly imaginative' and poetry's 'substantial' workings in Philip Sidney, *The Defence of Poesy*, in *'The Defence of Poesy' and Selected Renaissance Literary Criticism*, ed. Gavin Alexander (London: Penguin, 2004), p. 9.
28 Nashe, *Lenten*, sig. B2v.
29 Weimann, *Authority and Representation*, pp. 161–74.
30 Richards, *Voices and Books*, pp. 247 and 250.
31 Gina Bloom, *Voice in Motion: Staging Gender, Shaping Sound in Early Modern England* (Philadelphia: University of Pennsylvania Press, 2007), pp. 21–159; Paster, *Humoring*; see also Carla Mazzio, 'The History of Air: *Hamlet* and the Trouble with Instruments', *South Central Review*, 26 (2009), 153–96 (p. 159 and p. 182); and Carolyn Sale, 'Eating Air, Feeling Smells: *Hamlet*'s Theory of Performance', *Renaissance Drama*, 35 (2006), 145–68. On Nashe's involvement with *1 Henry VI*, a play that the fictional Pierce explicitly champions (Nashe, *Pierce Penniless*, sig. F3r), see Richards, *Voices and Books*, pp. 245–6.
32 See for instance Nashe, *Summer's*, sigs B1r–B2r, which includes the clown's recommendation that his fellow 'Actors' 'cleare your throats, blowe your noses, and wype your mouthes e're you enter' (sig. B2r); and the related discussion of *Summer's Last Will and Testament* in the Introduction above. My reading of pneumatic exchange in Nashe's prose works is indebted to Naya Tsentourou's argument that Shakespeare replicated a theatrical mode of pneumatic transmission and exchange

within his poem *The Rape of Lucrece*, which she has generously discussed with me in detail. See Naya Tsentourou, 'Untimely Breathings in *The Rape of Lucrece*', *Shakespeare*, 18 (2022), 385–407.
33 Nashe, 'Somewhat', sig. A3r; Bloom, *Voice in Motion*, p. 16.
34 Bloom, *Voice in Motion*, p. 68.
35 Bloom, *Voice in Motion*, esp. pp. 66–110.
36 Nashe, 'Christian', sig. D1v; Russell West, *Spatial Representations and the Jacobean Stage: From Shakespeare to Webster* (Basingstoke: Palgrave Macmillan, 2002), p. 35. See for example Nashe, *Pierce Penniless*, sig. E1v; Nashe, *Have With You*, sig. F1r; Nashe, *Lenten*, sig. K4v.
37 Nashe, *Pierce Penniless*, sig. I2v.
38 Kiernan Ryan, 'The Extemporal Vein: Thomas Nashe and the Invention of Modern Narrative', in *Thomas Nashe*, ed. Georgia Brown (Farnham: Ashgate, 2011), pp. 3–16 (p. 10); Charles Nicholl, *A Cup of News: The Life of Thomas Nashe* (London: Routledge & Kegan Paul, 1984), p. 272; Thomas Nashe, 'To his Readers', in Thomas Nashe, *Nashes Lenten Stuffe* (London, 1599), sig. A4v.
39 Thomas Nashe, *The terrors of the night* (London, 1594), sig. E3v.
40 Nashe, *Lenten*, sig. B4r.
41 Nashe, *Lenten*, sigs B4v and C1r. 'Sound' typically denotes something healthy, wholesome, or well-founded (*OED* 'sound' *adj.*); the verb form also has associations with maritime navigation (*OED* 'sound' *v.*2 2a). See too Douglas Clark, Chapter 3 below.
42 Nashe, *Lenten*, sig, B3r.
43 Nashe, *Lenten*, sigs C3v–C4r.
44 Nashe, *Lenten*, sig. D2r.
45 Nashe, *Lenten*, sig. I4v.
46 Nashe, *Lenten*, sig. L2r. Cf. Harvey's derisory comment that Nashe 'hath the winds of Aeolus at commaundement' (*Pierce's Supererogation*, sig. B3r).
47 Nashe, *Unfortunate Traveller*, sig. F3r.
48 Clark, Chapter 3 below; Nashe, *Lenten*, sig. C1v.
49 See for example Galen, *On the Usefulness of the Parts of the Body*, trans. and ed. Margaret Tallmadge May (Ithaca: Cornell University Press, 1968), pp. 279–80. The Roman physician Galen's theories importantly influenced early modern medical thinking, and were often cited by Nashe's contemporaries.
50 Nashe, *Lenten*, sig. L2r. Nashe is named on this edition's title page and in the mock-epistle. It is alternatively possible that the inverted layout reverses the asterism's usual meaning, denoting finality rather than omitted content, but the parenthetical framing – which elsewhere signals dialogic play with an imagined reader – seems to anticipate a response that remains textually imminent.
51 Gosson, *School*, sigs A6r and C5r; Harvey, *Pierce's Supererogation*, sigs V1v–V2r.
52 Nashe, *Lenten*, sig. B3v. See also Nashe, *Lenten*, sig. K2v.
53 Nashe, *Pierce Peninless*, sig. E1v; Richards, *Voices and Books*, p. 239. See also Thomas Nashe, 'To the Gentlemen Students of both Universities', in Robert Greene, *Menaphon Camillas alarum to slumbering Euphues* (London, 1589), sig. **1v; and Kettnich, 'Nashe's Extemporal Vein'.
54 See Hutson, *Thomas Nashe in Context*, p. 2; Alexandra Halasz, 'The Patrimony of Learning', in *Thomas Nashe*, ed. Brown, pp. 402–3; Richards, *Voices and Books*, p. 14; Nashe, *Pierce Penniless*, sig. F3r. On shared emotional experience at the early modern commercial theatre see Sale, 'Eating Air, Feeling Smells', pp. 145–68; and Steven Mullaney, 'Affective Technologies: Towards an Emotional Logic of

the Elizabethan Stage', in *Environment and Embodiment*, ed. Floyd-Wilson and Sullivan, pp. 71–89.
55 Laurie Ellinghausen, *Labor and Writing in Early Modern England, 1567–1667* (Aldershot: Ashgate, 2008), p. 45; Brown, *Redefining*, pp. 71 and 92.
56 Nashe, *Unfortunate Traveller*, sig. A2v.
57 Nashe, *Pierce Penniless*, sig. A2v.
58 Nashe, *Pierce Penniless*, sigs D3v–D4r. Cf. for instance Gianfrancesco Pico Della Mirandola, *On the Imagination*, trans. Harry Caplan (New Haven: Yale University Press, 1930), pp. 87–9.
59 Ellinghausen, *Labor and Writing*, p. 45.
60 Thomas Nashe, 'A private Epistle', in Nashe, *Pierce Penniless*, sigs ¶1r–¶1v.
61 Nashe, *Pierce Penniless*, sigs H2r and G2r. For a more detailed evaluation of this text's demonological and spectral discourse, see Salamone, Chapter 5 below. Cf. Nashe, *Pierce Penniless*, sig. A4r, where the Knight of the Post identifies himself as 'a spirite in nature and essence, that take upon me this humaine shame' (it is unclear whether the latter term is Nashe's own, or a compositorial misreading of 'shape').
62 Nashe, *Have With You*, sig. D4r.
63 William Fulke, *A goodly gallerye with a most pleasaunt prospect* (London, 1563), sig. F8r.
64 Nashe, *Have With You*, sig. D4r.
65 Puttenham, *Art*, sigs D3r–D3v, L4v, and L3v; see also sig. R4v. My examples refer to 'lightness' in the sense of lacking weight; in contrast, 'light' in the sense of shining rays almost invariably possesses positive connotations.
66 Sidney, *Defence*, p. 31.
67 Thomas Elyot, *The dictionary of syr Thomas Eliot knyght* (London, 1538), sig. Dd5v. See also Stephen S. Hilliard, *The Singularity of Thomas Nashe* (Lincoln: University of Nebraska Press, 1986), p. 200.
68 Harvey, *Pierce's Supererogation*, sigs T4r and V1r.
69 *Trimming*, sig. C4v.
70 Harvey, *Pierce's Supererogation*, C1r; Nashe, *Have With You*, sig. D3v; Nashe, 'Readers', sig. A4r.
71 Nashe, *Lenten*, sigs F2v and L1v; Thomas Nashe, 'To Master or Goodman Reader', in Nashe, *Terrors*, sig. A3r. The stylistic implications of the former example are discussed by Crewe, p. 96.
72 Nashe, *Terrors*, sig. G4r; Nashe, *Have With You*, sigs P1r–P1v.
73 Nashe, *Have With You*, sigs F1v and S2v.
74 Hadfield, 'Lenten Stuffe', p. 75; Nashe, *Strange News*, sig. G3r.
75 Thomas Nashe, 'To the most Orthodoxall ... Corrector', in Nashe, *Have With You*, sig. A3v.
76 Nashe, *Strange News*, sigs D1v and K4r.
77 I quote from Christopher Marlowe's Elizabethan-era translation: *All Ovids Elegies*, ed. Roma Gill, in *The Complete Works of Christopher Marlowe* (Oxford: Oxford University Press, 1986; 2012), I:I.21, 8, 31, 33.
78 Nashe, *Strange Newes*, sig. E1v.
79 Thomas Lodge, *A Treatise of the Plague* (London, 1603), sig. C2v; Francis Bacon, *Sylua syluarum: or A naturall historie In ten centuries* (London, 1627), sig. Ii2v.
80 Nashe, *Terrors*, sigs C2v–C3r.
81 Nashe, 'Readers', sig. A4r.
82 Lodge, *Treatise*, sig. B2v.

83 Gosson, *School*, sigs B6v–B7r; William Rankins, *A mirrour of monsters* (London, 1587), sigs A1r and B2v. See also Craik, '"The Material Point"', pp. 153–70.
84 Harvey, *Pierce's Supererogation*, sig. Y4v; Gabriel Harvey, *Foure letters, and certaine sonnets* (London, 1592), sig. B2r. For a comparative evaluation of Nashe's and Greene's print market reception see Lena Liapi, Chapter 4 below.
85 *Trimming*, sig. C2r.
86 Harvey, *Pierce's Supererogation*, sig. D1v; *Trimming*, sig. C4v. Cf. for instance Hugh Plat's warning that 'common seacole fiers… dooth make a hellishe smoke and smoder'. *A nevv, cheape and delicate fire of cole-balles* (London, 1603), sig. B4v.
87 Nashe, *Have With You*, sigs D1v and D4r. Elizabethan and Jacobean brew-houses were notorious for emitting thick clouds of noxious smoke. See William M. Cavert, *The Smoke of London: Energy and Environment in the Early Modern City* (Cambridge: Cambridge University Press, 2016), pp. 45–6.
88 Nashe, *Have With You*, sig. E3r. Nashe's interest in the physical cost of authorship is considered by Tamsin Theresa Badcoe in '"As many Ciphers without an I": Self-Reflexive Violence in the Work of Thomas Nashe', *Modern Philology*, 111 (2014), 384–407.
89 Nashe, *Strange News*, sig. L2v.
90 Nashe, *Have With You*, sig. N4v.
91 Hutson, *Thomas Nashe in Context*, p. 110.
92 Nashe, *Have With You*, sigs R1v–R2r; Nashe, *Pierce Penniless*, sig. I2v.
93 Nashe, *Strange News*, sig. L2v; Nashe, *Terrors*, sig. G1v.
94 Nashe, 'Gentlemen Students', sig. **2r; Nashe, 'Somewhat', sig. A3v. Cf. Clark's detailed analysis of the former quip (Chapter 3 below). On *Christ's Tears* see Groves, 'Laughter in the Time of Plague', esp. pp. 238–44.
95 Nashe, 'Christian', sig. D2v. See also Hutson, *Thomas Nashe in Context*, p. 110.
96 Lodge, *Treatise*, sig. C3v.
97 Nashe, *Have With You*, sig. E3r; Lodge, *Treatise*, sigs E4v and C4r.
98 J. B. Bamborough, *The Little World of Man* (London: Longmans, 1952), p. 30. Cited in Paster, *Humoring*, p. 12. See Rhodes, *Elizabethan Grotesque*; also Holbrook, *Literature and Degree*, p. 64; Hutson, *Thomas Nashe in Context*, pp. 15–17; and Salamone, Chapter 5 below.
99 Hutson, *Thomas Nashe in Context*, pp. 1–2. See also Landreth, 'Wit Without Money', p. 137.
100 Brown, *Redefining*, p. 97.
101 See Salamone, Chapter 5 below.
102 Nashe, 'Gentlemen Students', sig. **2r; Steve Mentz, 'Nashe's Fish: Misogyny, Romance, and the Ocean in *Lenten Stuffe*', in *Age of Thomas Nashe*, ed. Guy-Bray, Linton, and Mentz, pp. 63–73 (p. 70). See also Holbrook, *Literature and Degree*, pp. 34–5; Kettnich, 'Nashe's Extemporal Vein', p. 107; and Scott-Warren, 'Nashe's Stuff', esp. p. 215.
103 William Shakespeare, *Antony and Cleopatra*, ed. John Wilders (London: Arden Shakespeare, 1995), 2.2.242. Dyspnoea (shortness of breath) 'is often associated with hyperventilation and vice versa' (William N. Gardner and Alex Lewis, 'Hyperventilation and Disproportionate Breathlessness', in *Supportive Care in Respiratory Disease*, ed. Sam H. Ahmedzai and Martin F. Muers (Oxford: Oxford University Press, 2011), pp. 323–38 (p. 324)).
104 Nashe, *Pierce Penniless*, sig. I3r.
105 Nashe, *Have With You*, sig. P1r; Nashe, *Lenten*, sig. B3r.

106 Gabriel Harvey, 'To his very gentle and liberal frendes', in Harvey, *Pierce's Supererogation*, sig. **2v; Nashe, 'Somewhat', sig. A4v.
107 Thomas Nashe, *The Anatomie of Absurditie* (London, 1589), sig. A1v; Nashe, *Have With You*, sigs E1v and G1v.
108 Thomas Nashe, 'To the Reader', in Thomas Nashe, *Christs teares ouer Ierusalem* (London, 1594), sig. *2v; Scott-Warren, 'Nashe's Stuff', pp. 216–17. Cf. Scott-Warren, 'Nashe's Stuff', p. 218.
109 Nashe, *Unfortunate*, sig. F3r; Nashe, *Strange News*, sig. K4r.
110 Nashe, 'Christian', sig. D3v; Nashe, *Strange News*, sig. K4r; Nashe, 'Somewhat', sig. A3r.

2
A FLOOD IN A FURROW: NASHE, NEWS, AND MONSTROUS TOPICALITY

Kirsty Rolfe

Among the wide-ranging criticism of contemporary writing and scholarship in Thomas Nashe's *The Anatomy of Absurdity* (1589) – his first sustained piece of writing to reach print – is an anecdote about the production, dissemination, and effects of news.

> But lightly some newes attends the ende of every Tearme, some Monsters are bookt, though not bred against vacation times, which are straight waie diversly dispearst into everie quarter, so that at length they become the Alehouse talke of every Carter: yea the Country Plowman feareth a Calabrian floodde in the midst of a furrowe, and the sillie Sheephearde committing his wandering sheepe to the custodie of his wappe, in his field naps, dreameth of flying Dragons, which for feare least he should see to the losse of his sight, he falleth a sleepe, no star he seeth in the night but seemeth a Comet, hee lighteth no sooner on a quagmyre, but he thinketh this is the foretold Earthquake wherof his boy hath the Ballet.[1]

The imagined 'Calabrian floodde' indicates that the reference is, most directly, to *Strange News out of Calabria Prognosticated in the Year 1586, Upon the Year 87*, a short pamphlet of prophecies attributed to the fictional 'John Doleta', a learned 'Starre Maister' from Calabria, which predicted a variety of dire events for 1587.[2] His critique extends wider, though, towards an idea of idle, vacation-time 'newes', made up of spurious predictions, dispensed in books and ballads, which reaches those who interpret it incorrectly. It takes in both the news itself and the processes by which it moves. News – especially printed news – was itself topical in the 1580s and 1590s, when increasing numbers of news reports from the wars in France and the Netherlands arrived in the shops of London booksellers, along with pamphlets dealing with 'wonders' and disasters, and a range of astrological works that predicted dramatic and often dire future events.[3] These genres sat alongside one another on booksellers' stalls, often taking similar ballad or quarto pamphlet form, and drawing on and interacting with manuscript and oral forms of transmission. At the same time this increase in available news was met with an increase in discourse about it, which focused on ideas of idleness, sinfulness, and gullibility.

News haunts the edges of Nashe's work throughout his career: it is rarely defined or addressed directly, but its tropes and processes inform how he presents both his own writing and that of others (in particular, Gabriel Harvey). In this chapter I begin by exploring how we might understand the notoriously slippery category of 'news', with a particular focus on the place of prophecy – especially Doleta's *Strange News out of Calabria* – within both Nashe's works and late sixteenth-century news culture. Through this I examine how Nashe engages with contemporary cultures of news publication, looking especially at the satirical uses he makes of news's conceptual, material, and temporal slipperiness. In the second part I explore contemporary anti-news discourse to illustrate how people act on news and are acted on by news, concentrating on ideas that those who consumed or shared news might engage in idleness, disruptive behaviour, and dangerous misinterpretation – especially if they were from the lower classes. Finally I argue that understanding early modern stereotypes about news, and Nashe's use of them, deepens our understanding of Nashe's pamphlet war with Gabriel Harvey. I show that both writers deploy negative stereotypes about topical print both to mock their enemy and to protect – or, at least, to attempt to protect – their own authorial personas from accusations of dangerous, untruthful, 'monstrous' topicality.

STRANGE NEWS: NASHE, NEWS, AND PROPHECY IN THE 1580s–90s

'News' was, and remains, a capacious category and an inexact term. Joad Raymond and Noah Moxham note how difficult, if not impossible, it is to define.[4] Especially in a period before the advent of more professionalised, serialised news publication in England, it could indicate anything from tidings of a friend's good fortune to reports of a battle in France, to information about and interpretation of crime or natural disaster, to the 'good news' of the gospel.[5] These meanings inform one another, and shape how people talked about news. News could be stigmatised as gossip or as unacceptable meddling in affairs of state; at the same time it could be lauded as worldly information important for people to know, or as messages from the divine. The slipperiness of 'news' as a term is possible because news, conceptually speaking, is defined less by its content than by its processes. 'At an ideational level', Jenni Hyde notes, 'news is itself a construct, being simply what someone chooses to tell another person'.[6] It is 'essentially connective and dynamic', linking both places and people: whether it came in the form of a printed pamphlet, or a ballad heard in the street or purchased in print, or included in a sociable letter or in-person conversation, it was simultaneously an impetus for, evidence of, and the very matter of sociable and professional interaction.[7] The relationships news formed and reflected might cross significant international distances, as the work of numerous scholars demonstrates.[8] Joad Raymond stresses that news publications are not themselves *news*: they 'exist at the end of a network', and 'we need to study the processes that generate the products, and not the products alone'.[9] While Raymond's concern is the movement of news over far-flung distances via international postal and diplomatic networks, and Nashe's is a ploughman getting spooked by a puddle because he has read a prophetic pamphlet, in both cases the subject of investigation or criticism is the movement of information, the processes that allow intelligence (whether truthful or misleading) to spread. Nashe's 'newes' is ludicrous to start with, but what activates its ridiculousness – and perhaps even makes it dangerous – is the fact that it is 'straight waie diversly dispearst into everie quarter' and ends up in the hands of those who interpret it incorrectly.[10] Hyde's helpfully broad working definition fits Nashe's ridiculous 'news' rather well:

> Sixteenth-century news might then be defined as the broadcast or reporting of interesting events and information considered to be novel, relevant to contemporary society and/or worthy of discussion, in whatever way it was transmitted. Consumers may have believed information to be noteworthy because it could affect them in some way, or simply because they had an interest in gossip and rumour. Perhaps it just become newsworthy by the act of being passed by one person to another.[11]

If 'news' is defined by the processes of passing between people, and/or the idea that its content is novel, relevant, or discussion-worthy, then it makes sense to take Nashe's description of these prophecies as 'newes' seriously, even if the information they carry is misleading. The prophecies are treated as novel, and they move between people – the shepherd and his boy, the carters in the alehouse – creating and maintaining relationships through discussion, opinion, and shared fear. However, for Nashe, news is curiously and tellingly ill-defined: 'But lightly some newes attends the ende of every Tearme, some Monsters are bookt, though not bred against vacation times, which are straight waie diversly dispearst into everie quarter'.[12] It is not entirely clear what Nashe is designating as 'newes'. Is the news the 'Monsters' themselves – and what are they? The supernatural occurrences that Nashe's Carter, Ploughman and Shepherd read or hear about (and frighten themselves by imagining) fit the bill, but perhaps the texts in which they are described do, too. As we will see, the mutable, indefinable nature of 'news' – the fuzziness of its borders – allows

Nashe to explore the idea that topical texts and discourse can themselves be monstrous, in form, content, and effect.

The book that Nashe refers to in this passage from *Absurdity* – Doleta's *Strange News out of Calabria* – was registered to John Perrin in November 1586 and probably issued early the following year. It came on the heels of a surge in prophetic and 'wonder' literature in the earlier 1580s, in which Nashe's future nemeses, the Harvey brothers, were themselves involved. Richard Harvey's *Astrological Discourse* (1583), dedicated to Gabriel Harvey and with a supplement written by John Harvey, marred the reputations of the brothers when its predictions for the year failed to come true.[13] Doleta's *Strange News* prompted a 'Confutation' by one 'T.R.' later in the year, and was widely mocked – including by John Harvey, who punned on the closeness of 'Doleta' to 'Dolt' in his 1588 *A Discoursive Problem Concerning Prophesies* (a critical departure from his earlier astrological work): 'the reverend Astronomer and doughtie clarke, John Dolteta, Doleta I would say'.[14] Doleta's *Strange News* was itself newsworthy, an object of topical interest, but it also resembled other news pamphlets of the 1580s and 1590s in that it spoke to interest in 'foreign affairs'. Doleta's prophecy gets some of its newsworthiness, and some of its 'strangeness' (in the sense of 'foreignness'), from the fact that it has supposedly crossed Europe, bringing a 'Calabrian floodde' to an English furrow. Other prophetic literature from the 1580s was also international in nature: in particular, publications such as those by Richard and John Harvey were influenced by a much-discussed prophecy attributed to the German astronomer Regiomontanus (Johannes Müller von Königsberg, 1436–76), which predicted that cataclysmic events would take place in 1588.[15]

Nashe appears to have had an interest in these newsworthy prophecies. He ridicules 'our chiefe noted Augurers and Soothsayers in England at this time' as frauds in *The Terrors of the Night* (1594), and may have gone as far as predicting, and humorously interpreting, astrological phenomena for 1591 in the mock-prognostication *Fearful and Lamentable Effects of Two Dangerous Comets*, attributed to one 'Simon Smel-knave' but possibly authored by Nashe.[16] In particular Doleta was (as Matthew Steggle writes) 'a recurring figure in Nashe's imagination throughout his career'.[17] Nashe echoes Doleta's title in his own *Strange News* (1592), his response to Gabriel Harvey's *Four Letters, and Certain Sonnets* (1592). In *Strange News* he reports – or invents – a rumour that Gabriel's 'brother' in fact wrote the prophecies attributed to Doleta:

> The next weeke Maister Bird (if his inke-pot have a cleare current) hee will have at you with a cap-case full of French occurences, that is, shape you a messe of newes out of the second course of his conceit, as his brother

is said out of the fabulous abundance of his braine to have invented the newes out of Calabria (John Doletas prophesie of flying dragons, commets, Earthquakes, and inundations.)[18]

Nashe goes on to link Gabriel himself to Doleta in *Have With You to Saffron Walden* (1596), in which he calls Gabriel Harvey 'a base John Doleta the Almanack-maker'.[19] Crucially, as the quotation from *Strange News* above shows, Nashe associates Doleta's 'straunge newes' with other forms of news, such as the 'cap-case [travelling bag] full of French occurences' that he imagines Gabriel Harvey sending to his correspondent Christopher Bird. Here Nashe mocks Gabriel Harvey's promise in *Four Letters* to send Bird 'a letter of such French occurrences, and other intelligences, as the credible relation of inquisitive frendes, or imployed straungers shall acquaint me withall'.[20] Nashe aligns prophecies and foreign news through describing both as nonsense, each invented by an unscrupulous member of the Harvey circle. This attack on Harvey speaks to Nashe's ongoing interest in the production, movement, and consumption of 'news', broadly defined: information that ranged from reports of foreign 'occurences' to doubtful and fantastical prophecies, both of which Nashe treats as nonsense purposefully and misleadingly foisted upon the textual and conversational marketplace, which then circulates to ridiculous and possibly dangerous effect. As the final section of this chapter explores, news and the discourse around it become a means for Nashe to attack Harvey's engagements with the print market as idle, excessive, and monstrous.

Notably the prophetic 'news' in *The Anatomy of Absurdity* has not, in fact, been 'straight waie diversly dispearst': in fact, all of it is rather out of date by 1589. The 'foretold Earthquake wherof [the Shepherd's] boy hath the Ballet' might refer to the multiple 'great movings of the earth' predicted in Doleta's *Strange News* for 1587, which had not materialised.[21] This reference may also gesture towards the earthquake that south-east England had experienced in April 1580, which was widely commemorated in print, interpreted as a warning from God.[22] 'Foretold' is therefore heavily ironic: the Shepherd fears a disaster the predicted time for which has already been and gone, or which is nine years in the past. The Shepherd's fear demonstrates his poor knowledge of his sources: Doleta's *Strange News* and other prophetic astrological texts of the 1580s generally give precise dates for their 'foretold' events. Moreover, Doleta's pamphlet had far deeper chronological roots: Jonathan Green has demonstrated that the prophecy is based on the twelfth-century 'Toledo letter' – sometimes attributed to one 'John of Toledo', making 'Doleta' (more or less) an anagram. The 'Toledo letter', and prophecies drawing on it, circulated widely in medieval and early modern Europe, and Green has traced a large number of printed publications based on it circulating during the 1580s.[23]

News was time-bound at its very heart: old news was often derided as 'stale'. This time-boundedness is unclear and contingent, however. Whether news counted as novel depended on what one knew already, and what one expected from the news networks one accessed. It was not possible to delineate the point in its lifetime in which 'newes' stopped counting as such for all of the people who encountered it: 'old' news could be news if it was something the receiver did not already know. Meanwhile prophecy deals with time in the other direction: it promises future events, and, if the appointed time comes and goes without these happening, it proves false, matter for mockery rather than fear. However, when he aligns Harvey's promised 'French occurences' with Toledo's prophecies, Nashe elides this difference, and in doing so reveals something key about both forms of information: neither is as restricted to the past or the future as they at first appear. News deals with past events, but the currency of these events lies in the fact that they continue to develop and have consequences. News reports create, as Brendan Dooley has argued, a sense of 'contemporaneity' ('the perception, shared by a number of human beings, of experiencing a particular event at more or less the same time') across wide geographical spaces.[24] In turn this perception brings with it questions over what has happened in the time elapsed since the event, what is happening in the present, and what will happen next. News projects into the future, summoning expectations, predictions, and anxieties about what the next report (itself, necessarily, retelling the past) will bring. Harvey's promise to send Bird French news itself combines the past and the future, juxtaposing praise of Henri IV with the conjecture that '[t]he Spanyard, politique inough ...will bee advised, before he entangle himselfe with more warres attonce' at reports of English military heroism.[25] Harvey's rather bland and comforting prediction belies the anxiety news consumers may have felt as they navigated the partial and belated reports of major events available to them, trying to ascertain both what had happened and what it might mean for the future.[26]

News consumption shades into prophecy, and prophecy bleeds into news. There are two main 'newsworthy' points in the life of a prophecy: the moment of its divination (the sight and interpretation of a comet, for example) and the time at which that event(s) it foretells will supposedly take place. Until the latter point in time comes to pass the prophecy can function in a way analogous to news (and be presented as such): a report of a past event that allows one to predict the future. If that point in time comes and goes without the prophecy coming true, however, it becomes a different form of novelty: a joke, an anecdote passed between people to demonstrate the foolishness of those who prophesised floods and dragons, and those who believed them. Prophecy's predictions are specific and explicit (if sometimes confusing), while for the most part news prompts its consumers by implication to predict the future. However, both forms of information situate their consumers in an anxious present, looking to the past while awaiting disaster, comfort, or the cathartic release of laughter.

IDLENESS, NOSINESS, AND MISINTERPRETATION: NASHE AND ANTI-NEWS DISCOURSE

The 'newes' Nashe refers to is time-limited in a further sense: it is connected to – indeed, like a servant or seeker after preferment, 'attends' upon – the end of each university or legal term. Nashe also appears to make a connection between Doleta and the rhythms of university life, in *Terminus & Non Terminus*: a now-lost 'Show', which the Cambridge barber Richard Lichfield writes that Nashe both acted in and 'had a hand in' while at the university. This entertainment, Steggle has shown, appears to have placed Doleta as a comic figure on stage. Steggle's source is a lyric poem in manuscript by Nashe's contemporary at St John's, Richard Mills, which mentions a play containing both 'Lord Terminus', 'Lord Non Terminus', and 'the Jestes of merye Doleta'.[27] As Steggle points out, in early modern England 'non terminus' was used to refer specifically to the vacations between university or legal terms: '*Terminus & Non Terminus* does not mean, as has been thought, "the end and not the end": it means "Term and Vacation"'.[28] This lost play may – like Nashe's sole single-authored play, *Summer's Last Will and Testament* (probably performed 1592, published 1600), which dramatises the changing of the seasons – be part of 'a well-established tradition of allegorical drama in which seasons of the year, or other divisions of time, contend against each other'.[29] In the light of this, Doleta is – in both *Terminus & Non Terminus* and *The Anatomy of Absurdity* – 'not just a byword for foolishness, but specifically for foolishness linked to vacation time'.[30] Against ideas of freshness and staleness, or of ancient authority and prophetic future, this sets a different idea of the relationship between information, publication (in the broad sense of 'making public' as well as that of 'printing'), and the passage of time: in this case time flows inexorably onwards, but it is measured less by the calendar than by the use one makes of it. Nashe's use of Doleta connects *Strange News*, and (by implication) both prophecy and news more generally, to ideas of idleness and wastefulness that are key to discourse about the news in this period.

Nashe's connection of news to vacation-time idleness taps into common tropes that aligned news with triviality, time-wasting, untruth, and disruptive curiosity. Consuming, retailing, or distributing news – however one defined 'news' – was both ideologically and practically fraught in the latter years of the sixteenth century. Texts from this period abound in negative discourse about news: about what it might mean about, and do to, individuals and communities. The churchman Michael Cope exhorted his readers not to 'be like unto those that are desirous to heare newes, that they may passe away their time merily and carelesly, so vayne and unprofitable they are'.[31] News, in this interpretation, is treated simply as entertainment, a waste of time that could be used more purposefully. Seeking after and retelling news might give one a bad reputation, according to H. Roper: 'let every manne take heede, howe he doth tell or cary any newes, least hee be counted but a busie talker or a tatler: for he that is a teller of newes, is thoughte to be but a trifler, a very lyar, and a blabbe'.[32] This 'telling and carrying' could be dangerous to the individual and to their community. William Bullein aligns news-carrying with a range of other activities 'unprofitable to the commonwealth':

> Some men in misery straunge shiftes wil make,
> ...
> Furderers of Frayes, with longe Dagger or Sworde,
> Sowing of dissention, at eche mannes borde.
> Caryers of newes, proclaimers of lies,
> Livers by Lechery, blood sucker, and spyes.[33]

Not only is carrying news wasteful of time and effort, it also makes those who do it both sinful individuals and bad subjects. Those who spread news disseminate lies, misleading other subjects and prompting them to dissent from established authority. Here the sociable nature of news – its role as both marker and subject of exchange between individuals – becomes the means by which social roles are undermined. We see some of this in *The Anatomy of Absurdity*, when Nashe's 'silly Sheephearde' learns about 'the foretolde Earthquake' from a ballad in possession of 'his Boy'. The Shepherd, as the more senior person in the relationship, should instruct the youth in his charge to avoid wasting his time on such trivial and misleading things; however, instead of this he believes the 'news' uncritically.

Desire for news could endanger the commonwealth and the individual, too, especially if they were in an unfamiliar situation. John Lyly's *Euphues: The Anatomy of Wit* (1578) and its sequel *Euphues and His England* (1580) were (as the title of the former indicates) a major influence on Nashe's *The Anatomy of Absurdity*. In *Euphues and His England*, Euphues and Philautis are careful, upon visiting England, not to be 'too inquisitive of newes neither curious in matters of State'.[34] In part this is simply good practice when travelling: it is important for foreigners (in this case, a

Greek and a Neapolitan, respectively) to avoid being seen to meddle in affairs of another polity. Lyly's decision to stress this point, though, may reflect an impression that the English authorities, and maybe English people more generally, were especially keen to criticise and/or punish desire for news. This in turn may reflect the view – frequently expressed by English writers – that the English were especially susceptible to this desire, and thus needed to be particularly careful about the movement of information. In Nashe's *The Unfortunate Traveller* (1594) the banished English earl who rescues the narrator Jack from execution in Rome complains to him, in his lengthy oration on the dangers of travel, that 'our Englishmen are the plainest dealing soules that ever God put life in: they are greedie of newes, and love to be fed in their humors and heare themselves flattered the best that may be'.[35] The view that English people were subject to a particular national nosiness is also expressed by William Rankins, who posits that it was the influence of historical Norse invaders which filled England with 'carelesse cogitations', leading the nation to '[decline] from the proper estate of their natural good' to the extent that 'it may be thought that England ... hath brought more awaie, and pondered better of their neighbours newes, then any corner of all Christendom, besides'.[36] The eponymous protagonist of Nashe's *Pierce Penniless* (1592) meets the devil in the middle walk of St Paul's Cathedral, the most famous location for the exchange of news in early modern England, and displays 'an Englishmans appetite to enquire of news' in questioning his infernal interlocutor about hell.[37] Pierce's 'English' nosiness leads him to enquire into matters that are both beyond his human capacity and which might endanger his own soul – and, by implication, maybe the reader's soul as well. Pierce's interest in news already aligns him with the devil, who is described as 'a greedy pursuer of newes'.[38]

Seeking after news might make English men and women vicious, but it did not, according to its critics, make them smart. Cope's news consumers 'thinke verily they are not sluggish and sleepish, but are quicke and nimble', believing themselves to be capable and judicious when in fact they are slow and gullible. Worse, their credulous consumption of news causes them to spread untruths, and to misjudge their peers: '[a]s such men doe easily beleeve lyes, even so doe they delight to make others beleeve them also, and they thinke a man a verie foole, or that he doeth them wrong, when hee beleeveth not their words so easily, as did their jesters and flatterers.[39]

As well as acquiring an inaccurate view of their own intellectual capacity, credulous consumers of news were at risk of being manipulated into making fools of themselves, or worse. According to the banished earl in *The Unfortunate Traveller*, the plain-dealing gullibility of Englishmen abroad led them to 'devour any hooke baited for them' by canny Italians, to the great amusement of the latter.[40] Through the circulation of misleading publications like Doleta's *Strange News*, Nashe writes in *The Anatomy of Absurdity*, 'the ignorant [are] deluded, the simple misused, and the sacred Science of Astronomie discredited, & in truth what leasings will not make-shyfts invent for money? What wyl they not faine for gaine?'[41] Nashe connects deception specifically to 'low' forms of literary production:

> Hence come our babling Ballets, and our new found Songs and Sonets, which every rednose Fidler hath at his fingers end, and every ignorant Ale knight will breath foorth over the potte, as soone as his braine waxeth hote. Be it a truth which they would tune, they enterlace it with a lye or two to make meeter, not regarding veritie, so they may make uppe the verse, not unlike to Homer, who cared not what he fained, so hee might make his Countrimen famous. But as the straightest things beeing put into water, seeme crooked, so the crediblest trothes, if once they come with in compasse of these mens wits, seeme tales.[42]

This passage moves from the ill-defined 'news' with which Nashe started to the literary forms in which this news might take shape, or might inspire. It slides the idea of informational trickery into one of *metrical* trickery: it aligns the idea of adding 'feigned' details to a news report and adding syllables to 'make uppe the verse', playing on the fact that – in an era when news often moved in ballads intended to be sung – these could be one and the same.[43] This slippage allows Nashe to move into a diatribe on the ignorance of those who 'obtaine the name of our English Poets', running moral and aesthetic outrage together into a wide-ranging critique of contemporary print.[44] The 'straightest things', warped by the optical properties of water, are thus both distorted intelligence and sense warped into inelegant verse. 'Truth' becomes a matter both of informational accuracy and aesthetic form.

The expression of 'truth' in the 1580s might also, perhaps, be a matter of social degree and circumscribed expertise. Michael Cope, in his reading of Proverbs 12.17 ('He that speaketh truth, will show righteousness: but a false witness useth deceit'), connects 'speaking truth' to the idea of staying in, and speaking of, one's 'state and vocation':

> the manner of speaking trueth, in our common, familiar and private talke, is that wee shoulde talke togither of thinges and matters even so as they are, and as wee knowe them, without flattering and slaundering, without affection of telling newes, and without delighting to consume and passe away the time in reasoning and babbling ... must wee be sober in woordes, and also not to open our mouthes, but to talke and commen of thinges profitable and necessarie, as of thinges which may serve to the glory of

GOD, and profite of our neighbours, and of those matters which concerne our state and vocation, &c.⁴⁵

In a later section of *The Anatomy of Absurdity* (when criticising attempts, by those influenced by the French educational theorist Petrus Ramus, to overhaul the traditional, Aristotelian university curriculum) Nashe refers to a classical anecdote often marshalled to make a similar point, comparing those who challenge classical authorities from a position of (in Nashe's view) relative ignorance with the 'rude Cobler' who criticised the renowned Greek painter Apelles for representing a subject's sandals incorrectly. Apelles corrected his depiction of the sandals, but when the cobbler proceeded to critique how he had painted the subject's leg he refused to rework it, saying that a cobbler should not go beyond his last.⁴⁶ The anecdote appears in Erasmus's *Adages*, and was much-repeated in early modern texts as an example of how one should restain one's discourse within the bounds of individual expertise.⁴⁷

As Cope's prohibition on 'affection of telling newes' indicates, news activates these sorts of concerns: not only in terms of how one should profitably spend time but also in terms of questions over who should have access to news, and how they might discuss it, and at what point permissible curiosity became unacceptable 'meddling' in matters beyond one's last (what Fritz Levy calls 'the decorum of news').⁴⁸ This was especially fraught when news dealt with matters of politics and/or religion, and came to a head in the succeeding reign, when the developing market for international news in the 1620s came into conflict with the Stuart state's attempts to control flows and discussions of information.⁴⁹

Much of *The Anatomy of Absurdity* is concerned (rather ironically, given the author's inexperience) with ideas of capacity and expertise: of which talents and traits qualify someone to write, to speak, to interpret, on particular subjects. Nashe's discussion of 'newes' in *The Anatomy of Absurdity* is preceded by criticism of men who '[challenge] knowledge unto themselves of deeper misteries, when as with Thales Milesius they see not what is under their feete'.⁵⁰ This refers to the Greek philosopher Thales of Miletus, who fell into a well or ditch while observing the stars: an anecdote often deployed for ideas of intellectual overreach.⁵¹ Nashe uses it to attack those who search 'into the secrets of nature' in order to interpret and prophesy messages from the divine: 'Who made them so privie to the secrets of the Almightie, that they should foretell the tokens of his wrath, or terminate the time of his vengeaunce'.⁵² This overreaching is connected to ideas of bad *reading* and interpretation: a concern that Nashe returns to repeatedly throughout his career. In the address 'to the Gentlemen Readers' in *Strange News*, Nashe writes that, 'in these ill eide daies of ours', 'rash heads, upstart Interpreters, have extorted & rakte that unreverent meaning out of my lines, which a thousand deaths cannot make mee ere grant that I dreamd off'.[53]

This interest in correct interpretation and intellectual capacity runs throughout Nashe's oeuvre. In *The Anatomy of Absurdity* Nashe criticises 'our English Poets', for 'think[ing] knowledge a burthen, tapping it before they have halfe tunde it' (drawing it out before the barrel of it is half-filled; using knowledge before it is fully acquired and understood).[54] He connects this ignorance explicitly to rurality; the writers he attacks possess merely 'a little Countrey Grammer knowledge ... thanking God with that abscedarie Priest in Lincolnshire, that he never knewe what that Romish popish Latine meant'.[55] Nashe's 'Priest' appears to be apocryphal, and the details of his story unimportant: the same anecdote appears in *Strange News*, but there he is a parson from Lancashire, and deployed to mock Gabriel Harvey.[56] The salient points are that he is in a rural part of the country, and he is 'abscedarie': illiterate and/or lacking in basic knowledge, having received only some rudimentary education at a rural grammar school.[57] The fraudulent 'soothsayers' Nashe attacks in *The Terrors of the Night* are similarly under-educated, having only 'some little sprinkling of Grammer learning in their youth'.[58] The Carter, Ploughman, Shepherd, and Shepherd's boy in *The Anatomy of Absurdity* are all disqualified by class, profession, education, and location, in Nashe's schema, from interpreting the texts they read, or listen to, or hear second-hand versions of (none of these characters is necessarily literate, as the Shepherd's boy may 'have the ballad' by memory, rather than in printed form). By consuming and interpreting news, they pass, like Apelles's cobbler, 'beyond their lasts'. The use of these stock figures also gives a sense of commonality, of something being broadly discussed, which Nashe also uses in *Strange News* in order to mock the man he accuses of having written Doleta's pamphlet, John Harvey: 'I am sure it is not yet worne out of mens scorn, for every Miller made a comment of it, and not an oyster wife but mockt it'.[59]

Nashe's use of humble rural spaces and activities in *The Anatomy of Absurdity* also connects to the common negative stereotype of news being shared and discussed in inappropriately humble locations, and/or places associated with other vices. 'Where is the currant of newes but in tabling houses [inns used for gambling]?', George Whetstone asks, noting that such places are frequented by 'forraine explorers and faulse subjectes'.[60] In *The Anatomy of Absurdity* Nashe describes prophecies 'becom[ing] the Alehouse talke of every Carter', and in *Two Dangerous Comets* 'Simon Smel-knave' refers to 'Ale-knights' who 'tell Spanish newes over an Ale-pot'.[61] Ulpian Fulwell associates alehouse news with mendacious falsification: his 'Tom Tapster' claims 'I have in my taphouse both stale and fresh newes: yea, & if neede require, I have there a stamp to quoyne newes at all times'.⁶²

Both Nashe's Ploughman and Shepherd are distressed by the news they have learnt, and this distress manifests in ways that impede their everyday lives. The Ploughman pictures a puddle of water in a furrow as a disastrous flood, the sort of catastrophising that would not (one imagines) be terribly helpful when trying to plough a field. The Shepherd neglects his duties, leaving his sheep to be looked after by his 'wappe' (dog) while he snoozes. Influenced by Doleta's pamphlet, he 'dreameth of flying Dragons, which for feare least he should see to the losse of his sight, he falleth a sleepe': he dares not open his eyes, presumably due to Doleta's prediction that 'the Sunne shall be covered with the Dragon, in the morning from five a clocke untill nine, and will appeare like fire: therfore it is not good that any man doe behold the same: for by the beholding thereof you may lose your sight'.⁶³ The 'Dragons' he fears might be mythological winged lizards (Doleta's pamphlet contains a prefatory image showing such a 'dragon' in the sky) but might also refer to several astronomical phenomena, including a comet with a luminous train.⁶⁴ At any rate both he and the Ploughman are out of their depth, interpreting their everyday rural environments as sites of disaster. They have read (or heard) texts such as Doleta incorrectly, and now they read their surroundings incorrectly. Worse, their consumption of news warps the familiar features and processes of their lives, disrupts their normal patterns of rural understanding and labour. News and prophecy displace them temporally: Doleta's prophecy frightens the the Shepherd out of the rhythms and repetitions of the day, the season, and the needs of his flock, into news's anxious temporal linearity. It is part of Nashe's joke here that his response is *inaction*, idleness: he is paralysed by fear of an incomprehensible future. Nashe's characters are not necessarily rendered sinful by their consumption of news, in the way that Pierce Penniless is, but it does deepen their ignorance, upending the certainties of their lives. It works upon their idleness and gullibility, rendering them not just ridiculous but unable to function within their stations of life.

HEAVY NEWS: NASHE, HARVEY, AND MONSTROUS NEWS

In *Have With You to Saffron Walden* (1596) Nashe imagines a reader complaining that his text is no longer topical: '*Say, what are you reading?* Nashe *against* Harvey. Fo, thats a stale jeast, hee hath been this two or three yeare about it*'.⁶⁵ Nashe's joke here turns on his own delay: *Have With You* responds three years late to Gabriel Harvey's attacks in *Pierce's Supererogation* and *A New Letter of Notable Contents* (both 1593), contrasting to the speedy exchange of pamphlets between them in 1592–93. Nashe frames the dispute as topical entertainment that has turned 'stale' – like old news. Nashe returns, repeatedly, to the processes and forms of news in his writing against Harvey, using cultural assumptions and prejudices around newswriting and news consumption as means to mock Harvey's intellectual pretension.

The dispute between Nashe and Harvey began, arguably, with the topical.[66] Throughout their dispute topicality is a fraught issue. Both Nashe and Harvey are hyper-aware that the dispute they are engaged in is itself of trivial topical interest to readers, but both are also keen to turn attention to the longer term, claiming that there are much larger issues at stake: how they and their work will be viewed by posterity, and (in a wider sense) what sort of art is valuable, and what sort of art will be remembered. As Kate De Rycker has argued, anxiety over how posterity will remember them runs through Nashe's and Harvey's contributions to their dispute, especially visible in the determination of each writer to have the last word, and especially fraught in terms of their reliance 'on a material which was equal parts ephemeral and self-replicating': print. Ephemeral printed texts might be lost, and (more worryingly) the ever-increasing muliplicity of printed texts might confuse ideas of 'truth', or produce a biased or misleading version of events that become accepted 'fact'.[67] At the heart of the Nashe–Harvey dispute is a paradox: each writer reviles the excessive proliferation of topical print, but in doing so keeps the quarrel in the news, and keeps the presses running. To fail to have the last word is to consign one's literary posterity to the status of an unrealised prophecy – disproved and dispraised by later publications – and so neither writer is prepared to back down.

As mentioned above, in *Four Letters, and Certain Sonnets* (1592) Harvey promises his correspondent Christopher Bird that '[t]he next weeke, you may happily have a letter of such French occurrences, and other intelligences, as the credible relation of inquisitive frendes, or imployed straungers shall acquaint me withall'. Harvey goes on in this letter to provide Bird – and the reader of *Four Letters* – with some rather insipid points about foreign affairs:

> That most valorous, and brave king [Henri IV] wanteth no honourable prayses, or zealous prayers. Redoubted Parma was never so matched: and in so many woorthy histories, aswell new, as olde; how few comparable either for Vertue, or Fortune? The Spanyard, politique inough, and not over-rashly audatious, will bee advised, before he entangle himselfe with more warres attonce: knowing how the brave Earle of Essex, woorthy sir John Norrice, and their valiant knightes, have fought for the honour of England; and for the right of Fraunce, of the Low countries, and of Portugall.[68]

Harvey does not present his points here as actual *news*, per se – rather, this frames Harvey's proposed newsgathering activities, giving a sense of his own fitness to gather and interpret reports from multiple sources. Harvey stresses his own patriotic, protestant loyalty, and claims insight into the plans and motivations of foreign actors: the Spanish will be too 'politique' to tangle with the brave English nobility.

Harvey's claims are authoritative but simplistic, providing no real detailed insight, and thus serve as an easy target for Nashe's mockery. Nashe seizes upon Harvey's promised newmongering in his reply, *Strange News, of the Intercepting Certain Letters, and a Convoy of Verses, as They Were Going Privily to Victual the Low Countries* (1593).[69] In his title Nashe frames *Four Letters* as newsworthy secret correspondence. The joke here is in part about Harvey's earlier work, *Three Proper, and Witty, Familiar Letters* between him and Edmund Spenser (1580), which apparently offended both Edmund de Vere, Earl of Oxford, and Sir James Croft, the controller of the Queen's household, and landed Harvey in the Fleet prison.[70] In the third letter of *Four Letters* Harvey claims that his letters were intercepted and published without his consent: 'it was the sinister hap of those infortunate Letters, to fall into the left handes of malicious enemies, or undiscreete friends: who adventured to imprint in earnest, that was scribled in jest'.[71] However, Nashe also makes reference to the processes of foreign news: this generally moved via letters (sociable, diplomatic, mercantile, and professional manuscript newsletters), and the title pages of news pamphlets often advertised their contents as such. Correspondence that *hadn't* been intended to be seen – especially correspondence from opposing forces – was especially valuable, for what it revealed about the secret strategems and treacheries of one's enemies, and several extant publications from the 1580s and 1590s claim on their title pages to contain 'intercepted' letters.[72] Against Harvey's professed patriotism Nashe uses a trope of printed news texts to frame Harvey as an enemy to the commonwealth, and his *Four Letters* as scandalous proof of his treachery, which (rather than being openly published) has been 'intercepted' against Harvey's will.

What has been 'intercepted'? '[G]oing privilie to victuall the Low Countries' is a scatological pun: the letters are going to serve as toilet paper in a privy, supplying the 'Low Countries'. The image casts Harvey's work as both unimportant and topical: out-of-date, and thus fit only for the privy. At the same time there is another referential layer: Harvey's letters are imagined flowing over the North Sea to 'victual' – to feed – the Netherlands. Who is imagined receiving these letters/provisions is not clear. Given the context (and the military language of 'convoy') it is presumably soldiers fighting in the Dutch Revolt, but are these the English forces that Harvey is so keen to register his approval of, the armies of the States General, or perhaps – given the implication of treachery in the 'privy' sending of them – could the intended recipients be the Spanish forces under the command of 'redoubted Parma'? Nashe layers newsy implications in order to suggest that Harvey's work is simultaneously pointless and treacherous, his newsgathering and newswriting an inappropriate, indecorous intervention in foreign affairs by someone who (like the Shepherd and his boy in *Anatomy*) is not discerning enough to understand them.

Nashe also picks up on Harvey's promise to Bird later in *Strange News*, when he aligns it with the supposed 'invention' of Doleta's 'strange news' by Harvey's 'brother': 'The next weeke Maister Bird (if his inke-pot have a cleare current) hee will have at you with a cap-case full of French occurences, that is, shape you a messe of newes out of the second course of his conceit'.[73] Whereas in the title of *Strange News* Harvey's newsworthy intercepted letters had morphed into 'victuals', here it is the future news Harvey promises Bird that is imagined as food. Nashe puns on the idea of a 'second course' of a meal, served (as was typical in the sixteenth century) *à la française* (or its simplified cousin, *à l'anglaise*), in which a number of dishes were brought to the table simultaneously, in 'courses' probably determined largely by the capacity of the kitchen, though also potentially by early modern dietary theories. Diners were served 'messes' (servings) by the host, and/or servants, who selected food from the dishes in a way analogous to Harvey (as he describes his practice in *Four Letters*) choosing snippets of news from France from among the 'credible relation of inquisitive frendes, or imployed straungers' to send to Bird.[74] As Keith Botelho notes, 'the act of eating was often aligned with sharing and hearing news'; the image stresses that news is ephemeral, to be consumed, digested, and then excreted, a process repeated with each 'meal'.[75] That this is the 'second course' implies that this is the second – and thus inferior – production of Harvey's already-inferior wit, and also perhaps that this news is belated and 'stale', belying the pun on 'current'.[76] Nashe rewrites Harvey's promise to Bird, and in doing so rewrites Harvey's claim to a certain news identity. While in *Four Letters* Harvey attempts to establish himself as a discerning, patriotic, trustworthy source of foreign news, in *Strange News* he becomes a foolish, dangerous newsmonger, 'shaping' nonsense news out of his own muddled and inferior imagination to trivial or potentially even treasonous effect. Nashe's attacks on Harvey's ability to source and interpret news fits with his attacks on his background as the son of a ropemaker: the implication is that Harvey has moved beyond both his social place and his intellectual capacity.

Nashe returns to this connection between Harvey and news culture in *Have With You to Saffron Walden*, when he describes Gabriel Harvey in 'the first prime of his pamphleting ... capitulat[ing] on the births of monsters, horrible murders, and great burnings', in order to produce a kind of topical, morally suspect print not dissimilar from the 'Monsters ... bookt' in *Anatomy*.[77] Meanwhile Nashe characterises the lengthy *Pierce's Supererogation* itself as 'a whole Gravesend Barge full of Newes'.[78] Nashe's image aligns Harvey's work, again, with foreign news: Gravesend was the port by which most news (alongside other texts and commodities) from the continent entered England, travelling afterwards by barge to London. It allows Nashe to frame both news and Harvey's letters as everyday bulk commodities, moving through space alongside other goods. *Pierce's Supererogation* is 'a packet of Epistling, as bigge as a Packe of Woollen cloth, or a stack of salt-fish'.[79] Harvey's text is noteworthy for its bulk, rather than its erudition or utility: this 'heavie newes' – punning on both 'sad' and literally 'weighty' – cracks 'three axeltrees' of the cart it is transported in, and the carrier cannot wait to be rid of it.[80] Nashe's jokes on *Pierce's Supererogation*'s size continue, with Harvey's book morphing into increasingly fantastical forms: a 'gargantuan bag-pudding' filled with 'dogs-tripes, swines livers, oxe galls, and sheepes gutts'.[81] *Pierce's Superogation* is pointless – 'a whole Alexandrian Librarie of waste paper' – and it is colossal: 'the giant that Magellan found at Caput sancta crucis, or Saint Christophers picture at Antwerpe, or the monstrous images of Sesostres, or the Aegiptian Rapsinates, are but dwarffes in comparison of it'.[82]

Both the quotation from *Anatomy* with which I started and Nashe's description of Harvey's pamphleting activities connect news with monstrosity: Harvey 'capitulates on the birth of monsters', and in *Anatomy* 'some newes attends the ende of every Tearme, some Monsters are bookt, though not bred against vacation times'. The grammatical imprecision in *Anatomy* is telling: it is not clear whether the 'Monsters' are the events and figures being reported, or the news texts themselves. Nashe's treatment of *Pierce's Supererogation*'s immensity also draws on the idea of texts as monstrous: as Wes Williams notes, hugeness and monstrosity were intimately connected in the period, and '[t]o call something "monstrueux" in the mid-sixteenth century is, more often than not, to wonder at its enormous size'.[83] Framing *Pierce Penniless* as monstrous *news* connects news, through Harvey, to monstrous excess: by implication, both topical print and Harvey's text are overwhelming in extent, filling whole barges, resembling famous giants, demanding huge labour to comprehend and giving very little insight in return.

At the same time Nashe draws on other connected forms of monstrosity: that which is unnatural, depraved, misshapen, or absurd.[84] Topical print in the 1580s and 1590s often deals with the monstrous, the eruptive, the unusual, the wicked: the dragons and floods of *Anatomy*, the 'birth of monsters, horrible murders, and great burnings' that Nashe accuses

Harvey of 'pamphleting' on. At the same time it is itself inherently chimeric, drawing disparate topics together on the basis of perceived novelty (a battle, a flood, a dragon, and an invented prophecy are united by their status as 'news') and also connecting ordinary people (a shepherd, a carter, a Cambridge scholar wrongly convinced of his own ability to judge news reports) to major political and military figures and events. News is inherently unstable – constantly changing and renewing – and, as detailed above, inherently impossible to pin down. It is also – in sixteenth-century anti-news discourse, at least – potentially monstrous in its effects, disrupting ordinary temporalities and the 'natural order' of social and informational difference, and leading those who circulate and consume it into dangerous error.

Nashe and Harvey hurl accusations of textual monstrosity throughout their quarrel, beginning with Nashe's claim in *Pierce Penniless* that Richard Harvey's *Lamb of God* (1589) is 'Monstrous, monstrous, and palpable, not to bee spoken of in a Christian congregation'.[85] In *Pierce's Supererogation*, Harvey ascribes monstrosity both to Nashe's own style and to Nashe's treatment of Harvey's works. Nashe's rewriting of Harvey is 'monstrous knaverie': 'his only Art, & the vengeable drift of his whole cunning, to mangle my sentences, hack my arguments, chopp and change my phrases, wrinch my wordes, and hale every sillable most extremely; even to the disjoynting, and maiming of my whole meaning'.[86] Meanwhile Harvey characterises the 'monstrous Singularity' of Nashe's 'garish, and pibald stile' as a hellish chimera: it 'beginneth like a bullbeare, goethon like a bullocke, endeth like a bullfinch, and hath never a sparkle of pure Entelechy'.[87] Nashe's attack on the monstrous bulk of *Pierce's Supererogation* picks up this accusation, and turns it back upon Harvey, whilst also demonstrating his ability to deploy his 'piebald style' to produce not a misshapen monster but a laser-focused attack on his enemy. Picking apart (and, in truth, misrepresenting) *Pierce's Supererogation*, Nashe frames himself as the sort of discerning reader that, in his earlier mockery of Harvey's newsgathering activities, he claims Harvey is not.

Throughout the dispute accusations of textual monstrosity turn on a sort of monstrous topicality. Harvey's *Pierce's Supererogation* returns repeatedly to the idea that Nashe promises to produce lasting, artistically sound work, but produces only topical trash, 'such a gibbihorse of pastime, as Straunge Newes'.[88] Harvey claims, drawing on the connection of news to lower-class people and spaces, that Nashe has proved to be 'an oratour of the stewes ... a poet of Bedlam ... a knight of the alehowse ... a broker of baggage stuffe ... a pedler of straunge newes'.[89] Harvey reads the concluding couplet of the sonnet that ends *Strange News* – 'Awaite the world the tragedy of wrath, / What next I paint shall tread no common path' – as a vain promise to move beyond the topical, as indicated by the spaces in London most associated with the exchange of news: '[t]he next peece, not of his rhetorique, or poetry, but of his painture, shall not treade the way to Poules, or Westminster, or the Royall Exchange; but [will] sett the world an everlasting sample of inimitable artificiality'.[90] For Harvey the 'monstrous' style of Nashe renders his works trivial and topical, the sort of art that will not last. Meanwhile, for Nashe, the monstrous bulk of *Pierce's Supererogation* both reveals and belies the work's topical triviality: it resembles the excess of news, and while pretending to be a work of lasting erudition it in fact speaks only to a present quarrel. Nashe complains that in *Pierce's Supererogation* Harvey has 'in a superlative degree made me a monster beyond him': a topical 'monster' to be stared at, to be shared and misinterpreted by the masses, like the dragon in *Anatomy*.[91] Nashe and Harvey each resist the other's accusation that they are topical writers, and claim to produce work more lasting than mere 'news', while their scandalous and newsworthy quarrel threatens to turn both of their authorial personas into that saddest of printed things: out-of-date news, a disproved prophecy, 'a stale jeast'.

CONCLUSION: A CUP OF NEWS

Doleta's *Strange News* might be associated, in *The Anatomy of Absurdity*, with vacation idleness: but so is *Anatomy* itself. Near the start of the book Nashe gives an account of how he came to compose it:

> I, having laide aside my graver studies for a season, determined with my selfe beeing idle in the countrey, to beginne in this vacation, the foundation of a trifling subject, which might shroude in his leaves, the abusive enormities of these our times.[92]

Examining Nashe's treatment of news provides insight into his fraught relationship with his own topicality. Throughout his career he engages with the forms and features of topical print, while he critiques them. This is perhaps most visible in *Strange News*, which both treats Harvey's *Four Letters* as news and presents Nashe's own excoriation of them as news, too. Much like Harvey's newsworthy texts – which morph into military rations and 'messes' of food – Nashe's news is intended for consumption. In the mock-dedication to 'Maister Apis Lapis', he offers the text as a toast: 'I am bold in stead of new wine, to carowse to you a cuppe of newes'.[93] *Strange News* is pleasurable, intoxicating, and soon gone.

Nashe's treatment of news draws, as I have shown, on contemporary fears over what the movement of information might do to the commonwealth. Nashe uses news to explore fears over interpretation, and to express deeply conservative ideas of intellectual capacity. News functions in his works as an exemplar of artistic and social excess and inappropriateness, of speech, writing, and behaviour that is comically and dangerously out of place. It breaks bounds and clear definitions, pushing to satiric extremes the curious, undefined status of news as explored by Hyde, Raymond, and Moxham. For Nashe news moves between people, creating and consolidating real and conceptual relationships (between Gabriel Harvey and Christopher Bird; between a Calabrian flood and an English furrow) but also warping these relationships, and the commonwealth more widely. For Nashe, whether news dealt with tales (or prognostications) of monsters or not, it was itself *monstrous* in extent, form, and effect, and he uses accusations of topical monstrosity to attack both Harvey's texts and Harvey's intellectual authorial persona. However, Nashe's mercurial, chimeric style, and his engagement with topical print, lay him open to accusations of monstrosity himself. While he might claim in *Anatomy* to be dealing with important 'enormities', the book cannot entirely shake off the stigma of vacation-time idleness, and both *Strange News* and *Have With You to Saffron Walden* attack news while both they, and their author, become newsworthy scandals.

NOTES

1 Thomas Nashe, *The Anatomie of Absurditie* (London, 1589), sigs B3v–B4r.
2 John Doleta [?], *Straunge Newes out of Calabria Prognosticated in the Yere 1586, Upon the Yere 87* (London, 1587).
3 See Joad Raymond, *Pamphlets and Pamphleteering in Early Modern Britain* (Cambridge: Cambridge University Press, 2003), pp. 98–108.
4 Joad Raymond and Noah Moxham, 'News Networks in Early Modern Europe', in *News Networks in Early Modern Europe*, ed. Joad Raymond and Noah Moxham (Leiden: Brill, 2016), pp. 1–16 (pp. 1–4).
5 For discussion of the development of serialised news publication in England see Carolyn Nelson and Matthew Seccombe, 'The Creation of the Periodical Press 1620–1695', in *The Cambridge History of the Book in Britain, vol. 4: 1557–1695*, ed. John Barnard and D. F. McKenzie (Cambridge: Cambridge University Press, 2002), pp. 533–50.
6 Jenni Hyde, *Singing the News: Ballads in Mid-Tudor England* (London: Routledge, 2018), p. 107.
7 Raymond and Moxham, 'News Networks in Early Modern Europe', p. 3.
8 See the essays collected in *News Networks in Early Modern Europe*, ed. Joad Raymond and Noah Moxham (Leiden: Brill, 2016), in particular Nikolaus Schobesberger et al., 'European Postal Networks' (pp. 17–63); Brendan Dooley, 'International News Flows in the Seventeenth Century: Problems and Prospects' (pp. 158–77); Ruth Ahnert, 'Maps Versus Networks' (pp. 130–57); and Raymond, 'News Networks: Putting the "News" and "Networks" Back In' (pp. 102–29). See also Paul Arblaster, 'Posts, Newsletters, Newspapers: England in a European System of Communications', in *News Networks in Seventeenth-Century Britain and Europe*, ed. Joad Raymond

(London: Routledge, 2006), pp. 19–34; Arblaster, *From Ghent to Aix: How They Brought the News in the Habsburg Netherlands, 1550–1700* (Leiden: Brill, 2014); S. K. Barker, '"Newes Lately Come": European News Books in English Translation', in *Renaissance Cultural Crossroads: Translation, Print and Culture in Britain, 1473–1640*, ed. S. K. Barker and Brenda M. Hosington (Leiden: Brill, 2013), pp. 227–44; Carmen Espejo, 'European Communication Networks in the Early Modern Age: A New Framework of Interpretation for the Birth of Journalism', *Media History*, 17.2 (2011), 189–202; Andrew Pettegree, *The Invention of News: How the World Came to Know About Itself* (New Haven: Yale University Press, 2014); Yann Ciarán Ryan, '"More Difficult from Dublin than from Dieppe": Ireland and Britain in a European Network of Communication', *Media History*, 24 (2018), 458–76.
9 Raymond, 'News Networks: Putting the "News" and "Networks" Back In', p. 110.
10 Nashe, *Anatomy*, sig. B4r.
11 Hyde, *Singing the News*, p. 108.
12 Nashe, *Anatomy*, sigs B3v-B4r.
13 Richard Harvey, *An Astrological Discourse* (London, 1583); John Harvey, *An Astrologicall Addition* (London, 1583). See Bart Van Es, *Spenser's Forms of History* (Oxford: Oxford University Press, 2002), pp. 189–92; Margaret Aston, 'The Fiery Trigon Conjunction: An Elizabethan Astrological Prediction', *Isis*, 61 (1970), 159–87; Don Cameron Allen, *The Star-crossed Renaissance: The Quarrel about Astrology and Its Influence in England* (London: Frank Cass, 1966), pp. 121–5.
14 T. R., *A Confutation of the Tenne Great Plagues, Prognosticated by John Doleta from the Country of Calabria* (London, 1587); John Harvey, *A Discoursive Probleme Concerning Prophesies* (London, 1588), sig. O2r.
15 See Aston, 'The Fiery Trigon Conjunction'; Walter B. Stone, 'Shakespeare and the Sad Augurs', *The Journal of English and Germanic Philology*, 52 (1953), 457–79.
16 Thomas Nashe, *The Terrors of the Night* (London, 1594), sig. E3r; Simon Smel-knave [Thomas Nashe?], *Fearfull and Lamentable Effects of Two Dangerous Comets* (London, 1590).
17 Matthew Steggle, *Digital Humanities and the Lost Drama of Early Modern England: Ten Case Studies* (London: Routledge, 2016), p. 37.
18 Thomas Nashe, *Strange Newes* (London, 1592), sig. F1v. Steggle suggests that the specific brother referred to here is John, presumably because he shared a forename with the Anglicised name given to Doleta (Steggle, *Digital Humanities and the Lost Drama*, p. 38). However, Nashe may have meant 'brother' in a non-literal sense, simply meaning a writer that is similar, or allied, to Gabriel.
19 Thomas Nashe, *Have with You to Saffron-Walden* (London, 1596), sig. L3v.
20 Gabriel Harvey, *Foure letters, and certaine sonnets* (London, 1592), sig. B4v.
21 Nashe, *Anatomie*, sigs B3v–B4r. Doleta, *Straunge Newes*, sigs A4r–A4v.
22 See Alexandra Walsham, *Providence in Early Modern England* (Oxford: Oxford University Press, 1999), pp. 130–5.
23 Jonathan Green, 'Toledo, Toledo Letter, am Toledosten', *Research Fragments*, 5 November 2010, researchfragments.blogspot.com/2010/11/toledo-toledo-letter-am-toledosten; 'The Toledo Letter in Print', *Research Fragments*, 16 May 2014, researchfragments.blogspot.com/2014/05/the-toledo-letter-in-print. See also Green, *The Strange and Terrible Visions of Wilhelm Friess: The Paths of Prophecy in Reformation Europe* (Ann Arbor: University of Michigan Press, 2014), p. 117; Steggle, *Digital Humanities and the Lost Drama*, pp. 35–6.
24 Brendan Dooley, 'Preface', in *The Dissemination of News and the Emergence of Contemporaneity in Early Modern Europe*, ed. Dooley and Sabrina A. Baron (Farnham:

Ashgate, 2010), pp. xiii–xiv (p. xiii). Dooley draws here on Benedict Anderson's notion of 'simultaneity' (*Imagined Communities: Reflections on the Origin and Spread of Nationalism* (rev. edn. London: Verso, 2000), p. 24).

25 Harvey, *Foure letters*, sig. B4v.
26 For an examination of this kind of 'news anxiety' see Kirsty Rolfe, 'Probable Pasts and Possible Futures: Contemporaneity and the Consumption of News in the 1620s', *Media History*, 23.2 (2017), 159–76.
27 Steggle, *Digital Humanities and the Lost Drama*, p. 33; quoting Bodleian Library: MS Rawlinson Poet. 85, fols 77v–78r.
28 Steggle, *Digital Humanities and the Lost Drama*, p. 33.
29 Steggle, *Digital Humanities and the Lost Drama*, p. 35.
30 Steggle, *Digital Humanities and the Lost Drama*, p. 37.
31 Michael Cope, *A godly and learned exposition vppon the Prouerbes of Solomon* (London, 1580), sig. 2R1r.
32 R. Hoper, *The instruction of a Christian man* (London, 1580), sig. I4v.
33 William Bullein, *Bulleins bulwarke of defence* (London, 1579), sig. 2A6r.
34 John Lyly, *Euphues and his England* (London, 1580) sig. D3v; see also sig. E2v.
35 Thomas Nashe, *The Unfortunate Traveller* (London, 1594), sig. L3v.
36 William Rankins, *The English Ape, the Italian Imitation, the Footesteppes of Fraunce* (London, 1588), sig. B1v.
37 Thomas Nashe, *Pierce Penilesse* (London, 1592), sig. I3r.
38 Nashe, *Pierce Penilesse*, sig. A3r.
39 Cope, *A Godly and Learned Exposition*, sig. 2R1v.
40 Nashe, *Unfortunate Traveller*, sig. L3v.
41 Nashe, *Anatomie*, sig. B4r.
42 Nashe, *Anatomie*, sig. B4r.
43 See Hyde, *Singing the News*, and also Una McIlvenna, 'When the News Was Sung: Ballads as News Media in Early Modern Europe', *Media History*, 22 (2016), 317–33, and *Singing the News of Death: Execution Ballads in Europe 1500–1900* (Oxford: Oxford University Press, 2022).
44 Nashe, *Anatomie*, sig. B4r.
45 Cope, *A Godly and Learned Exposition*, sig. 2K7v.
46 Nashe, *Anatomie*, sig. E1v; Pliny the Elder, *Natural History*, trans. H. Rackham, Loeb Classical Library 394 (Cambridge, MA: Harvard University Press, 1952), IX:35.36 85.
47 Desiderius Erasmus, *Adages*, 1.6.16, in *Collected Works of Erasmus: Adages: Ivii to Ix100, Volume 32*, trans. and ed. R. A. B. Mynors (Toronto: University of Toronto Press, 1989), p. 14.
48 Fritz Levy, 'The Decorum of News', in *News, Newspapers and Society in Early Modern Britain*, ed. Joad Raymond (London: Frank Cass, 1999), pp. 12–38.
49 See Nelson and Seccombe, 'The Creation of the Periodical Press 1620–1695'; Sabrina A. Baron, 'The Guises of Dissemination in Early Seventeenth-Century England: News in Manuscript and Print', in *The Politics of Information in Early Modern Europe*, ed. Brendan Dooley and Sabrina A. Baron (London: Routledge, 2001), pp. 41–56; Richard Cust, 'News and Politics in Early Seventeenth-Century England', *Past & Present*, 112 (1986), 60–90.
50 Nashe, *Anatomie*, sig. B3v.
51 Babrius [Aesop], *Fables*, trans. Ben Edwin Perry, Loeb Classical Library 436 (Cambridge, MA: Harvard University Press, 1965), pp. 428–9; Diogenes Laertius, 'Thales', *Lives of Eminent Philosophers*, trans. R. D. Hicks, Loeb Classical Library

184 (Cambridge, MA: Harvard University Press, 1925), I:1.1.34; Plato, *Theaetetus*, in *Theaetetus, Sophist*, trans. Harold North Fowler, Loeb Classical Library 123 (Cambridge, MA: Harvard University Press, 1921), 174 A.
52 Nashe, *Anatomie*, sig. B3v.
53 Nashe, *Strange Newes*, sig. B1r.
54 Nashe, *Anatomie*, sig. B4r.
55 Nashe, *Anatomie*, sig. B4r.
56 Nashe, *Strange Newes*, sig. L1v.
57 abscedarie, *OED*[3] 2.
58 Nashe, *Terrors*, sig. D4v.
59 Nashe, *Strange Newes*, sig. F1v
60 George Whetstone, *The enemie to vnthryftinesse* (London, 1586), sig. K2v.
61 Smel-knave, *Fearfull and Lamentable Effects*, sig. B1v.
62 Ulpian Fulwell, *The First Parte, of the Eyghth Liberall Science* (London, 1579), sig. G3r.
63 Doleta, *Straunge Newes*, sig. A3v.
64 Doleta, *Straunge Newes*, sig. A2r; see 'dragon', *OED*, 8c.
65 Nashe, *Have With You*, sig. C4r.
66 See the Introduction, above.
67 Kate De Rycker, 'Commodifying the Author: The Mediation of Aretino's Fame in the Harvey-Nashe Pamphlet War', *ELR*, 49.2 (2019), 145–71 (pp. 169–70).
68 Harvey, *Foure letters*, sig. B4v.
69 *Strange Newes* was reissued some time after April 1593 with the title *The Apologie of Pierce Pennilesse. Or Strange Newes, of the Intercepting Certaine Letters, and a Convoy of Verses, as they were Going Privilie to Victuall the Lowe Countries* (London, 1593). 'The Apologie of Pierce Pennylesse or strange newes of the intercepting certen letters' is the title the publication was entered into the the Stationers' Register under in January 1593 (the work was published some time before the turn of the old-style year at the end of March).
70 Jason Scott-Warren, 'Harvey, Gabriel (1552/3–1631), Scholar and Writer', *ODNB* (Oxford: Oxford University Press, 2016) (https://www.oxforddnb.com/view/10.1093/ref:odnb/9780198614128.001.0001/odnb-9780198614128-e-12517).
71 Scott-Warren, 'Harvey, Gabriel'; Nashe, *Foure Letters*, sig. C2v.
72 See *Newes From Antwerp, the 10 Day of August 1580, Contayning, a Speciall View of the Present Affayres of the Lowe Countreyes: Revuealed and Brought to Lyght, by Sundrie Late Intercepted Letters* (London, 1580); *Letters Conteyning Sundry Devises Touching the State of Flaunders and Portingall: Written by Card. Granvelle and Others, and Lately Intercepted and Published* (London, 1582); *A True and Plaine Declaration of the Horrible Treasons, Practised by William Parry the Traitor ... Together With the Copies of Sundry Letters of His and Others, Tending to Divers Purposes, for the Proofes of His Treasons* (London, 1585); George Ker, *A Discoverie of the Unnaturall and Traiterous Conspiracie of Scottisch Papists ... Whereunto are Annexed, Certaine Intercepted Letters, written by Sundrie of that Factioun* (Edinburgh, 1593).
73 Nashe, *Strange Newes*, sig. F1v. Steggle suggests that the specific brother referred to here is John, presumably because he shared a forename with the Anglicised name given to Doleta (Steggle, *Digital Humanities and the Lost Drama*, p. 38). However, Nashe may have meant 'brother' in a non-literal sense, simply meaning a writer that is similar, or allied, to Gabriel.
74 Nashe, *Foure Letters*, sig. B4v.

75 Keith Botelho, *Renaissance Earwitnesses: Rumor and Early Modern Masculinity* (New York: Palgrave Macmillan, 2009), p. xii.
76 See Robert Appelbaum, *Aguecheek's Beef, Belch's Hiccup, and Other Gastronomic Interjections: Literature, Culture, and Food Among the Early Moderns* (Chicago: University of Chicago Press, 2006), pp. 88–9.
77 Nashe, *Have With You*, sig. L2r.
78 Nashe, *Have With You*, sig. F1r.
79 Nashe, *Have With You*, sigs F1r–F1v.
80 Nashe, *Have With You*, sig. F1v.
81 Nashe, *Have With You*, sig. F1v.
82 Nashe, *Have With You*, sigs F2r–F2v.
83 Wes Williams, *Monsters and Their Meanings in Early Modern Culture: Mighty Magic* (Oxford: Oxford University Press, 2011), p. 1.
84 See 'monstrous', OED^3 1, 2, 4, 5.
85 Nashe, *Pierce Penilesse*, sig. E1v.
86 Gabriel Harvey, *Pierces Supererogation* (London, 1593), sig. I1r.
87 Harvey, *Pierces Supererogation*, sigs Z4v, Z4r, and 2A3v.
88 Harvey, *Pierces Supererogation*, sig. V4v.
89 Harvey, *Pierces Supererogation*, sig. D1r.
90 Nashe, *Strange Newes*, sig. M2v; Harvey, *Pierces Supererogation*, sig. I2r.
91 Nashe, *Have With You*, sig. T2r.
92 Nashe, *Anatomie*, sig. A1r.
93 Nashe, *Strange Newes*, sig. A1r. 'Maister Apis Lapis' refers to either William or Christopher Beeston, the name disguised as 'Apis (bee), Lapis (stone)' (Benjamin Griffin, 'Nashe's dedicatees: William Beeston and Richard Lichfield', *Notes & Queries*, 44 (1997), 47–9).

3
TEXTUAL SUPERFICIALITY AND SURFACE READING IN NASHE'S PROSE

Douglas Clark

Thomas Nashe was concerned with the threat that superficial interpretation posed to his place in late sixteenth-century literary culture. His disquiet with those who display neither critical acumen nor decorum in their reading is evident in his preface to *The Terrors of the Night* (1594), where he states that 'a number of you there bee, who consider neither premisses nor conclusion, but piteouslie torment Title Pages of everie poast: never reading farther of anie Booke, than Imprinted by Simeon such a signe, and yet with your dudgen judgements will desperatelie presume to run up to the hard hilts through the whole bulke of it'.[1] Here Nashe imagines a browsing reader who pays more attention to the imprint information of a publisher ('Simeon such a signe') than the quality of the work. The title page forms the primary interpretative site for the ignorant reader, as Nashe directs his authorial ire towards members of both the 'book trade *and* the amorphous body of the reading public'.[2] An author may hope for those with 'winy wits' and 'dull tricks' to avoid their text, but control over their product is seemingly relinquished as soon as it finds its way to the bookstalls of 'Poules Church-yard'.[3] Architectural surfaces ('everie poast' of a bookstall) become locations where whole books are tormented through their exteriors: the 'whole bulke' of an edition may be skewered by a reductive appraisal of the title page that has been separated from the rest of its leaves. Some readers lack the ability to venture beyond this world of surfaces created by the material conditions of the market, and some, as shown through his pointed reference to 'Martin Momus', may actively look to 'betouse' or mistreat texts.[4] Knowing that it is impossible to defend oneself completely from undue criticism, Nashe gives any prospective buyer of his *Terrors* the freedom to 'stop mustard pots with my leaves if they will'.[5] This pointed reflection suggests that all texts risk having their contents effaced by analytical negligence, or their material surface sullied with mustard. From post to pot, books will endure bitter critics or the 'bite' of sharp mustard.[6]

It is ironic that Nashe's assessment of facile interpretative misjudgement does not directly succeed the *Terror of the Night*'s title page, but instead follows an opening dedicatory epistle to Elizabeth Carey. Nashe's detractors would, in his estimation, never even read this far into his book. It is apparent, however, for those who delve beyond Nashe's title pages that he is attentive to the cultural significance of surface reading, and the effects it may have upon his own literary reception. The commentary he provides on the labour of writing reveals the opportunities and risks posed by print technologies. As David Scott Kastan proposes, Nashe's responsiveness 'to the ways texts come into being and circulate in the newly commodified world of print publication' in early modern England is 'arguably the central preoccupation of his fiction'.[7] One way to develop Kastan's claim would be to attend to the significance that acts of superficial reading take in Nashe's evaluation of print market politics. Offering one's work to a public audience, while trying to mediate its reception through a potentially futile lesson concerning interpretative decorum, illustrates a particular authorial fear for Nashe in his *Terrors*: 'poore fellowes as I … must have our work dispatcht by the weeks end, or els we may go beg'.[8] You will either rush to publish a text that will be quickly skewered by the ignorant, or you will starve. Textual surfaces are politicised territories whose use may have immediate personal consequences.

My chapter explains the broader significance that the facile analysis of surfaces takes in Nashe's canon. It argues that scrutinising the external properties of books as both material and literary entities is pivotal to the way he justifies acts of literary creation. Primary focus is placed on Nashe's engagement with distorted surfaces of poorly executed writing, the outward attire of texts, the generation of waste paper, and presentation of texts as appetising commodities in his first and last works, *The Anatomy of Absurdity* (1589) and *Lenten Stuff* (1599). I consider the significance of the contradictions that emerge in Nashe's satirical appraisal of surface reading, in light of Georgia Brown's assertion that 'in place of inherited and unchanging meanings' Nashe situates the 'foundation of truth' upon the 'endless process of criticism'.[9] His oeuvre is indeed underpinned by a vitriolic energy, though he does not always illustrate a 'self-conscious triviality' that conveys 'playful, but simultaneously meaningful, gestures of paradox'.[10] Where Chloe Preedy deftly conveys how Nashe's prose style is deployed in purposeful 'resistance to influential formulations of literary value', I contend that Nashe's engagement with concepts of ornamentality and excess are often contradictory, without exhibiting any self-consciously edifying reflection on the slippery nature of literary value or truth.[11]

Incongruity can nevertheless be illuminating. Lorna Hutson, for instance, has already identified the 'apparent shapelessness' of Nashe's playfully

TEXTUAL SUPERFICIALITY AND SURFACE READING 69

splenic style, and its 'lack of continuity and coherence' to 'function as a politically and morally significant aesthetic in its own right'.[12] I draw upon the notion of Nashe's 'plasticity of discourse' to show how this stylistic feature of his writing facilitates slippage into contradiction.[13] I do not advocate that Nashe's work should be uniformly viewed as a site 'wherein the Spirit of Contradiction reigneth', as Gabriel Harvey would describe of his own 'Martinish and Counter-martinish age'.[14] Moments of logical discord are, however, a commonplace feature of Nashe's extemporal style. These tendencies, exhibited in his critique of rhetorical superficiality, are aptly exposed through Nashe's fixation with surfaces as sites of meaning, in and beyond his prefatory writing.

This chapter determines how Nashe critiques the specious eloquence of writers, while simultaneously defending his own literary style by giving precedence to the merits of outward appearances. Nashe's contested relationship with literary interpretation reveals a willingness to revel in the freedom of expression that he denies or denounces in those he criticises. Examining the significance of facile eloquence and textual value in Nashe's work elucidates how he plays capriciously with the imputed boundaries between surface and depth. My exploration of this topic is sensitive to recent developments in surface reading, as exhibited in Stephen Best and Sharon Marcus's remark that 'a surface is what insists on being looked *at* rather than what we must train ourselves to see *through*'.[15] I agree with Best and Marcus's attempt to eschew a 'depth model of truth, which dismisses surfaces as inessential and deceptive', but my reading of Nashe's surfaces does not wholly align with their rather diffuse critical methodology[16] One problem with their proposal to perform 'literal readings that take texts at face value', and the subsequent claim that 'surface reading ... strives to describe texts accurately', is that, as Crystal Bartolovich describes, this aspiration 'cannot in itself decisively authorise one reading over another, since the same text will support many plausible ones'.[17] My chapter instead simply considers the place that both literal and metaphorical surfaces take as places where 'the generation of meaning' may occur.[18] Attending to Nashe's fixation with surfaces will establish the significant role they take as sites of contested interpretation, and how Nashe deploys his own surface reading to defend his texts from analytical negligence. Nashe, as I show, is preoccupied with the materials that allow for surface thinking and reading to occur.

Jennifer Richards reminds us that contemporary criticism has been dedicated to untangling Nashe's 'preoccupation with the materiality of his world and his words', and suggests that we may instead consider how his wit 'enlivens a pamphlet more than the paper that it appears on', in order to 'rethink what a book can be – less a material object than a live experience'.[19] A book is not just an object to be held, but 'a "thing" we can perform (or imagine as a performance)', yet the imagined acoustic qualities of a text's contents represents but one aspect of the sensory dynamics applicable to reading practices.[20] I argue that haptic contexts equally inform the performance of textual analysis that Nashe imagines being enacted by his readers, and that he uses these features to establish the critical legitimacy of his own writing. I begin this study of Nashe's lively materials by considering the self-reflexive commentary offered on literary artifice and surface logic in *The Anatomy of Absurdity*.

ARTISTRY AND *THE ANATOMY OF ABSURDITY*

The Anatomy's polemical digressions into the 'sundry follies of our licentious times' have led readers to interpret this text as a poorly organised patchwork of ideas, marking a transition from older 'forms of repentant prodigality' into a 'new mood of scepticism and discontent' of the 1590s.[21] The 'ornate euphuism' of *The Anatomy* and the barbs it directs against facets of late sixteenth-century literary culture have also been traditionally thought to inhibit rather than enhance its remonstrative objectives.[22] G. R. Hibbard has additionally suggested that the 'complaints' that feature in the *Anatomy* 'only take on relevance and reality when the diction of common speech ruffles the smooth surface of literary artifice'.[23] In Hibbard's estimation plain speech is a more appropriate way to express the 'relevance and reality' of Nashe's social critique, since it helps to break the illusion of the 'smooth surface' to his style. Nashe is nonetheless aware of the place that stylistic simplicity takes as a foundational feature of his prose, as addressed at the end of the text's dedicatory epistle to his patron, Charles Blount:

> And as the foolish painter in Plutarch, having blurred a ragged Table, with the rude picture of a dunghill Cocke, willed his boy in any case to drive away all lyve Cocks, from that his worthles workmanship, least by the comparison he might be convinced of ignorance: so I am to request your worship, whiles you are perusing my Pamphlet, to lay aside out of your sight, whatsoever learned invention hath heretofore bredde your delight, least their singularitie reflect my simplicitie, their excellence convince mee of innocence.[24]

Nashe draws attention to the crude and 'blurred' nature of his writing that has blemished the surface of the printed 'Pamphlet' as part of a commonplace act of performative humility. This 'request' takes on additional significance because it marks the first instance of Nashe's repeated attempt to emphasise the dangers of mimesis by associating authorial creation to acts of misrepresentation.

The conceit concerning the apparent 'simplicitie' of Nashe's *Anatomy* draws on an episode from Plutarch's *Moralia*, mimicking the phrasing of its translation in John Marbeck's *A Book of Notes and Common Places* (1581), rather than its depiction in Jacques Amyot's influential vernacular translation of Plutarch *Les Oeuvres Morales & Meslees de Plutarque* (1572). Where Amyot refers only to 'un mauvais peintre [a bad painter] … qui avoit fort mal peint des cocqs [who had badly painted cocks]', Marbeck comments on the painter's poorly 'proportioned … painted Henne' that demonstrates his 'evill workmanship'.[25] In the Greek, French, and Philemon Holland's 1603 English translation of Plutarch a cock is mentioned instead of the reference to a 'painted Henne' that appears in Marbeck's commonplace book.[26] This is to say that placid hens, rather than presumptuous cocks, are more fitting to the pious moral invective that guides Marbeck's reformulation of Plutarch's instruction. Marbeck uses this parable to assert that we 'chase awaie Gods word' to protect the integrity of our own inventive 'fancie'.[27] A deference to God's word is paramount to Marbeck's work; Nashe, conversely, encourages Charles Blount to drive the 'learned invention' of the other 'Cocks' from his sight, so that Nashe's 'dunghill' of 'simplicitie' will be read more favourably. Where Plutarch uses the tale of the painter to advise that a 'flatterer will doe what he can to chase away true friends', Nashe deploys it with the hope of advancing his favour with Blount by chasing away his textual competitors.[28] His preface concludes thus with an attempt to pre-emptively prohibit an act of comparative analysis, for fear that *The Anatomy*'s 'soveraigne content' would be ruined.[29] In this opening dedication Nashe focuses on the primacy of inventive 'delight' while signalling the naivety of his own 'workmanship'.[30] This rhetorical tactic reminds the reader of the conceptual divisions within, and dimensional depth of, the text as a whole, while simultaneously signalling the text's status as a site of interpretation associated with the artistic merit of a 'rude picture of a dunghill Cocke'.

Likening his own work to the product of a 'foolish Painter' forms part of a convention of authorial humility, yet Nashe's attitude towards literary creation through the rest of the *Anatomy* would suggest that 'Every cocke is proude on his owne dounghyll'.[31] Like 'Zeuxes' – the Grecian painter who gathered the 'fayrest' 'Maydes' to 'drawe the counterfeit of Juno' – Nashe addresses the work of the 'unlearned Idiots' of his day who 'are every quarter bigge wyth one Pamphlet or other' in his own attempt to 'anatomize Absurditie'.[32] In Nashe's literary portrait the 'brainlesse Bussards' who fill the print market with 'emptie' 'Egge[s]' of their creation are likened to 'Asses, who bring forth' valueless work 'all their life long'.[33] Taking a 'view of sundry mens vanitie' exposes the self-conceited nature of their writing, in addition to how they are 'voide of all knowledge'.[34]

It is rather fitting that Nashe censures such vacuous texts by imitating the figure of Zeuxis in his denouncement of false eloquence – an artist whom Aristotle, when speaking of the imitative quality of poetry, refers to as one whose skill may be impossible to replicate.[35]

Nashe's self-important portrayal of his own literary skill is a notable feature in his early work, as seen in his prefatory contribution to Robert Greene's *Menaphon* (1589). In this preface Nashe pours scorn on the place that facile eloquence takes in his age, berating those who take their '*ut vales* [greetings] from the inke-horne' while liberally sprinkling his prose with sententious Latin phrases that illuminate his own erudition.[36] English literary culture is apparently marked by the 'servile imitation' of 'vaine-glorious Tragedians' and the 'idiot Art-masters' of their playwrights, whose 'swelling bumbaste' of 'bragging blanke verse' has made 'every Mechanicall mate abhorreth the English he was borne to'.[37] Empty-headed grammarians, rhetoricians, and orators are also targeted as those who produce derivative work, and who have been made subject to a slavish devotion to 'Apish devices' borrowed from Ariosto and Cicero.[38] Nashe's preface to Sidney's *Astrophel and Stella* (1591) continues in this vein: '*Tempus adest plausus aurea pompa venit* ['The shout is nigh, the golden pomp comes here'], so ends the Sceane of Idiots, and enter Astrophel in pompe'.[39] The entrance of Sidney's work into the cultural milieu of early modern marketplace in a golden procession, figured through Nashe's own allusion to Ovid, should help rid the literary scene of 'Idiots'.[40] In a moment of self-conscious reflection at the end of his preface to *Astrophel* Nashe states that he has 'beene too bold, to stand talking all this while in an other mans doore':[41] he must move out of the way for Sidney's procession to begin. This statement may be read as a moment of deference, but it is figured in a manner that indicates the power that prefatory writers hold as mediators of any given text's social value. This particular paratextual space offers a chance for praise and dispraise alike through the architectural imagery it deploys.

Nashe's earlier preface to *Menaphon* is equally concerned with the significance that thresholds and surfaces take in framing acts of literary interpretation. In *Menaphon* Nashe proposes that those who have been 'surfetted unawares with the sweete sacietie of eloquence' could remedy their numbed sense of taste with the '*sublime dicendi genus* [elevated style of speech], which walkes abroad for wast paper in each Serving-mans pocket, and the otherwhile perusing of our Gothamists barbarisme'.[42] This satirical quip follows on from an earlier piece of praise addressed to the 'attyre' of *Menaphon* and its '*temperatum dicendi genus* [moderate style of speech], which Tully in his *Orator* tearmeth true eloquence'.[43] A restrained, and seemingly ideal, style of speech which is 'not so stately, yet comely' evidences the true merit of Greene's work.[44] Jonathan Crewe posits that 'such decorum is essentially hollow or that outward appearances may be meaningless, contradictory, or treacherous', yet the contrary does have a purpose here.[45] Nashe advises that one solution for the indulgence in overblown rhetoric is to read the type of printed works that are kept in the pockets of serving-men for use as toilet paper – materials reflective of their 'barbarisme', which would revive one's appreciation of literary eloquence. Similarly, to 'expell the infection of Absurditie', one should focus their attention on works of stylistic 'Puritie'.[46] The 'over-racked Rhetoricke' of other writers would thus 'bee the Ironicall recreation of the Reader' who engages with works of modest clarity.[47] This scenario substantiates 'the remedie of contraries' that texts may produce for their readers, which, in turn, places the material surface of Nashe's contribution to Greene's work in danger of being turned into waste paper, or receive the waste of its users.[48] Even 'wast paper' may have value.

This preoccupation with the interpretation of textual surfaces is further developed when Nashe takes the opportunity to promote *The Anatomy* at the end of his preface to *Menaphon*: 'If you chance to meete it [*The Anatomy*] in Paules, shaped in a new sute of similitudes, as if like the eloquent Apprentice of Plutarch, it were propped at seven yeeres end in double apparrell, thinke his Master hath fulfilled covenants, and onely cancelled the Indentures of dutie'.[49] The discursive apparel that gives structure to his *Anatomy* denotes its worth as a product of Nashe's education – a personified text that is presented as an apprentice and 'a walking commodity, dressed well and hoping to be recirculated into the protection of employment'.[50] Self-advancement is chosen over reiterating the virtues of Greene's work to the reader. This particular allusion to Plutarch helps, in Alexandra Halasz's terms, to 'formulate a relation between his rhetorical wealth and the marketplace' of print circulating around St Paul's.[51] Imagining his book being found by a reader of Greene's work serves to replace the ragged edges of paper (found in the traditionally serrated edges of the legal 'Indentures of dutie' that figuratively holds him in service to his craft and to his reader) with the sartorial finery of his book's 'double apparrell'. The worth of Nashe's *Anatomy* is thus rationalised through a reading of its outer appearance as a textual surface associated with mature erudition, and one promoted within another book's paratextual material.

Each of Nashe's prefaces are devised to reflect upon the merits of literary style and the benefits of the knowledge that they offer their readers, and to undermine the form and content of other texts. I agree with Jason Scott-Warren that Nashe's approach to rhetorical ornamentation in his early work conveys 'the force of superficies', though his presentation of material surfaces in his early prefatory work differs from how bodies and clothes are depicted as the 'ever-proliferating and often absurdly incoherent assemblages' in later texts like *Christ's Tears over Jerusalem* (1593) and *The Unfortunate Traveller* (1594).[52] There is a continuity in the way that Nashe presents the book as apparelled by its preface, licensing it with a sense of cultural authority which validates its status in the literary marketplace. Contrariness itself is part of the logic that grants coherence to his prefaces, as it is embraced as a stylistic remedy and a beneficial rhetorical tool.

TEXTUAL SURGERY

Nashe's preface to Greene's *Menaphon* states that the *Anatomy* will expose 'the diseases of Arte' that have infected the writing of 'our maimed Poets', and that by reading the *Anatomy* these poets should be compelled to 'put together their blankes unto the building of an Hospitall'.[53] His prescribed treatment for 'the diseases' produced by bad writing is the creation of a structure that may cure through its blank constitution; empty leaves would do more good than filled pages. This pointed interest in literary production provides a sense of structural cohesion to the *Anatomy* as a whole, as he attempts to show his own 'skill in surgerie'.[54]

We are made aware that a process of 'pensivenes', not of 'vain-glory', has compelled Nashe's 'wit to wander abroad' in the 'satyricall disguise' he adopts to dissect the work of his contemporaries.[55] Adopting this disguise — what was previously described as a 'sute of similitudes' in his preface to *Menaphon*[56] — allows him to rectify the mistakes of others who 'sette before us, naught but a confused masse of wordes without matter, a Chaos of sentences without any profitable sence'.[57] In doing so he determines that the 'painted shewe' of those 'Authors of eloquence' and their 'lust' filled 'leaves' should be dispensed, since 'the Presse should be farre better employed'.[58] He reasons that no 'Morall of greater moment, might be fished out of their fabulous follie' for they hide vice under a 'visard of vertue'.[59] Looking past these façades while in his own disguise reveals that the work of such authors resemble 'drummes … being emptie with in, sound big without'.[60] Examining the skins of these books and the facile eloquence within them verifies their emptiness, and exposes their lack of moral virtue.

Aim is also taken at men who 'anatomize abuses, and stubbe up sin by the rootes', making 'the Presse the dunghill, whether they carry all the muck of their mellancholicke imaginations'.[61] Their didacticism exemplifies only personal vanity and foolishness, 'because they place praise in painting foorth other mens imperfections'.[62] Nashe criticises those who 'overshoote themselves too much wyth inveighing against vice', but shows himself to be engaged in this very act of making the press a 'dunghill' by performing an anatomy of his contemporaries' imperfections.[63] He seems more invested in saving those readers of 'nobler wits' who are enticed by 'Poets wanton lines' and the 'inticements of pleasure and vanitie', than resolving the conflicted logic of his relationship with the triviality of studied eloquence.[64] If '[y]oung men are not so much delighted with solide substances, as with painted shadowes', should they listen more intently to Nashe's guidance because it is presented as an imperfect painting (as shown in his previous references to Zeuxis)?[65] His *Anatomy* does not seem concerned with portraying his artistic enterprise as a part of the remedy of contraries that he advocates in Greene's *Menaphon*. The *Anatomy* instead draws attention to the dangerous validity of the Horatian adage, *ut pictura poesis* (as is painting so is poetry).[66] Poets corrupt the wits of the country's '[y]oung men' through the delightful redundancy of their 'painted shadowes', encouraging them to internalise the teachings of 'vanitie' and 'those thinges which are goodly to the viewe', rather than seeking out 'Fountaines of truth'.[67] Where Horace's dictum suggests that poetry's sweet utility derives from the clarity and cultural value of what it figures forth, Nashe emphasises the alluringly facile poetic pictures that are most commonly generated.

The *Anatomy*'s polemic against the visual nature of poetical practice engages with contemporary debates over how the concept of image-making was used to 'conceptualise and articulate the poet's relation to the truth'.[68] The 'chief prayse and cunning of our Poet' as George Puttenham states in his *Art of English Poesy* (1589), is 'in the discreet using of his figures, as the skilfull painters is in the good conveyance of his coulours and shadowing traits of his pensill, with a delectable varietie'.[69] Nashe vilifies those who do not use discretion in their writing, but who only offer a 'delectable varietie' of words that sully young minds.[70] If Sidney's theory about poetry acting as a 'speaking Picture, with this end to teach and delight' represents 'a kind of utopian poetics, a dream that poetry can do just about anything' as Leonard Barkan suggests, then Nashe's *Anatomy* helps indicate the beguiling nature of the 'lascivious ... English devise of verse'.[71] As Nashe declares, forsaking 'sounder Artes' for 'excessive Studies of delight' may leave one only with 'a newe painted boxe, though there be nothing but a halter in it'.[72] The painted surface of such verse is a captivating veneer whose 'smoother eloquence' causes our estrangement from 'profounde knowledge', and whose hidden 'halter' symbolises the hazards associated with unprofitable pleasures.[73] The instructive impulse to disregard the painted show of literary eloquence also frames Nashe's misogynistic denouncement of women: 'But what should I spend my ynck, waste my paper, stub my penne, in painting forth theyr ugly imperfections, and perverse peevishnesse ... how many eyes, so many allurements. What shall I say?'[74] Anatomising women's bodies and moral vices leads him to question the purpose of his own authorial voice, presenting it as insufficient to the task of adequately 'painting forth' the flaws of women.[75] The *Anatomy* reminds us to be wary of captivating surfaces, even as it draws attention to its own textual surface as a space where wasted thoughts proliferate. This particular castigation of women's behaviour accentuates Nashe's deference to his own self-conceited display of cocky literary exceptionalism.

Nashe's prose emphasises how paper should be valued for its role as a receptacle for knowledge rather than merely its base material properties. Its surface has cultural currency because it may receive wisdom from those who inscribe their opinions upon it. So where does this leave a text like the *Anatomy*, as a poorly painted dunghill cock associated with the inconsequential wastepaper of the 'dunghill' printing 'Presse'?[76] When considering the network of associations crafted between his preface to Greene's *Menaphon* and the *Anatomy*, it is not so much the case, as Socrates remarks in Plato's *Phaedrus*, that writing is 'truly analogous to painting … when it is ill-treated or unfairly abused it always needs its parent to come to its aid, being unable to defend or help itself'.[77] Nashe's early work conversely needs to be protected from its own creator. Consider his comments regarding print culture in *Pierce Penniless* (1592):

> Should we (as you) borrowe all out of others, and gather nothing of our selves, our names should bee baffuld on everie Booke-sellers Stall, and not a Chandlers Mustard-pot but would wipe his mouthe with our wast paper. Newe Herrings, new, we must crye, every time wee make our selves publique, or else we shall bee christened with a hundred newe tytles of Idiotisme.[78]

Each new book should be presented as 'newe' to avoid an association with 'Idiotisme', offering a pre-emptively fishy inflection to the modernist dictum attributed to Ezra Pound – 'make it new'.[79] An unproductive borrowing of *sententiae* and commonplaces will doom a text. Writers must therefore make sure their work is fresh or risk its transformation into 'wast paper' tarnished with mustard or, as suggested in *Menaphon*, the excrement of serving-men.

The defence of new writing presented in *Pierce* demonstrates how 'all writers, regardless of genre of status, are subject to the whims of the market' as Samuel Fallon remarks. This section also conveys, I contend, how a satirist may eventually be made subject to the tools of his own trade.[80] Nashe's particular invocation for innovation, taken alongside the text's critique of literary originality, reflects poorly on the apparent lack of novelty and rhetorical creativity in the *Anatomy*: an early work that should have helped demonstrate his ability for a decorously creative use of *imitatio*. Looking back upon Nashe's discursive tendencies in the *Anatomy* in this light would show that it not only 'cuts apart the general corpus of early modern English literature to investigate its formal components and expose them to scrutiny' as John Nance suggests, but that it also exhibits potential points of weakness in its own rhetorical structure.[81] Nashe consistently recognises the inescapable dynamic that plays out in the early modern print market between the deceptive textual aesthetics deployed by writers to sell their books and the facile critical judgements of their intended readers. In *Pierce* the promise of a delectable fish is necessary to distinguish one's work from the reductively imitative creations of other writers. Seemingly palatable covers for literary material may, nevertheless, prove to be derivatively insubstantial fare upon further inspection. The 'crye' of originality issued by the opening pages of this text reveals the dual role its veneer plays as a primary selling point and evidence of its central flaw.

LENTEN STUFF'S SUBSTANCE

Evaluating the utility of textual surfaces, the political consequences of surface reading, and the consumption of literary fish also features prominently in Nashe's last work, *Lenten Stuff*. Its opening signals the importance that the reception of this 'tribute of inke and paper' takes as a piece of 'rhetorical food'.[82] This preface presents the text as a dried 'redde herring' that should be appropriate 'meate' for its readers, standing in direct contrast to the opening epistle of his earlier *Anatomy*, which proposes that it represents an 'undisgested endevour'.[83] Where Lena Liapi argues that Nashe cultivates 'a reputation for biting satire and vindictiveness' in the early modern print market, it is also clear that Nashe's own works are meant to be bitten.[84] The herring stands as a metaphorical representation of the *Lenten Stuff* itself, where its imputed worth forms the baseline from which all other goods will be valued.

Lenten Stuff should nourish its reader, and allow Nashe to evaluate the worth of his reputation in the 'worldes outwarde apparance' as a 'deade man' to be fed upon by the 'contemptible stickle-banck' of his 'enemies'.[85] The public presentation of literary matter is an act of self-display that renders one's physical and literary body vulnerable to acts of consumption. Here Nashe underscores the risks associated with literary production, yet his work may constitute the fishy curative to thwart those sticklebacks (tiny fish) who busy themselves in 'nibbling about' his 'fame'.[86] His ruined reputation is 'no smoothred secret', though 'with light cost of rough cast rethorieke [rhetoric] it may be tollerabley playstered over', if Nashe were to be granted the indulgence of his audience to shape his own fate.[87] The rhetorical aptitude displayed in a text like *Lenten Stuff* may help to partially repair his cracked reputation, and prove himself to be a 'cunninger diver then they [his detractors] are aware'.[88] Cunning is needed to remedy his past actions, to justify his current output, and to aptly plunge his critics into their own 'bryne, or a piteous pickle'.[89] Brown's contention that the defence of herring fishing presented here acts as a 'facsimile for the defense of rhetoric … one which is skilful, cunning, trivial and superficial' is compelling.[90] I would, however, also underscore the significance that superficiality takes in the rhetorical framework for this mock encomium. The fantasy of a reputation mended through literary guile conveys the importance that outer appearances take for *Lenten Stuff*'s recuperative and vitriolic objectives as a whole.

The depiction of his and his text's materiality (as objects to be read, interpreted, and gobbled up by the public) takes a grotesque turn when Nashe imagines the posthumous analysis of his legacy. Nashe first proposes that only fragments of his essence, 'like the crums in a bushy beard after a greate banquet,' will inhabit his papers once he is dead, and then states that 'the bare perusing of which, infinite posterities of hungry Poets shall receive good refreshing, even as Homer by Galatæon was pictured vomiting in a bason … and the rest of the succeeding Poets after him, greedily lapping up what he disgorged'.[91] Counter to the 'scurvie pedling' poets in *Pierce Penniless* who only offer 'purgations and vomits wrapt uppe in wast paper', Nashe envisions his own literary excretion as coveted material in *Lenten Stuff*.[92] Future readers will be able to sustain themselves merely by the 'bare perusing' of these textual scraps.[93] In this light *Lenten Stuff* forms the basin from which the regurgitated 'taste of such a dainty dish as the redde Herring' is collected.[94] Nashe affirms the instructive potential of painted images, rather than depicting them as a corrupting form of artifice associated with the obscuration of truth: paint is a technology of revelation, not occlusion. Homer's insides are brought forth into the world and used as an instructive tool for Nashe's own rhetorical schemes. This ekphrastic commentary on excretions thus validates his writing as both exceptional and strangely delectable, and presents his text as a receptacle filled with import, rather than merely covered in the veneer of a new herring (as commented upon in *Pierce Penniless*).

Lenten Stuff is punctuated by comments concerning its textual substance and how it should be navigated by the reader, as first made evident when we are reminded of the personal documents Nashe relies on to create the text: 'My Tables are not yet one quarter emptied of my notes out of their Table … a Sea Rutter diligently kept amongst them from age to age'.[95] The 'Sea Rutter', a sailing chart or notebook, records the 'ebbs and flowes' of his life and helps form an anchor point for him to 'tie my selfe to more precisely' as the narrative 'leadeth on'.[96] This glimpse of the potential for narrative disorientation is countered by another piece of self-reflexive commentary regarding the text's structural integrity: 'I woulde be loth to builde a laborinth in the gatehouse of my booke, for you to loose your selves in, and therefore I shred of[f] many thinges'.[97] Nashe once again deploys spatial and architectural metaphors to signal the dimensional depth of his work, this time in the main content of the book rather than its paratextual façade as seen in his prefaces to the *Anatomy* and Sidney's *Astrophel*.

The opening of *Lenten Stuff* encourages its reader to think of it as a composite whose form is governed by editorial mindfulness, and whose narrative is unified through the 'priority and prevalence' of Yarmouth's red herring.[98] Despite this gesture towards its careful construction *Lenten Stuff* is still presented as being deficient of certain material. We learn that Nashe's 'intellectuall faculties' are bereaved of his 'note-books and all books else here in the countrey ... whereby I might enamell and hatch over this device more artifically and masterly, and attire it in his true orient varnish and tincture'.[99] The application of discursive varnishes, derived from the knowledge in his abandoned notebooks, would provide the main 'device' of his text with its rightful 'attire'. Stylistic attire has been previously used to signal the insubstantial offering of Greene's *Menaphon* and the false sense of erudition of his own *Anatomy*. Such embellishment would help to glaze over *Lenten Stuff*'s deficiencies, but we are aware that this excuse is, in itself, a rhetorical gesture designed to defend the content of the text. Appearances are crucial even when Nashe directs us to acknowledge the insufficiencies of what lies beneath the mandatory veneer of refinement.

SWALLOWING THE RED HERRING

Rhetorical ornamentation is fundamental to the integrity of *Lenten Stuff* but Nashe is acutely aware of its vulnerability to acts of misinterpretation. It is apparently at risk from those with the 'title of learned' who – 'not looking into the text itselfe' – would 'disjoynt and teare every sillable betwixt their teeth severally'.[100] Such 'lawyers, and selfe-conceited misinterpreters' fail to properly attend to a text's complexity before tearing it to pieces, running 'over al the peeres of the land in peevish moralizing and anatomizing it'.[101] Nashe fears being gnashed. It is apt that such a scenario is mentioned just after he has referred to his previous 'discourses' as textual substances associated with 'mingle mangle cum purre'.[102] The deformation of the text is correlated to personal defamation. Nashe acknowledges that his career, in one respect, has moved from the pig trough to the fishing net – from jumbled, 'mingle mangle' outputs to whole red herrings – though the development of his writing has not deterred those who wish to render it into base matter. Where acts of anatomisation generate vaccuous texts that make 'the Presse' a 'dunghill' in the *Anatomy*, the depiction of 'anatomisation' in *Lenten Stuff* shows how critics ruin legitimate textual meat by their 'ilfavoured mouthing and missounding' of it.[103] Instead of turning texts into profitable matter, superficial readers turn books into material and acoustic waste. Nashe's particular oral fixation provides an alternative teleology to the convention of textual digestion as moral edification that was commonplace in the period.[104] Even by the conclusion of *Lenten Stuff* Nashe is still thinking about a time and place where a reader might 'heare mee mangled and torne in mennes mouthes'.[105] This vision of improper textual mastication implies that superficial critics chew without swallowing, and speak without sense. Nashe's concern over the disintegration of *Lenten Stuff* offers an image of the text being macerated into material 'stuffe' that, unlike the stuff or textual pulp that was used to form sheets of paper, would be left worthless after human intervention.

Despite this fear Nashe invites potential detractors to construe the value of his work, offering up his writing to 'a Legion of mice-eyed decipherers and calculators uppon characters' so that they may 'augurate' its meaning.[106] Professing ignorance to the broader significance of his digressions, Nashe states that his 'readers peradventure may see more into it then I can' for 'nothing from them is obscure'.[107] This sardonic reflection on the ability of his readers to ascertain the depth of his writing aptly succeeds a metafictional reflection on the importance of the aims, structure, and spatial dimensions of *Lenten Stuff* as a whole: 'Stay, let me looke about, where am I in my text, or out of it? ... I thinke I am out indeede. Beare with it, it was but a pretty parenthesis of Princes and theyr parasites, which shalt doo you no harme, for I will cloy you with Herring before wee part.'[108] The parenthetical nature of his asides take him off course or 'out' of his work, before reassuring the reader that he will stuff them full of herring before the text's conclusion. Henry Turner proposes that these self-reflexive comments 'divert our gaze from the object before our mind's eye to the physical page beneath our nose', but both have been presented to the reader as one and the same since the text's introduction: 'Heere I bring you a redde herring'.[109] Attending to the materiality of print is to attend the herring as well as a text that is presented as a consumable good – the page is a printed surface swimming with Nashe's own rhetorical fish which should apparently satiate his readers. This rupture in the text's narrative progression reminds us of the control that Nashe wields over its structure, despite his presentation of it as a depository of inconsequential tales of 'loose, digressive quality'.[110] Nashe conveys the potency of his authorial voice, and his powers of interpretation (as opposed to his detractors) through this play with spatial dislocation.

The vital relationship between paper-text and fish-text is reiterated near the conclusion of the work when Nashe compares the skin of the smoked red herring to that of the legendary Colchian ram. It is said that the 'skinne of the sheepe that bare the golden fleece' has a 'booke of Alcumy written upon it', just as the 'redde Herrings skinne' contains the 'accidens of Alcumy' when smoked: 'which is a secret that all Tapsters will curse mee for blabbing, in his skinne there is plaine witchcraft, for doe but rubbe a kanne or quarte pot round about the mouth wyth it, let the cunningest lickespiggot swelt his heart out, the beere shal never foame or froath in the cupp, whereby to deceyve men of their measure, but be as setled as if it stoode al night'.[111] The esoteric inscription occupying the surface of the ram's hide is reflected in the 'redde Herrings skinne', though the herring's alchemical qualities have a more practical application since its 'plaine witchcraft' is evident in its use to clarify beer. Applying smoked herring skin to the rim of a 'kanne or quarte pot' will rid beer of its frothy head, and allow for a 'Tapsters' patron to ascertain the true dimensions and contents of their drinking vessel. Through this logic, herring skin acts as a counter to deception, elucidating rather than obscuring the true nature of things.

So, if Nashe repeatedly presents *Lenten Stuff* as a herring, what is its particular utility as a site of inscription and interpretation? Lorna Hutson advocates for the socially liberating principles of Nashe's work, arguing that it offers an alternative mode of literary value to the 'habits of moralizing or reading for "profit"' fostered by Elizabethan grammar schools: '*Lenten Stuff* is about redefining prosperity as a kind of freedom of movement' which is apparent when 'oratical affluence ... redefines itself as a capacity to stimulate and be stimulated by words without having them manipulated against oneself'.[112] Hutson's point concerning the reciprocal freedom of expression conveyed by Nashe's style is persuasive. We should, nevertheless, remember how the conclusion of *Lenten Stuff* is structured around a mode of economic exchange between reader and author which accentuates Nashe's authority to dictate the value and meaning of his herring-text. This section raises the issue of whether a reader should swallow what Nashe has produced.

The correlation between text and herring is extended through the vision Nashe offers of packing fish into a barrel: 'wee call it the swinging of herrings when hee cade them ... If the text will beare this, we wil force it to beare more, but it shall be but the weight of a strawe'.[113] In spite of this apparently light cognitive load Nashe encourages his 'weary Readers' by the end of the work to 'Be of good cheere ... for I have espied land, as Diogenes said to his weary Schollers when he had read to a waste leafe'.[114] Where Diogenes ends his lesson at a 'waste' or blank 'leafe', Nashe rationalises the length and content of *Lenten Stuff* through the claim that it may actually represent something worthwhile, for he is 'the first that ever sette quill to paper in prayse of any fish or fisherman'.[115] This claim is, however, set alongside an imagined scenario where a slow-witted philistine might think Nashe had instead 'writte of a dogges turde'.[116] *Lenten Stuff* may then be viewed as excrement rather than a fishy delicacy.[117] In order to defend the inspiration behind his text and its structuring conceit Nashe states that he would 'take mine oath uppon a redde herring and eate it, to proove' that his potential detractors' families 'were scullions dishwash, & durty draffe and swil set against a redde herring'.[118] Consuming the red herring therefore confirms the refinement of one's palate and verifies what is 'draffe' (refuse) or a textual 'turde'.

Ruminating upon the imagined distaste for his textual herring leads Nashe to suggest that he must depart, since his 'conceit' has been 'cast into a sweating sickenesse, with ascending these few steps of his renowne'.[119] He has apparently made himself ill in the act of generating this substance, and thus holds back from spending 'the whole bagge of my winde' on his work.[120] Rhodes helpfully outlines how this passage speaks to the 'uncontrollability of his imaginative creations' and the profusion of thoughts 'which is a chief stimulant of the grotesque'.[121] I would contend that Nashe's allusion to the production and packaging of his text actually highlights the very deliberate command that he holds over the 'fountaines of eloquence' which he harnesses to extol the virtues of the red herring.[122] *Lenten Stuff* still has more of its own wind to blow: it is in literary surplus at its end, just as it was in its opening where Nashe states that he was 'not yet one quarter emptied of my notes'.[123] Rather than demonstrating Nashe's 'sensitivity' to the effects that his text may have on its reader, this conclusion stresses how *Lenten Stuff*'s central conceit is primarily attuned to exhibiting his extensive rhetorical flair.[124] Nashe, swollen with self-conceit, produces a red herring that brings him to the brink of sickness, while offering the same fish-text for his readers to consume. Spending too much mental energy on this mock-encomium exposes the limit of his creative faculties and casts doubts over the reader's appetite for such textual fare. Despite investing in the image of the red herring as delectable meat, the text may after all be unfit for human consumption.

My aim here has been to show how we might navigate Nashe's 'overracked Rhetoricke' by attending to the consistency in which he uses acts of surface reading to conceive of literary value and rhetorical integrity.[125] Nashe displays a deep-rooted commitment to both self-display and self-reflexive commentary on his place in the 'worldes outwarde apparance' throughout his career.[126] He repeatedly denounces facile interpretative acts in an attempt to defend himself from superficial scrutiny, while promoting the worthiness of outward appearances to validate his own texts as valuable products. I've also shown how his writing is typified by metacritical reflections on the envisioned fate of his work as a consumable material which is threatened by acts of misinterpretation. The interrogative energy of his extemporal style thus creates (and is defined by) moments of logical discord concerning the appraisal of outward appearances. Attending to his concern with the significance of outer appearances exposes the ironical inconsistencies of Nashe's prose, as he continually relies upon an orthodox schema of vapid surface and complex depth while trying to invert the hierarchy of this relationship for his own benefit. Nashe's work is simultaneously wary of but indebted to the appeal of surface logic.

NOTES

1 Thomas Nashe, *The terrors of the night* (London, 1594), sig. A4r.
2 Helen Smith, '"Imprinted by Simeon such a signe": Reading Early Modern Imprints', in *Renaissance Paratexts*, ed. Helen Smith and Louise Wilson (Cambridge: Cambridge University Press, 2011), pp. 13–33 (p. 23).
3 Nashe, *Terrors*, sig. A4r.
4 Nashe, *Terrors*, sig. A4r. Martin Momus (Momus, Greek god of mockery) forms another descriptor for Martin Marprelate. Momus figures also appear in 'contemporary texts to signify the carping critic': Lori Newcomb, 'What Is a Chapbook?', in *Literature and Popular Culture in Early Modern England*, ed. Matthew Dimmock and Andrew Hadfield (Farnham: Ashgate, 2009), pp. 57–72 (p. 55).
5 Nashe, *Terrors*, sig. A4r.
6 Nashe gives us an insight into the sharp 'bite' of 'Tewkesburie mustard' later on in *Terrors* (sig. B4v).
7 David Scott Kastan, 'The Body of the Text', *ELH*, 81.2 (2014), 443–67 (p. 448). See also Lena Liapi's exploration of Nashe's place in the early modern print market in Chapter 4 below.
8 Nashe, *Terrors*, sig. A4r.
9 Georgia Brown, *Redefining Elizabethan Literature* (Cambridge: Cambridge University Press, 2004), p. 80.
10 Brown, *Redefining Elizabethan Literature*, p. 56.
11 Chloe Kathleen Preedy, Chapter 1 above.
12 Lorna Hutson, *Thomas Nashe in Context* (Oxford: Clarendon Press, 1989), p. 5.
13 Hutson, *Thomas Nashe in Context*, p. 4.
14 Gabriel Harvey, *Foure Letters, and certaine sonnets* (London, 1592), sig. E3r.
15 Stephen Best and Sharon Marcus, 'Surface Reading: An Introduction', *Representations*, 108 (2009), 1–21 (p. 9).
16 Best and Marcus, 'Surface Reading', p. 10.
17 Best and Marcus, 'Surface Reading', pp. 12 and 16; Crystal Bartolovich, 'Humanities of Scale: Marxism, Surface Reading – and Milton', *PMLA*, 127 (2012), 115–21 (p. 118). The flaws of Best and Marcus's vision of surface reading have been laid out in some detail in Bruno Penteado, 'Against Surface Reading: Just Literality

and the Politics of Reading', *Mosaic*, 52 (2019), 85–100, and Ellen Rooney, 'Live Free or Describe: The Reading Effect and the Persistence of Form', *Differences*, 21 (2010), 112–39.
18 Taking inspiration from Tim Ingold's emphasis on the restorative function that a preoccupation with surfaces may have for our understanding of the world, in 'Surface Visions', *Theory, Culture & Society*, 34 (2017), 99–108 (p. 100).
19 Jennifer Richards, *Voices and Books in the English Renaissance* (Oxford: Oxford University Press, 2019), p. 232.
20 Richards, *Voices and Books*, p. 282.
21 Thomas Nashe, *The Anatomie of Absurditie* (London, 1589), sig. ¶2r; Hutson, *Thomas Nashe in Context*, pp. 10–11.
22 Donald J. McGinn, *Thomas Nashe* (Boston: Twayne, 1981), p. 18.
23 G. R. Hibbard, *Thomas Nashe: A Critical Introduction* (London, Routledge and Kegan Paul, 1962), p. 18.
24 Nashe, *Anatomy*, sig. ¶4v.
25 Jacques Amyot, *Les Oevvres Morales & Meslees de Plutarque* (Paris, 1572), sig. I1v; John Marbeck, *A Booke of Notes and Common Places* (London, 1581), sigs Ll7r–Ll7v. Nashe's reference to 'worthles workmanship' seems to echo the phrasing of Marbeck's work.
26 See also Plutarch, *The philosophie, commonlie called, the morals*, trans. Philemon Holland (London, 1603), sig. I4v.
27 Marbeck, *A Book of Notes and Common Places*, sig. Ll7v.
28 Holland, *The Morals*, sig. I4v.
29 Nashe, *Anatomy*, sig. ¶4v.
30 Nashe, *Anatomy*, sig. ¶4v.
31 John Heywood, *Two Hundred Epigrammes, Vpon Two Hundred Prouerbes* (London, 1555), sig. D5v.
32 Nashe, *Anatomy*, sig. A1r.
33 Nashe, *Anatomy*, sig. A1r.
34 Nashe, *Anatomy*, sigs A1r–A1v.
35 Aristotle, *Poetics*, trans. Stephen Halliwell (Cambridge, MA: Harvard University Press, 1995), 1461b 14–15. As Spenser relates to the reader in his *Faerie Queene*, 'living art may not least part express / Nor life-resembling pencill' can 'paint' what 'Zeuxis' was capable of producing: Edmund Spenser, *The Faerie Queene*, ed. Thomas P. Roache Jr and C. Patrick O'Donnell, Jr (London: Penguin, 1987), Book III, Canto I, Verse 2, ll. 1–2.
36 Thomas Nashe, 'To the Gentlemen Students', in Robert Greene's *Menaphon* (London, 1589), sig. **1r. As Day reminds us, 'the creative use of the paratext was part of the skill of writing' for Nashe: Matthew Day, 'Hakluyt, Harvey, Nashe: The Material Text and Early Modern Nationalism', *Studies in Philology*, 104 (2007), 281–305 (p. 295).
37 Nashe, 'Gentlemen Students', sig. **1r.
38 Nashe, 'Gentlemen Students', sig. **2r.
39 Thomas Nashe, 'Somewhat to reade for them that list', in Philip Sidney's *Syr P. S. His Astrophel and Stella* (London, 1591), sig. A3r.
40 Marlowe would later translate these lines from Ovid's *Amores* as 'the shout is nigh, the golden pomp comes here' (III.2, l. 44). See *Christopher Marlowe: The Complete Poems and Translations*, ed. Stephen Orgel (London: Penguin, 2007).
41 Nashe, 'Somewhat', sig. A4v.
42 Nashe, 'Gentlemen Readers', sig. **2r.

43 Nashe, 'Gentlemen Readers', sig. **1v.
44 Nashe, 'Gentlemen Readers', sig. **1v.
45 Jonathan V. Crewe, *Unredeemed Rhetoric: Thomas Nashe and the Scandal of Authorship* (Baltimore: Johns Hopkins University Press, 1982), p. 27.
46 Nashe, 'Gentlemen Readers', sig. **2r.
47 Nashe, 'Gentlemen Readers', sig. **2r.
48 Nashe, 'Gentlemen Readers', sig. **2r.
49 Nashe, 'Gentlemen Readers', sig. A3r.
50 Michael Saenger, *The Commodification of Textual Engagements in the English Renaissance* (Aldershot: Ashgate, 2006), p. 114.
51 Alexandra Halasz, *The Marketplace of Print: Pamphlets and the Public Sphere in Early Modern England* (Cambridge: Cambridge University Press, 1997), p. 96.
52 Jason Scott-Warren, 'Nashe's Stuff', in *The Oxford Handbook of English Prose 1500–1640*, ed. Andrew Hadfield (Oxford: Oxford University Press, 2013), p. 210.
53 Nashe, 'Gentlemen Readers', sig. A3r.
54 Nashe, *Anatomy*, sigs A1v and E4r.
55 Nashe, *Anatomy*, sig. ¶3r.
56 Nashe, 'Gentlemen Readers', sig. A3r.
57 Nashe, *Anatomy*, sig. A1v.
58 Nashe, *Anatomy*, sig. A1v.
59 Nashe, *Anatomy*, sig. A1v.
60 Nashe, *Anatomy*, sig. A1v.
61 Nashe, *Anatomy*, sig. B2r.
62 Nashe, *Anatomy*, sig. B2v.
63 Nashe, *Anatomy*, sigs B2r–B2v.
64 Nashe, *Anatomy*, sigs E2v–E3r.
65 Nashe, *Anatomy*, sig. E3r.
66 Horace, *Art of Poetry*, trans. H. Rushton Fairclough (Cambridge, MA: Harvard University Press, 1926), line 361, p. 480.
67 Nashe, *Anatomy*, sig. E3r.
68 Jane Partner, *Poetry and Vision in Early Modern England* (London: Palgrave, 2018), p. 12.
69 George Puttenham, *The arte of English poesie* (London, 1589), sig. Q4r.
70 Such 'artificers ... debase the art of poesy by publishing vulgar verse'. See Rayna Kalas, *Frame, Glass, Verse: The Technology of Poetic Invention in the English Renaissance* (Ithaca: Cornell University Press, 2007), p. 62.
71 Philip Sidney, *The Defence of Poesie* (London, 1595), sig. C1v; Leonard Barkan, 'Making Pictures Speak: Renaissance Art, Elizabethan Literature, Modern Scholarship', *Renaissance Quarterly*, 48 (1995), 326–51 (p. 327); Nashe, *Anatomy*, sig. C3v.
72 Nashe, *Anatomy*, sig. C3v.
73 Nashe, *Anatomy*, sig. C3v.
74 Nashe, *Anatomy*, sig. A4r. See also Steven Mentz's observations on Nashe's misogyny in 'Nashe's Fish: Misogyny, Romance, and the Ocean in Lenten Stuffe', in *The Age of Thomas Nashe*, pp. 63–76.
75 Nashe also critiques authors who would defend or show an 'affinity with women' in their works (like Robert Greene): Helen Hackett, *Women and Romance Fiction in the English Renaissance* (Cambridge: Cambridge University Press, 2000), p. 98.
76 Nashe, *Anatomy*, sig. B2r.

77 Plato, *Phaedrus*, trans. Robert Hackforth (Cambridge: Cambridge University Press, 1972), 275e.
78 Thomas Nashe, *Pierce Penilesse* (London, 1592), sig. D3r. A similar use of texts to stop mustard pots occurs in William Page's translation of Celio Curione's *Pasquine in a Traunce* (London, 1584) where a priest's works are found in a shop that sells pilchards as a domestic rather than a literary material. The marginal comment on this story states: 'Good wares to stop mustard pots' (sigs I4v–K1r).
79 Pound's motto was ironically a borrowed phrase from a classical Chinese historical source. See Michael North's *Novelty: A History of the New* (Chicago: University of Chicago Press, 2013), pp. 162–4.
80 Samuel Fallon, *Paper Monsters: Persona and Literary Culture in Elizabethan England* (Philadelphia: University of Pennsylvania Press, 2019), p. 131.
81 John V. Nance, 'Gross Anatomies: Mapping Matter and Literary Form in Thomas Nashe and Andreas Vesalius', in *The Age of Thomas Nashe*, pp. 115–31 (p. 117).
82 Thomas Nashe, *Nashes Lenten stuffe* (London, 1599), sig. A2r; Andrew Hadfield, '"Not without Mustard": Self-publicity and Polemic in Early Modern Literary London', in *Renaissance Transformations: The Making of English Writing, 1500–1650*, ed. Margaret Healy and Thomas Healy (Edinburgh: Edinburgh University Press, 2009), pp. 64–78 (p. 67).
83 Nashe, *Lenten Stuff*, sigs A3r–A3v; Nashe, *Anatomy*, sig. ¶4v.
84 See Liapi, Chapter 4 below.
85 Nashe, *Lenten Stuff*, sig. B1r.
86 Nashe, *Lenten Stuff*, sig. B1r.
87 Nashe, *Lenten Stuff*, sig. B1v.
88 Nashe, *Lenten Stuff*, sig. B1r.
89 Nashe, *Lenten Stuff*, sig. B1r.
90 Brown, *Redefining Elizabethan Literature*, p. 86.
91 Nashe, *Lenten Stuff*, sigs B1v–B2r.
92 Nashe, *Pierce Penniless*, sig. I2v. This reference to Homer forms part of Nashe's pointed critique of Gabriel Harvey's *Pierce's Supererogation* (1593). See Andrew Hadfield, 'Lenten Stuffe: Thomas Nashe and the Fiction of Travel', *YES*, 41 (2011), 68–83 (p. 79).
93 Nashe, *Lenten Stuff*, sig. B2r.
94 Nashe, *Lenten Stuff*, sig. B4r.
95 Nashe, *Lenten Stuff*, sig. C1v.
96 Nashe, *Lenten Stuff*, sig. C1v.
97 Nashe, *Lenten Stuff*, sig. D1v.
98 Nashe, *Lenten Stuff*, sig. D3r.
99 Nashe, *Lenten Stuff*, sig. D4r.
100 Nashe, *Lenten Stuff*, sigs I3v–I4r. This approbrium for Nashe's work is realised in the *Isle of Dogs* debacle of 1597, and in the later 'widespread assault on literary culture' following the 1599 Bishops' Ban: see Hadfield, '"Not without Mustard": Self-publicity and Polemic in Early Modern Literary London', p. 68.
101 Nashe, *Lenten Stuff*, sigs I4v–K1r.
102 Nashe, *Lenten Stuff*, sig. I3v. J. B. Steane notes that 'cum purre' is '[s]aid to be a call to pigs to come to the trough'. Thomas Nashe, *Nashe's Lenten Stuff*, in *'The Unfortunate Traveller' and Other Works*, ed. J. B. Steane (London: Penguin, 1971), p. 444 (n. 459).
103 Nashe, *Anatomy*, sig. B2r; Nashe, *Lenten Stuff*, sig. I4r.
104 For a recent study on the trope of textual digestion see Jan Purnis, 'The Belly-Mind Relationship in Early Modern Culture', in Laurie Johnson, John Sutton, and Evelyn

Tribble (eds), *Embodied Cognition and Shakespeare's Theatre* (London: Routledge, 2014), pp. 235–52.
105 Nashe, *Lenten Stuff*, sig. L1v.
106 Nashe, *Lenten Stuff*, sig. K2r.
107 Nashe, *Lenten Stuff*, K3r.
108 Nashe, *Lenten Stuff*, sig. K2v.
109 Henry S. Turner, 'Nashe's Red Herring: Epistemologies of the Commodity in "Lenten Stuffe" (1599)', *ELH*, 68 (2001), 529–61 (p. 536); Nashe, *Lenten Stuff*, sig. A3r.
110 Hutson, *Thomas Nashe in Context*, p. 246.
111 Nashe, *Lenten Stuff*, sig. K3v.
112 Hutson, *Thomas Nashe in Context*, p. 261 and p. 266.
113 Nashe, *Lenten Stuff*, sig. K3v.
114 Nashe, *Lenten Stuff*, sigs K4v–L1r.
115 Nashe, *Lenten Stuff*, sig. L1r.
116 Nashe, *Lenten Stuff*, sig. L2r.
117 Remember that he begins *Lenten Stuff* by stating that 'Heere I bring you a redde herring' (sig. A3r).
118 Nashe, *Lenten Stuff*, sig. L2r.
119 Nashe, *Lenten Stuff*, sig. L2r.
120 Nashe, *Lenten Stuff*, sig. L2r. Preedy eloquently shows how pneumatic metaphors and 'respiration's role in generating fictional matter' underpins Nashe's prose style in *Lenten Stuff*: see Chapter 1 above, esp. p. 28.
121 Neil Rhodes, *Elizabethan Grotesque* (London: Routledge & Kegan Paul, 1980), p. 53.
122 Nashe, *Lenten Stuff*, sig. L2r.
123 Nashe, *Lenten Stuff*, sig. C1v.
124 Day, 'Hakluyt, Harvey, Nashe', p. 303.
125 Nashe, 'To the Gentlemen Readers', sig. A3r.
126 Nashe, *Lenten Stuff*, sig. B1r.

4
'WHEN PRINTS ARE SET ON WORK, WITH GREENS & NASHES': NASHE'S 'POPULARITY' REVISITED

Lena Liapi

Writing more than a hundred years after the Martin Marprelate debate, Anthony Wood revisited this controversy, passing judicious judgement on its ultimate conclusion. Wood claimed that even though 'learned and sober Men' had answered most of Marprelate's works,

> yet they did not so much work on the author and his disciples, make them ridiculous, and put him and them to silence, more than those answers which were written in a buffooning stile; as (1) that written by Tom Nash, intit. *Pappe with an hatchet* ... these buffoonries and Pasquils did more *non-plus* Penry and his disciples, and so consequently made their Doctrine more ridiculous among the common sort, than any grave or learned answer could do.[1]

Here Wood views Nashe's 'buffooning stile' as the main element of what made his works appealing to the common sort. Wood's words also suggest that this style of writing is employed in order to court 'popularity' and ensure that the attack on Martinism will have a wide (if potentially 'lowly') audience.

This comment brings into focus the debate on the meaning of 'print popularity' in early modern England. Despite an often-stated reluctance to use the term, it keeps cropping up in edited volumes such as *The Elizabethan Top Ten* or *Literature and Popular Culture in Early Modern England*.[2] 'Print popularity' has been a frustratingly difficult term to define. Andy Kesson and Emma Smith define it as 'that which might either confirm or subvert communal value, or confirm and subvert it, remembering that for early modern politics communality itself was viewed suspiciously by those who saw hierarchy, monarchy and patronage as guarantees of social stability'.[3] This is a very dense synthesis of a wide range of approaches to popularity. It is impressive in its attempt to combine a wide range of viewpoints, but it obscures how the different elements of this definition point to different attitudes towards 'popularity'. This difference of opinion on what the term means is made apparent in the other contributions to

Kesson and Smith's volume. In their piece Alan Farmer and Zachery Lesser examine 'popularity' in terms of best-selling works and their market share, gauging how successful particular kinds of texts were by estimating the number of editions published, the rate at which they were reprinted, and how profitable these works were for the publishers.[4] Helen Smith connects popularity to the way in which texts were collected and preserved, while Neil Rhodes focuses more on the social and literary status of the author, suggesting that writing for the market, rather than for a patron or a learned coterie, was 'popular' but less valuable.[5]

Rhodes's approach echoes earlier scholarship on the development of the professional author in sixteenth-century England. For scholars such as Charles Nicholl and Stephen Hilliard, writing for the market was connected to 'popularity': newly emerged professional authors (chief among them Nashe) targeted a wider audience than previously desired, in order to increase the sales of their works on which they depended for their living. By consequence – so the argument goes – such writers sacrificed their elite cultural status by writing more accessible and less erudite texts, which could be enjoyed by an audience that included the middling and even the lower sorts.[6] Stephen Hilliard stretched further the definition of this audience by claiming that Nashe's ideal readers were 'the displaced young men of the city, perhaps a literally masterless man, disrespectful of authority and prone to disruptive behaviour'.[7] Dubbing such authors as 'hacks' (implying poor-quality writing and writing for consumption rather than for praise) who often worked on such 'low' genres as satire or romance solidified the equation between print popularity, 'lowly' genres, and 'lowly' readers.

This connection between addressing a wide audience and writing for the market has been made more positively recently, and print popularity analysed as a tactical move, a deliberate exploitation of publicity for political purposes, implying that it was not only possible but also desirable to affect 'the people'.[8] This approach often focuses on the Marprelate controversy, which created new ways of targeting a broad audience. Joseph Black has argued that the Marprelate pamphlets sought to make Presbyterian agenda accessible to a wide audience 'through the use of fictional strategies, a racy, colloquial prose, anecdotes anchored in the everyday details of their readers' lives, and a willingness to put into print the personal failings of individual bishops'.[9] The anti-Martinist campaign, in which Nashe took part, answered in kind, by appropriating Martin's polemical mode and targeting the same audience in a bid to influence public opinion. In this context Peter Lake views Nashe as a hack writer, using Marprelate's language and techniques in order to gain access to a socially mixed ('popular') audience and defeat Martin. Thus the anti-Martinist campaign was a result of official sanction and popular demand, because 'the immense impact of Marprelate's hilarious and scabrous satires had created a considerable popular market which could be exploited', and this was achieved by the anti-Martinist camp by recourse 'to the scurrilities and lewdness of the popular mode'.[10] Within this tradition Nashe's 'popularity' does not stem from his grotesque sympathy for all that was 'low', but is a symptom of his ability to draw in readers to theological debate through the emulation of Marprelate. This brief overview of approaches to print popularity shows that it is a multifaceted concept which has been approached through different lenses.

Adding another dimension to print popularity, this chapter argues that print popularity can be connected to cultural visibility. I analyse Thomas Nashe's vexed relationship with his audience and argue that, even though Nashe's works were not popular, Nashe's afterlife made him 'popular' in terms of notoriety and cultural visibility. Focusing on typographical and authorial choices, I examine how Nashe attempted to restrict the audience of his works and distinguish himself from other writers, whom he viewed as more 'lowly'. Nashe used populist moves to create notoriety and to push a particular agenda, without necessarily inviting a wide audience. Nonetheless I argue that there is a way in which we can talk about popularity in Nashe's case. Through Nashe's use of invective he gained a reputation as a contentious writer. This carefully cultivated characteristic became so pronounced that Nashe's name became a synonym for 'gall in print'.[11] If we think of popularity in terms of visibility, being ubiquitous in early modern culture, then Nashe was popular for establishing a brand name which not only was well known but also employed throughout the early modern period to connote a biting writing style. As we will see, Nashe's legacy was cemented on a kind of popularity based on notoriety.

NASHE'S INTENDED AUDIENCE: TYPOGRAPHY AND 'MARKETABILITY'

For a writer seen as the archetypal 'hack', Nashe's works were not easy to sell, and the typographical choices made for their packaging did not make them accessible to a wide audience. Examining the size and, consequently, estimated price of these texts, it becomes apparent that Nashe's works were not best-sellers, nor were they intended for a wide audience. The point will become clearer through the comparison of Nashe's works with Greene's works published or reprinted between 1589 and 1601 (the same period as Nashe's writing) and with sermons preached in London and published in the same time frame. Robert Greene was chosen as another example of a market-oriented reader, who was regularly identified with Nashe by rivals such as Gabriel and John Harvey as well as modern scholars. Sermons were very successful in terms of their sales and were intended to appeal to a wide audience. Both kinds of publication were speculative and non-monopolistic, so they were competing in the same market as Nashe's works.[12] Of course this comparison has some issues: given that few of Nashe's works were published, we cannot examine how his works compare to the total number of editions appearing in this period or their market share (as Lesser and Farmer have done), as the numbers would be insignificant. In addition, even though Robert Greene's works fall into the same genres as the ones Nashe worked on (drama, satire, polemic), sermons are a different genre. However, I posit that the comparison between Nashe, Greene, and London sermons serves to indicate that Nashe was significantly less interested in producing works which would target or be purchased by a wider audience.

This does not mean that Nashe was indifferent to having best-selling works. In *Have With You to Saffron Walden* (1596) Nashe brags about the economic performance of his *Pierce Penniless* (1592), claiming that Gabriel Harvey 'borrows my name, and the name of *Piers Pennilesse* (one of my Bookes), which he knew to be most saleable (passing at the least through the pikes of sixe Impressions)'.[13] However, such illusions of 'saleability' were shattered by the overall performance of his works in the marketplace of print. Even though the involvement of twelve printers and eight booksellers in the publication of Nashe's works suggests an expectation that his works would attract readers' interest, such interest was short-lived, as evidenced by the few reprints of his works. Most of his works were published only once, with few exceptions: *Pierce Penniless* (1592), which was Nashe's breakaway hit, went through six editions, and *Christ's Tears over Jerusalem* (1593) was reprinted three times. However, comparing them to Greene's works published or reprinted in the same period, we can see that texts by Greene appear more frequently and are reprinted more often. Between 1589 and 1601 twenty-five works by Greene were printed. From those works fourteen were reprinted at least twice, and often more than that, with particular hits being *A Quip for an Upstart Courtier* (1592); *Menaphon* (1589); and *Greene's Never Too Late* (1590) which were reprinted no fewer than five times. It is clear that Greene's works regardless of genre (his best-selling works included a play, a satire, and a prose repentance) were selling significantly better than Nashe's.

Even though Nashe talked about 'prostitute[ing]' his pen for gain, choices about the format of his texts show that he was selective in the clientele he sought to attract.[14] For the archetypal 'hack', the size – and, by consequence, price – of his texts surprises. If we examine Figure 4.1, we can establish that only four of Nashe's works were smaller than ten sheets: *The Anatomy of Absurdit, An Almond for a Parrot, Summer's Last Will and Testament*, and *The Terrors of the Night*. Of the rest, three (*Nashe's Lenten Stuff, Strange News, Pierce Penniless*) could barely be considered pamphlets, being just shorter than twelve sheets. I am using twelve sheets as a cut-off point for pamphlets, as this was the limit at which a text need not be bound as a book, but stitched.[15] *The Unfortunate Traveller* (in different editions, either thirteen or fifteen sheets long), *Have With You to Saffron Walden* (twenty-one sheets), and *Christ's Tears over Jerusalem* (twenty-four sheets in 1593 and 1594, twenty-five in 1613) were all substantial works. Nashe himself wrote disparagingly about short works: Nashe describes the eight-sheet *Terrors of the Night* (1594) as a 'Pamphlet (no bigger than an old Præface) speedily botcht up and compyled'.[16] If we contrast these works with the twenty-five works published by Robert Greene in the same period, we note that, even though Greene also had some longer works, the majority of his works fall between six and nine sheets (fifteen works) and that his three longer works, *Greene's Never Too Late* (1590), *Gwydonius* (reprinted in 1590), and *Mamillia* (reprinted in 1593), are all between fourteen and seventeen sheets. The difference is far more pronounced if we compare Nashe's works to sermons: of the thirty-seven extant sermons the majority (twenty-two) are shorter than six sheets, with twelve being five sheets long. Of the rest ten were between six and nine sheets and only two were longer than this. Even if we concede that the size and format depended on the publisher of Nashe's texts (and I will discuss how Nashe was personally involved in the publication of his texts), they knew the audience his texts were intended for.

Length of text is an important indicator of the intended audience, because it determined the price of texts. If we accept Francis Johnson's comments that the prices for books were about a halfpenny per sheet, with an additional retail mark-up of as much as 50 per cent, we can assume that Nashe's works cost between 4½d and 1s 7d. This is a very speculative estimation, because we cannot be certain about book prices. Given the difference in size, this shows that both sermons and Greene's works were far cheaper than most of Nashe's works. Nashe did not attempt to make even his best-selling *Pierce Penniless* more accessible: the last part of the pamphlet is a *Discourse on Spirits*, a translation of Georgius Pictorius's work, which did not add anything to the meaning of the text (and it was a substantial part of the work, being two and a half sheets long).[17] This part could have easily been cut off, thus making the rest cheaper. The decision to include it shows that the expected audience was a more affluent one.

Nashe consciously sought to have title pages which did not 'sell' his works. Even though (or, perhaps, because) Nashe was aware that a number of readers 'consider neither premisses nor conclusion, but piteouslie torment

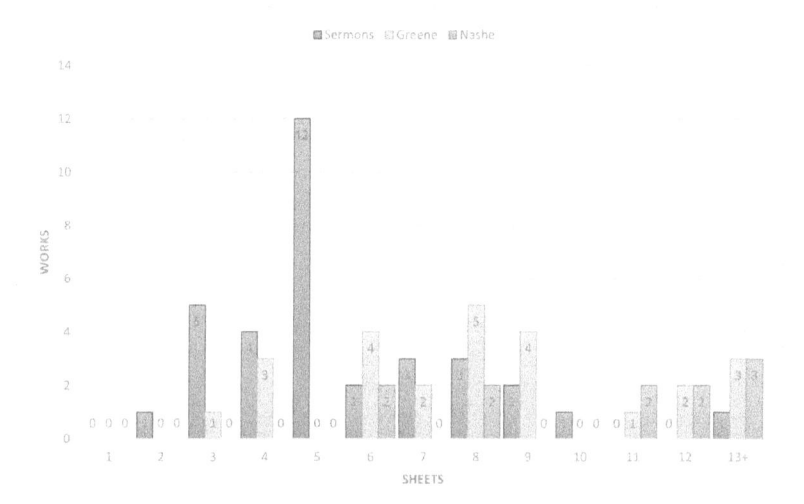

4.1 Comparative extents of works by Nashe, Greene, and sermon-writers

Title Pages on everie poast: never reading farther of anie Booke, than Imprinted by Simeon such a signe',[18] he did not try to make the title pages attractive to his prospective readers. The first edition of *Pierce Penniless*, which was printed without Nashe's consent, at least advertised its contents by mentioning that it described 'the over-spreading of Vice, and suppression of Vertue. Pleasantly interlac't with variable delights: and pathetically intermixt with conceipted reproofes'. This title page was rejected by Nashe, who asked the printer in the next edition to 'cut off that long-tayld Title, and let mee not in the forefront of my Booke, make a tedious Mountebanks Oration to the Reader', thus disassociating himself from a characteristic kind of sales speech encountered in markets and fairs.[19] This is particularly interesting if we think about the 'performability' of Nashe's style; Jennifer Richards persuasively argues that Nashe's writing style was highly performative, a quality achieved partly through imitation of the Elizabethan clown Richard Tarleton.[20] Throughout his literary career Nashe vocally disassociates himself from Tarleton and Greene, while emulating their style. In the second edition of *Pierce Penniless* Nashe shows ambivalence about his own style and a fear that it might be taken as a sales pitch.

Nashe's editorial intervention on *Pierce Penniless* was successful, and the next editions were as bare as the other works by Nashe, which do not include descriptions of their contents or advertisements to the reader.[21] As Kate De Rycker has shown, Nashe was very good at employing print to his benefit. In *Have With You to Saffron Walden* (1596), Nashe leaves an empty frame for the readers to put their own negative comments about the brothers Harvey, and also formats part of his text to look like a marketplace sign of a dyer, in order to ridicule the Harveys.[22] Consequently his choice to have his title pages bare, with no attempt to market their 'wares', was conscious. Nashe's personal (rather than the publisher's) engagement with the title pages of his works is evident in the one exception to his toned-down title pages: in *Have With You to Saffron Walden*. The title page aggressively advertises its contents as '*Containing a full Answere to the eldest sonne of the Halter-maker*'.[23] This, however, is a far more personal and direct address to the reader, claiming that this is '*As much to say, as* I sayd I would speake with him'.[24] This is not a sales pitch but a declaration of war, something that fits with Nashe's overall 'brand', as I will show in the last section.

If this is compared to Greene's works, it is clear that the choice of title pages was intended to draw in the readers. We can see this in Greene's cony-catching pamphlets, which use woodcuts of rabbits engaged in illegal activities as their trademark, to make different pamphlets an easily recognisable part of the whole. In addition Greene's works use phrases advertising their contents, such as *A DISPUTATION, Betweene a Hee Conny-catcher, and a Shee Conny-catcher, whether a Theefe or a Whoore, is most hurtfull in Cousonage, to the Common-wealth. DISCOVERING THE SECRET VILLA-nies of alluring Strumpets. With the Conversion of an English Courtizen, reformed this present yeare, 1592. Reade, laugh, and learne* (1592).[25] This is the case with other kinds of Greene's writing: in *Pandosto* (1588), the title page reads: *PANDOSTO. The Triumph of Time. WHEREIN IS DISCOVERED by a pleasant Historie, that although by the meanes of sinister fortune Truth may be concea-led, yet by Time in spight of fortune it is most manifestly revealed. Pleasant for age to avoyde drowsie thoughts, profitable for youth to eschue other wanton pastimes, and bringing to both a desired content.* Both title pages not only advertise the contents of the pamphlet but also emphasise that reading them is pleasant and useful; this is very similar to the initial title page of *Pierce Penniless*, which was denounced by Nashe as a sales pitch. This could still be an advertising technique, with Nashe seeking to woo readers in a far more aggressive and novel way. If so, Nashe tried to market his works to appeal to those who enjoyed irreverence and the denigration of his opponents and even his readers.

NASHE'S POPULISM AND MUCH MALIGNED READERS

Nashe attempted to walk a difficult tightrope in his writing: he criticised other writers for not being sufficiently learned, but he also tried to sound street-savvy and print-savvy. *The Anatomy of Absurdity* (1589) is the signature text in terms of Nashe's criticism of other writers. He accused John Stubbs and similar pamphleteers of making 'the Presse the dunghill, whether they carry all the muck of their mellancholicke imaginations'.[26] He was even more scathing towards the readers of such publications, claiming that they took such 'trifling Pamphlet[s]' as serious: 'each trifling Pamphlet [seems] to the simpler sorte, a most substantiall subject, whereof the wiser lightly account, and the learned laughing contemne'.[27] Here Nashe divides the audience of printed works to the 'simpler sorte', the wiser and the learned. 'Simpler sorte' was often employed as a synonym for the 'lower sort' (apprentices, labourers, peasants), or to denote those with little learning. This is not just a comment on their position and learning, it is a downright dismissal of their intelligence. Nashe discredits such readers by claiming that writers of pamphlets 'seeme learned to none but to Idiots'.[28] Separating the audience into different segments was not unusual in this period, as well as flattering those readers who viewed themselves as wise or learned.[29] However, Nashe's attack against readers of 'trifling Pamphlet[s]' suggests an attempt to disassociate himself from such an audience.

Such sentiments may be expected in one of Nashe's first eponymous works, where his attempt to draw a line between himself and other popular writers is intended as a salvo to his reputation as a serious writer, which was already tarnished by participation in the Marprelate debate. However, similar statements are also evident in *Pierce Penniless* (1592), where Nashe not only accuses 'poore latinlesse Authors' for being clueless but again dismisses those who read their works: these readers 'no sooner spy a new Ballad, and his name to it that compilde it: but they put him in for one of the learned men of our time'.[30] Attempting to distinguish himself from such writers, he claims 'For my part I do challenge no praise of learning to my selfe, yet have I worne a gowne in the Universitie, and so hath *caret tempus non habet moribus* [no time and no manners]'.[31] The speed with which Nashe's claim of seeking no praise for learning is undermined by his mention of his university studies and his use of Latin suggests that this is merely a self-congratulatory pat on the back.

Nashe's claims of an elite cultural status were complicated, however, by the ways in which he employed populist techniques in his works, such as using traditional framing devices (such as jest-books or anatomy of sins) and simplifying historical and mythological examples.[32] Such techniques were used by the Marprelate tracts in the 1580s, in order to heap abuse on the church establishment and to court a wider audience by making texts easier to understand.[33] Nashe's use of such techniques could imply that he was also aiming at a wider audience, but a circumscribed one. It is possible that he sought to appeal to the middling sort, but his continuous references to the wise and learned, along with his disparaging comments against the 'simpler sorte', could undermine such an ambition. I suggest that Nashe was trying to develop his brand as a writer who could use populist techniques in order to differentiate himself from others.

Nashe employed a structure resembling jest-books, which narrated different 'jests' or 'pranks' in the format 'how X did Y'. Nashe used this to great effect in order to illustrate his statements against either the hypocrisy of Puritans or the corruption of society at large. In *An Almond for a Parrat*, he gleefully narrated how 'a brother in Christ ... tombled his wife naked into the earth at high noone, without sheete or shroude to cover her shame, breathing over her in an audible voice: Naked came I out of my mothers wombe, and naked shall I returne againe'.[34] His characterisation of that incident as a 'prank' connects it to the jest-book tradition and to the iconoclastic discourse of anticlericalism, using the style championed by the Marprelate tracts against them. He does the same in *Pierce Penniless*, when he narrates 'A tale of a wise Justice', 'A merry tale of a Butcher & his Calves' and 'A rare wittie jest of Doctor Watson', all of them meant to exacerbate his criticism against London society.[35] This format could appeal to different audiences: it was part of a learned tradition which had been popularised for a long time.[36] In Nashe's hands, however, it received a new twist through his irreverence and biting satire.

The same can be said about some of the ways in which Nashe inserted classical reading in his texts. Nashe adopted a scoffing manner and a jesting attitude which playfully transformed even more lofty material to an everyday idiom. In *Pierce Penniless* Nashe castigates early modern London's prostitution trade by claiming that 'Lais, Cleopatra, Helen, if our clyme hath any such, noble Lord warden of the witches and jugglers, I commend them with the rest of our uncleane siffers [sisters] in Shorditch, the Spittle, Southwarke, Westminster, & Turnbull streete'.[37] In this passage Nashe displays his knowledge of the classics, but by connecting these famous women of antiquity to London spaces notorious for prostitution he turns this into an everyday reference. This technique of twisting classical references out of shape through the use of hyperbole and a colloquial style is manifested in *Terrors of the Night*: 'Socrates (the wisest man of Greece) was censured by a wrinckle-wyzard for the lumpishest blockehead that ever went on two legs'.[38] A reference to Socrates and physiognomy is brought down to earth through vulgar phraseology and used as a punchline. Nashe employs his knowledge of the classics elastically, flaunting his learning but also developing his own style.

Nashe often winks at his more learned readers, referencing the classics and expecting to be understood by discerning readers.[39] When railing against adultery, Nashe states: 'Menelaus hospitalitie mooved young Paris to adulterie. I say no more you knowe the rest, the wiser can apply it.'[40] Here Nashe expects his readers to be aware of the classical allusion and then adds that it is not enough to know it but to apply it, flattering those who consider themselves 'wise'. An even more covert reference to the classics is the well-known allusion to Aretino: 'of all stiles I most affect & strive to imitate Aretines, not caring for this demure soft *mediocre genus* [mediocrity], that is, like water and wine mixt togither'.[41] Nashe shows his desire to emulate Aretino's satirical style, but he is also implicitly dismissing ancient Greek philosophers' emphasis on the golden mean, the avoidance of extremes, and connecting it to the ancient Greek practice of mixing wine and water in order to avoid inebriation.[42] This would be understood only by readers who knew philosophy and history, establishing Nashe's credentials while also suggesting different expected audiences: readers who would get this reference, and those who would not, but could still read on.

Nashe attacked Robert Greene for his indiscriminate appeal to 'lowly' audiences: he accused Greene of being a 'Homer of women' and writing works intended for 'Serving mens pockets'.[43] We cannot be certain about authors' intentions. We can, however, say that by peppering his texts with classical allusions and disparagements of 'lowly' readers Nashe would be more appealing to an elite audience (or at least, not a popular one). Some of his attacks against less discerning readers seem disingenuous, as his use of populist techniques suggests. This echoes Anna Bayman's argument that writers such as Nashe occupied a literary middle ground, mocking 'both ill-educated, superstitious, "popular" culture and earnest, moralizing, learned culture'.[44] Nonetheless it seems likely that the use of such techniques was designed to produce outrage and to highlight Nashe's literary status and his characteristic style.

NOTORIETY AND VISIBILITY: NASHE'S LEGACY

So far we have examined the ways in which Nashe's authorial and editorial choices attempted to limit the intended audience for his works. Despite his attempts at populism, which were borrowed from the Marprelate controversy, Nashe did not seem to welcome or even tolerate a wide audience. This, of course, could be a rhetorical move; in this case, it seems to be less about endearing himself to his audience than about antagonising other readers and authors. This, however, was his most lasting legacy: Nashe became synonymous with his style.

Nashe sought to control his reputation by staking a claim as a serious writer and was – to an extent – successful, as can be seen from comments by contemporary critics. At the same time his name became associated with his style, rather than his works. Even though Nashe tried to shape his reputation, he could not control how it evolved. By courting controversy and cultivating a reputation for biting satire and vindictiveness, Nashe became notorious. Even though his works stopped being reprinted soon after his death, his name lived on as a synonym for gall in print. I argue that, by becoming a highly visible reference in early modern English culture, Nashe became 'popular' in the sense put forward by Adam Smyth. Smyth examines almanacs' ubiquity in early modern culture and posits that we can understand popularity as 'the instantly recognisable'; Smyth argues that 'this recognizability was dependent on almanacs in discourse being symbolically stable'.[45] Similarly Nashe's name after his death became fixed, signifying a satirical and vindictive writing style.

Pietro Aretino and Robert Greene also suffered the same fate. Kate De Rycker explores the transformation of Aretino from famous writer, wit, and scourge of princes to a pornographer and atheist. Even though Aretino personally cultivated a reputation as a professional writer, his name morphed into a synonym for pornographical writing.[46] Nashe was more sceptical about this process, as he was worried that his name would be remembered by what Harvey wrote about him.[47] In Chapter 3 above Douglas Clark shows how in *Lenten Stuff* Nashe is particularly worried about his reputation and the way in which readers will construct it.[48] Nashe had also seen how Robert Greene's reputation had been transformed: Greene sought to shape and commodify his reputation, employing his prodigal past and late-day repentance as selling points. However, this resulted in Greene's fictional persona as repentant prodigal becoming conflated with his actual self. Consequently other writers used Greene's name to signify writing for the market and prodigal criminality.[49]

Nashe's reputation went into two directions: critics acknowledged his status as a learned writer, but his most lasting legacy was as a synonym for gall in print. From the posthumous references to Nashe we can see that Nashe was considered as part of a learned coterie. Ben Jonson in a manuscript elegy characterised Nashe as a 'deare friend' and focused on his wit.[50] This sense that Nashe was part of the company of literati of his day is evident in the poem prefacing Humphrey King's *An Half-pennyworth of Wit, in a Penny-worth of Paper* (1613). The anonymous poet calls Nashe 'famous Nash, so deare unto us both'.[51] This quotation suggests personal knowledge of Nashe but also draws attention to Nashe's fame, also evident in John Taylor's eulogy 'noble Nash thy fame shall live alwayes'.[52] Chris Salamone also examines how early Stuart authors such as Thomas Middleton, Thomas Dekker, and John Taylor employed Nashe's ghost as a satirical device.[53]

Nashe had clearly made a name for himself among critics, something corroborated by his inclusion in anthologies and biographies of Elizabethan writers published throughout the sixteenth and seventeenth century. Francis Meres in *Palladis Tamia* (1598), an early account of poets and authors, calls Nashe a 'brave ... witte' and compares him to classical writers and mythical figures, focusing on his satirical style: 'As Eupolis of Athens used great libertie in taxing the vices of men: so dooth Thomas Nash, witnesse the broode of the Harveys'.[54] Robert Allott's anthology *England's Parnassus: Or the Choicest Flowers of Our Modern Poets* (1600) included passages from Nashe, acknowledging his status as a poet.[55]

Nashe's claims to a literary status through his writing style are highlighted in Michael Drayton's poem 'To my most dearely-loved friend HENRY REYNOLDS Esquire of *Poets and Poesie*'. Drayton includes Nashe in the company of writers such as Spenser and Sidney and argues:

> And surely Nashe, though he a Proser were,
> A branch of Lawrell yet deserves to beare,
> Sharply Satirick was he, and that way
> He went, since that his being, to this day
> Few have attempted, and I surely thinke
> Those words shall hardly be set downe with inke;
> Shall scorch and blast, so as his could, where he,
> Would inflict vengeance[56]

Drayton suggests that Nashe deserves praise not because of the genre in which he was writing (even though Nashe also wrote poetry, Drayton refers here to Nashe's published satires and polemics) but because of the function of his works: satire is expected to fulfil the same role as poetry, of inculcating ethical behaviour and civic consciousness.[57] Drayton does not stop there, however, but also describes the effect of Nashe's words in striking terms. His words are so violent that they resist being confined to print.

Nashe's reputation did not just reach critics of the next generation. His name also featured in biographies of authors published towards the end of the seventeenth century. Edward Phillips mentions Nashe off-handedly, with little interest in his merits: 'Thomas Nash, one of those that may serve to fill up the Catalogue of English Dramaties Writers: his mention'd Comedies are *Summers Last Will and Testament*, and *See me and see me not*'.[58] Even though Phillips rates Nashe's literary achievement very poorly, including him in his catalogue suggests that Nashe's name still had currency as a writer. Others had a better opinion of Nashe: William Winstanley, in his *Lives of the Most Famous English Poets, or, The Honour of Parnassus* (1687) mentions Nashe directly after Robert Greene, implying a closeness of style between the two. Even though Nashe's description is brief, Winstanley highlights Nashe's most distinctive characteristic: 'a man of a quick apprehension and Satyrick Pen'.[59]

This emphasis on Nashe's style becomes more evident in *An Account of the English Dramatic Poets* (1691). In it Gerard Langbaine presents a biography of Nashe focusing almost exclusively on his satirical writing and his wit: '[h]is Genius was much addicted to Dramatick Poetry and Satyr; and he writ some things in Prose; all which gain'd him the Reputation of a Sharp Wit'.[60] Langbaine also included in his biography the stanzas from Drayton's poem that Nashe's words would 'scorch, and blast'.[61] It is interesting that, when this work was reprinted in 1699 by an anonymous editor who 'improv'd and continued' it, Nashe's entry was significantly shortened.[62] The new editor did not mention anything about his style, limiting Nashe's biography to his studies at Cambridge and his two plays. The only qualitative comment about Nashe is in comparing him to the previous entry, Thomas Nabbes: the editor states that Nashe was 'A contemporary with the former, tho' of a more eminent Character'.[63] Should we assume that Nashe has an 'eminent Character' because of his value as a writer? Given how Nashe's works are presented here, mentioning only the two plays with no comments about their quality, this seems unlikely. It seems more plausible to suggest that the emphasis on 'Character' here refers to Nashe's personality, and the fact that his name was notorious even ninety years after his death. These comments suggest a place of notoriety in the public imagination as a poet of note.

Nashe cultivated a reputation for biting satire and vindictiveness. This was a conscious choice, as Nashe was keenly aware of how reputations were made in print.[64] In *Pierce Penniless* Nashe warns any patron who dismisses him that:

> if I bee evill intreated, or sent away with a flea in mine eare, let him looke that I will raile on him soundly: not for an houre or a day, whiles the injury is fresh in my memory: but in some elaborate pollished Poem, which I will leave to the world when I am dead, to be a living Image to all ages, of his beggerly parsimony and ignoble illiberaltie[65]

Nashe boasts of his ability to rail at his opponents, but also exhibits his belief that his poem will live for ever and that the memory of the person who has slighted him will be stamped by Nashe's words. His boast came to pass, as Harvey is often remembered through Nashe's words. More importantly this comment is accurate in terms of how Nashe himself was remembered not only by critics, as we have already seen, but also by other contemporaries. These qualities of his persona as sharp, witty, acidic, were understood as what made Nashe's style distinctive from others. In the epigram 'Of Tho. Nash', Thomas Freeman claims:

> For why there lived not that man I thinke,
> Usde better, or more bitter gall in Inke.[66]

Freeman's play with words casts further light on Nashe's style. Nashe's attempt at self-promotion was successful, perhaps more than he intended, as throughout the seventeenth century his name became a synonym for bitterness in print.

This is more evident in off-handed references to Nashe's name, such as the comment by Samuel Sheppard that the newsbook *Mercurius Aulicus* was able 'in a sweet Satyrick vain to lash, / Better then ere flow'd from the quill of Nash'.[67] Other commentators used Nashe as a synonym for scurrility, railing, and controversy, in order to discredit their opponents by comparing them to Nashe. When Samuel Harsnett published a tract attacking the alleged exorcisms of John Darrell, the latter chose to respond by characterising the text as follows: 'the whole boke from the first leafe to the last, is written in such scoffing and raylinge characters, that it might seme rather to have bene compiled by Nash Pasquil, or some Interlude-maker, then any other of sobriety & judgment'.[68] The term 'Nash Pasquil' draws attention to the Marprelate debate and conflates Nashe, the writer, with Pasquil, the authorial persona. In this quotation Nashe becomes his writing but also a figurative space for debate: pasquils were libels pinned on posts.[69] Conflating Nashe with a physical space shows that Nashe is not seen as a person but as a space that can be inhabited and inscribed by others in order to create their own definitions of triviality and scurrility.

Darrell was not the only one to do this: as late as 1637 Peter Heylyn compared the writing style of the book *The Holy Table, Name, & Thing* with 'The stile composed indifferently of Martin Marre-Prelate, and Tom: Nash: as scurillous and full of folly, as the one; as scandalous and full of faction, as the other was'.[70] In the polemical work *The Jesuit's Downfall* (1612) Thomas James claims that Parsons 'might have left such scoggerie, as he hath set out in this Book, to Tarleton, Nash, or els to some Puritan Mar-prelate'.[71] In both of these quotations Nashe is connected to contentious publications through evoking the Marprelate debate. However, he is also associated with a clownish kind of speaking and writing reminiscent of Tarleton. Here James's intention is to disparage his opponent by claiming that he resorted to 'low' ways of speaking.[72]

It might not be surprising in this context that in 1630 a medical tract called *The Newlanders' Cure* used Nashe as an example of a man imbibing inappropriate beverages:

It is reported, that Thomas Nash a scurrilous pamphleter in Q. Elizabeths dayes, used to drinke Aqua vitæ with Gun-powder to inspire his malicious spirit with rayling matter to shame Doctor Harvey, and other Adversaries of his: which inflaming Potion wrought so eagerly uppon his Braine, that hee would often beate himselfe about the noddle, and scratch the Walls round about him, untill hee met with some extravagant furious Termes, which as he imagined would blurre and lay sufficient aspersions upon them.[73]

This is a paraphrase of Nashe's own words, 'I have tearmes (if I be vext) laid in steepe in Aquafortis, & Gunpowder', and is indicative of the ways in which Nashe's satirical self-presentation acquired an afterlife of its own.[74] These examples show the qualities of Nashe's writing which left a lasting impression on people: his railing and scoffing style, his lack of sobriety, his scurrility, and his scandalous prose.

CONCLUSION

John Harington, in an epigram written in the 1590s and titled *A Prophesy when Asses Shall Grow Elephants*, makes the following critique on contemporary society:

> When Monopolies are giv'n of toyes and trashes:
> ...
> When clergy romes to buy, sell, none abashes,
> When fowle skins are made fair with new found washes,
> When prints are set on work, with Greens & Nashes,
> ...
> When plainnesse vanishes, vainenesse surpasses,
> Some shal grow Elephants, were knowne but Asses.[75]

Harrington here trivialises Nashe and Greene by suggesting that their works are made only for the marketplace of print. Nashe is seen as an author who is selling something that should have no market price (literature) in the same way that the church should not be selling faith. This is a critique of Nashe's writing but has the added effect of turning Nashe into an object. Here Nashe becomes his works, synonymous to trivial and market-oriented writing.

This is another example of how Nashe's name had become its own brand, indicating a particular kind of writing. De Rycker mentions that Nashe realised that a writer 'was remembered for their style rather than for what they wrote' and connects it to what Ian Frederick Moulton dubs 'scandalous authorship', a combination of 'political authority and disorderly eroticism'.[76] However, we have seen that Nashe's reputation – at least in print – was not specifically associated with eroticism. Even though

Harvey tried to portray him as such, we saw that most references to Nashe in print do not focus on eroticism.[77] Nashe's provocative style meant to whip up outrage, laughter, uneasiness. This made him notorious and turned his name into a brand, associated with his style.

In this chapter I have shown that Nashe was not popular in terms of market share or accessibility to a wide audience, nor did he necessarily intend to. Nashe wanted to be notorious more than popular, probably under the assumption that this would bring him most success in terms of being well known and distinctive. Judging by the fact that critics up to the end of the seventeenth century included him in books about great writers, this was a partially successful strategy. Nonetheless his style is what was remembered and emphasised, and he acquired a brand name. Throughout this chapter we have seen that assessments of value, style, and reputation of his work among his near contemporaries have given Thomas Nashe an afterlife in print that exceeds the 'popularity' that he achieved while he was alive. In the end Nashe became a 'living Image to all ages' of a particular kind of acidic writing.[78] Nashe's case allows us to reconsider print popularity in terms of cultural visibility. Popularity and notoriety were connected; for authors willing to court controversy, such an avenue could turn them into cultural icons, famous for what they symbolised and the outrage they caused.

NOTES

I would like to thank Helen Smith, Mark Jenner, and Joel Sodano for discussing the themes of this chapter with me; the result is all the better for their input.

1 Anthony Wood, *Athenae Oxonienses* (London, 1691), vol. 1, sig. P3v.
2 *The Elizabethan Top Ten: Defining Print Popularity in Early Modern England*, ed. Andy Kesson and Emma Smith (Farnham: Ashgate, 2013); *Literature and Popular Culture in Early Modern England*, ed. Matthew Dimmock and Andrew Hadfield (Farnham: Ashgate, 2009). See also Joad Raymond, 'Introduction', in *The Oxford History of Popular Print Culture*, ed. Joad Raymond (Oxford: Oxford University Press, 2011), pp. 1–14 (p. 4).
3 Andy Kesson and Emma Smith, 'Introduction: Towards a Definition of Print Popularity', in *The Elizabethan Top Ten*, ed. Kesson and Smith, pp. 1–16 (p. 8).
4 Alan B. Farmer and Zachary Lesser, 'What Is Print Popularity? A Map of the Elizabethan Book Trade', in *The Elizabethan Top Ten*, ed. Kesson and Smith, pp. 19–55.
5 Helen Smith, '"Rare poemes ask rare friends": Popularity and Collecting in Elizabethan England', in *The Elizabethan Top Ten*, ed. Kesson and Smith, pp. 79–100; Neil Rhodes, 'Shakespeare's Popularity and the Origins of the Canon', in *The Elizabethan Top Ten*, ed. Kesson and Smith, pp. 101–22 (p. 103).
6 Charles Nicholl, *A Cup of News: The Life of Thomas Nashe* (London: Routledge, 1984), pp. 3–5.

7 Stephen S. Hilliard, *The Singularity of Thomas Nashe* (Lincoln: University of Nebraska Press, 1986), pp. 9–10.
8 Raymond, 'Introduction', pp. 5–6.
9 *Martin Marprelate Tracts*, ed. Joseph L. Black (Cambridge: Cambridge University Press, 2008), pp. xxvii–xxviii. See also Kate De Rycker, 'The Political Function of Elizabethan Literary Celebrity', *Celebrity Studies*, 8 (2017), 157–61.
10 Peter Lake with Michael Questier, *The Antichrist's Lewd Hat: Protestants, Papists and Players in Post-Reformation England* (New Haven: Yale University Press, 2002), p. 519 and p. 535.
11 Cf. Thomas Freeman's claim in *Rubbe, and a great cast Epigrams* (London, 1614) that 'there lived not that man I thinke, / Usde better, or more bitter gall in Inke' than Nashe (sig. K3v).
12 Alan B. Farmer and Zachary Lesser, 'The Popularity of Playbooks Revisited', *Shakespeare Quarterly*, 56 (2005), 1–32 (p. 21); Peter W. M. Blayney, 'The Alleged Popularity of Playbooks', *Shakespeare Quarterly*, 56 (2005), 33–50.
13 Thomas Nashe, *Haue with you to Saffron-vvalden* (London, 1596), sig. F2r.
14 Nashe, *Have With You*, sig. E3v.
15 Joad Raymond, *Pamphlets and Pamphleteering in Early Modern Britain* (Cambridge: Cambridge University Press, 2003), pp. 81–3.
16 Thomas Nashe, *The terrors of the night* (London, 1594), sig. G4v.
17 Thomas Nashe, *The Works of Thomas Nashe*, ed. R. B. McKerrow, 2nd edn, rev. F. P. Wilson. 5 vols (Oxford: Basil Blackwell, 1958), IV.140. About the significance of the spectral in Nashe's writing see Chris Salamone, Chapter 5 below.
18 Nashe, *Terrors*, sig. A4r.
19 Thomas Nashe, *Pierce Penilesse his supplication to the diuell* (London, 1592), sig. ¶1r. See also Douglas Clark, Chapter 3 above, about how *Pierce Penniless* simulated the cries of the marketplace.
20 Jennifer Richards, *Voices and Books in the English Renaissance* (Oxford: Oxford University Press, 2019), p. 281.
21 The only exceptions are *An almond for a parrat* (London, 1589) and *The Anatomie of Absurditie* (London, 1589), which have longer titles and advertise their contents. It seems likely that this is because Nashe did not feel equally confident in these first works to diverge from a common style.
22 Kate De Rycker, 'Guide to Folger's *Have With You to Saffron Walden*', *The Thomas Nashe Project*: https://research.ncl.ac.uk/thethomasnasheproject/resources/digitisednasheeditions/guidetofolgershavewithyoutosaffronwalden/#d.en.429655 (accessed 17 January 2024).
23 Nashe, *Have With You*, sig. A1r.
24 Nashe, *Have With You*, sig. A1r.
25 Lena Liapi, *Roguery in Print: Crime and Culture in Early Modern London* (Woodbridge: Boydell & Brewer, 2019), pp. 39–43.
26 Thomas Nashe, *The Anatomie of Absurditie* (London, 1589), sig. B2r.
27 Nashe, *Anatomy*, sig. B3r.
28 Nashe, *Anatomy*, sig. B2v.
29 Zachary Lesser, *Renaissance Drama and the Politics of Publication: Readings in the English Book Trade* (Cambridge; Cambridge University Press, 2004), p. 1.
30 Nashe, *Pierce Penniless*, sig. D4r.
31 Nashe, *Pierce Penniless*, sig. D4r.
32 Sandra Clark, *Elizabethan Pamphleteers; Popular Moralistic Pamphlets 1580–1640* (Rutherford: Fairleigh Dickinson University Press, 1983).
33 Raymond, *Pamphlets and Pamphleteering*, p. 44.

34 Thomas Nashe, *An almond for a parrat* (London, 1590), sigs B1r–B1v.
35 Nashe, *Pierce Penniless*, sigs D1v, D2r, and E2v.
36 Lori Newcomb, '"Social Things": The Production of Popular Culture in the Reception of Robert Greene's *Pandosto*', *ELH*, 61 (1994), 753–81 (p. 765).
37 Nashe, *Pierce Penniless*, sig. G1r.
38 Nashe, *Terrors*, sig. F1v.
39 Gerard Genette, *Paratexts: Thresholds of Interpretation*, trans. Jane E. Lewin (Cambridge: Cambridge University Press, 1997), p. 194.
40 Nashe, *Anatomy*, sig. B1v.
41 Thomas Nashe, *Nashes Lenten stuffe* (London, 1599), sig. A4v.
42 Alfred D. Menut, 'Castiglione and the Nicomachean Ethics', *PMLA*, 58 (1943), 309–21 (p. 320). About Aretino see Kate De Rycker, 'Commodifying the Author: The Mediation of Aretino's Fame in the Harvey-Nashe Pamphlet War', *ELR*, 49 (2019), 145–71 (pp. 153).
43 Steve Mentz, *Romance for Sale in Early Modern England: The Rise of Prose Fiction* (Farnham, Ashgate, 2006), pp. 125, 156–7, and 177; Newcomb, '"Social Things", p. 761; Nashe, *Anatomy*, sig. A2v; Thomas Nashe, *Strange newes, of the intercepting certaine letters* (London, 1592), sig. L4r.
44 Anna Bayman, 'Printing, Learning, and the Unlearned', in *The Oxford History of Popular Print Culture*, ed. Raymond, pp. 76–87 (p. 86).
45 Adam Smyth, 'Almanacs and Ideas of Popularity', in *The Elizabethan Top Ten*, ed. Kesson and Smith, pp. 125–34 (p. 128 and p. 133). A similar point is made in Peter Kirwan in the same volume (Kirwan, '*Mucedorus*', pp. 223–34 (p. 227)).
46 De Rycker, 'Commodifying the Author', pp. 145–71.
47 De Rycker, 'Commodifying the Author', p. 147.
48 Clark, Chapter 3 above.
49 Mentz, *Romance for Sale*, pp. 180–2, and 219. Bryan Reynolds and Henry S. Turner also consider this, but mostly as a strategy to corner the market: 'From *Homo Academicus* to *Poeta Publicus*: Celebrity and Transversal Knowledge in Robert Greene's *Friar Bacon and Friar Bungay* (c.1589)', in *Writing Robert Greene: Essays on England's First Notorious Professional Writer*, ed. Kirk Melnikoff and Edward Giesk (Farnham: Ashgate, 2008), pp. 73–94 (p. 74).
50 Charles Nicholl, 'Thomas Nashe', *ONDB* (Oxford: Oxford University Press, 2020): https://www.oxforddnb.com/view/10.1093/ref:odnb/9780198614128.001.0001/odnb-9780198614128-e-19790.
51 Humphrey King, *An halfe-penny-worth of vvit, in a penny-worth of paper. Or, The hermites tale* (London, 1613), sig. B2r.
52 John Taylor, *A verry merry vvherry-ferry-voyage* (London, 1622), sig. A5r.
53 Salamone, Chapter 5 below. See also Rachel Willie, Chapter 7 below, on Taylor's appropriation of the 'ghost' of Nashe.
54 Francis Meres, *Palladis tamia. Wits treasury being the second part of Wits common wealth* (London, 1598), sig. Oo6r.
55 Robert Allott, *Englands Parnassus: or the choysest flowers of our moderne poets* (London, 1600), sigs Cc7r and Hh3r.
56 Michael Drayton, *The battaile of Agincourt Fought by Henry the fifth of that name* (London, 1627), sig. Dd1v.
57 Andrew McRae, *Literature, Satire and the Early Stuart State* (Cambridge: Cambridge University Press, 2009), p. 5.
58 Edward Phillips, *Theatrum poetarum, or, A compleat collection of the poets* (London, 1675), sig. Hh7r.

59 William Winstanley, *The lives of the most famous English poets* (London, 1687), sig. F7r.
60 Gerard Langbaine, *An account of the English dramatick poets* (London, 1691), sig. Aa7v.
61 Langbaine, *Account*, sig. Aa8r.
62 Gerard Langbaine, *The lives and characters of the English dramatick poets* (London, 1699), sig. A1r.
63 Langbaine, *Lives*, sigs H4r–H4v.
64 De Rycker, 'Commodifying the Author', p. 146.
65 Nashe, *Pierce Penniless*, sigs D4r–D4v.
66 Freeman, *Rubbe*, sig. K3v.
67 Samuel Sheppard, *God and Mammon, or, No fellowship betwixt light and darknesse* (London, 1646), sig. A2r. Italics from the original. I am grateful to Marissa Nicosia for this reference.
68 John Darrel, *A detection of that sinnful, shamful, lying, and ridiculous discours, of Samuel Harshnet* (London, 1600), sig. C2r.
69 Randle Cotgrave, *A Dictionarie of the French and English Tongues* (London, 1611), sig. Nnn4r.
70 Peter Heylyn, *Antidotum Lincolniense· or An answer to a book entituled, The holy table, name, & thing* (London, 1637), sig. A3r.
71 Thomas James, *The Jesuits downefall threatned against them by the secular priests* (London, 1612), sig. H2r.
72 See comment about Richards and Tarleton.
73 William Vaughan, *The Newlanders cure* (London, 1630), sig. B2v.
74 Nashe, *Pierce Penniless*, sig. D4v.
75 John Harington, *The most elegant and witty epigrams of Sir Iohn Harrington* (London, 1618), sig. D5r.
76 De Rycker, 'Commodifying the Author', pp. 154 and 156; Ian Frederick Moulton, *Before Pornography: Erotic Writing in Early Modern England* (Oxford: Oxford University Press, 2002), p. 158; Georgia Brown, 'Sex and the City: Nashe, Ovid, and the Problems of Urbanity', in *The Age of Thomas Nashe: Text, Bodies and Trespasses of Authorship in Early Modern England*, ed. Stephen Guy-Bray and Joan Pong Linton (Farnham: Ashgate, 2013), pp. 11–26.
77 Maria Teresa Micaela, 'Promiscuous Textualities: The Nashe-Harvey Controversy and the Unnatural Productions of Print', in *Printing and Parenting in Early Modern England*, ed. Douglas A. Brooks (Farnham: Ashgate, 2005), pp. 173–96.
78 Nashe, *Pierce Penniless*, sigs D4r–D4v.

5
THOMAS NASHE AND HIS TERRORS OF THE AFTERLIFE

Chris Salamone

It is a critical commonplace that material stuff pervades the language of Nashe's works, his style being synonymous with substance, physicality and grotesque corporality.[1] Obscured by this materiality, however, lies a facet of his work that has evaded sustained attention: Nashe's interest in the insubstantial world of spirits. Spectres haunt his work thematically and formally. We see this explicitly in his discourse on apparitions, *Terrors of the Night* (1594), and the demonology that abounds in his Lucianic satire, *Pierce Penniless* (1592). But Nashe's recourse to the supernatural goes beyond the occasional dabbling in demonological discourse. The spectral frequently functions in his work as a metaphor – an economy of representation – through which to figure authorial presence, posthumous reputation, and a concern over the power to live beyond death through literary production. For Nashe a text, whether printed or performed, can be powerfully, and problematically, undying and ghostly.

THE NECROMANTIC POTPOURRI

Nashe was well read on the subject of spirits. *Pierce Penniless* and *Terrors* both contain discussions of demonology and spectres likely gleaned from contemporary treatises on either side of the confessional divide. The account of the spirit world in *Pierce Penniless* is translated almost wholesale from Gregorius Pictorius's *De Illorum Daemonum qui sub lunari collimitio versantur Isagoge* (1563). *Terrors*, meanwhile, contains traces of Henry Howard's *A Defensative against the Poison of Supposed Prophesies* (1583) and Reginald Scot's *Discovery of Witchcraft* (1584). There are also possible debts to *Of Ghosts and Spirits Walking by Night*, by the Swiss Calvinist theologian Lewes Lavater (trans. 1572), and Pierre le Loyer's 1586 *Discourse of Spectres* (trans. 1605), the latter of which offers a Catholic viewpoint on the interpretation of apparitions.[2] Tracing a writer's reading habits on this topic, however, is problematic when theories and superstitions regarding spirits are repeated across tracts and circulated at a popular level orally.[3] Even if one identifies a key source for *Terrors* in Howard's *A Defensative*, the arguments, examples, and rhetorical tropes used in this text are shared throughout the cultural discourse on the nature of spirits.[4] Lavater's *Of Ghosts and Spirits*, so often identified by critics as a source-text for literary depictions of the supernatural in this period, contains stock examples found in other printed texts, with Pliny the Younger's ghost story, for instance, also featuring in Pictorius's *Isagoge*. The cultural transmission and recycling of supernatural beliefs and tropes both within and beyond literate audiences therefore makes a precise inventory of Nashe's reading habits – and a source study of *Terrors* and *Pierce Penniless* – difficult, with Ann Pasternak Slater bringing our attention to McKerrow's own editorial dismay at hunting 'for the originals of Nashe's necromantic *pot pourri*'.[5]

Does this syncretic assortment of possible sources, which offer conflicting and overlapping arguments from across the theological spectrum, impact our ability to sniff out – to persist with Slater's metaphor – a consistent theological scent, a trademark aroma, to the figuration of the spirit world in Nashe's works? Before answering that question it is worth remembering that one need not expect consistency from an early modern individual's engagement with the period's ghost controversy. The Catholic position on ghosts was, in the first place, riddled with hermeneutic uncertainty: distinguishing between the returning dead, dissembling devils, and angelic apparitions was problematic given that the forces behind an apparition could be considered heavenly or diabolic regardless of the shape it took. Whilst Protestantism narrowed the interpretative possibilities by allowing for only diabolic or rational explanations for ghostly visions, between the zealous wrangling of Puritan polemic and Catholic counter-argument we nevertheless find conceptual crossover and a recycling of the same ghost stories serving as evidential arguments on either side of the confessional divide. These changing, contradictory, but at times overlapping frameworks for interpreting apparitions 'spread confusion', Gillian Bennet notes, 'because not only did it undermine established belief systems, but it also left people unable to interpret their experiences'.[6] Furthermore historians have stressed that Protestantism's doctrinal rebuttal of the dead's ability to haunt the living percolated only slowly down to popular local habits of thought and custom. Contemporary accounts indicate that individuals did not whole-heartedly accept reforms to the living's relationship with the (non-returning) dead following the dismissal of Purgatory.[7] Reformers such as William Perkins articulate despair that 'many ignorant persons' still believe that 'dead men doe often appeare and walke after they are buried'.[8] The haunting continuity of a traditional belief system has been stressed by the folklorist Ronald Hutton, who suggests that the habitual need and belief in the supernatural slowly shifted away from prohibited Catholic beliefs and rituals, and transmuted into popular folklore and customs.[9] Theo Brown's analysis also reveals a medley of coexisting ideas regarding the existence of spirits, 'a mixture of ancient pagan belief, half-remembered old Catholic teaching and later Puritan doctrine possibly distorted as a result of misleading sermons'.[10] It is a mixture that contributes to what David Cressy describes as a 'hybrid religious culture in which reformed and unreformed elements intermingled whilst being pressured towards conformity'.[11]

'WILL SUMMERS GHOST I SHOULD BE ...'

The spirits that feature in Nashe's texts – which vary between the returning dead, disguised diabolic spirits, and the misperceptions of the melancholic – are indicative of this hybridity. The Catholic concept of communicative and returning denizens of the afterlife can be found, but only with a decidedly literary, notably Protestant, twist, achieved by heightening the audience's awareness of the fictionality and representational status of such hauntings. The result is a playful gallimaufry of appropriated classical, theological, and folkloric images that, taken as a whole, nonetheless bears the stamp of that pressure towards Protestant conformity outlined by Cressy. The ghost of Will Summers in *Summer's Last Will and Testament* (performed c. 1592; printed 1600) is a case in point. Henry VIII's jester haunts the stage by skirting the threshold between fiction and the reality of dramatic representation, declaring that he will 'sit as a Chorus, flowte the Actors', playing 'the knave in cue' to put his fellow performers off their parts.[12] The interruptions function as comic checks against any imaginative investment the audience may have in the play's fiction. This foregrounding of representational artifice is inaugurated by his very entrance, coming onstage '*in his fooles coate but halfe on, comming out*', and announcing that 'I am a Goose or a Ghost at least'.[13] Half-attired in a costume representative of Will Summers, the character and actor are here liminally co-present. This is, and is not, the ghost. Spectators are invited to perceive both the semi-costumed actor – possibly Archbishop Whitgift's own clown, Toy – and the character simultaneously in a moment of incomplete signification. Hence the conditional nature of his claim that 'Will Summers Ghost I should be'.[14] Indeed he 'should', but Nashe never allows the audience to be fully immersed in an illusion of spectral presence, not least because the ghost soon after calls our attention to the name of the actor likely performing the role ('I that have a toy in my head, more then ordinary').[15] Nashe is toying with the device of the ghost-as-chorus, uniting, as Beatrice Groves puts it, 'the clown of comedy and the ghost of tragedy' by way of metatheatrical winks that undercut the notion of the dead's return.[16] The play therefore serves as a useful illustration for what Andrew Gordon, discussing the function of ghosts in early modern dramatic comedy, sees as a temporary comic 'accommodation for the conceptual place of Purgatory', through which 'culturally pervasive' beliefs, not doctrinally prescribed, 'may be re-housed within an orthodox landscape'.[17] Part of that toleration is achieved by these moments of foregrounded artifice, the Catholic possibility of the returning dead coexisting within a literary, Protestant scepticism that humorously highlights the representational status of spectres.

A heightened awareness of dramatic artifice characterises, too, Cornelius Agrippa's conjuration of the spectral dead in Nashe's prose fiction *The Unfortunate Traveller* (1594). The 'proto-spiritualist séance' that Wilton witnesses, where each spectator is asked by Agrippa to 'keepe him in his place without moving' while a spirit in the likeness of Cicero ascends to deliver the requested oration, would no doubt remind a 1590s readership of onstage necromantic entertainments seen in performances of Marlowe's *Doctor Faustus* (c. 1592).[18] There are striking similarities between Nashe's Agrippa episode and the *Faustus* B-Text, where the Emperor, instructed to sit 'in dumb silence', is told by Faustus that the apparitions of Alexander the Great and his paramour 'are but shadows, not substantial'.[19] Furthermore, although supposedly supernatural in origin, Agrippa's attendant spirit is nevertheless performing the role of a deceased historical personage as a stage-player would, taking on a counterfeit, illusory appearance in such a way that unites actor and apparition as 'shadows'. The association between Agrippa's necromantic shows and theatrical representation, implied too by the language of representation used to describe his previous conjuration of 'the nine worthies, David, Salomon, Gedeon, and the rest, in that similitude and lykeness that they lived upon earth', is evidenced elsewhere in the period.[20] The prologue to a production of John Lyly's *Campaspe* at court in 1584 compares the play's representation of Alexander the Great (called up 'from his grave') to 'the daunsing of Agrippa his shadowes, who in the moment they were seene, were of any shape one woulde conceive'.[21] The tradition of Agrippa's necromancy therefore comes to Nashe already loaded with the association of representational artifice, even if Nashe's narrator, Jack Wilton, eschews articulating scepticism explicitly. To more fully locate a sceptical viewpoint that gestures towards the fictionality of Agrippa's apparitions, we must recognise the implication of Wilton's comparison of Agrippa to 'Scoto'. The musician and court legerdemain artist Girolano Scotto (1505–72) – who 'did the jugling trickes here before the Queene' – never, we are told 'came neere him [Agrippa] one quarter in magicke reputation'.[22] It is a comparison that damns with faint praise, deflating the occult philosopher's necromancy as being only a more elaborate and esteemed form of juggling theatrics.[23]

DIABOLIC REPRESENTATIONS

The supernatural fiction undercut by these allusions to theatricality is one that, in any case, rests upon dissemblance, for the revenants presented by Agrippa, like those conjured by Marlowe's Faustus, are diabolic counterfeits appearing in the 'similitude' of the deceased. Protestant explanations for ghostly visitations frequently rely on the figure of a deceptive diabolic spirit, and we certainly find Nashe steering readers towards that interpretation of the spectral (un)dead. During *Terrors* dissembling demonic spirits are said to present themselves 'in the likenes of ones father or mother, or kinsfolks' after they are deceased, adopting the 'shapes' that are 'most familliar unto us, and that wee are inclined to with a naturall kind of love'.[24] These apparitional representations, Nashe argues, are rhetorical strategies staged by the devil to persuade the bereaved to 'sooner harken to him'.[25] We likewise find the idea of evil spirits masquerading for persuasive purposes in *Pierce Penniless*, where a devil, upon request, gives Pierce a run-through of the shape-shifting capabilities of different ungodly 'creatures incorporall', which 'transform themselves into all kind of shapes, wherby they maie more easilie deceive our shallow wits and senses'.[26] Those of the 'under-earth' do 'terrifie men in the likenesse of dead mens ghostes in the night time', while 'spirits of the water', this devil explains, 'desire no forme or figure so muche, as the likenesse of a man', it being 'the neerest representation to God'.[27]

Although both texts therefore have recourse to diabolic explanations for apparitions, we should be cautious against necessarily assuming this in itself signifies Nashe's strict adoption of doctrinal Protestant orthodoxy on the subject. The same concept circulates, after all, amongst Catholic tracts in this period: Le Loyer's admission that 'divells are capable to clothe themselves, and to put on a certaine similitude of humane bodie', reiterates Lavater's suggestion that 'devil ... can (as the Poets faine of Proteus) chaunge himselfe into all shapes and fashions'.[28] Owen Davies's assertion that Nashe's diabolic 'explanation was only satisfactory if one rejected the possibility that the spirits of the dead returned', therefore needs recalibrating.[29] Belief in both Purgatory and malevolent spectral simulacra coexists in the early modern Catholic viewpoint. What can be considered a more meaningful marker of doctrinal Protestant conformity in Nashe's works, however, is the combined frequency of both the diabolic explanation and those moments of foregrounded fictionality, discussed earlier, that comically heighten our awareness of the spectre as representational artifice.

FALSE OBJECTS AND COUNTERFEIT NOISES

In a logical extension of Nashe's manoeuvring of the spectral dead to the representational realm, a playful and occasional scepticism moves beyond the concept of diabolic similitude towards natural explanations for why individuals misconstrue accidental likenesses of the deceased for their true spectral return. While careful not to undermine the sincere interest shown in the supernatural by his patron, Sir George Carey and wary of scepticism's potential slide into atheism, Nashe's *Terrors* nevertheless touts the imagination's power to freely project and construe fears and superstitions cued up accidentally by external stimuli, which can make us believe we 'heare the complaint of damned ghosts', when in reality we hear only a dog's howl.[30] Explanations of this kind were accommodated within both Protestant and Catholic discourses on spirits, although Le Loyer's Catholicism does inform his rebuttal of Girolamo Cardano's argument that supposed spirits in the damp climate of Iceland are merely 'vapours which are ingendred by reason of the colde'.[31] Nashe's rational explanations for supernatural sightings owe more to emerging conceptions of psychological affect than the contested effects of bad weather. Melancholy, in particular, is seen as a condition that yields 'up our intellective apprehension to be mocked and troden under foote, by everie false object or counterfet noyse that comes neere it'.[32] Far from diabolic similitude, 'counterfet' spectral representations of this sort are the result of a kind of synaptic misfire whereby the mind's 'ordained embassadours, doo not their message as they ought', leading our senses to 'faile in their report, and deliver up nothing but lyes and fables'.[33]

The misinterpretation of natural phenomena as the haunting dead combines with religious mockery in *Lenten Stuff* (1599), when we read of the Pope and his consort mistaking the smell of a stinking herring for a supernatural presence returning from beyond the grave. Their initial belief that the stench derives from 'some evill spirit of an heretique' escalates into an elaborate explanatory narrative involving 'the distressed soule of some king that was drownd, who, being long in Purgatorie', sought charitable dirges by imparting an olfactory sense of his Purgatorial 'combustion and broyling'.[34] We see here that demonological tropes in Nashe are not entirely evacuated of theological significance. He is hardly sitting on the fence with this mad-cap anti-Catholic satire, with the clergy falling prey to their own self-deceiving superstition. However, there is also a sense that Nashe is rather enjoying the absurdity of this satirical performance, not least as he playfully reconfigures contemporary anxieties over infectious and noxious vapours into a hysterical fear of contagious possession, with the clergy fretting that the foul-smelling evil 'spirit' 'penetrates our holy fathers nostrils'.[35] Early modern debate surrounding the authenticity of spirits surfaces therefore as a site of play through which Nashe can make good on the promise that he 'will make you laugh your hearts out'.[36]

NECROMANTIC PERFORMANCES

Nashe's hodgepodge combination of comically deflating rational scepticism, parroted diabolic explanations, and self-consciously fictitious spectral revenants can be viewed as collectively indicative of the writer's ludic performativity. To do so chimes with a critical tradition that emphasises a mercurial style-over-substance quality to his work.[37] James Nielson refers to this as the central 'Nashe problem' – that he 'seems to be all style and no content'.[38] Nashe's turn to the apparitional spirit-world could in that light be read as a self-conscious reflection on his own literary practice: 'spirits of the aire', he tells us in *Terrors*, 'are in truth all show and no substance, deluders of our imagination, & nought els'.[39] Such a charge and comparison may, to an extent, be misplaced: as shown, there is some consistency in Nashe's sceptical, broadly Protestant comic emphasis upon illusory, performative, insubstantial spectres. However, a degree of hybridity is apparent when one considers, as I do below, how thoroughly haunting as a metaphorical trope is absorbed into Nashe's argumentative arsenal. Under the auspices of rhetorical figuration, pushed to the realm of representation – of rhetorical 'show' and 'imagination' – the ghost returns to offer Nashe a multifaceted image reflecting not just a culture marked by imitation and literary resurrections but the formation and circulation of authorial identities, including his own.

The conceit of the dead's haunting return, although steeped in Catholic connotations, gives Nashe an appealingly versatile metaphor through which to explore modes of representation and authorship. Indeed the debate over the representational status of the spectre only furthers its suitability for such purposes. It is utilised explicitly in *Pierce Penniless* when Nashe draws attention to the ghostly quality of theatrical performance. Arguing that drama – and in particular *1 Henry VI* (perf. 1592), which he co-authors with Shakespeare – provides moral and courageous exemplars for audiences to emulate, he applauds how 'valiant' historical personages, such as 'brave Talbot', can through performance be 'raised from the Grave of Oblivion, and brought to pleade their aged Honours in open presence'.[40]

Metaphorically attributing necromancy to the act of theatrical representation, Nashe's description of the staging of Talbot re-purposes demonological – and theologically loaded – tropes, for the purpose of literary praise. As with Agrippa's conjurations and the ghost of Will Summers, Nashe goes out of his way to emphasise the representational status of such stage 'hauntings': in performance Talbot's bones are 'newe embalmed with the teares of ten thousand spectators ... who in the Tragedian that represents his person, imagine they behold him fresh bleeding'.[41] The illusory presence of the deceased is never complete, for Nashe's description of spectatorship foregrounds the simultaneous perception of both the actor's body – the 'Tragedian that represents' – and the deceased historical figure.[42] To invoke necromancy as a metaphor in the defence of theatrical representation is to bring into focus the multivalence of the term 'shadow', which in this period signifies not just representation and imitation but also actors and spirits.[43] The theatrical sense, partly informed by Platonic theory, derives from a notion that performers function as shadows or representations of characters. The stage, from this viewpoint, becomes a space haunted by 'shadows' or representations of absent figures. Nashe puns on these multiple senses of the term in *The Unfortunate Traveller* when Jack Wilton, having masqueraded as the Earl of Surrey, congratulates himself for having enough undetected 'art in my budget, to separate the shadowe from the bodie'.[44] To imitate the personage of another is to become their shadow, a performative representation circulating 'separate[ly]' from the substantial original body.

Although necromancy provides, in *Pierce Penilesse*, an evocative metaphor with which to defend drama against Puritan polemicists, elsewhere in Nashe's oeuvre the same conceit is a figurative vehicle not for literary praise, but satiric critique.[45] Agrippa's conjuration of Cicero in *The Unfortunate Traveller*, it should be remembered, is framed by Jack Wilton's critique of those universities that consider orators 'excellent eloquent, who stealeth not whole phrases but whole pages out of Tully', nurturing scholars who have 'No invention or matter ... of theyr owne, but tacke up a stile of his stale galimafries'.[46] The humanists' slavish imitation of dead writers is parodically symbolised in their desire for the resurrection of these authors. One Doctor of Wittenberg requests to see the spirit of 'pleasant Plautus', while another 'had halfe a moneths minde to Ovid', with Nashe teasingly half-evoking the Catholic tradition of the 'month's mind', whereby the deceased were commemorated with the celebration of a requiem mass one month from the date of the death or funeral.[47] It is Erasmus, finally, who 'requested to see Tully in that same grace and majestie he pleaded his Oration *pro* [for] *Roscio Amerino*'; the duly summoned apparition of Cicero, who 'declaimed verbatim the fornamed Oration', also functions as a thinly veiled attack on the rhetorical habits of Gabriel Harvey.[48] In the previous year, Nashe's *Strange News* (1592) jeeringly predicts that Harvey will walk through the street followed by the cry, 'there goes the Ape of Tully: uh he he, steale Tully, steale Tully'.[49] Necromancy, in Nashe's hands, offers a metaphorical motif through which to emblematise aping, hollow, insubstantial classical imitation.

SHEETED SPIRITS

Rhetorically figuring authorial textual presence and imitation as a kind of supernatural haunting is an effective method of undermining those voices and styles that make unwelcome, troublesome returns in print. Nashe adopts the analogy early in his career when attacking the pseudonymous, imitable and therefore seemingly irrepressible, anti-episcopal persona known as Martin Marprelate. The metaphor's use in this controversy is partly set up by the various figurative 'deaths' of Marprelate written and staged during 1589. The publication of *Theses Martinianae* in July 1589, presented as a collection of his works compiled by his successor, 'Martin Junior', prompts the conceit that Marprelate himself had 'died', defeated by antagonists in print and stage lampoons. Soon after, *A Countercuff Given to Martin Junior* (1589) – included in McKerrow's edition of Nashe's works – supposes that 'the Monster be deade' and in October 1589 the anti-Marprelate *Martin's Month's Mind* announces a 'certain report, and true description of the death, and funeralls, of olde Martin Marreprelat'.[50] We notice, again, the comic appropriation of the Catholic 'month's mind' tradition of ritualised remembrance, which gives an ironically un-Reformed frame for this caustic mock-biography of the supposedly vanquished Puritan persona. The publication in late October, however, of yet another Marprelate pamphlet, *The Protestation* (1589), proved the pronounced figurative 'death' of this authorial persona premature, prompting Nashe to describe the return of the anti-episcopal voice in spectral terms as an unwanted revenant. Writing as 'Cuthbert Curry-Knave' in *An Almond for a Parrot* (1590), he welcomes 'Mayster Martin from the dead', opening the text with a sarcastic salutation ('much good joy may you have of your stage-like resurrection'), that mocks the print persona for being both insufferably unending in its capacity for revival, and, through the comparison to tragicomic supernatural dramatic spectacle, clownish in its performativity.[51] The textual reappearance of Martin marks – as it will for John Taylor in the 1640s when the persona is resurrected alongside reprints of Marprelate pamphlets – the noisy return and troubling spectral afterlife of a once-thought quashed authorial identity.[52]

The analogy can also be invoked, conversely, to laud the textual afterlife of a praiseworthy writer. Nashe's reassurance to Thomas Churchyard in *Strange News* that whilst 'Shores wife is yong, though you be stept in yeares, in her shall you live when you are dead' pivots the metaphor away from the author-as-troublesome-spirit, towards a longed-for afterlife in which the voice of the dead achieves a posthumous, absent-presence via the reproducibility of text.[53] Some returns, it seems, are more welcome and hoped for than others. Churchyard's poem 'Shores Wife' initially appeared in the 1563 edition of William Baldwin's collection of first-person ghost-complaints, *The Mirror for Magistrates*, and was repeatedly reprinted with that ever-expanding compilation in subsequent editions for the remainder of the century. And just months after Nashe's praise a 'yong' and newly amended version of the poem appears independently of *The Mirror* in *Churchyard's Challenge* (1593), a collection offering a response to those who contested Churchyard's authorship of the assembled poems.[54] It is telling that Nashe imagines Churchyard as living on, posthumously, through a poem in which the poet has already adopted the pose of a deceased, haunting speaker: in Nashe's figuration, Jane Shore and Churchyard thereby coalesce as ghosts within one text. Critics have been rightfully attentive to Nashe's presentation of texts as physical and ephemeral objects; yet texts are, as we have seen, also figured as haunting entities, playing on the notion of a textual afterlife and posthumous absent-presence that is prompted by the iterability of print. The conceit is not unique to Nashe. Thomas Thorpe's dedication to Edmund Blount in Marlowe's translation of Lucan's *Pharsalia* (1600) plays on the analogy with the declaration that the 'ghoast or Genius' of that 'pure Elementall wit Chr. Marlow' 'is to be seene walke the churchyard in (at the least) three or foure sheets'.[55] St Paul's Churchyard is thus at once inhabited by booksellers' sheets of printed literature, and as a graveyard, figuratively haunted by absent authors in their winding 'sheets'.

Seeking moments when authorial identity and textual circulation are metaphorically presented as spectral hauntings runs counter to a critical trend that has emphasised Nashe's place in the emergence of an interchangeable connection between the author's name and body, and their printed output and style.[56] Valuable studies on early modern metaphors for production and authorial identity repeatedly turn to figures of embodiment: Steve Mentz notes, for example, the 'intensely physical relationship Nashe sees between writing, printing, and human bodies', whereby 'Books are prosthetic extensions of their authors'.[57] His argument builds upon Douglas Bruster's earlier observation that the 'personalization of print' saw an increased connection between author and text, to the extent that the latter was frequently figured as the embodied presence of the author.[58]

Nashe's corporeal imagery provides valuable evidence of this, yet it is worth remembering that the imitation of that rhetoric of substance allows John Taylor to effectively adopt the persona of Nashe's disembodied spirit in *Tom Nashe His Ghost* (1642). Nashe's projection of a persona in print facilitates later apparitional appropriations. An author's imitable style and voice is metaphorically associated not only with the author's body, therefore, but also with their disembodied, spectral shadow, as something that circulates, haunts, influences, and communicates in their absence. If, as Mentz argues, entry into print – or indeed 'all new writing technologies' – brings into formation 'new human-mechanical hybrids', then this posthuman identity extends, in Nashe's rhetoric, both into and necessarily beyond materiality and bodily presence. James Nielson's reading of Nashe's construction of a 'prosopopeic pseudo-presence', brought about by what Lorna Hutson terms the satirist's 'effect of intimacy', is helpful here, for he draws attention to how 'this form of deixis creates at the same time (or rather, of course, in a different moment) a sense of pseudo-*absence*, as the actual sender of the utterance refers to textual circumstances that are purely virtual at the time of inditing'.[59] It is the pseudo-absence of the author, who is not present at the moment of the affected textual 'presence', that encourages a ghostly conception of authorial identity and voice: the more Nashe's texts foreground their physical 'presence' in the hands of the reader, the more forcefully they gesture towards his own absence. This dynamic describes, from a Derridean perspective, the spectral condition of all writing and representation, whether verbal or visual. It is a condition that Derrida explores most forcibly in relation to photographic representation, arguing that 'once it has been taken, captured, this image will be reproducible in our absence, [and] because we know this *already*, we are already haunted by this future. Our disappearance is already here.'[60] Derrida's remarks on the 'logic of the spectre' pertains, as Cary Wolfe highlights, to '*any* form of representation, any semiosis whether of the word or the image'. '[S]uch is the price', continues Wolfe, 'of a futurity in which our media, our archives, are to be legible in our absence'.[61] As we shall see, the text's capacity to function in the absence, and as an extension, of the author is for Nashe a cause of empowerment but also unease.

IMMORTAL INVECTIVES

Nashe foresees himself – 'captured or possessed by spectrality in advance' – haunting his readers and enemies as a ghostly absent-presence, adopting spectral metaphors to evoke a sense of his textual afterlife.[62] In *Have With You to Saffron Walden* (1596), for example, the rhetoric of vengeful

Senecan spirits combines with self-deification when Nashe posits a future wherein his text compels enemies to 'fall downe and worship mee ere I cease or make an end, crying upon their knees *Ponuloi nashe*, which is in the Russian tongue, Have mercie upon us'.[63] The ambition of revenge, even whilst punning on his name's presence in the Russian Orthodox mass, elevates Nashe's voice to that of a wrathful God. Yet the passage also has hitherto unnoted diabolic connotations, appropriating as it does Satan's demand in his temptation of Christ that the latter should 'fall down and worship me' (Matthew 4.9). Nashe actually provides this very section of scripture in *Pierce Penniless*: translated in Pictorious's *Isosogue*, it is in turn quoted verbatim when a devil explains to Pierce that a 'monarchizing spirit … said to Christ, *If thou wilt fall downe and worship me, I wil give thee al the kingdoms of the earth*'.[64] '[S]uch a spirit it was', continues Nashe via Pictorious, 'that possest the Libian Sapho, and the Emperor Dioclesian, who thought it the blessedest thing that might be, to be called God'.[65] We can thus assume that Nashe is aware of the demonic implication of his phrasing in *Have With You*, imagining his printed voice not as embodied substance, but rather as a diabolic spirit, inspiring awe and idolatry amongst its readers. Similarly, in *Strange News*, having warned Harvey that he shall 'be haunted and coursed to the full … [for] as long as I am able to lift a pen', Nashe then picks up the supernatural connotation of 'haunt' to frame his invectives as incessantly unending diabolic entities: '*All the invective and satericall spirits*', writes Nashe of his own verbal assaults, '*shall then bee thy familiars*, as the furies of hell are the familiars of sinfull ghosts to follow them and torment them without intermission'.[66]

The text-as-spirit motif weaponises Nashe's invectives with threatening gestures of textual futurity. To point this out is not to contest critical readings that focus on the themes of material ephemerality and images of waste paper in his works. Nashe's satirical approach accommodates antithetical rhetorical tropes: dismissing an opponent's pamphlet as destined for the privy one moment, he is equally capable of figuring his own invective, or an opponent's slander, as attaining an unending presence through print's iterability. *Have With You*, for example, warns Harvey that additional invectives against him are 'in a readines' to be inserted into *Strange News* when that text is 'renewed and reprinted againe'.[67] In *Pierce Penniless*, that prospect of repeat printings affords Nashe the possibility of framing his persona as an undying spirit, as he warns each detractor to 'look his life be without scandale', or else he shall 'live as their evil Angel, to haunt them world without end, if they disquiet me without cause'.[68] The satirist's revenge is couched in terms familiar to demonological discourse, where one repeatedly reads of apparitions of the 'disquieted' and disturbed dead, particularly in debates surrounding the description of Samuel's ghost in 1 Samuel 18.[69] To collocate the terms 'disquiet' and 'haunt', as Nashe does, is therefore to form an image of the satirist as a restless spirit, whose vengeful railings will re-appear – 'without end' – beyond the author's death thanks to the reproducibility of the printed pamphlet.

POSTHUMOUS REPUTATIONS

Yet the spectral threat of satire cuts both ways. The terror of an undying textual voice that Nashe threatens to wield strikes fear into the satirist himself, vexed as he is that printed slanders against him will attain an afterlife read by future generations. Although Keith Thomas evidences a pervasive early modern aspiration to outlive the 'ends of life' through posthumous memorial, it is Nashe in particular whom Gabriel Harvey singled out as fixated on posterity, with the title page of *Pierce's Supererogation* (1593) presenting Nashe's muse as 'St. Fame'.[70] Concern over his posthumous fame and reputation is especially apparent in *Lenten Stuff*, wherein he complains that in his absence 'the silliest millers thombe, or contemptible stickle-bank of my enemies' have been 'busie nibbling about my fame, as if I were a deade man throwne amongst them to feede upon'.[71] Although here a metaphor for the exploitation of his momentary corpse-like textual silence, elsewhere Nashe explicitly addresses the desecration of the dead's reputation in print. It is this anxiety over posthumous fame that fuels his fantasy of communicating with dead writers so they may write back to redress damages done to their reputations. Nashe admits in the second edition of *Pierce Penniless* that he had previously hoped to include a letter 'to the Ghost of Robert Greene, telling him, what a coyle there is with pamphleting on him after his death', while the spirits of Deloney and Armin are later called upon in *Strange News* to revenge Gabriel Harvey's slander of Elderton.[72] The desire to defend posthumous reputations becomes, rhetorically, a matter of caring for, and communicating with, ghosts.

Indeed, the Nashe–Harvey quarrel is very much haunted by the presence of the absent dead and preoccupied with the contestation of their posthumous reputations. Despite insisting that 'The dead bite not: and I am none of those, that bite the dead', within three days of Greene's death Harvey writes a scandalous account of his demise.[73] Harvey's *Four Letters* (1592) rolls out terms of abuse for the deceased, 'ever brainsick' writer, claiming that he both lodged with a poxed sex worker and fathered an illegitimate son, Infortunatus.[74] The repeated rhetorical resurrection of, and addresses to, Greene's spirit in the mid-1590s are, to a large degree, a consequence of these defamatory remarks. His ghost, like Nashe's after him, was frequently depicted as restlessly entreating obligations from the living. Most notably Greene is one of five spirits that appear in Henry Chettle's *Kind-Hart's Dream* (1593), wherein he passes the dreamer, Kind-Hart, a letter addressing Nashe, or 'Pierce Penilesse'.[75] The spectral 'Greene' upbraids Nashe in the epistle for his delay in replying to Harvey's attacks against each of them. In the Senecan tradition of a vengeful father's spirit, he calls Nashe to action, demanding that his 'secure boy' 'Awake ... revenge thy wrongs, remember thine: thy adversaries began the abuse, they continue it'.[76] Chettle forges this fiction of ghostly communication so as to actually restate a call-to-arms already uttered in the posthumously published pamphlet, *Greene's Groatsworth of Wit* (1592), from which the voice of Greene would have been heard, beyond the grave, ordering his 'Sweet boy', Nashe, to 'inveigh against vaine men, for thou canst do it, no man better, no man so well'.[77]

Defending Greene against the charges set at his grave, Nashe's approach is twofold. Firstly, he rectifies Greene's posthumous identity in print by 'taking upon me to be Greenes advocate', reassuring readers that 'with any notorious crime I never knew him tainted'.[78] Secondly, he writes vengefully against Harvey on behalf of Greene. Although momentarily admitting to Greene's ghost that he 'can spare thy revenge no more roome in this booke', he nonetheless frequently derides 'Gabriel Grave-digger' as being one who will 'never leave afflicting a dead Carcasse'.[79] Accused of rhetorically raking the departed from their rest, Harvey is portrayed as neurotically preoccupied with disgracing the absent dead.[80] The dead hover over this literary feud because their reputations are neither left to rest nor respectfully interred by the living, much like the unquiet spirit of Caligula described in *Pierce Penniless*:

> bicause he was onlie covered with a few clods, and unreventlie thrown amongst the weeds, he mervelouslie disturbed the owners of the garden, & woulde not let them rest in their beds, till by his Sisters returned from banishment, he was taken up, and intoombed solemnlie.[81]

Absent from Greene's deathbed and funeral, Nashe's defence of his friend's reputation is an attempt to solemnly carry out his own duty to the dead, countering Harvey's invectives to lay Greene's disquieted ghost to rest.

The fantasy of an afterlife functioning as a textual forum where the dead rail against each other and transmit demanding epistles to the living reveals a paradoxical yearning for endurance and reform. The early modern authorial persona accrues a posthumous absent-presence in print that may last, and communicate to the living, yet the dead are unable to correct slanders or misattributions that taint their posterity. Nashe's imagined literary afterlife – prompted by Chettle's *Kind-Hart's Dream* and, ultimately, Lucian's *Dialogues of the Dead* – evokes a space where that paradox can, through fiction, be resolved: within it we find not just Greene's spirit arguing with the dead John Harvey, but also 'so indefinite a spirite' as Aretino, who 'should have no peace or intermission of paines, but be penning Ditties to the Archangels in another world'.[82] The implication is that their argumentative zeal cannot be quashed by death, and, furthermore, that their causes were valid. Indeed, as Kate De Rycker shows, Aretino would have had good reason for a posthumous rant. Besmirched by accusations of blasphemy – perpetuated by the false attribution to Aretino of the nonexistent 'Black Book', *De Tribus Impostoribus Mundi*, in Richard Harvey's *The Lamb of God* (1590) – his authorial identity is transformed through critical reception into, to borrow Harvey's phrase, that of 'a very incarnat devill'.[83]

The unease over the Harvey brothers' mistreatment of posthumous reputations signposts a more pervasively articulated fear in Nashe's work that his own textual afterlife will be tainted. In *The Anatomy of Absurdity* (1589), Nashe concedes it unlikely that 'a mans after life shall be without blemish', and the satirical quarrels that followed in the 1590s made its participants acutely aware of how easily reputation may be forever tarnished in print.[84] 'Spittle may be wip't off', bemoans Nashe's interlocutor in *Have With You*, Importuno, 'but to be a villaine in print' is 'an attainder that will sticke by thee for ever'.[85] Nashe's legalistic terminology emphasises the enduring legacy of slander: descendants of the attainted are denied the right to inherit the latter's property, which is forfeited on conviction. Iterability makes printed slander not ephemeral waste paper but potentially an everlasting blot on one's family name. For this reason, Nashe laments, one cannot even take solace in the 'bad sale' of Harvey's books: in his 'owne Deske they may bee founde after his death', and 'while Printing lasts, thy disgrace may last, & the Printer (whose Copie it is) may leave thy infamie in Legacie to his heyres'.[86] It is the 'immortality of the Print', as he later calls it, that will continue to 'baffull and infamize my name when I am in heaven'.[87]

SPECTRAL NASHE

Following his death in 1601, the idea of Nashe's spirit in heaven, hell, or Elysium proved irresistible for satirists. Middleton provides a brief fiction of supernatural communication with Nashe's ghost in *Father Hubburd's Tales* (1604), while in *News from Hell Brought by the Devil's Carrier* (1606) Dekker directly alludes to Nashe's invocation of Aretino's influencing spectral presence when summoning Nashe's spirit for inspiration.[88] Dekker's *A Knight's Conjuring* (1607), an enlarged edition of *News from Hell*, extends the engagement with spirits further still. Reconfiguring Nashe's supernatural metaphor for the endurance of textual voice, Dekker portrays Nashe's ghost in Elysium, 'still haunted with the sharpe and Satyricall spirit that followed him here upon earth ... accusing them ['dry-fisted Patrons'] of his untimely death'.[89] Lawrence Manley views these ghosts of Nashe as a symptomatic effect of his involvement in the 'socio-economic marginality of popular writing' – a bugbear, so to speak, befitting his destabilising and culturally subversive presence in print.[90] Yet, another influencing factor behind these literary resurrections must have been the appeal of continuity with Nashe's own attraction to the figure of the ghost and the conceit of textual haunting. Nashe's warning to miserly patrons and enemies that he will live on in print as an 'evil Angel, to haunt them world without end', gets actualised by his satirical descendants, not least John Taylor, whose pamphlets against religious separatists in the early 1640s adopted the voice of Nashe's ghost to add comic zest and a triumphant – in hindsight misplaced – sense of inevitability to the quelling of re-emergent religious nonconformists.[91] Middleton, Dekker, and Taylor inherit from Nashe a culturally syncretic and metaphorical use of haunting influenced, but not determined, by the period's controversy over the ghost's representational status: shifted towards fiction and the figurative, the ghost now spoke of representational modes, and ultimately, literature itself, capturing its capacity to conjure absent voices, and its terrifying but potent power to bestow upon authors and enemies a life beyond death.

NOTES

1 See Neil Rhodes, *Elizabethan Grotesque* (London: Routledge and Kegan Paul, 1980), p. 40; Lorna Hutson, *Thomas Nashe in Context* (Oxford: Clarendon Press, 1989), p. 19; John V. Nance, 'Gross Anatomies: Mapping Matter and Literary Form in Thomas Nashe and Andreas Vesalius', in *The Age of Thomas Nashe: Text, Bodies and Trespasses of Authorship in Early Modern England*, ed. Stephen Guy-Bray, Joan Pong Linton, and Steve Mentz (Farnham: Ashgate, 2013), pp. 115–31.
2 R. B. McKerrow remarks upon Nashe's likely familiarity with these tracts in his edition of *The Works of Thomas Nashe*, 5 vols (Oxford: Blackwell, 1958), IV.197.
3 See Wilson and Yardley, 'Introduction', in Lewes Lavater, *Of Ghostes and Spirites Walking by Nyght* (1572), ed. J. Dover Wilson and May Yardley (Oxford: Oxford University Press, 1929), pp. vii–xxviii (pp. ix–x).
4 C. G. Harlow, 'A Source for Nashe's *Terrors of the Night*, and the Authorship of *I Henry VI*', *SEL*, 5 (1965), 31–47 (p. 39).
5 Ann Pasternak Slater, '*Macbeth* and the *Terrors of the Night*', *Essays in Criticism*, 28 (1978), 112–28 (p. 116). McKerrow laments that 'works of demonology, witchcraft,

and related subjects borrow so largely from one another that it is a matter of considerable difficulty to discover from what source a particular thing is taken' (IV.197).
6 Gillian Bennett, 'Ghost and Witch in the Sixteenth and Seventeenth Centuries', *Folklore*, 97 (1986), 3–14 (p. 8).
7 See Peter Marshall, 'Deceptive Appearances: Ghosts and Reformers in Elizabethan and Jacobean England', in *Religion and Superstition in Reformation Europe*, ed. Helen Parish and William G. Naph (Manchester: Manchester University Press, 2002), pp. 188–208 (pp. 195–6).
8 William Perkins, *A discourse of the damned art of witchcraft* (Cambridge, 1608), sigs C1r–C1v.
9 Ronald Hutton, 'The English Reformation and the Evidence of Folklore', *Past & Present*, 148 (1995), 89–116 (p. 113).
10 Theo Brown, *The Fate of the Dead* (Ipswich: D. S. Brewer, 1979), p. 83.
11 David Cressy, *Birth, Marriage and Death: Ritual, Religion, and the Life-Cycle in Tudor and Stuart England* (Oxford: Oxford University Press, 1997), p. 402.
12 Thomas Nashe, *A pleasant comedie, called Summers last will and testament* (London, 1600), sig. B2r.
13 Nashe, *Summer's*, sig. B1r.
14 Nashe, *Summer's*, sig. B1r.
15 Nashe, *Summer's*, sig. B1r.
16 Beatrice Groves, 'Laughter in the Time of Plague: A Context for the Unstable Style of Nashe's *Christ's Tears over Jerusalem*', *Studies in Philology*, 108 (2011), 238–60 (p. 259).
17 Andrew Gordon, 'The Ghost of Pasquill: The Comic Afterlife and the Afterlife of Comedy on the Elizabethan Stage', in *The Arts of Remembrance in Early Modern England: Memorial Cultures of the Post Reformation*, ed. Andrew Gordon and Thomas Rist (Aldershot: Ashgate, 2013), pp. 229–46 (p. 241).
18 Simon During, *Modern Enchantments: The Cultural Power of Secular Magic* (Cambridge, MA: Harvard University Press, 2002), p. 57; Thomas Nashe, *The vnfortunate traueller* (London, 1594), sig. F3v.
19 Christopher Marlowe, *Doctor Faustus, B-Text (1616)*, in *Christopher Marlowe: 'Doctor Faustus' and Other Plays*, ed. David Bevington and Eric Rasmussen (Oxford: Clarendon Press, 1995), 4.1.95; 4.1.103.
20 Nashe, *Unfortunate Traveller*, sig. F4r.
21 John Lyly, *Campaspe* (1584), in *The Works of John Lyly*, ed. R. Warwick Bond, 3 vols (Oxford: Clarendon Press, 1902), II.302–61 (II.316).
22 Nashe, *Unfortunate Traveller*, sig. F3r.
23 On Nashe's comparison of Agrippa to Scotto, see During, *Modern Enchantments*, pp. 57–8.
24 Thomas Nashe, *The terrors of the night* (London, 1594), sig. B3r.
25 Nashe, *Terrors*, sig. B3r.
26 Thomas Nashe, *Pierce Penilesse his supplication to the diuell* (London, 1592), sig. H4v.
27 Nashe, *Pierce Penniless*, sigs H3v and H4v.
28 Pierre Le Loyer, *IIII Livres de Spectres* (Angers, 1586), trans. Z. Jones, *A Treatise of Specters or straunge Sights* (London, 1605), sig. N1r; Ludwig Lavater, *Of ghostes and spirits walking by night ... translated into Englyshe by R.H.* (London, 1572), sig. M4v. Citations from Le Loyer and Lavater taken from the 1605 and 1572 English translations of their tracts, respectively.

29 Owen Davies, *The Haunted: A Social History of Ghosts* (Basingstoke: Palgrave, 2006), p. 17.
30 Nashe, *Terrors*, sig. C4v. On Nashe and the relationship between scepticism and atheism see Melissa Caldwell, *Skepticism, Belief and the Reformation of Moral Value in Early Modern England* (Abingdon: Routledge, 2016), pp. 142–67.
31 Le Loyer, *IIII Livres*, sigs M1r–M1v. Le Loyer is here quoting from Cardano's *De Subtilitate* (1550) in a moment of animadversion that perhaps informs Nashe's description of Icelandic ghost-belief. McKerrow (IV.202) suggests Sebastian Münster's *Cosmographia* (1572 edn) as Nashe's possible source. Chapters VII and VIII (Book 1) of Le Loyer's work are devoted to instances when natural phenomena are misconstrued for spirits.
32 Nashe, *Terrors*, sig. C3r.
33 Nashe, *Terrors*, sig. C3r.
34 Thomas Nashe, *Nashes Lenten stuffe* (London, 1599), sigs I1r–I1v.
35 Nashe, *Lenten*, sig. I1v. On the period's figurative association between foul contagious air and the ghostly see Chloe Kathleen Preedy, 'The Smoke of War: From *Tamburlaine* to *Henry V*', *Shakespeare*, 15 (2019), 152–75, esp. p. 154.
36 Thomas Nashe, 'To his Readers', in Nashe, *Lenten*, sig. A4r.
37 See Jonathan Crewe, *Unredeemed Rhetoric: Thomas Nashe and the Scandal of Authorship* (London: Johns Hopkins University Press, 1983), pp. 1–5.
38 James Nielson, *Unread Herring: Thomas Nashe and the Prosaics of the Real* (New York: Peter Lang, 1993), p. 17.
39 Nashe, *Terrors*, sig. C2r.
40 Nashe, *Pierce Penniless*, sig. F3r.
41 Nashe, *Pierce Penniless*, sig. F3r.
42 See Brian Walsh, '"Unkind Division": The Double Absence of Performing History in *1 Henry VI*', *Shakespeare Quarterly*, 55 (2004), 119–47.
43 See *OED*, 'shadow', n., sense 6.b and 7.
44 Nashe, *Unfortunate Traveller*, sig. H2r.
45 On Nashe and legitimising literary judgement see Samuel Fallon, *Paper Monsters: Persona and Literary Culture in Elizabethan England* (Philadelphia: University of Pennsylvania Press, 2019), pp. 123–8.
46 Nashe, *Unfortunate Traveller*, sig. F3r. For the satirical implications of this episode see Patricia Parker, '*The Merry Wives of Windsor* and Shakespearean Translation', *MLQ*, 52 (1991), 225–61 (p. 244).
47 Nashe, *Unfortunate Traveller*, sig. F3v.
48 Nashe, *Unfortunate Traveller*, sig. F3v.
49 Thomas Nashe, *Strange newes, of the intercepting certaine letters* (London, 1592), sig. F2v.
50 *A countercuffe given to Martin Junior* (London, 1589), sig. A2r; *Martins months minde* (London, 1589), sig. A1. On McKerrow's attribution of *Countercuffe* and *Month's Mind* to Nashe see, respectively, V.55–8 and V.58–9.
51 Thomas Nashe, *An almond for a parrat, or Cutbert Curry-knaves almes* (London, 1589), sig. B1r. On Nashe's likely authorship of *Almond*, see Donald McGinn, 'Nashe's Share in the Marprelate Controversy', *PMLA*, 59 (1944), 952–84.
52 See Joad Raymond, *Pamphlets and Pamphleteering in Early Modern Britain* (Cambridge: Cambridge University Press, 2004), pp. 204–5.
53 Nashe, *Strange News*, sig. I1r.
54 Matthew Woodcock, *Thomas Churchyard: Pen, Sword and Ego* (Oxford: Oxford University Press, 2018), pp. 248–9.

55 Thomas Thorpe, 'To the Kind and True Friend: Edmund Blunt', in Christopher Marlowe, trans., *Lucan's First Book* (London, 1600), ed. Roma Gill, in *The Complete Works of Christopher Marlowe*, 5 vols (Oxford: Clarendon Press, 1987–98), I.93.
56 See Douglas Bruster, 'The Structural Transformation of Print in Late Elizabethan England', in *Print, Manuscript & Performance*, ed. Michael D. Bristol and Arthur F. Marotti (Columbus: Ohio State University Press, 2000), pp. 49–89.
57 Steve Mentz, 'Day Labor: Thomas Nashe and the Practice of Prose in Early Modern England', in *Early Modern Prose Fiction: The Cultural Politics of Reading*, ed. Naomi Conn Liebler (New York: Routledge, 2007), pp. 18–32 (p. 19).
58 Bruster, 'Structural Transformation', p. 63, p. 69.
59 Hutson, *Nashe in Context*, p. 2; Nielson, *Unread Herrings*, p. 97.
60 Jacques Derrida and Bernard Stiegler, *Echographies of Television*, trans. Jennifer Bajorek (Cambridge: Polity Press, 2002), p. 117.
61 Cary Wolfe, *What Is Posthumanism?* (London and Ann Arbor: University of Minnesota Press, 2010), p. 294.
62 Derrida and Stiegler, *Echographies*, p. 117.
63 Thomas Nashe, *Haue vvith you to Saffron-vvalden. Or, Gabriell Harueys hunt is vp* (London: John Danter, 1596), sig. G1r.
64 Nashe, *Pierce Penniless*, sig. H2v.
65 Nashe, *Pierce Penniless*, sig. H2v.
66 Nashe, *Strange News*, sigs K2v–K3r.
67 Nashe, *Have With You*, sig. X3v.
68 Thomas Nashe, 'A private Epistle', in Nashe, *Pierce Penniless*, sig. ¶1v.
69 Lavater, *Of Ghostes and Spirits*, p. 207; p. 138; Reginald Scot, *The discouerie of witchcraft* (London, 1584), pp. 140–50. Translations of this biblical passage use the term 'disquieted' from the 1558 Bishops Bible onwards, as in 'And Samuel said to Saul, Why hast thou disquieted me, to bring me up?' (Geneva Bible, 1587).
70 Keith Thomas, *The Ends of Life: Roads to Fulfilment in Early Modern England* (Oxford: Oxford University Press, 2009), pp. 235–67. Gabriel Harvey, *Pierces Supererogation* (London, 1593), sig. A1r. See also sig. Ff4r.
71 Nashe, *Lenten*, sig. B1r.
72 Nashe, 'A private Epistle', *Pierce Penniless*, sig. ¶1r; Nashe; *Strange News*, sig. D4v.
73 Gabriel Harvey, *Foure letters, and certaine sonnets* (London, 1592), sigs B3r–B4r.
74 Harvey, *Four Letters*, sigs A4v and B2v.
75 See also John Dickenson, *Greene in Conceipt* (London, 1598).
76 Henry Chettle, *Kind-Harts Dreame* (London, 1593), sig. E2r.
77 Robert Greene [with Henry Chettle], *Greenes groats-vvorth of witte, bought with a million of repentance* (London, 1592), sig. F1v.
78 Nashe, *Have With You*, sig. T3r; Nashe, *Strange News*, sig. E4v.
79 Nashe, *Strange News*, sigs G4r and G3v; McKerrow, II.181.
80 Harvey viewed Greene's *A quip for an vpstart courtier* (London, 1592) as itself desecrating the memory of John Harvey, his recently deceased brother (see *Four Letters*, sigs A2r–A2v). The pamphlet depicts the ghost of their father criticising his three sons.
81 Nashe, *Pierce Penniless*, sig. H4r.
82 Nashe, *Have With You*, sig. G4r; Nashe, *Unfortunate Traveller*, sig. H1v.
83 Kate De Rycker, 'Commodifying the Author: The Mediation of Aretino's Fame in the Harvey-Nashe Pamphlet War', *ELR*, 49 (2019), 145–71 (pp. 166–8).
84 Thomas Nashe, *The Anatomie of Absurditie* (London, 1589), sig. C4r.
85 Nashe, *Have With You*, sigs E1r–E1v.

86 Nashe, *Have With You*, sig. E1v.
87 Nashe, *Have With You*, sigs E3v–E4r.
88 Thomas Dekker, *Newes From Hell Brought by the Diuells Carrier* (London, 1606) sigs C2r–C2v; see Nashe, *Pierce Penniless*, sig. I3v.
89 Thomas Dekker, *A knights coniuring* (London, 1607), sig. L1r.
90 Lawrence Manley, *Literature and Culture in Early Modern London* (Cambridge: Cambridge University Press, 1995), p. 320.
91 See John Taylor's three pamphlets *Differing worships* (London, 1640), *Tom Nash his ghost* (London, 1642), and *Crop-eare Curried* (Oxford, 1645), discussed by Rachel Willie in Chapter 7 below. See also Chris Salamone, 'Nashe's Ghosts & the Seventeenth Century', in *The Oxford Handbook of Thomas Nashe*, ed. Andrew Hadfield, Jennifer Richards and Kate De Rycker (Oxford: Oxford University Press, forthcoming 2025).

6
THOMAS NASHE AND THE VIRTUAL COMMUNITY OF ENGLISH WRITERS

Kate De Rycker

It is by now a critical commonplace that a 'public' is not only a literal collection of people but also a virtual entity, imagined into being through textual discourses.[1] As a published author Thomas Nashe can therefore be said to create a virtual public simply by addressing his imagined readers in his prefatory materials. Wes Folkerth, for example, has demonstrated how both Nashe and his Italian precursor, Pietro Aretino, used conversational interjections in their writing to produce an illusion of intimacy between author and reader despite the anonymity of print.[2] What this chapter is interested in, however, is that Nashe goes beyond these generally applicable strategies of print authorship, to create an emphatically textual community of like-minded writers and readers. This can be seen most clearly in one of Nashe's prefaces to *The Unfortunate Traveller* (1594), addressed to the 'dapper Monsier pages of the court', in which it soon appears that these 'pages' are not, as we might first expect, necessarily servants of the court but literal inhabitants of a paper landscape.[3] This conceit is continued in the main text with Wilton's acknowledgement that he was a 'certain kind of an appendix or page' to the Henrician court.[4] I quote from the preface at length, to demonstrate how Nashe's pun on 'pages' builds:

> Gallant Squires, have amongst you. [A]t mumchance [dice] I meane not, for so I might chaunce come to short commons, but at *novus, nova, novum* [new, new, new], which is in English, newes of the maker. A proper fellow Page of yours called Jacke Wilton, by mee commends him unto you, and hath bequeathed for wast paper heere amongst you certaine pages of his misfortunes. In any case keep them preciously as a privie token of his good will towards you. If there be some better than other, he craves you would honor them in their death so much, as to drie and kindle tobacco with them ... *Memorandum*, everie one of you after the perusing of this pamphlet, is to provide him [Wilton] a case of ponyards, that if you come in companie with any man which shall dispraise it [*The Unfortunate Traveller*] or speake against it, you may straight cry *Sic respondeo* [Thus I answer], and give him the stockado. It stands not with your honors (I assure yee)

to have a gentleman and a page abusde in his absence ... [I]t shalbe lawfull for anie whatsoever to play with false dice in a corner on the cover of this foresaid Acts and monuments ... Every stationers stall they passe by whether by day or by night they shall put off their hats too, and make a low leg, in regard their grand printed Capitano is there entoombd.[5]

Nashe here presents himself not as the creator but rather as the messenger of his story's fictional narrator, Jack Wilton. The virtual community that we find in this preface is a rowdy one, in which young men are equally as likely to be found gambling as poring over the newest pamphlet to hit the bookshops. As we read on, the scene becomes less convivial, and more threatening. These men are armed with poniards and sworn to defend any text containing 'their grand printed Capitano' Jack Wilton, now described as lying in state within the paper tomb of a pamphlet.[6] The threat of violence was a real one, as Chris Fitter has demonstrated in his political reading of *Romeo and Juliet*. The 1590s saw an escalation of 'inter-class youth violence' exacerbated by food shortages, boiling over into weeks of riots in June 1595.[7]

This community of armed young men are not being asked to defend the text because it is necessarily something they understand and enjoy, but because they must prove their membership to a fraternity through loyalty to its leader. They are allowed, for example, 'to play with false dice in a corner on the cover of this foresaid Acts and Monuments', *The Unfortunate Traveller* here presented as an irreverent version of John Foxe's *Book of Martyrs*, making it both a foundational text and one that Nashe does not expect its adherents to fully read.[8] While outsiders who 'dispraise' the book are to be attacked, insiders can treat this paper however they wish, whether to 'kindle tobacco', and – as 'privie' or toilet paper – presumably also to wipe their arses with.[9]

This imagined community is a satirically exaggerated version of what I am here calling a 'virtual' community of freelance writers that Nashe belonged to in the 1590s. Nashe was associated with various communities in his life, as a Cambridge student, and as a writer residing at aristocratic households like those of Archbishop Whitgift and Sir George Carey. However, none of these allegiances was long-lived. Instead Nashe's career as a freelance writer is defined by impermanence and movement, often involuntarily, such as his flight to Great Yarmouth after the *Isle of Dogs* scandal of 1597. Given the instability of his chosen career, in this *Unfortunate Traveller* preface, Nashe creates a virtual print community of 'masterlesse men' such as himself.[10] Because this community lacks the institutional structure of a guild or household, it is bound instead by a code of aggressively defending all its paper denizens, even the dead. It is also a community which, despite being splintered along different social groups, can momentarily come together in the virtual space of the page to defend, as we will see when Nashe evokes the balladeers at St Paul's Churchyard in *Strange News* (1593).

AN AFTERLIFE IN PRINT: DEFENDING THE DEAD

Much has already been written about the way that the authorial personae of Elizabethan writers such as Thomas Nashe, Robert Greene, Edmund Spenser, and Philip Sidney helped to animate the relatively new field of published fiction in the late sixteenth century.[11] As Samuel Fallon's *Paper Monsters* has convincingly demonstrated, the 'projections of personality onto the page' of the 'serial, semi-fictional personae of the 1580s and 1590s' both 'conjur[ed] public sociality into being' and 'conferred on their reading publics a sense of durability'.[12] Nashe was fascinated by this power that a fictional persona held over readers, a power which he often reminded them was constructed by authors and actors. To do this Nashe used the device of narrative metalepsis to undermine the mimetic illusion of narrative and 'foreground the nature of the narrative as *fictio*, the narrator's invention'.[13] For example, in *The Terrors of the Night* (1594) he breaks off his narration to declare that he has grown 'wearie of it, for it hath caused such a thicke fulsome Serena to descend on my braine, that now my penne makes blots as broad as a furd stomacher, and my muse inspyres me to put out my candle and goe to bed'.[14] This strategy was often (but not exclusively) combined with a trope of the author's power to transgress temporal and spatial boundaries, that of haunting and mediumship, because it emphasised the virtual nature of an author's presence on the page.

For Jacques Derrida, writing can be understood in terms of haunting because, like the liminal figure of a ghost, it disrupts numerous binaries: presence/absence, living/dead, past/present.[15] Writing, and subsequent communication technologies, not only confer material permanence on the absent writer, but crucially it does not remain static. Rather, like a ghostly messenger, writing continues to enact change on its living audience: 'to write is to produce a mark that will constitute a sort of machine which is productive in turn, and which my future disappearance will not, in principle, hinder ... For a writing to be a writing it must continue to "act" and to be readable even when what is called the author of the writing no longer answers for what he has written.'[16] As Fallon argues, the trope of ghosts and haunting was used to construct a textual durability for the persona of Robert Greene, who had died suddenly in 1592, amid a growth in published fiction. His ghostly appearance as a character in the work of other authors was used as a framing device to claim a lineage between Greene and writers such as Henry Chettle, Barnabe Rich, and

John Dickenson who presented their texts as the result of otherworldly communications with the dead author. The implication was that Greene's authorial persona had been so evocatively rendered in his own writing that it retained enough life-force to outlive him on the page.[17]

The trope of haunting provides the recently dead author with a transgressive power in its acknowledgement that the textually contingent persona will outlive the physical author. The corollary of haunting is possession, the agency moving from the dead author, and on to the living ones who mediate on their behalf, and who justify their position in the 'virtual community' through this created lineage. Another form of relationship which cements this group identity for professional writers is that of vengeance. The very existence of ghosts implies that a soul has unfinished business on earth, often a wrong which must be righted by their living relatives, before they can pass on. In these three interlocking tropes of haunting, possession, and vengeance Nashe and indeed the other two 'Thomases' who followed in his footsteps – Middleton and Dekker – helped to forge a virtual community of freelance writers.

The association between ghosts and authorial influence has a long legacy. The classical model for otherworldly conversation is Lucian of Samosata's *Dialogues of the Dead* in which ghosts act as messengers to the living. Numerous early modern texts were written in this tradition, such as *The Mirror for Magistrates* (first printed in 1563) in which the ghosts of the powerful recount their downfall as a warning to those living in the present. Nashe himself discussed writing to the dead in the demonic *Pierce Penniless, His Supplication to the Devil* (1592), claiming that his plans to write 'certayne epistles to orators and poets [such as] … the ghost of Machevill, of Tully, of Ovid, of Roscius, of Pace, the Duke of Norfolks jester; and lastly, to the ghost of Robert Greene, telling him, what a coyle there is with pamphleting on him after his death', had been scuppered by his printer going to press too quickly.[18] In a letter to the reader embedded at the end of *Pierce Penniless*, Nashe also promises to write to Aretine's 'ghost by my carrier, and I hope hele repaire his whip, and use it against our English peacockes'.[19]

Nashe's evocation of the satirist and 'scourge of princes' Pietro Aretino also highlights the theme of vengeance that runs through many of these ghostly encounters. On the stage the Senecan tradition of ghosts inciting relatives to avenge their deaths was revived in revenge tragedies such as Thomas Kyd's *The Spanish Tragedy* (c. 1590) and William Shakespeare's *Hamlet* (1603). Nashe alludes to this tradition through his use of a ghost clown, Will Sommers as a heckler in *Summer's Last Will and Testament* (first performed 1592). Unlike the ghost of Don Andrea in *The Spanish Tragedy*, who acts as a chorus to the action from beyond the veil, the ghost of Sommers crosses narrative boundaries between the reality of the audience and the fiction of the performance. At the beginning of this play the audience is directly addressed by the professional comic actor, Toy, as he struggles into his costume, the *'fooles coate'* which denotes the long dead jester of Henry VIII, Will Sommers: 'I am a goose or a ghost at least ... Will Summers ghost I should be, come to present you with Summers last will, and testament'.[20] Nashe satirises the character of the vengeful ghost of Senecan tragedy by clarifying that it is the actor Toy who is seeking revenge on the play's author (i.e. Nashe), for having given him only a prologue rather than a meatier role: 'He were as good have let me had the best part: for Ile be reveng'd on him to the uttermost, in this person of Will Summer, which I have put on to play the Prologue, and meane not to put off till, the play be done'.[21] Toy, dressed as the 'ghost' of Sommers, then continues to heckle the other actors' speeches for the rest of the play, potentially from a position in the audience. As such he is a truly liminal character, speaking as himself, the supposedly scorned actor, Toy, while dressed as a dead clown, from the 'margins' between audience and actors.

While both the theme of history as a dialogue with the dead and the association between ghosts and revenge influenced Nashe, it is in scenes of conjuration and possession that we can see how ghosts work as a useful trope of authorship. If for Derrida an actors' writing is itself ghostly because it continues to function separately from its originator, for early modern writers the emphasis was instead on the necessity of the living to act as mediators of ghostly directions. One author may be ghost-like in their ability to create a vivid persona that outlives them (like Greene) but even in this scenario a mediator is deemed necessary to reanimate the persona left behind in the text. Nashe demonstrates this in *The Unfortunate Traveller* when he literalises what he sees as the lazy recycling of Ciceronian rhetoric. In front of an audience at Wittenberg university, the ghost of Cicero or 'Tully' is conjured up by the polymath and magician Cornelius Agrippa to deliver his famous speech in defence of Roscio Amerino.[22] Preceding this conjuration the narrative voice of Jack Wilton merges with that of Nashe's, when he mocks university students for recombining lines from Cicero and passing them off as their own: 'A most vaine thing it is in many universities at this daye, that they count him excellent eloquent, who stealeth not whole phrases but whole pages out of Tully ... No invention or matter have they of theyr owne, but tacke up a stile of his stale galimafries.'[23]

If this description of the recycling of Cicero's writing as 'gallimaufry' has become too dead a metaphor (gallimaufry being both a meat stew and, figuratively, a confused mixture), then Nashe underlines its staleness by contrasting it with a scene of conjuration which demonstrates good oratory's ability to make language come to life. Various academics ask Agrippa to allow them to see classical figures like Plautus and Ovid in the flesh, until Erasmus's request to see Cicero is accepted. There is no dialogue between the living and the conjured figure; instead it is a performance: 'at the time prefixed in entered Tully, ascended his pleading place, and declaimed verbatim the forenamed oration, but with such astonishing amazement, with such fervent exaltation of spirite, with such soule-stirring jestures, that all his auditours were readie to install his guiltie client for a God'.[24] What is missing from the amateur recycling of Cicero's phrases is the skill of delivery, demonstrated by his ghost's ability to match 'soule-stirring jestures' to his words, and to express them with a 'fervent exaltation of spirite'.[25] It was the importance of *pronuntiatio* – the skilful use of voice and gesture in rhetorical training – that Nashe here imagines to be apparent only when Cicero is seen as an orator rather than as text which can be cherry-picked for useful phrases. As Jennifer Richards has demonstrated, Nashe is one of a number of writers who attempt to 'animate the material book even for silent readers' through their knowledge of *pronuntiatio*.[26] Think of the way that Nashe uses a metaphor of resurrection in the following description of Gabriel Harvey's supposedly comatose written style: 'Squeise thy heart into thy inkehorne, and it shall but congeal into clodderd garbage of confutation, thy soule hath no effects of a soule, thou canst not sprinkle it into a sentence, & make everie line leape like a cup of neat wine new powred out, as an orator must doe that lies aright in wait for mens affections'.[27] Harvey's writing is here described as soulless, congealing as soon as it touches the paper, and this is because it lacks the spoken rhythms of oratory that Nashe implies he can better capture in his own writing. His own style, he suggests, leaps off the page, so much so that one can almost taste and hear it, like a cup of freshly poured wine.

Nashe again likens the skills of oratory to the revivification of a dead figure from the past when his satirical persona, Pierce, defends the theatre industry in *Pierce Penniless*. Nashe describes an actor's power to move an audience to tears in one performance:

> [T]he subject of them [plays] (for the most part) it is borrowed out of our English chronicles, wherein our forefathers valiant acts (that have line long buried in rustie brasse and worme-eaten bookes) are revived, and they themselves raised from the grave of oblivion, and brought to pleade their aged honours in open presence ... How would it have joyed brave Talbot (the terror of the French) to thinke that after he had lyne two hundred yeares in his tombe, hee should triumphe againe on the stage, and have his bones newe embalmed with the teares of ten thousand spectators at

least (at severall times), who in the tragedian that represents his person, imagine they behold him fresh bleeding.[28]

To emphasise the power of the stage, Nashe contrasts this shared experience of performing and watching a history play against the stillness of 'worme-eaten bookes', which are equated with 'rustie brasse' coffins, unread and thus passively holding the dead. As well as a plug for *1 Henry VI* (1591) – a play which is now supposed to have been co-written by Shakespeare, Marlowe, and Nashe – this quotation also demonstrates Nashe's interest in the communal, embodied experience of live performance.[29] It is the grisly sight of a wounded body 'fresh bleeding' which moves the audience to tears. The capacity to revive the dead is attributed not only to the actor's transformative talents of representation but also to the audience's physical response of weeping which 'newe[ly] embalm[s]' the memory of the dead warrior and raises him from his 'tombe'. The ability to revive the dead is in this case a relational experience: an audience is necessary for the 'magic' of resurrection to work. Thomas Heywood uses a similar analogy in his description of the power actors hold over their audience, who look on them 'as if the Personater were the man Personated, so bewitching a thing is lively and well spirited action, that it hath power to new mold the harts of the spectators'.[30]

It was, however, in Nashe's most sustained exploration of communicating between this world and the next, *Pierce Penniless*, that his portrayal of the freelance writer as an alienated observer of urban society comes across most clearly. The Pierce persona of a university student turned freelance satirist was almost immediately treated as a thinly veiled version of the author. Gabriel Harvey regularly elided 'Nashe' with his haunted persona, 'Pierce', even naming one of his attacks on Nashe *Pierce's Supererogation* (1593). We can see how Harvey slips easily between 'Nashe', 'Mr Penniles', and 'Mr Pierce', blurring the line between reality and fiction in the following quotation: 'Well, my maisters, you may talke your pleasure of Tom Nash ... but assure your selves, if M. Penniles had bene deeply plunged in a profound exstasic of knavery, M. Pierce had never written that famous worke of Supererogation, that now stayneth all the bookes in Paules-churchyard, and setteth both the uniuersites to schoole'.[31] Harvey writes that this blending of fictional persona and author was initiated by Nashe: 'His Life daily feedeth his Stile; & his stile notoriously bewraieth his Life.'[32] Nashe played along with Harvey's elision of his persona and his own reputation in his 1596 pamphlet *Have With You to Saffron Walden*. This pamphlet is presented as a dialogue between five friends, one of whom, Nashe explains, is 'my selfe, whom I personate as the Respondent', or 'Piers Pennilesse Respondent' in the list of characters.[33]

None of the other characters, however, addresses him as 'Piers'; they instead call him 'Tom' and 'Nashe'.[34] Nashe here enjoys the metaleptic overstepping of the boundary between the world that is doing the narrating, and the world which is being narrated, just as he had explored in *Summer's Last Will* through the interjections of 'Toy' as a prologue who has overstayed his welcome, insulting Nashe as 'a beggerly poet' who has so little paid work that he must 'licke dishes' clean.[35] Today we might call this 'autofiction', in that Nashe returns time and again to a slippery form of writing which blurs the boundary between fiction and biography, paratext and narrative.

Given that Pierce was already a persona associated with otherworldly transgression in writing to the devil for money, after Nashe's death in *c.* 1600 it was inevitable that other writers would publish their continuations of *Pierce Penniless*. Thomas Middleton's *The Black Book* (1604) especially demonstrates Derrida's point about writing as a form of productive machine, because it continues to develop the fictionalised 'beggerly' persona that Nashe had originated in *Pierce Penniless*. *The Black Book* opens with Lucifer on stage at the Globe playhouse, then searching for Pierce amongst London's 'tipsy taverns, roosting inns, and frothy alehouses'.[36] Middleton writes in the grotesque style associated with Nashe, but aims his satire at a newly Jacobean London, demonstrating that many of the urban sins identified in *Pierce Penniless* have continued into the next decade. His Lucifer meets a bawd in the Pickt-hatch brothel in Turnmill Street whose 'fat-sag-chinne hang[s] downe like a Cowes Udder':[37] phrasing reminiscent of Nashe's description of a stereotypical Danish 'flaberkin face' as having 'cheekes that sag like a womans dugs over his chin-bone'.[38] When Lucifer finally meets Pierce, however, the language used to describe his new abode suggests that the tenement and its inhabitants are part of a ghostly, textual, version of London.

Lucifer finds Pierce renting a room at the house of 'Mistress Silver-pin'. This is a sobriquet for a sex worker, used in the 1601 doggerel that described the then Lord Chamberlain as having played around with 'his Joan Silverpin / She makes his cockscomb thin / And quake in every limb'.[39] A fictional persona, Mistress Silver-pin's house is both a ghost-house and a stage upon which she and Pierce live: 'we knocked up the ghost of Mistress Silver-pin, who suddenly risse out of two white sheets, and acted out of her tiring-house window. But having understood who we were ... she presently, even in her ghost's apparel, unfolded the doors, and gave me my free entrance.'[40] It is significant that her 'ghost's apparel' is 'two white sheets' as this suggests both the winding sheets that the dead were buried in and the sheets of paper in which this fictional persona primarily circulates. The same association between winding sheets, ghosts, and paper is made in the dedication to Marlowe's translation of *The First Book of Lucan* (1600), when its printer, Thomas Thorpe, describes the authorship of the book in terms of haunting: 'that pure Elementall wit Chr. Marlow; whose ghoast or *Genius* [spirit] is to be seene walke the Churchyard in (at the least) three or foure sheets'.[41] As Sarah Wall-Randell has noted, 'three or four sheets' is the estimated quantity of paper needed to print that pamphlet, and 'So Marlowe's ghost wears the Lucan translation, the very text Thorpe is presenting and we are now reading, as a winding-sheet', as he wanders around the bookstalls of St Paul's Churchyard, both book and ghost.[42]

Heading upstairs, Lucifer finds Pierce in a room decked in material culled from both the stage and the cemetery:

> [T]he bare privities of the stone-walls were hid with two pieces of painted Cloth ... [T]he spindle-shank spiders ... went stalking over his head, as if they had been conning of Tamburlaine ... [T]here was many such sights to be seen and all under a penny ... [I]n this unfortunate tiring-house lay poor Pierce ... the sheets smudged so dirtily, as if they had been stolen by night out of Saint Pulcher's churchyard when the sexton had left a grave open ... [T]he coverlet was made of pieces o' black cloth clapped together, such as was scattered off the rails in Kings-Street at the queen's funeral.[43]

Just as Mistress Silver-pin is dressed in the costume of a stage ghost, 'acting' out of her tiring house, so too is Pierce's room reminiscent of the backstage or 'tiring house' of a theatre, bedecked in stage cloth, the spiders likened to the long-legged Edward Alleyn in his role as Tamburlaine, and all visible for 'under a penny': the cheapest price of admission to the theatre. It is also a ghostly world. Pierce is, like his hostess, one of the living-dead, sleeping in sheets that look like they have been removed from a grave and a coverlet that reminds Lucifer of the dramatic swathes of black that marked Elizabeth I's funeral. As a literary character living on beyond the life of his author, Pierce is in a liminal space between death and life, and, when roused by Lucifer, speaks words 'between drunk and sober ... [and] between sleeping and waking'.[44] Elizabethan London and its key literary persona continues, it seems, to haunt the newly Jacobean London in textual form.

While Middleton makes it clear that he is writing of the persona 'Pierce' through his emphasis on the theatrical nature of Lucifer's visit to London, Thomas Dekker's *News from Hell Brought by the Devil's Carrier* (1606) introduces both Nashe *and* Pierce as fictional characters, and, in doing so, amplifies the dead author into a muse for subsequent satirical writers.

Dekker's narrator dreams that he is transported to hell, where Mephistopheles is informed that 'during his absence both Pierce Pennyles and the Poet that writ for him, have bene landed by Charon' in the underworld.[45] Posthumously it seems that Nashe's virtual existence on the page has reduced him to the same level as his persona, Pierce, so that both arrive simultaneously in the underworld. Dekker's dreamer goes on to invoke the ghost of Nashe to aid him in his composition:

> And thou, into whose soule (if ever there were a Pithagorean Metempsuchosis) the raptures of that fierie and inconfinable Italian spirit were bounteously and boundlesly infused, thou sometimes Secretary to Pierce Pennylesse, and Master of his requests, ingenious, ingenuous, fluent, facetious, T. Nash: from whose aboundant pen, hony flow'd to thy friends, and mortall Aconite to thy enemies ... get leave for thy Ghost, to come from her abiding, and to dwell with me a while, till she hath carows'd to me in her owne woted ful measures of wit, that my plump braynes may swell, and burst into bitter Invectives against the Lieftennant of Limbo, if hee casheere Pierce Pennylesse with dead pay.[46]

As Fallon points out, one of the unusual aspects of this invocation is the way in which the relationship between author and persona is inverted: 'Nashe is presented not as Pierce's begetter, but instead as a secretary in his service – a writer doing the bidding of a character who has at last outgrown him.'[47] Nashe, we might remember, similarly presents himself as a secretary for his character Jack Wilton in his prefatory letter to *The Unfortunate Traveller*. This illusory power balance does, however, shift in *News from Hell*. The rest of the invocation recasts Nashe, previously the 'master of [Pierce's] requests' and 'poet that writ for him' as a muse, capable of transforming the dreamer into a powerful satirical writer. Just as Nashe had once invoked the satirical spirit of Aretino to help him 'strip' miserly patrons or 'golden asses out of their gaie trappings' and 'leave them on the dunghill for carion',[48] so too does this new scribe invoke Nashe, creating a chain of ghostly mediations. The former invocation resulted in Nashe becoming so closely associated with 'that fierie and inconfinable Italian spirit', Aretino, that Dekker describes their relationship as a form of metempsychosis. Dekker's scribe might hope for a similar transformational process between himself and Nashe by executing the work that Nashe had once promised (i.e., 'the devils answer to the supplication'), but which was never published.[49] This transaction is so consuming that the scribe imagines himself bursting with Nashean invective; Nashe's 'Ghost' is a fertile 'she', able to impregnate a poet's brains till they become plump and swelling with the power to create paper progeny, or rather the 'Paper-monsters' which both Nashe and

Dekker claim to have generated, pamphlets which have posthumous lives of their own.[50]

VIRTUAL COUNTER-PUBLICS

In his continuation of *Pierce Penniless* in *News from Hell*, Dekker demonstrates how the ghost trope could be used to express a commonality of purpose between writers, especially when they otherwise lacked an institutional connection through belonging to a guild or (nominally) to an aristocratic household, as in the case of their closest collaborators: printers and actors. Freelance writers were clearly each other's competitors. Pierce, for example, complains that 'every grosse braind idiot is suffered to come into print ... How then can we chuse but be needy, when ther are so many droans amongst us?'[51] However, they were also aware that they needed to distinguish themselves from other forms of freelance textual producers such as ballad writers, who, as we shall see, are described by Nashe as being bound by the same code of honour as his imagined textual defenders of that 'grand printed Capitano' Jack Wilton.[52] This sense of shared purpose between otherwise masterless men is conducted through the imagery of vengeful ghosts inciting their aggressive followers to defend their honours.

Dekker recycled sections of *News from Hell* into an expanded pamphlet called *A Knight's Conjuring* (1607), and in this augmented version his dreamer takes the reader even further into the underworld. In the 'Fields of Joye' various social types (forlorn lovers singing ballads under willow trees, soldiers who died honourably in battle) now dwell. Finally the dreamer reaches a grove of laurel trees, where he finds groups of poets and musicians. Our attention is focused on two virtual communities of English writers. In one Geoffrey Chaucer sits encircled by 'all the Makers or Poets of his time' who, like the audiences described by Heywood and Nashe, are bewitched by his oratory: 'their eyes fixt seriously upon his, whilst their eares are all tied to his tongue, by the golden chaines of his Numbers'.[53] Because this is a virtual, textual, community, time can be collapsed to allow the 'Grave' Edmund Spenser into this 'Chappell of Apollo' and to be sat at the right hand side of Chaucer, who names him his 'son'. The attention of these fourteenth-century poets now shifts to silently listening to Spenser as he 'sing[s] out the rest of his Fayrie Queenes praises'.[54] Spenser had indeed presented himself as Chaucer's successor, even invoking his spirit to aid him in completing his unfinished 'Squire's Tale' in Book Four of the *Faerie Queene* (1590):

> Then pardon, O most sacred happy Spirit,
> That I thy Labours lost may thus revive,

> And steal from thee the Meed of thy due Merit,
> That none durst ever whilst thou wast alive,
> And being dead, in vain yet many strive:
> Ne dare I like, but through Infusion sweet
> Of thine own Spirit (which doth in me survive)
> I follow here the footing of thy Feet,
> That with thy meaning so I may the [thee] rather meet. (4.2.34)[55]

Like Dekker's use of metempsychosis to describe the continuation of Aretino's spirit into Nashe, and Nashe's spirit into Dekker's, Spenser here suggests that Chaucer's spirit survives in him, and therefore only once he is dead could Chaucer continue his 'Labours' through his Elizabethan successor.

In Dekker's dream vision, other groups of writers are seated separately, associated through their connection to certain theatre companies, as well as the conviviality of drink and song. Together they sit 'carowsing to one another at the holy well', in an apparent reference to Holywell Street near the Theatre playhouse in Shoreditch.[56] In one group sit the Queen's Men dramatists from the early 1580s, such as Thomas Watson, Thomas Kyd, and Thomas Achelley, who are joined by the Queen's Men tragedian, John Bentley. In another likely reference to a tavern sign Christopher Marlowe, Robert Greene, and George Peele, all dramatists associated with the Admiral's Men, sit 'under the shades of a large vyne' laughing as they greet Thomas Nashe who has 'but newly come to their Colledge'.[57] Nashe is described as:

> still haunted with the sharpe and Satyricall spirit that followd him heere upon earth: for Nash inveyed bitterly (as he had wont to do) against dry-fisted Patrons, accusing them of his untimely death, because if they had given his Muse that cherishment which shee most worthily deserved, hee had fed to his dying day on fat Capons, burnt sack and Suger, and not so desperately have ventur'de his life, and shortend his dayes by keeping company with pickle herrings.[58]

This is Nashe as 'Pierce Penilesse', the archetypal freelance writer, attempting to survive on the meagre rations afforded to him by ungenerous patrons. Nashe is again associated with Robert Greene through the allusion that subsisting on pickled herrings – a common tavern snack – had led to both their 'untimely death[s]'. Speaking to Marlowe, Greene, and Peele, Nashe reminds them that although they may all have worked with theatre companies, as freelance writers their association with the collective enterprise of the theatre was tangential. When asked 'how Poets and Players agreed now', Nashe's ghost confirms that although they necessarily must work together, the actors have no real need of the writers beyond their provision of material. Their relationship is likened to that of 'Phisitions and patients' in that 'the patient loves his Doctor no longer then till hee get his health', 'and the Player loves a Poet, so long as the sicknesse lyes in the two-penie gallery when none will come into it': that is, good plays are needed to cure the theatres of empty galleries. Writers are also set up in opposition to public audiences. Nashe says that writers still 'wast [their] braines, to earne applause' from their audience which, like an unthinking and destructive 'Asse ... stands by and bites [his work] in sunder'.[59]

That the spirits questioning Nashe are Marlowe, Greene, and Peele is significant, because it is the same collective who are addressed in *Greene's Groatsworth of Wit*, a text published soon after Greene's death in 1592. That pamphlet had also set up a clear opposition between 'Poets' and 'Players' in its infamous dismissal of William Shakespeare as an 'upstart Crow, beautified with our feathers', the animosity seemingly because he was an actor turned playwright.[60] Both *Groatsworth* and this section of *Knight's Conjuring* attempt to strengthen the sense of fellowship between freelance writers by opposing them to actors, a group with whom they have a financial relationship, but not always a sense of common purpose.

The authorship of *Groatsworth* was contested almost immediately, as we can see in Henry Chettle's declaration of innocence in the preface to *Kind-Hart's Dream* (1593). Here he explained his part in *Groatsworth* as a form of revision while he prepared Greene's work for publication. Chettle, himself a playwright, prose author, and compositor, is included in Dekker's imagined community of modern English writers, appearing in the afterlife (having only recently died in 1607) to interrupt Nashe's diatribe. He arrives 'sweating and blowing, by reason of his fatnes, to welcome whom ... all rose up, and fell presentlie on their knees, to drinck a health to all the Lovers of Hellicon'.[61] In his prefatory letter to *Kind-Hart's Dream*, the real Chettle addresses his working relationship to Greene and Nashe, explaining that on his death Greene had left behind 'many papers in sundry Booke sellers hands', one of which was *Groatsworth*. Chettle claims he then 'writ it over' as a fair copy and that he 'protest[s] it was all Greene's, not mine nor Master Nashes as some unjustly have affirmed'.[62] The reason why this had become so controversial was because of the pamphlet's veiled address to Marlowe, Nashe, and Peele to warn them against being taken advantage of by actors, 'those apes' who 'imitate your past excellence'.[63] Chettle claims that this 'letter written to divers play-makers, is offensively by one or two of them taken, and because on the dead they cannot be avenged, they wilfully forge in their conceits a living author: and after tossing it to and fro, no remedy, but it must light on me'.[64] Whatever the truth of *Groatsworth*'s authorship, the *Kind-Hart* preface here acknowledges that posthumous print authorship is necessarily contested because publication is in essence a collaborative act, and so any surviving collaborators might find themselves responsible for the 'authorship' of controversial works.

The main text of *Kind-Hart's Dream* sets up yet another liminal convocation of ghostly authors and living mediators.[65] The subtitle explains that it contains 'five apparitions' or 'severall ghosts' who appear to Chettle's narrator and require him to publish their invectives. It is nominally a continuation of Nashe's *Pierce Penniless*, in that the ghostly authors claim they had to come to Kind-Hart in person because the 'knight of the post' who carried Pierce's letter to the devil 'repulsed them wrathfully ... for he had almost hazarded his credit in hell, by being a Broker between Pierce Penilesse and his Lord'.[66] Chettle establishes himself in yet another literary controversy caused by Greene's death: the pamphlet war between Gabriel Harvey and Thomas Nashe, initiated because Nashe had promised to defend Greene's reputation against Harvey's attack.

One of Kind-Hart's ghostly visitors is Robert Greene, who has a letter for 'Pierce Penilesse' (i.e., Thomas Nashe). Greene's ghost chastises Nashe for his slowness in responding to Gabriel Harvey's invective against Nashe and Greene in his *Four Letters* (1592): 'the longer thou deferst, the more greefe thou bringst to thy frends, and givest the greater head to thy enemies ... Awake (secure boy) revenge thy wrongs, remember mine: thy adversaries began the abuse, they continue it: if thou suffer it, let thy life be short in silence and obscuritie, and thy death hastie, hated, and miserable.'[67] It is likely that Chettle knew Nashe was preparing *Strange News*, his response to Harvey, given that it was being published by John Danter, for whom Chettle had been both a business partner and later a journeyman compositor. In either case the ghostly Greene's warning to Nashe not to delay his published defence any longer is yet again tied up in the language of ghostly revenge and honour.

In *Strange News* Nashe attempts to resurrect Greene's spirit in a less literal way than Chettle to respond to Harvey's attack:

> Had hee liv'd, Gabriel, and thou shouldst so unarteficially and odiously libeld against him as thou hast done, he would have made thee an example of ignominy to all ages that are to come, and driven thee to eate thy owne booke butterd, as I sawe him make an apparriter once in a tavern eate his citation waxe and all, very handsomly serv'd twixt two dishes.[68]

The emphasis is here on the conditional: *had* Greene lived, then he *would have* force-fed Harvey his own *Four Letters*. Greene is associated here with the same sort of playful aggression as the 'dapper Monsier pages of the court' who Nashe imagines will defend the fictional Jack Wilton against public attacks. Greene's performative vengeance takes place in a tavern, a common scene of writerly conviviality because it is an identifiable and stable location in which otherwise mobile freelance writers can be imagined as gathering together, as implied throughout Dekker's presentation of dead English writers 'carowsing' and drinking to each other's health in the afterlife. A little over a decade later Ben Jonson would repeatedly identify taverns as the location of informal drinking societies of writers, such as when Littlewit curses other 'pretenders to wit, your Three Cranes, Mitre, and Mermaid men!' in the opening to *Bartholomew Fair* (1614).[69]

If the tavern is one location where the virtual community of English writer might be imagined to convene, then the other imagined space is St Paul's Churchyard, an area replete with bookshops where Nashe describes Pierce Penilesse distributing his 'unperusde papers' only to be picked up by 'the ape Gabriel, who made mops and mows at them ... but coulde not enter into the contents'.[70] It is both an actual meeting space for writers and a space where their ghostly doubles, their books, continue to circulate. We have seen this dual circulation of virtual and real authors in Thomas Thorpe's description of Marlowe's translation of Lucan as a 'ghoast' walking around the Churchyard in 'three or foure sheets', and in Nashe's locating of Jack Wilton and his defenders, bowing at 'stationers stall[s]' where their 'grand printed Capitano' is 'entombd' in copies of *The Unfortunate Traveller*.[71] The bookshops of St Paul's Churchyard therefore makes it a liminal space which, as per Derrida, disrupts the binaries of authorial presence and absence, past and present, living and dead. By locating the virtual community of often mobile freelance writers in identifiable spaces such as the taverns of Cheapside and the bookshops of St Paul's Churchyard, Nashe and his network provide readers with an imagined meeting space to compensate for their lack of identifiable workspace.

For university-educated writers like Nashe, the ballad writer, as a mobile freelancer associated with the print trade, was in a worryingly similar line of work. Equally driven by a code of honour, Nashe presents them as a counter-public to his own group of writers in *Strange News*, because they had recently lost a famous member, William Elderton, in the same year as Nashe's virtual community had lost Robert Greene. Gabriel Harvey had described both Greene and Elderton as 'two notorious mates, & the very ringleaders of the riming, and scribbling crew'.[72] In response Nashe calls upon this 'scribbling crew' to join what amounts to a street brawl. Nashe rallies his troops – 'List Pauls Churchyard (the peruser of everie mans works & exchange of all authors) you are a many of you honest fellows, and favour men of wit' – and sets them on Harvey:[73]

> We are to vexe you mightely for plucking Elderton out of the ashes of his ale, and not letting him injoy his nappie muse of ballad-making to himselfe,

but now when he is as dead as dead beere, you must bee finding fault with the brewing of his meeters.

    Hough, Thomas Delone[y], Philip Stub[b]s, Robert Armin, &c. Your father Elderton is abus'd. Revenge, revenge on course paper and want of matter, that hath most sacriligiously contaminated the divine spirit & quintessence of a penny a quart.

    Helter skelter, feare no colours, course him, trounce him, one cup of perfect bonaventure licour will inspire you with more wit and schollership than hee hath thrust into his whole packet of letters.[74]

Nashe is no defender of ballads as a literary form; they are still made on 'course paper and want of matter', while Elderton and his fellow ballad makers are mocked for their reputation as heavy drinkers. In *Pierce Penniless*, for example, Pierce scoffs at 'poore latinlesse authors' who 'no sooner spy a new ballad, and his name to it that compilde it: but they put him in for one of the learned men of our time'.[75] And yet Nashe is angered that Harvey should attack a dead man who is unable to answer for himself, a theme threaded throughout *Strange News* and Chettle's *Kind-Hart's Dream*. In his response to Harvey, Nashe creates a vivid and locatable public scene. This 'congregation' are a 'we' being called on ('Hough, Thomas Delone[y] ... Revenge, revenge') and directed to attack ('Helter skelter ... course him, trounce him').[76] The comparison of the printed page to a public square continues when Nashe describes his potential readers as voyeurs: 'You that bee lookers on perhaps imagine I talke like a mery man, and not in good earnest when I say that Eldertons ghost and Gabriel are at such ods: but then you knowe nothing, for there hath beene monstrous emulation twixt Elderton and him time out of mind'.[77]

    Elderton's 'ghost' is itself unable to retaliate, as ballads are especially ephemeral form of text. We only now know that Elderton wrote 'whole bundles of ballets' scorning or 'bearbayting' Gabriel Harvey and his brothers thanks to Nashe's mentioning of them in *Pierce Penniless* and *Strange News*, but none has survived.[78] The onus, then, is on the living balladeers such as Thomas Deloney to produce new work in defence of their predecessor. The reason that Nashe is involved in rallying this group of writers is primarily due to his animosity against Harvey, but we could also interpret it (as Kenneth Friedenreich suggests) as 'a call to defend the institution of the professional writer'.[79] Nashe's dismissal of ballad makers in the rest of his writing is really, as Alexandra Halasz has demonstrated, an anxiety about his work's 'loss of distinction' from other professional writers, producing other cheaply printed texts.[80] Setting such anxieties aside in this representation of the 'scribbling crew' congregating in the 'exchange of all authors', St Paul's Churchyard, Nashe here creates a virtual community of freelance writers staking out their territory in the book trade, and aligning themselves with the ghosts of their predecessors through this language of vengeance and honour.[81]

The ghostliness of writing is in its ability to produce a visceral sense of an author's presence, despite their physical absence. The posthumous continuations of the 'Pierce' persona by Middleton and Dekker work because Nashe had himself worked hard to capture a sense of intimacy between reader and writer through an animated writing style ('make everie line leape like a cup of neat wine'),[82] and by experimenting with a form of autofiction, blurring the line between paratext and narrative, between autobiography and fiction. Yet in the *News from Hell* continuation especially we can see that the trope of ghostly possession or (in Dekker's words) 'metempsychosis' is also about creating an imagined lineage and sense of virtual community between freelance writers, who had a less stable professional identity than their sometime collaborators, printers and actors. In Nashe's own writing this acknowledgement of the printed page as a virtual space where freelance writers can 'meet' is explored through yet another ghostly trope, that of the duty of living relatives to avenge their predecessors for a perceived wrong. In a career which was otherwise built on competition and attempts to distinguish cheap printed forms through claims to literary value, the creation of a virtual community on the page arguably provided the otherwise marginal status of freelance writers with a sense of social identity.

NOTES

1 Benedict Anderson's *Imagined Communities: Reflections on the Origin and Spread of Nationalism* (London and New York: Verso, 1991), which examines the imaginary construction of the modern nation state. Anderson's work influenced Charles Taylor's *Modern Social Imaginaries* (Durham, NC: Duke University Press, 2004), which added the market and the public sphere as additional societies to Anderson's focus on the nation. Michael Warner's *Publics & Counterpublics* (New York: Zone Books, 2002) emphasises that a public is rhetorically constituted by dint of being addressed.
2 Wes Folkerth, 'Pietro Aretino, Thomas Nashe, and Early Modern Rhetorics of Public Address', in *Making Publics in Early Modern Europe: People, Things, Forms of Knowledge*, ed. Bronwen Wilson and Paul Yachnin (Oxford and New York: Routledge, 2010), pp. 68–78.
3 Thomas Nashe, 'The Induction to the dapper Monsier Pages', in *The vnfortunate traueller* (London, 1594), sig. A3v.
4 Nashe, *Unfortunate Traveller*, sig. B1r.
5 Nashe, *Unfortunate Traveller*, sigs A3v–A4r.
6 Nashe, *Unfortunate Traveller*, sig. A4r.
7 Chris Fitter, '"The quarrel is between our masters and us their men": *Romeo and Juliet*, Dearth, and the London Riots', *ELR*, 30 (2000), 154–83 (p. 155).
8 Nashe, *Unfortunate Traveller*, sig. A4r.

9   Nashe, *Unfortunate Traveller*, sigs A3vA4r.
10 Thomas Nashe, *Pierce Penilesse his supplication to the diuell* (London, 1592), sig. D4r.
11 See for example Katharine Wilson, *Fictions of Authorship in Late Elizabethan Narratives: Euphues in Arcadia* (Oxford: Oxford University Press, 2006); Douglas Bruster, *Shakespeare and the Question of Culture: Early Modern Literature and the Cultural Turn* (Basingstoke: Palgrave Macmillan, 2003), pp. 65–93; Georgia Brown, *Redefining Elizabethan Literature* (Cambridge: Cambridge University Press, 2004).
12 Samuel Fallon, *Paper Monsters: Persona and Literary Culture in Elizabethan England* (Philadelphia: University of Pennsylvania Press, 2019), p. 18.
13 Monica Fludernik, 'Scene Shift, Metalepsis, and the Metaleptic Mode', *Style*, 37 (2003), 382–400 (p. 384).
14 Thomas Nashe, *The terrors of the night* (London, 1594), sig. H1v.
15 Jacques Derrida's theory of 'hauntology' is most fully outlined in his *Spectres of Marx: The State of the Debt, the Work of Mourning, & the New International*, trans. Peggy Kamuf (New York and London: Routledge, 1994).
16 Jacques Derrida, 'Signature, Event, Context', *Limited Inc.*, trans. Samuel Webster and Jeffrey Mehlman (Evanston, Il.: Northwestern University Press, 1988), pp. 1–23 (p. 8).
17 Fallon, *Paper Monsters*, pp. 25–53, also published as 'Robert Greene's Ghosts', *MLQ*, 77 (2016), 193–217.
18 Thomas Nashe, 'A private Epistle', in Nashe, *Pierce Penniless*, sig. ¶1r.
19 Nashe, *Pierce Penniless*, sig. I3v.
20 Thomas Nashe, *A pleasant comedie, called Summers last will and testament* (London, 1600), sig. B1r.
21 Nashe, *Summer's*, sig. B2r.
22 Nashe, *Unfortunate Traveller*, sig. F3v.
23 Nashe, *Unfortunate Traveller*, sig. F3r.
24 Nashe, *Unfortunate Traveller*, sig. F3v.
25 Nashe, *Unfortunate Traveller*, sig. F3v.
26 Jennifer Richards, *Voices and Books in the English Renaissance: A New History of Reading* (Oxford: Oxford University Press, 2019), p. 239.
27 Thomas Nashe, *Strange newes, of the intercepting certaine letters* (London, 1592), sig. H4r.
28 Nashe, *Pierce Penniless*, sig. F3r.
29 Matthew Steggle described how this emotive experience 'act[s] as a chain, making the spectators into a collective' in *Laughing and Weeping in Early Modern Theatres* (Aldershot: Ashgate, 2007), p. 86.
30 Thomas Heywood, *An apology for actors* (London, 1612), sig. B4r.
31 Gabriel Harvey, *Pierces supererogation or A new prayse of the old asse* (London, 1593), sig. C3v.
32 Harvey, *Pierce's Supererogation*, F2v.
33 Thomas Nashe, 'To the reader', in Thomas Nashe, *Haue vvith you to Saffron-vvalden. Or, Gabriell Harueys hunt is vp* (John Danter, 1596), sig. D3r; Nashe, *Have With You*, sig. D4r.
34 See Nashe, *Have With You*, sigs D4r and H3r.
35 Nashe, *Summer's*, sig. C1v.
36 Thomas Middleton, *The Black Book*, ed. G. B. Shand, in *Thomas Middleton: The Collected Works*, gen. eds Gary Taylor and John Lavagnino (Oxford: Oxford University Press, 2007), pp. 204–18 (p. 208).
37 Middleton, *The Black Book*, p. 208.

38 Nashe, *Pierce Penniless*, sig. C1v.
39 Anonymous, quoted in *Elizabethan and Jacobean Journals 1591–1610*, ed. G. B. Harrison (Abingdon: Routledge, 1999), III:174.
40 Middleton, *The Black Book*, p. 212.
41 Thomas Thorpe, 'To his Kind, and True Friend: Edmund Blunt', in Christopher Marlowe, trans., *Lucans first booke translated line for line, by Chr. Marlow* (London, 1600), sig. A2r.
42 Sarah Wall-Randell, 'Marlowe's Lucan: Winding-sheets and Scattered Leaves', in *Christopher Marlowe, Theatrical Commerce and the Book Trade*, ed. Kirk Melnikoff and Roslyn L. Knutson (Cambridge: Cambridge University Press, 2018), pp. 11–25 (p. 15).
43 Middleton, *The Black Book*, pp. 212–13.
44 Middleton, *The Black Book*, p. 212.
45 Thomas Dekker, *Newes From Hell, Brought by the Diuells Carrier* (London, 1606), sig. F2v.
46 Dekker, *News from Hell*, sigs C2r–v.
47 Fallon, *Paper Monsters*, p. 150.
48 Nashe, *Pierce Penniless*, sig. I2v.
49 Thomas Nashe, 'A private Epistle', in Nashe, *Pierce Penniless*, sig. ¶1v.
50 Nashe writes: '[I] lette him bloud with my penne ... and so ... was this paper-monster Pierce Penilesse begotten' (Nashe, *Pierce Penilesse*, sig. A3r). Dekker echoes this in his dedication to John Hamden: 'the begetting of Bookes, is as common as the begetting of Children ... Theise Paper-monsters are sure to be set uppon, by many terrible encounters' (*Newes from hell*, sig. A3r).
51 Nashe, *Pierce Penniless*, sigs A1v–A2r.
52 Nashe, *Unfortunate Traveller*, sig. A4r.
53 Thomas Dekker, *A knights coniuring* (London, 1607), sig. K4v.
54 Dekker, *Knight's Conjuring*, sig. K4v.
55 Edmund Spenser, *The Faerie Queene*, ed. A. C. Hamilton (Abingdon: Routledge, 2006), p. 424.
56 Dekker, *Knight's Conjuring*, sig. L1r.
57 Dekker, *Knight's Conjuring*, sig. L1r.
58 Dekker, *Knight's Conjuring*, sig. L1r.
59 Dekker, *Knight's Conjuring*, sigs L1r–L1v.
60 Robert Greene [?], *Greenes groats-worth of witte, bought with a million of repentance* (London, 1592), sig. F1v.
61 Dekker, *Knight's Conjuring*, sig. L1r.
62 Henry Chettle, *Kind-harts dreame* (London, 1593), sig. A3v. For discussion of the Groatsworth controversy see John Jowett, 'Johannes Factotum: Henry Chettle and Greene's *Groatsworth of Wit*', *Bibliographical Society of America*, 87(1993), 453–86; Steve Mentz, 'Forming Greene: Theorizing the Early Modern Author in the *Groatsworth of Wit*', in *Writing Robert Greene: Essays on England's First Notorious Professional Writer*, ed. Kirk Melnikoff and Edward Gieskes (Aldershot: Ashgate, 2008), pp. 115–32.
63 Greene [?], *Greene's Groatsworth of Wit*, sig. F1v.
64 Chettle, *Kind-hart's Dream*, sig. A3v.
65 For an in-depth analysis of the text as an exploration of the various forms of print authorship see Alexandra Halasz's *The Marketplace of Print: Pamphlets and the Public Sphere in Early Modern England* (Cambridge: Cambridge University Press, 1997), pp. 46–81.
66 Chettle, *Kind-hart's Dream*, sig. B3v.

67 Chettle, *Kind-hart's Dream*, sig. E1v.
68 Nashe, *Strange News*, sig. C3v.
69 Ben Jonson, *Bartholomew Fair*, in Ben Jonson, *'The Alchemist' and Other Plays*, ed. Gordon Campbell (Oxford: Oxford World Classics, 1995), 1.1.30.
70 Nashe, *Strange News*, sig. H3r.
71 Nashe, *Unfortunate Traveller*, sig. A4r.
72 Gabriel Harvey, *Foure letters, and certaine sonnets* (London, 1592), sig. A4r.
73 Nashe, *Strange News*, sig. D3r.
74 Nashe, *Strange News*, sig. D4v.
75 Nashe, *Pierce Penniless*, sig. D4r.
76 Nashe, *Strange News*, sigs E1r and D4v.
77 Nashe, *Strange News*, sig. D4v.
78 Nashe, *Pierce Penniless*, sig. E1r; cf. Nashe, *Strange News*, sig. I2r.
79 Kenneth Friedenreich, 'Nashe's Strange Newes and the Case for Professional Writers', *Studies in Philology*, 71 (1974), 451–72 (p. 466).
80 Halasz, *The Marketplace of Print*, p. 123.
81 Harvey, *Four Letters*, A4r; Nashe, *Strange News*, sig. D3r.
82 Nashe, *Strange News*, sig. H4r.

7
THOMAS NASHE BEYOND THE GRAVE

Rachel Willie

At the height of the Marprelate controversy in the late sixteenth century ephemeral print was used to stage protest against church and state through drawing from established tropes and literary personas. Such personas, Samuel Fallon argues, were central to the development of publicity: 'they were virtual persons called forth by emerging forms of virtual community'.[1] Fallon takes as a starting point the character Pierce Pennilesse, Nashe's 'paper monster' alter ego, to consider how a variety of monsters outgrew their original contexts and had afterlives as charismatic literary personas within the public realm and the marketplace of print. Yet the textual persona of Nashe also outgrew his original context and he and his writing were invoked frequently and reimagined by later audiences. This chapter addresses Thomas Nashe's afterlife to consider the use and abuse of Nashe's literary authority in addressing religious and political controversy in the early 1640s. In the lead-up to civil war and shortly after war broke out, several tracts by John Taylor the Water Poet were printed, each invoking the ghost of Tom Nashe, something that EEBO seems to take all too literally through attributing Nashe as the post-mortem author. Through addressing the literary agency and textual persona of Nashe, each pamphlet takes Nashe from his sixteenth-century context and transplants him into mid-seventeenth-century political discourse. As we will see, both Nashe and the Marprelate controversy are revived in the 1640s as a way to comprehend civil war: Nashe's voice is inexpertly ventriloquised by those more confident with the voice of Marprelate even as they adopt Nashe's authorial persona to support Archbishop William Laud. The first half of this chapter is dedicated to outlining the Marprelate controversy to provide some context for these later writings before considering how Nashe's literary persona is brought into later discourses where parallels between past discords and present discontents are identified. The discussion of the Marprelate controversy is divided into two parts: in the first section I tease out the textual performativity of a tract attributed to Nashe before turning to the broader political and cultural context of the controversy to show some of the points that forged Nashe's literary persona and how his writing was received in the seventeenth century. Through introducing the Marprelate controversy 'backwards' – starting with the specific before moving to the general – the ripples of the Marprelate controversy and Nashe's involvement in it will be more readily identifiable. What I hope to reveal is that the continued legacy of Nashe in the seventeenth century is a complex one that is as much bound up with the Marprelate controversy and its resonances with later religious and political dissent as it is with Nashe's writing.

RAILING IN RHYME: *MAR-MARTINE*

MAR-MARTINE,

I know not why a trueth in rime set out
Maie not as wel mar Martine and his mates
As shameslesse lies in prose-books cast about
Marpriests, & prelates, and subvert whole states
    For where truth builds, and lying overthroes,
    One truth in rime, is worth ten lies in prose.[2]

Thus declares the title page of an anonymous tract printed in 1589 and at one time attributed to Thomas Nashe and/or John Lyly but now attributed to Nashe.[3] Despite this somewhat muddled attribution history, since this tract was understood in the seventeenth century as the work of Nashe, it and similar anti-Martinist tracts feed into Nashe's afterlife and literary persona irrespective of whether they were actually written by him.[4] I have presented the text as it appears on the title page (Figure 7.1) because the way it has been typeset is significant. The clear Roman type is printed without ornament, but even these blank spaces are purposeful since, as Claire Bourne notes, 'setting a piece of type to produce a blank space required of the compositor the same amount of labour as setting a special character like a pilcrow'.[5] The blank space draws attention to the absence of any of the features we might expect to find on a title page – there is no mention of who the author is, or who printed the text (though this is to be expected in the context of the Marprelate controversy), and no other paratextual markers that would tell the reader that this is a title page. Even the purpose the words serve on the title page is ambiguous. A glance at the bibliographical details for the tract on EEBO and on the British Library catalogue present all of the words on the front page as the title of the tract.[6] Yet another entry in the British Library catalogue, of a 1912 reprint, has the title as *Mar-Martine*.[7] The ambiguity is further heightened by the way in which the layout of the bibliographical details on EEBO

MAR-MARTINE,

I know not why a trueth in rime set out
Maie not as wel mar Martine and his mates,
As shamelesse lies in prose-books cast about
Marpriests, & prelates, and subvert whole states.
   For where truth builds, and lying overthroes,
   One truth in rime, is worth ten lies in prose.

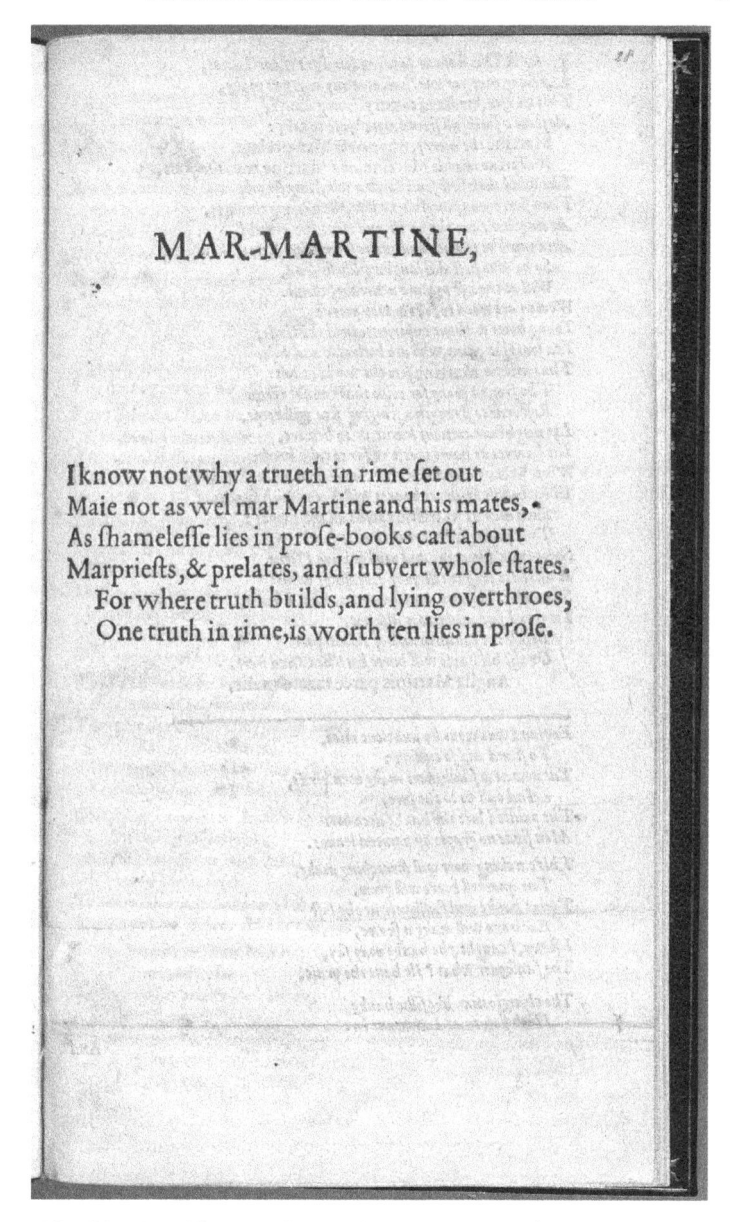

7.1 *Mar-Martine* title page. From *Mar-Martine*. London: [s.n.], 1589; STC [2nd edition] 17461, sig. A1r. RB 62525, The Huntington Library, San Marino, California

and on the library catalogue transforms the poetry into prose. There is a structural precision to the typography that is lost in its replication and this precision correlates rhetorically with the words on the page. In this attention to typesetting, the pamphlet is echoing the Martinists, who used spoof running heads and errata, as well as publication details.[8] For example *Hey Any Work for Cooper*, printed in Coventry by Robert Waldegrave in 1589, states on its title page that it was 'Penned and compiled by *Martin the Metropolitane*', and 'Printed in Europe / not farre from some of the Bounsing Priestes'.[9] What both Martinist and anti-Martinist tracts illustrate is the performative quality of text and how the rhetorical function of typography underpins the argument of the tract.[10]

The poem on the title page of *Mar-Martine* pits poetry against prose, presenting poetry as truth triumphant and battling the deceit embedded in prose. Marprelate tracts are positioned as setting lies in prose in a malicious attempt to overthrow church and state, but the one key truth argued in rhyme can demolish these untruths. Different forms of writing are thus placed in opposition to each other, suggesting that poetic form has a higher intrinsic value than prose works. The page is used as a performative space for a type of railing and invective that, paradoxically perhaps, asserts its refined honesty before the poem continues the argument as laid out on the title page. Instead of the title page catching the eye through decorous ornamentation or through salutary description, it presents its reader with a provocation that gives the argument shape. While it might not 'look' like a title page, it scaffolds the pamphlet by vocalising its substance. As the pamphlet progresses, it works its way through the offices of state, the church, and everyday life to castigate 'Martine, a traitorous Libeler'.[11] Towards the end of the poem, however, a different performative space is invoked:

> These tinkers terms, and barbers jests first Tarlton on the stage,
> Then Martin in his bookes of lies, hath put in every page:
> The common sort of simple swads [country bumpkins], I can there
>   state but pitie:
> That will vouchsafe, or deyne to laugh, at libelle so unwittie.
> Let Martin thinke some pen as badde, some head to be as knavish:
> Some tongue to be as glibbe as his, some rayling all as lavish,
> And be content: if not, because we know not where to finde thee:
> We hope to se thee where deserts of treason have assignd thee.[12]

The previous stanza ends, 'My rithme shall be as dogrell, as unlearned is thy prose', suggesting an equivalency between Martin's prose and the speaker's verse.[13] The preposition 'these' that begins the stanza quoted above ambiguously connects the poetry and prose mentioned at the end of the previous stanza to foolish utterances found in 'tinkers terms' and 'barbers jests'. Textual words and spoken words weave together as words on and off the page influence each other symbiotically. Stage, page, books, and ink are all presented as 'ingredients' for the production of performative spaces, but another performative space is also brought into the narrative: the gibbet. As such railing is presented as an evil that has corrupted all forms of oral and literate culture and can be remedied only through executing the culprits, exposing the ubiquity of a type that Maria Teresa Micaela Prendergast identifies as belonging to a coherent body of railing literature. 'While such texts', Prendergast writes, 'might not constitute a fully articulated genre in their own right, texts dominated by railing do share certain generic traits – traits which ... often contradict each other. These include a strong moral stance, a saucy vituperative persona, hurling invective at a known opponent, and doing so with an arsenal of elaborate rhetorical figures.'[14] *Mar-Martine* revels in these contradictions, castigating writing that has a similar railing tone.

Such hurling of invective and use of elaborate rhetorical figures like 'glibbe tongue' has a distinctly oral feel: words on the page echo words on the stage as Martin is accused of appropriating the tenor of jests that reverberated through the playhouse via the mouth of Richard Tarlton. Given Gabriel Harvey's jibe at Nashe's 'Tarltonizing wit' and the many other references to Tarlton in Marprelate tracts, the referencing of Tarlton here is by no means unique.[15] The reference to Tarlton, paradoxically perhaps, may even have strengthened its connection to Nashe for early readers. As Karen Kettnich reminds us, the persona of Tarlton and his particular brand of clownish, stylised, precise, rehearsed 'spontaneous' extemporising is appropriated frequently in railing texts, even as the name of the celebrated Elizabethan actor was used to discredit opponents. Rhetorically dexterous yet reminiscent of the Vice figure in medieval morality plays, Tarlton's carnivalesque performances could go as far as singling out members of the audience to be the subject of his jests for audience-pleasing laughs. To mimic Tarlton was to debase yourself by producing cheap jibes.[16] *Mar-Martine* criticises such Tarltonising wit, even as the tract appropriates the spirit of such rhetorical dexterity. These rhetorical flourishes outlived the Elizabethan context of the Marprelate controversy, as did Harvey's jibes: although Nashe rejected Harvey's attack, the slur stuck.[17]

While Nashe's style later came to be associated with Tarlton, as the referencing of Tarlton in *Mar-Martine* indicates, Tarlton was also presented as the Lord of Misrule behind the Marprelate tracts. Here we see invective and railing carefully targeted despite the semblance of unstructured rambling. The tract gradually layers points of critique to present carefully crafted argumentation that looks like careless extemporising. An argument is not developed so much as words are unleashed at a breathless pace: the words beg to be uttered aloud and the timbre and texture of the voice add further inflections to the satire. Yet the poem is given structure through horizontal line rules breaking it up into various sections that introduce different poetic metres: visually these line rules help to break up the poem, slowing down the apparently breathless verse on the page, while the use of punctuation further helps to regulate verbal utterances and the pace of the voice in reciting the text. The invective settles with a desire to see Martin brought to justice. Stage, page, and literary personas collide as the carefully crafted narrative and measured rhyme schemes appear to jumble into rambling, borderline inarticulate speech. Prose, poetry, and drama collapse into the personas presented on the page.

The Tarltonising muse thus infuses the aural, textual, and visual structure of the tract, which in turn feeds into Elizabethan politics and poetics. Nashe's wit, Tarlton, and Marprelate become inextricably linked as religion, politics, and poetics collide. The forms of protest forged in the heat of the Marprelate controversy would be recycled in the seventeenth century. To understand how, we first need to consider some of the circumstances that created the paper monster that was Martin Marprelate.

STAGING RELIGIOUS DISSENT: MARTIN MARPRELATE

Since the beginnings of the Church of England, debates over how it should be constituted abounded, coming to a head at various crunch points. One such pressure point came with the appointment of John Whitgift as Archbishop of Canterbury in 1583. Whitgift was a long-standing opponent of Presbyterianism and implemented reforms with the intention of creating conformity in church worship. While those opposed to episcopal worship had been engaged in polemical battles in print for decades, between October 1588 and September 1589 six pamphlets and a broadsheet were printed. Under the pseudonym of Martin Marprelate, the Presbyterian Martinists attacked Whitgift's reaffirmation of episcopacy and endeavours to impose uniformity on the church. While the criticisms laid out in the Marprelate tracts were not exactly new, they were possibly the most sensational attack on episcopal worship to spring from the printing presses in the late sixteenth century. The Martinists primarily satirised bishops, attacking Whitgift's and the church's attempts to suppress nonconformist literature while also calling for reforms in church worship and governance. They appropriated aspects of Menippean discourse such as dialogic confrontation, scandal and lack of decorum in adhering to generic conventions as a way of deriding the Elizabethan Settlement, bishops and episcopal worship.[18] Social levelling prevails and this lack of deference to authority renders the hierarchies present in the episcopal church irrelevant and destroys any claim the bishops may have laid to intellectual and theological authority.

The Marprelate tracts were produced on an underground printing press, angering the bishops and the authorities, who sought out the printers, writers, and those who harboured the Martinists as they moved around the country. On 4 August 1589 some moveable type fell out of a cart near Warrington. John Hodgkins, one of the printers, tried to persuade onlookers that the strange bits of metal 'were shott', but news of the incident spread. About ten days after the printers accidentally dropped their paper bullets at Warrington, the guerrilla press was traced to a safe house near Manchester, three printers were arrested, and the Marprelate controversy began to come to an end.[19] One final tract was produced in September 1589. Prior to this and as the printing and circulation of the tracts was gathering momentum, Richard Bancroft suggested that the bishops should bring in the paid expertise of professional writers such as Nashe, John Lyly, Anthony Munday, and Robert Greene to fight fire with fire, and Gabriel Harvey 'wrote on the side of "proper authority"' of his own volition.[20] What resulted were a series of pamphlets that both appropriated and derided the rhetoric of the Martinists, which, Alexandra Halasz argues, attempted to reaffirm the position of the orator within discursive fields that were no longer confined to highly literate audiences moulded by institutional spaces.[21] Rejecting the well-honed rhetoric that underpinned the humanist education of the sixteenth-century universities, these tracts played nastily with their adversaries. In so doing they attempted – and partially succeeded – in realigning the discourse back into an authority-conscious sense of the carnivalesque and the grotesque.[22] Anti-Martinists more readily flirted with the grotesque, bodily deformity, and monstrous births. As Jason Scott-Warren notes, Nashe, in particular, gave body to Marprelate.[23] But, as Marprelate's description of the conception of his textual adversary Mar-Martin attests, Marprelate also revelled in this type of satire:

> from Saraum came a gooses egg
> with specks and spots bespatched
> A priest of Lambeth coutcht thereon:
> thus was Mar-Martin hatched[24]

The Sarum Missal was primarily used in the English church before the introduction of the Book of Common Prayer; the grotesque imagery of the Catholic rite producing a fool's (goose's) egg on which an unnamed Archbishop of Canterbury – presumably Whitgift – copulates to produce the monstrous Mar-Martin, coupled with the ABCB rhyming scheme, lends the narrative an absurd playfulness, but it also reinforces the satire of the prose that precedes it in the pamphlet. The tract as a whole serves as both a counterattack on Mar-Martin and a criticism of social hierarchies and wealth.

Andrew Hadfield notes how Benedict Anderson's pathbreaking investigation into the origins of nationalism has been criticised for failing to grasp how print culture and the mass circulation of news have a longer prehistory than Anderson's study suggests.[25] Partly taking his cue from Anderson, Hadfield provocatively traces the relationship between literature and class through historical crunch points and how class conflict is represented in English literature to put pressure on our understanding of how class functions in the premodern period. The context of the Marprelate controversy would certainly seem to back Hadfield's contentions, as the tenor of the tracts create imagined communities that reflect on wealth and class as well as church and state, and this can also be seen in Nashe's work.[26] As Lorna Hutson observes, Nashe abandoned 'the protestant-humanist notion of reading for profit to pursue his own "festive" notion of reading as a recreative purgation of received images and ideas' pretty much at the start of his career and instead favoured Menippean satire.[27] Such recreative purgation suggests a symbiotic relationship between the Marprelate tracts and the development of Nashe's notoriously slippery style. There is a precision to the festive satire that brings protest into the marketplace. Ironically, in hiring wits to appropriate and develop the rhetoric adopted by the Martinists, the bishops did not gain control of the debate. Rather they temporarily allowed a liminal space to be created that moved beyond the traditional boundaries of authority and the home. In moving beyond Protestant-humanist rhetoric to instead develop and revel in an exchange that is designed to inform, misinform, and entertain the reading public, the Marprelate controversy spoke to its readers in a way that could never be controlled fully by Elizabethan censorship. Where the Martinists subverted the licensing regulations, the anti-Martinists attempted to beat them at their own rhetorical game. Such satiric imagery would be echoed in the 1630s and early 1640s, where anti-Laudian libels would figure the hapless archbishop as the devil incarnate, vomiting up books, eating the ears of those who criticised him, or being locked in a bird cage.[28]

As well as echoing the Marprelate controversy, some adopted the persona of Marprelate or of the anti-Martinists as a way of directly responding to the religious and political climate of the mid-seventeenth century. In the 1640s (and in the Restoration) some of the Marprelate tracts were reprinted and their rhetorical strategies were redeployed in the new political context.[29] This illustrates how remembrance of previous events can feed into the present: the Elizabethan past collides with the Stuart present and any sense of teleological or chronological difference collapses under the weight of contemporary anxieties regarding the place and function of church and state. Yet it also shows us the possibilities for satire to be recycled and reappropriated as a way of making sense of different political and cultural moments. Writing of the relationship between literary works, memory and culture, Astrid Erll notes how literary genres encode our understanding of cultural memory: 'Literature', Erll writes, 'takes up existing patterns, shapes and transforms them, and feeds them back into memory culture'.[30] Genres too shape cultural memory and remembrance:

> Genres are also a method of dealing with challenges that is [sic] faced a memory culture. In uncommon, difficult, or dangerous circumstances it is especially traditional or strongly conventionalized genres which writers draw upon in order to provide familiar and meaningful patterns of representation for experiences that would otherwise be hard to interpret. For example, in late-nineteenth-century British fictions of empire, the genre patterns of romance provided a ready format for dealing with colonial anxieties ... By the same token, the emergence of new genres can also be understood as an answer to mnemonic challenges.[31]

Erll's wide-ranging study provides a brief history of memory studies and its social, cultural, historiographical, material, and psychological institutions before turning to media and literature, but what I am most interested in here is how memory studies and literary studies can help us to understand the connections between the Marprelate controversy and later social and civil unrest. Dermot Cavanagh has traced three distinct phases of prose satire in the sixteenth century, starting with Erasmus's *Praise of Folly* (1509; printed 1511 and translated into English by Thomas Chaloner in 1549), then Stephen Gosson's *The School of Abuse* (1579) followed by Nashe, *Christ's Tears over Jerusalem* (1594) and *The Unfortunate Traveller* (1594).[32] What emerges is 'the capacity to scrutinize contemporary values is a crucial quality of sixteenth-century satire', enabling it to interrogate received wisdom about the relationship between authority and morality.[33] These intertextual and generic resonances illustrate how the prehistory of the Marprelate tracts was forged not only in the heat of religious controversies and polemical debate but also in the literary forms that circulated in the sixteenth century. The long, stuffy polemics that provided the Martinists with fuel for their satirical pens were also not immune from colloquial and satiric flourishes: while many scholars have noted the dry tedium of John Bridge's *c*. fifteen-hundred-page *Defence of the Government Established in the Church of Englande for Ecclesiastical Matters* (1587), Eric Vivier has drawn attention to how aspects of Marprelate rhetoric were indebted to the *Defence*, despite or perhaps because it was frequently ridiculed by the Martinists.[34] The satire in these forms of writing thus clings to a type of literary tradition while simultaneously breaking the decorum of public discourse: the Marprelate tracts are embedded within genre patterns well-established in prose even as they emerge as a form of radical political and doctrinal protest that is indebted to colloquial extemporising derived from the stage and especially Tarlton's jigs. The nebulous quality of the tracts within memory culture meant that, by the 1640s, the radicalism of Marprelate had become tradition and therefore could be used as a way of understanding Stuart controversies. Some Marprelate tracts were thus reissued and Thomas Nashe also made a ghostly appearance.

THE GHOSTS OF NASHE AND OF MARPRELATE IN THE 1640S

When William Laud was appointed Archbishop of Canterbury in 1633, he began instigating unpopular reforms in church worship, which proved disastrous when he attempted to impose episcopal worship on Presbyterian Scotland. Tensions abounded until in 1639 the Bishops' Wars broke out between Scotland and England. While the Archbishop had the support of the King, he did not have the confidence of Parliament. In 1641 he was impeached and imprisoned in the tower of London. When discontent with Charles's reign eventually led to the outbreak of civil war in 1642, Laud's position became even more precarious and the hapless prelate was executed for treason in 1645.[35]

This brief summary of Laud's later career and death inevitably skips over much detail and offers no room for caveats, but I am mostly concerned with how Laudian reforms were perceived as bringing the Church of England closer to Catholicism, something that even Pope Urban VIII seems to have recognised as, in 1633, he twice offered to make Laud a cardinal.[36] While Laud asserted his opposition to Roman Catholicism, his critics censured him for his 'Catholic' reforms: those opposed to Laud seized upon parallels between Whitgift's endeavours at uniformity in the late sixteenth century and Laudian reforms in the mid-seventeenth century. Laud's aim was to restore the church to its 'first Reformation' and appealing to Elizabethan precedent allowed Laudian reforms to be packaged as a conservative return to the church's founding principles.[37] Yet this also meant the types of satire used to attack Elizabethan reforms could be recycled to critique Laud. Both Laud and his detractors believed they were upholding the traditional values of the Church of England, even if the ultimate result of Laudian reforms meant that the fragile Jacobean consensus collapsed and 'Elizabethan ecclesiastical tradition' effectively became marginalised.[38] A tension arose between two polarising factions that both laid claim to (and drew from) ecclesiastical and literary tradition as a means of asserting the integrity of their way of practising faith. The ghostly ventriloquised voice of Nashe was heard in these debates. John Taylor, in particular, revelled in his self-styled persona as inheritor of the Nashean mantle; one way he drew from Nashe was to appropriate the ghost of Nashe to be the authority figure who offers commentary on religious and political discontents. Taylor was not unique in producing tracts by the ghosts of dead figures: in the 1640s and 1650s, conversations were staged between the ghosts of Charles I, Oliver Cromwell, Thomas Wentworth Earl of Strafford, Henry VIII, and many more.[39] Perhaps what makes Taylor's ghost unique is that, in assuming the persona of Nashe, Taylor is appealing to literary authority rather than political authority. As Michelle O'Callaghan has argued in her reading of Taylor's positioning of Thomas Coryate as a Gabriel Harvey to Taylor's Nashe, the binaries between the learned scholar poet and the unlearned sculler or water poet (and between elite culture and popular culture) are not as clear as they may at first appear.[40] This fluidity between 'educated' and 'uneducated', 'popular' and 'elite' is also present in how writers engaged with mid-seventeenth century politics. Taylor frequently references Nashe in his political commentaries as a way of asserting his textual and literary authority, and gains influence in print through constructing a connection between himself and the Elizabethan wit. This is, perhaps, most forcibly apparent in two tracts, *Differing Worships, or The Odds, Between some Knight's Service and God's. Or Tom Nash His Ghost (The Old Martin Queller) Newly Roused, and Is Come to Chide and Take Order with Non Conformists, Schismatics, Separatists, and Scandalous Libellers*, and *Crop-ear Curried, or Tom Nash His Ghost*. Printed in 1640 and 1644 respectively, these two texts establish a connection between Nashe and Taylor as a way of engaging with contemporary anxieties regarding church and state. *Differing Worships* defends episcopal worship and the Church of England against what is perceived as the twin evils of Catholicism and Presbyterianism. The pamphlet details kneeling in prayer and as part of worship, anointing with the sign of the cross in baptism, and the wearing of surplices by priests to argue that such displays of faith conform with the scriptures and the 'authentique old' ways of practising faith.[41] The pamphlet criticises nonconformists who pretend to follow Calvinist doctrine but fail to grasp Calvin's teachings. Far from adhering to Calvinism, proponents of 'severe Geneva Anarchie'[42] must learn humility and kneel to their God:

> Those unkneeling saucy Separatists
> Are often falsly called Calvinists:
> For master Calvin's flat against their side;
> And they are all from his directions wide[43]

Anabaptists, Presbyterians, and those practising the various other forms of Christianity that emerged in the mid-seventeenth century are conflated under the umbrella title of 'Schismatique Separatists'.[44] Their failure to adhere to what the pamphlet identified as the traditional and authentic modes of worship as articulated by Richard Hooker and Whitgift along with the canons and ordinances passed during the reigns of Elizabeth I and her successor to the English throne, James, are here attacked. Tellingly, Taylor refers to the separatists as holding 'Amsterdamnable opinions'.[45]

According to a deposition of 1589, an unnamed Dutchman sold a printing press to John Penry, one of the Martinists.[46] Many illicit books were printed in Amsterdam, including reprints of Elizabethan pamphlets.[47] In his study of Dutch responses to the execution of Charles I in 1649, Helmer Helmers has illustrated how the relationships between the Low Countries and England were complex and close, binding each nation together in a political and cultural Anglo-Dutch public sphere.[48] Whereas later writers sought to establish a geographical connection between a paradoxical royalist republic and defeated royalists, here 'Amsterdamnable opinions' establishes a geographical and temporal connection between Martinists and later English and European nonconformists where the Netherlands becomes the space for ecclesiastical sin. However, the pamphlet also turns its satire to Catholicism, asserting that Catholics are equally blameworthy as they have moved away from the true tenets of Christianity:

> The Romish Church was Right, for many yeares,
> Till ('mongst the wheat) the Envious men sow'd tares:
> Wherefore we first began to leave her quite,
> When shee began to mingle wrong with right[49]

In this reading the Church of England becomes a way of sanitising Catholicism of the corruption that has gradually infiltrated its offices. Kneeling and making the sign of the cross in baptism are therefore rightfully used as part of church worship by good Christians, despite the long association with Catholicism of these forms of ritual. Although the wearing of the surplice by those in holy orders is, in the pamphlet, presented as a 'Romish' invention, it is sanitised of this association because 'when the Church was in her prime perfection, / This vestment was ordain'd by good direction'.[50] The colour white's biblical associations with purity and the surplice's connection to early Christian martyrs means that, contrary to what those opposed to Laud's 'Catholicising' of the Church of England may think, his reforms enable the Church to negotiate safely what are perceived to be the twin evils of nonconformism and Catholicism. In making these claims Taylor is making assertions about the public nature of worship. Church ritual is called into question and Taylor firmly sides with Laud and projects himself as the upholder of tradition. By invoking the memory of Nashe and of the Marprelate controversy Taylor is underpinning this sense of being the gatekeeper of the authentic church by suggesting that the Church of England is in constant need of a textual bodyguard. Nashe served this function in the previous generation and Taylor is both the inheritor and the guardian of this kind of engagement with ecclesiastical politics; Taylor becomes the protector of true governance in church and state. Four years later Taylor was to make this role more emphatic with the publication of *Crop-ear Curried*. Here, we see a shift from the focus upon church reforms to offer censure and commentary upon parliamentarian concerns. The eponymous 'Crop-Eare' who finds himself curried is William Prynne. Eleven years previously Prynne had offended the court through the publication of his lengthy anti-stage play diatribe *Histriomastix* as the Crown had read it as a covert attack on Henrietta Maria and her ladies in waiting who performed amateur dramatics at court.[51] For his efforts Prynne was duly fined, imprisoned, had his tongue split and his ears cropped. From the tower, a sympathetic gaolor kindly helped Prynne to continue circulating his texts. This earned Prynne a branding and further mutilation of his ears. The punishment of Prynne was judged by many contemporaries as too severe and the resultant public outcry – including satires against Laud – was a contributory factor in the Archbishop's downfall.[52] Taylor, however, presents Prynne as a far from sympathetic figure.

The title page to *Crop-ear Curried* asserts that it serves the function of mutilating Prynne's text in a similar manner to which the Crown set about relieving the lawyer of his ears:

> Crop-Eare Curried. Or *Tom Nash* His Ghost, Declaring the pruning of *Prinnes* two last Parricidicall Pamphlets, being 92 Sheets in *Quarto*, wherein the one of them he stretch'd the Soveraigne Power of Parliament; in the other, his new-found way of opening the counterfeit Great Seale.[53]

Here Prynne's tracts are dismissed because Prynne's writing assumes Parliament holds authority. The sheer length of Prynne's texts becomes a means of ridiculing him and reducing his significance and the intellectual integrity of his arguments. However, far from pruning the text, the title page then goes on to advertise that the rebuttal takes the form of 'a short survey and ani-mad-versions of some of his falsities, fooleries, non-sense blasphemies'.[54] Contradictions abound as Taylor insists that he is both cropping Prynne's text and appropriating the format of the lengthy animadversion to engage with, and refute, Prynne's arguments. Yet Taylor is selective in his recourse to Prynne and the animadversion proves a fragmentary and incomplete rebuttal of Prynne's text. Loosely connecting to the appropriation of Menippean discourse and under the supervision of Nashe's ghost, Taylor subverts the generic conventions of the animadversion and in so doing negates the lengthy prose style of Prynne.

Nashe's ghost does not only serve as the persona through which the rebuttal is served. The pamphlet echoes and inverts the opening of Shakespeare's *Richard III* by setting the scene 'In this Mad, Sad, Cold Winter of discontent'.[55] Such a scene is ripe for spectral hauntings and what, in Chapter 5 above, Chris Salamone terms the 'spectral threat of satire'.[56] The spectre of Marprelate also haunts the tract: as Joad Raymond notes, in *Crop-ear Curried* Taylor identifies 'Elizabethan contention over reformed church government' and the Marprelate controversy as marking the origins of pamphlet wars in the mid seventeenth century.[57] Taylor marries allusion to the stage with textual spectres as the apparition of Nashe implores for a rebuttal of Prynne's work:

> Concerning William Prinne, he hath lately write two damnable and detestable Books, stuft with as much Hipocrysie Villany, Rebellion and Treason as the Malice of the Divill, and his own mischievous braine could invent ... *Jack* (kind *Jack*) I Conjure three to take this Railing fellow in hand, look upon his wicked works, view his villanies, squeeze the Quintessence of his eighty and odde sheets of printed Confusion into 12 leaves in Quarto, that the abominable charge or his worthlesse high priz'd Volumes (at ten or twelve shillings) may by thee be Epitomized, Abreviated, and Curtall'd in Bulk, and price to six-pence a peece. Fear not, go on Boldly. I will leave my *Genius* with thee, which shall Inspire thee, and infuse into thee such Terrible, Torturing, Tormenting, Termagant flames and flashes as shall Firk, Ferret and force Prinne and his partners run quite out of that little wit that is left them, and desperately save the Hangman a Labour, farewell.[58]

Central to the notorious quarrel between Nashe and Harvey was a sense that literary discernment had broken down.[59] In *Pierce Penniless* (1592) Nash laments how 'every grosse braind Idiot is suffered to come into print' while scholars are unable to earn a living by the pen.[60] Prynne's sulphur-riddled books, infused with devilish art, would seem to be further example of how an indiscriminate reading public has been infected with detestable books. Prynne's books are 'stuft', implying a lack of discernment by the author to regulate their prose in part due to their diabolical muse. But this conversation between the quick and the dead, where the ghostly Nashe 'conjures' the living Taylor to vanquish Prynne, suggests Prynne is not the only writer to be influenced by devilish art. The abrasive and alliterative infusing of Taylor with Nashe's '*Genius*' to drive Prynne and his associates to a painful death before they can be executed for treason suggests a desire to restore literary order to print, yet, ultimately, this decorum is negated through one 'railing fellow' being replaced by another.

A ghostly Nashe thus lays down the gauntlet to Taylor. Nashe's pseudo-absence facilitates a textual presence when Taylor is handed the Nashean authorial identity and voice to truncate and refute Prynne's pamphlets.[61] By rendering Prynne's prose into cheap print Taylor will negate its market value and transform it from costly tome to an ephemeral text. However, this also means that Prynne's words will be more readily available to a wider audience through its broader circulation in the marketplace. Far from diminishing the importance of Prynne's pamphlets, Taylor's glosses add a sense of urgency to the tracts and enforce the view that they are a matter for public debate.

In dismissing Prynne's arguments, Taylor looks to the past as a way of supporting his refutations. Yet again precedence, tradition, and biblical exegesis are invoked as a way of challenging Prynne. The dual epistemological stalwarts of tradition and the Bible become a means of verifying the credibility (or lack thereof) of Prynne's arguments, but Nashe's presence lends the text a literary authority that draws Taylor's work into Nashe's literary canon even as, rhetorically, Taylor's texts are distinctly unNashean in style. This is further emphasised by the prophecy upon which the tract ends. Not content with refuting the claims of the 'running-witted, rolling-headed, raling-tongu'd, rattle-brain'd Roundhead', Taylor foretells 'The king shall prevail in the end'.[62] Conflating early modern cosmographical truths with classical mythology and the current political moment, Taylor imagines a future where Prynne (presented as the offspring of a Centaur) and his ilk are thwarted. Past, present, future, and the mythological all conjoin as Taylor seeks to gain a textual victory over critics of the King. However, Taylor also alludes to the commercial nature of the printed word:

> and although Lilbourne the Libeller, or a Mushroom hatched by this blazing star in the blacke Night of sedition, and that sincere upright verst man Withers with the rest of the Rabble of railing Poets be retained in fee by the Rebells to write weekly Lyes for them: yet Tom Nash his Ghost returning to this Charon, with some distilled wilde-fire-water in an inke-horne, shall provide such a whip for this proud Horse, such a Bridle for this senseless Asse, and such a rod for this mad fooles backe, as shall tame Cerberus[63]

Harking back to the kinds of insult-throwing that became a characteristic of the Marprelate controversy and the Nashean grotesque, Taylor renders those who write for the parliamentarians as deformed beasts. Taylor fulfils the function of detractor, but only until Nashe's ghost rises again. With his 'wilde-fire-water' – possibly an allusion to the rumour that Nashe drank aqua vitae with gunpowder to 'inspire his malicious spirit with rayling matter'[64] – Nashe will tame the beast of sedition and mete out painful punishments through instilling the pen with a railing voice. Nashe thus becomes the order-restoring focal point of the narrative, but 'wilde-fire-water in an inke-horne' also focuses attention on the physicality of writing and the capacity for it to be a messy and error-fuelled activity where words are deliberately scratched out or accidentally blotted out through ink spills. Inkhorn additionally suggests inkhornism, or a love of pedantic language infused with neologism.[65] The inkhorn evokes a scholarly industry that seems to be at odds with the marketplace, which is further underscored by the reference to the 'Rabble of railing poets' being in the employ of Parliament. Mercantile transactions underpin the production and reproduction of these texts, but this in turn reminds the reading public through inference that Nashe's interventions in the Marprelate controversy were also commissioned.

The pamphlet thus begins by staging a visitation by Nashe's ghost and ends with a prophecy that Nashe's spirit will return to spar with the King's adversaries. Such representations assert Nashe's considerable textual authority. In being constructed as an authority figure this representation of Nashe becomes a means of establishing a connection between mid seventeenth-century political conflict and the past, but in lacking physicality within the corporeal world, the textual apparition is not tied to current affairs and can therefore also be used to imagine a future where the parliamentarians have been defeated. Tradition and prophecy conjoin to assert the integrity of the royalist cause. The fact that parliamentarian writers also looked to precedent as a means of asserting their position does not negate this. Rather, it emphasises the plurality of voice and textual performances as the authority of Nashe's literary persona is affirmed.

To varying degrees Nashe becomes the focal point of anxieties regarding how to construct satirical images of those in conflict with church and Crown. This is further emphasised by an anonymous tract, printed first in York and then in London around 1642. This final pamphlet has also been attributed to Taylor and, as with the other pamphlets, *Tom Nash His Ghost* affords Nashe textual authority in the past and the present.[66] In the pamphlet Nashe appears before 'Anabaptists, Libertines and Brownists' and remonstrates with them regarding their rejection of the Book of Common Prayer.[67] Directly alluding to the Marprelate controversy, the tract establishes a teleological connection between Martinist error and anti-Laudian strife. However, the text is also prefaced with a poem that directly engages with the textual/spectral Tom Nash's lack of physical form:

> I am a Ghost, and Ghosts doe feare no Lawes;
> Nor doe they care for popular Applause:
> I liv'd a Poet poore, long time agoe;
> And (living a poore Poet) I dy'd so.
> ...
> In those dayes, we had desperate madmen here,
> Who did the Queene, State, Church and Kingdom jeere.
> And now a Crew are up as wise as those
> Who do all Rule and Government oppose.
> In those dayes I did bring those men in frame;
> An not my Ghost is come to doe the same[68]

Nashe thus comes to harangue the inheritors of Martinist strife. The textual warfare occurs because discontents with the Caroline church and state are believed to directly echo Elizabethan controversy. Nashe's experiences of the Marprelate controversy mean he is depicted as having special insights that can only aid his successors in refuting latter-day Martinists. However, the opening couplet asserts that Nashe holds authority beyond that afforded to him as a poster boy of the Marprelate controversy. Nashe may trouble himself with Caroline affairs, but he is not troubled by concerns of the corporeal. Since he no longer inhabits a place in the material world, neither the law nor a desire to gain popularity from the reading public can inhibit his words. Unlike living critics the ghostly Nashe is presented as being able to write pamphlets comprising universal truths and unbiased appraisals of ecclesiastical and state controversy. The pamphlet speaks to cultural memory and claims its veracity through ventriloquising Nashe and by blending the political events of the dead poet's past with the anonymous living author's present.

A SWEET SATYRICK VAIN?

In the opening to *God and Mammon* (1646) Samuel Sheppard reflects on the power of words. Echoing an invocation to the muses, Sheppard seeks 'purpose' to 'inspire' his mind. Listing various rhetorical strategies to combat hypocrisy, 'a sweet Satyrick vain' is called upon, but one that is 'Better then ere flow'd from the quill of Nash'.[69] Once again the persona of Nashe is invoked, but here Nashe is presented as someone whose prose is to be emulated and surpassed. Whereas the ghost pamphlets assert Nashe's prominence as the universal truth-sayer and slayer of the kinds of folly that breeds discontent within the body politic, Sheppard resituates Nashe as a writer with his own distinct voice. Conversely the ghost narratives assert that, post-mortem, Nashe has no definable place in the public realm and this affords him a privileged position. However, this very attempt to eschew publics becomes a form of performativity that reaffirms the drama of print and Nashe's Tarltonising wit. By actively engaging with contemporary debates these texts embrace textual performativity, railing, and invective. John Taylor's pamphlets may be more broadly indebted to Marprelate than to Nashe stylistically, but, in giving Nashe's apparition a voice, later writers (to reshape Erll's observations) took up Nashe's rhetorical patterns, reshaped, and transformed them, before feeding them back on to the page and into memory culture.

NOTES

I would like to thank Joseph Black, Douglas Clark, Chloe Preedy, and Kirsty Rolfe for their comments on an earlier draft of this chapter.

1 Samuel Fallon, *Paper Monsters: Persona and Literary Culture in Elizabethan England* (Philadelphia: University of Pennsylvania Press, 2019), p. 17.
2 *Mar-Martine* [1589], title page [sig. A1r], STC 17461.
3 The text's attribution to Nashe and Lyly stems from R. Warwick Bond's 1902 edition of the complete works of Lyly (*Complete Works of John Lyly*, ed. R. Warwick Bond, 3 vols (Oxford: Clarendon, 1902), I:387–8). Ronald McKerrow de-attributes Nashe (see 'The Marprelate Controversy' in *The Works of Thomas Nashe*, ed. R. B. McKerrow, 2nd edn, rev. F. P. Wilson, 5 vols (Oxford: Basil Blackwell, 1958), V.34–65 (p. 63)); however, in the forthcoming *Complete Works of Thomas Nashe* Joseph Black re-attributes Nashe, making a compelling case for him being the sole author. Shared by Joseph Black in personal correspondence (April 2023).
4 Alexandra Halasz, *The Marketplace of Print: Pamphlets and the Public Sphere in Early Modern England* (Cambridge: Cambridge University Press, 1997), p. 85.
5 Claire L. Bourne, *Typographies of Performance in Early Modern England* (Oxford: Oxford University Press, 2020), p. 71.
6 *I know not why a trueth in rime set out Maie not as wel mar Martine and his mates, As shamelesse lies in prose-books cast about Marpriests & prelates, and subvert whole states. For where truth builds and lying overthroes, One truth in rime, is worth ten lies in prose.* [By T. Nashe?] Martin Marprelate [London?], [1589]. BL Shelfmark 702.g.20.
7 *Mar-Martine* [A reprint of the complete text of the tract, the authorship of which is here attributed to John Lyly and Thomas Nash, together with the text of 'Marre Mar-Martin,' an anonymous rejoinder to the above. With an introduction by T. G. Crippen. Reprinted from the Transactions of the Congregational Historical Society]. BL Shelfmark 11630.ee.20. An additional textual muddle comes from the fact that another tract missing the terminal 'e' in its title, *Mar-Martin*, was also printed in 1589, the opening stanza of which castigates 'a frutelesse lye in print', whether that print be poetry or prose (*Mar-Martin* (London, 1589), STC 17461.5, sig. A1r).

8 Joad Raymond, *Pamphlets and Pamphleteering in Early Modern Britain* (Cambridge: Cambridge University Press, 2003), p. 40. Raymond gives *Oh Read Over D. John Bridges, for it is a Worthy Worke: or an epitome of the fyrste booke, of that right worshipfull volume, written against the puritanes, in the defence of the noble cleargie, by as worshipfull a prieste, Iohn Bridges* (London, 1588), more commonly known as *The Epistle* as an example of one of the two tracts with a spoof list of errata. See also *The Martin Marprelate Tracts*, ed. Joseph L. Black (Cambridge University Press, 2008), pp. xxiiii–xxix.

9 Attributed to Job Throckmorton and John Penry, *Hay any worke for Cooper: or a briefe pistle directed by waye of an hublication to the reverende byshopps counselling them, if they will needs be barrelled vp, for feare of smelling in the nostrels of her Maiestie [and] the state, that they would use the aduise of reuerend Martin, for the prouiding of their cooper* ([Coventry, 1589]), title page, sig. A1r.

10 Jennifer Richards notes that Nashe has a similar attentiveness to page layout and the connections this has with performance and Nashe's oralism. See Richards, *Voices and Books in the English Renaissance: A New History of Reading* (Oxford: Oxford University Press, 2019), p. 241.

11 *Mar-Martine*, sig. A4v.

12 *Mar-Martine*, sig. A4v, italics inverted.

13 *Mar-Martine*, sig. A4v.

14 Maria Teresa Micaela Prendergast, *Railing, Reviling, and Invective in English Literary Culture, 1588–1617: The Anti-Poetics of Theatre and Print* (Farnham: Ashgate, 2012), p. 2.

15 Gabriel Harvey, *Foure letters, and certaine sonnets* (London, 1592), sig. E2v.

16 Kettnich, 'Nashe's Extemporal Vein and his Tarltonizing Wit', in *The Age of Thomas Nashes: Text, Bodies and Trespasses of Authorship in Early Modern England*, ed. Stephen Guy-Bray, Joan Pong Linton, and Steve Mentz (Farnham: Ashgate, 2013), pp. 99–114 (p. 103). See also *The Martin Marprelate Tracts*, ed. Black, xxvii.

17 Kettnich, 'Nashe's Extemporal Vein and his Tarltonizing Wit', p. 113.

18 Joseph Navitsky, 'Disputing Good Bishop's English: Martin Marprelate and the Voice of Menippean Opposition', *Texas Studies in Literature and Language*, 50 (2008), 177–200. For an account of Nashean 'literary theory' and how this connects to Menippean satire and rhetoric see Lorna Hutson, *Thomas Nashe in Context* (Oxford: Oxford University Press, 1989), chapters 6 and 7.

19 There are numerous summaries of the Marprelate controversy, the most authoritative of which is Black's introduction to *The Martin Marprelate Tracts*. See also Joseph Black, 'The Marprelate Controversy', in *The Oxford Handbook of English Prose*, ed. Andrew Hadfield (Oxford: Oxford University Press, 2013), pp. 544–59. Other studies include Leland H. Carson, *Martin Marprelate, Gentleman: Master Job Throkmorton Laid Open in his Colors* (San Marino: Huntingdon Library, 1981), pp. 8–21 and 210–36; Antoinina Bevan Zlatar, *Reformation Fictions: Polemical Protestant Dialogues in Elizabethan England* (Oxford: Oxford University Press, 2011), pp. 167–75.

20 Halasz, *The Marketplace of Print*, p. 86. Conversely Prendergast observes that, despite appearing relatively neutral, Harvey 'showed respect for the Martinists (Prendergast, *Railing, Reviling, and Invective*, p. 76).

21 Halasz, *The Marketplace of Print*, pp. 86–7.

22 The classic study on the carnivalesque remains Mikhail Bakhtin's *Rabelais and His World*, trans. Hélène Iswolsky (Bloomington: Indiana University Press, 1984). In her discussion of Shakespeare's Falstaff as a carnivalesque figure inspired by elements

of Martin Marprelate and the Lollard Sir John Oldcastle, Kristen Poole establishes Martin Marprelate as the carnivalesque Puritan, noting that the Marprelate Tracts caused the 'greatest harm' to the clergy through 'not taking them seriously' (Poole, *Radical Religion from Shakespeare to Milton: Figures of Nonconformity in Early Modern England* (Cambridge: Cambridge University Press, 2000), p. 23).

23 Jason Scott-Warren, 'Nashe's Stuff', in *The Oxford Handbook of English Prose, 1500–1640*, ed. Andrew Hadfield (Oxford: Oxford University Press, 2013), pp. 204–18 (p. 205).

24 *The iust censure and reproofe of Martin Iunior. Wherein the rash and undiscreete headines of the foolish youth, is sharply mette with, and the boy hath his lesson taught him, I warrant you, by his reverend and elder brother, Martin Senior, sonne and heire unto the renowmed Martin Mar-prelate the Great. Where also, least the springall shold be utterly discouraged in his good meaning, you shall finde, that hee is not bereaved of his due commendations* (1589), sig. D3r.

25 Andrew Hadfield, *Literature and Class: From the Peasants' Revolt until the French Revolution* (Manchester: Manchester University Press, 2021), p. 13. See also Benedict Anderson, *Imagined Communities: Reflections on the Origin and Spread of Nationalism* (London: Verso, 1983).

26 Hadfield notes how many writers, including Nashe, can be considered in relation to 'shifting/unstable class positions' and how 'Class was a significant and obvious factor in the lives of most writers, structuring their relationship to everyday reality' (p. 126).

27 Hutson, *Thomas Nashe in Context*, p. 120 and esp. chapters 6 and 7.

28 For discussions of anti-Laudian satires and visual culture see Helen Pierce, 'Anti-Episcopacy and Graphic Satire in England, 1640–1645', *The Historical Journal*, 4 (2004), 809–48; Rachel Willie, 'Sensing the Visual (Mis)representation of William Laud', *SPELL: Swiss Papers in English Language and Literature*, 34 (2017), 183–210.

29 Raymond, *Pamphlets and Pamphleteering*, p. 125, pp. 211–13 and pp. 365–8; *The Martin Marprelate Tracts*, ed. Black, pp. lxxxv–lxxix.

30 Astrid Erll, *Memory in Culture*, trans. Sara B. Young (Basingstoke: Palgrave, 2011), p. 148.

31 Erll, *Memory in Culture*, pp. 148–9.

32 Dermot Cavanagh, 'Modes of Satire', in *The Oxford Handbook of English Prose, 1500–1640*, ed. Andrew Hadfield (Oxford: Oxford University Press, 2013), pp. 380–95.

33 Cavanagh, 'Modes of Satire', p. 382.

34 Eric D. Vivier, 'John Bridges, Martin Marprelate, and the Rhetoric of Satire', *ELR*, 44 (2014), 3–35.

35 For biographies of Laud see Charles Carlton, *Archbishop William Laud* (London: Routledge, 1987), Hugh Trevor Roper, *Archbishop Laud*, 3rd edn (Basingstoke: Palgrave Macmillan, 1988), and Anthony Milton's *ODNB* entry ('Laud, William (1573–1645), Archbishop of Canterbury', *ONDB* (Oxford: Oxford University Press, 2009), https://www.oxforddnb.com/view/10.1093/ref:odnb/9780198614128.001.0001/odnb-9780198614128-e-16112.

36 William Laud, *The history of the troubles and tryal of the Most Reverend Father in God and blessed martyr, William Laud, Lord Arch-Bishop of Canterbury wrote by himself during his imprisonment in the Tower; to which is prefixed the diary of his own life* (London, 1695), sig. Gggg4v.

37 Kenneth Fincham, 'Episcopal Government, 1603–1640', in *The Early Stuart Church, 1603–1642*, ed. Kenneth Fincham (Basingstoke: Macmillan, 1993), pp. 71–92 (pp. 77–80).

38 Anthony Milton, 'The Church of England, Rome and the True Church: The Demise of a Jacobean Consensus', in *The Early Stuart Church, 1603–1642*, ed. Kenneth Fincham (Basingstoke: Macmillan, 1993), pp. 187–210 (p. 203).

39 For discussions of these see, for example, Laura Lunger Knoppers, *Constructing Cromwell: Ceremony, Portrait and Print, 1645–1661* (Cambridge: Cambridge University Press, 2000); Elizabeth Sauer, 'Paper Contestations' and Textual Communities in England, 1640–1675 (Toronto: University of Toronto Press, 2005); Raymond; Rachel Willie, *Staging the Revolution: Drama, Reinvention and History, 1647–72* (Manchester: Manchester University Press, 2015), pp. 52–79; Susan Wiseman, *Drama and Politics in the English Civil War* (Cambridge: Cambridge University Press, 1998).

40 Michelle O'Callaghan, '"Thomas the Scholer" versus "John the Sculler": Defining Popular Culture in the Early Seventeenth Century', in *Literature and Popular Culture in Early Modern England*, ed. Matthew Dimmock and Andrew Hadfield (Farnham: Ashgate, 2009), pp. 45–56.

41 John Taylor, *Differing worships* (London, 1640), sig. C2v. For a discussion of scurrilous Protestant polemic across Europe in the sixteenth century, see Bevan Zlatar, *Reformation Fictions*.

42 *Differing Worships*, sig. C3v.

43 *Differing Worships*, sig. C2v.

44 *Differing Worships*, sig. C3v.

45 *Differing Worships*, sig. C4v.

46 'A breiffe of the Depositions allredy taken, touching the printing and publishing of Martins Libelles, and of the supposed Author thereof.' Lambeth Palace Fairhurst Papers MS 3470, fols 105–6. Transcription available: *The Martin Marprelate Press: A Documentary History*, ed. Joseph Black (University of Massachusetts Amherst), https://people.umass.edu/marprelate/documentfifteen.html (accessed 17 January 2024).

47 Keith L Sprunger, *Trumpets from the Tower: English Purtian Printing in the Netherlands, 1600–1640* (Leiden, New York, and Cologne: E. J. Brill, 1994); Raymond, *Pamphlets and Pamphleteering*, pp. 179–81; David Como offers a corrective to some received wisdom that links the prominent Leveller Richard Overton's works (perhaps especially his use of the 'ghosts' of Martin and Margery Marprelate), printed on the Cloppenburg Press to the Cloppenburg bookselling dynasty in Amsterdam. Nevertheless, many illicit and scurrilous materials were printed in Amsterdam and smuggled into England. See David R. Como, 'Secret Printing, the Crisis of 1640, and the Origins of Civil War Radicalism', *Past & Present*, 196 (2007), 37–82.

48 Helmer Helmers, *The Royalist Republic: Literature, Politics, and Religion in the Anglo-Dutch Public Sphere, 1639–1660* (Cambridge: Cambridge University Press, 2015). Esther van Raamsdonk takes a complementary approach, focusing on how Dutch influences and connections anchor canonical English writers within a European framework (van Raamsdonk, *Milton, Marvell, and the Dutch Republic* (London: Routledge, 2021)) and collaborations between Dutch and English speakers in the medieval and early modern period, and the influence of Dutch migrants on English literary culture has been examined in Sjoerd Levelt and Ad Putter, *North Sea Crossings: The Literary Heritage of Anglo-Dutch Relations 1066–1688* (Oxford: Bodleian Library, 2021).

49 *Differing Worships*, sig. C4v.

50 *Differing Worships*, sig. D3r.

51 Martin Butler, *Theatre and Crisis, 1632–1642* (Cambridge: Cambridge University Press, 1984), p. 84.

52 For a contemporary account see John Rushworth, *Historical Collections From The Year 1628 to the Year 1638, Abridg'd and Improv'd*. vol. 2 (London, 1706), sigs V3r–V3v.
53 John Taylor, *Crop-eare Curried. Or Tom Nash His Ghost, Declaring the pruning of Prinnes two last Parricidicall Pamphlets, being 92 Sheets in Quarto, wherein the one of them he stretch'd the Soveraigne Power of Parliament; in the other, his new-found way of opening the counterfeit Great Seale* (1644), title page [sig. A1r]. *Crop-Eare Curried* appears to be a revision or reprint under a different title of an earlier pamphlet, though only a fragment of this earlier pamphlet appears to have survived. See *Tom Nash his ghost: or The currying of crop-eare. The pruining of Prinnes prurient parricidicall pamphlets wherein he stretch'd the soveraigne prower of Parliaments and his new found way of opening the Great Seal* (London, 1643).
54 *Crop-ear Curried*, title page.
55 *Crop-ear Curried*, sig. A2r.
56 Christopher Salamone, Chapter 5 above.
57 Raymond, *Pamphlets and Pamphleteering*, p. 27.
58 *Crop-ear Curried*, sig. A3r.
59 For an in-depth discussion of Nashe, and the persona of Pierce Penniless in relation to literary discrimination, value, and the quarrel between Nashe and Harvey see Fallon, *Paper Monsters*, chapter 4.
60 Thomas Nashe, *Pierce Penilesse his supplication to the diuell* (London, 1592), sig. A1v.
61 For more on the Derridean impulses that underpin the rhetorical figuration of the author, see Salamone, Chapter 5 above. See also Kate De Rycker, Chapter 6 above.
62 *Crop-ear Curried*, sig. E4r.
63 *Crop-ear Curried*, sigs F1r–F1v.
64 William Vaughan, *The Newlanders cure* (London, 1630), sig. B2v.
65 Miriam Jacobson, *Barbarous Antiquity: Reorienting the Past in the Poetry of Early Modern England* (Philadelphia: University of Pennsylvania Press, 2014), pp. 30–1.
66 For attribution see *The Martin Marprelate Tracts*, ed. Black, p. lxxxix n. 276.
67 *Tom Nash his Ghost. To the three scurvy Fellowes of the upstart Family of the Snuffleers, Rufflers and shufflers; the thrice Treble-troublesome Scufflers in the church and State, the onlye Lay Ecclesi-Ass, I call Generallissimos* (London, 1642), title page [sig. A1r].
68 *Tom Nash His Ghost*, sig. A1v, italics inverted.
69 S[amuel] S[heppard], *God and Mammon. Or No Fellowship betwixt Light and Darknesse* (London, 1646), sig. A2r. See also Lena Liapi, Chapter 4 above, on Nashe's posthumous reception as a satirist.

AFTERWORD

Jennifer Richards

How did an influential writer from the age of Shakespeare – a collaborator *with* Shakespeare no less – become so unpopular in the present age? By 'unpopular' I mean unknown not just to the wider public, but also to students of English Literature. There was a promising flurry of interest in Nashe in the second half of the twentieth century. Literary scholars engaging with the modern moment found in Nashe a fellow traveller. Nashe has a place in Marshall McLuhan's story about the changing technologies of communication in *The Gutenberg Galaxy* (1962).[1] Jonathan Crewe studied Nashe's subversive strategies in 1992, and Neil Rhodes the influence of his 'grotesque' style on the development of comic Shakespeare in 1980.[2] More recently Andrew Hadfield interviewed the playwright Thomas Kilroy about the importance of Nashe to him.[3] Nashe has also proved an illuminating writer for those who contributed to the historical turn in literary studies from the 1980s. Lorna Hutson gave us *Thomas Nashe in Context* in 1989, shaping ongoing interest in Nashe as a writer who provides unusual access to the materiality as well as economic precarity of his world.[4] In 1993 Reid Barbour took this emphasis on the materiality of Nashe's writing in a new direction, describing it as 'somatic', suggesting that his 'writings are virtually present in the cloths, organs, and metals of the world',[5] while in 2000 Ian Moulton emphasised the physicality of his writing in a different way, focusing on his contribution to erotic writing.[6] Yet this quintessentially Elizabethan writer, who gives us a glimpse of the world of 1590s London while also seeming to talk to us – quite literally with the asides of trickster narrators like Jack Wilton – has not had a lasting renaissance of his own in the early twenty-first century. This collection, and the forthcoming new edition of *The Works of Thomas Nashe* with Oxford University Press, of which I am one of the General Editors, might just change that.

Still, my opening question stands. Why is Nashe, a formative writer for the English language, whose style was widely admired and imitated by his contemporaries, so rarely taught in English departments today?

One answer may be that his reputation as a 'minor' Elizabethan writer, noted by Chloe Kathleen Preedy and Rachel Willie in their Introduction, still lingers.[7] Another is likely the challenge that his writing poses to readers. Nashe is a difficult writer to read, and, as Preedy and Willie remind us, he also has a reputation for being 'difficult to teach'.[8] This is in part because his writing is so highly rhetorical.

Nashe grew up in a village in West Harling, Norfolk, where his father was the vicar. The nearest grammar school was in Thetford, seven miles away, and too far for a small boy to walk to daily, so it is likely he was tutored at home by his father, perhaps alongside other boys from the village as well as the sons of the local squire.[9] In his lessons he would have learned how to pronounce Latin, to conjugate verbs, and decline nouns; he would likely also have practised saying Latin sentences of the *vulgaria* as a prelude to reading and writing, perhaps first 'coolly' or calmly, and then producing the same again 'in a fierce and heated manner'.[10] He would have studied rhetoric, identifying figures and tropes, perhaps matching his voice to them to express emotion; if he advanced any further, he may also have written and performed letters and orations. These schoolroom habits of collecting and performing were developed further at the University of Cambridge, where he matriculated as a sizar scholar in 1582, graduating with a BA in 1586. The ambitious reading lists for schools included a range of Latin authors and texts: Terence, Cicero's *Epistles*, *De officiis*, *De amicitia*, and *De senectute*, Virgil's *Eclogues* and *Aeneid* and the *Georgics*, Caesar or Sallust, Ovid and Horace.[11] At university he would have encountered an even 'broader range of classical Greek and Latin authors and rhetorical theorists' as well as 'their more recent Latin counterparts who were busily editing and translating ancient rhetorical works'.[12] He would also have acquired skills in dialectic: the analysis of the argumentative structure of writings.[13]

Nashe's schooling does not entirely explain why he is such a challenging writer, of course. His male peers went to grammar school too, and a few also went to university, yet we still enjoy reading and teaching their drama, primarily in modern editions. Yet Nashe is different. It is not just that he writes mainly prose pamphlets, employing 'a structure resembling jest-books, which narrated different "jests" or "pranks" in the format "how X did Y"', as Lena Liapi reminds us in Chapter 4 above, so he will seem less familiar to twenty-first-century readers.[14] Nor is it that his meaning is also embodied in the mise-en-page, making a fully modernised edition unhelpful. One example of this is the strange punctuation found in the jokey dedication of the first edition of *The Unfortunate Traveller* to the Earl of Southampton, to which colleagues at the University of Geneva first drew my attention: 'How wel or ill I have done in it, I am ignorant:(the eye that sees round about it selfe, sees not into it selfe): only your Honours applauding encouragement hath power to make mee arrogant'.[15] The colons outside the parentheses arguably represent the eyes seeing 'round ... not into' the self of the proverb. Rather than silently correcting this possible 'error', as R. B. McKerrow did in his revered edition (1904–10), we read it as an example of expressive typography.[16] (Or is it the first ever emoticon?) The same applies, of course, to Willie's focus on the meaningful blank space of *Mar-Martine*'s title page, an anonymous anti-Martinist tract that our edition attributes to Nashe, in Chapter 7 above.[17] Nor are the challenges the result of the hundreds of neologisms we find across his writings, which, Preedy reminds us, require 'extra breath' – and energy – to 'enunciate'.[18] Some of these, like 'balderdash', have stayed with us, but many of them have not: 'Heggledepegs' for hedgehogs; 'twittle cum-twattles' for chatter or nonsense, 'snudgery' for miserliness etc. It is the combination of all of these that makes Nashe a difficult read, and no doubt hard to teach, and we might add to this list his habit of writing 'long-running sentences', to quote Liapi.[19]

Nashe's sentences certainly are long-running, but they are not without craft. Indeed they can carry a thought, or a series of thoughts, that change direction, just as thinking out loud in the moment does; this is integral to our reading experience, contributing to the sense of the 'liveness' of his prose writing. Crucially Nashe gives his sentences structure in two different ways, which can help readers understand what he is doing, and knowing something about his rhetorical training can help. He structures his sentences, firstly, with figures of speech, and, secondly, perhaps in collaboration with a compositor, with rhetorical punctuation, which helps us to pace delivery rather than identify the grammatical relationship between clauses. Quite simply, in Nashe's writing the colon or semicolon marks a longer pause, the comma a shorter one. Notable are figures of reversal, like chiasmus, perhaps marked out with stronger punctuation by Nashe or his printer, and of repetition like anaphora, where the same word is repeated at the beginning of successive clauses, *conduplicatio*, the repetition of words in adjacent clauses or phrases, or, one of my favourites, the pun *antanaclasis*, the repetition of the same word in two or more different senses. (There are many other figures of repetition used by Nashe, of course, too many to mention here.)

A good example of *antanaclasis*, to which Kate De Rycker draws our attention in Chapter 6 above, concerns the word 'page'.[20] The meaning it is made to carry in *The Unfortunate Traveller* builds gradually, so the distinction between our tricksy narrator, Jack Wilton, a page or servant of a noble master (the Earl of Surrey in this narrative), and the material page we are holding in our hand begins to blur in ways that will become embedded. So too does the distinction between Wilton and the actual reader, you and me, as we step into the character Nashe has prepared for us in 'The Induction to the dapper Mounsier Pages of the Court'. Yes, we are pages too! As De Rycker explains, we join a rowdy 'virtual community' of young men who 'are equally as likely to be found gambling as poring over the newest pamphlet to hit the bookshops'.[21] This sounds like fun, right? Yet, as De Rycker explains, the text becomes 'less convivial, and more threatening' when we read on.[22] We may think we are at the side of our tricksy narrator, laughing at the foolish dolts he tricks along the way, as well as the 'popular' literature Nashe is parodying, including, as Kirsty Rolfe reminds us in Chapter 2 above, the 'capacious category' of news.[23] But soon we will find we are being tricked too *and* compromised by what we see and hear, transformed into peeping Toms.

The Unfortunate Traveller becomes increasingly disturbing and uncomfortable as we read on. Scenes of torture, executions, massacres, and rape lie ahead for the reader who ventures into its murky world. We also have to wrestle with language that is both misogynistic and antisemitic. What may have seemed like an entertaining romp when we started soon turns into something much darker. What also becomes clear, however, is that Nashe means us to be uncomfortable: his relationship with his readers, both real and imagined, as Liapi points out, is 'vexed' and antagonistic.[24] Our responses to his supposedly entertaining narratives – and the popular genres he is parodying – are being scrutinised; in short, we are also 'pages' to be read in this fiction. One scene from *The Unfortunate Traveller*, which I often use to illustrate this point, is the grotesque description of the rape of a Roman matron called Heraclide by a Spanish bandit who has broken into her house during a time of plague, from which her husband has died, leaving her vulnerable to assault. We witness the scene and hear her attempts to dissuade Esdras before the attack; then we hear her lamentation afterwards. We also witness what happens next: like Lucrece, on whom she is clearly modelled, she commits suicide. So lengthy is the scene, and so vocal is Heraclide, that it is likely we forget whose voice is telling her story: it is Wilton's. A final sentence in three parts or cola concludes this story, two of which describe sequential actions, while the third positions us: Heraclide stabs herself, falling on her husband's corpse; this unexpectedly revives him; we learn from which vantage point we witness all of this, discovering we are not *at* Heraclide's side but at Wilton's, spying on the scene through a 'crannie' in the floor:

> So throughly stabd fell she downe, and knockt her head against her husbands bodie: wherewith, he not having beene ayred his full foure and twentie houres, start as out of a dreame: whiles I through a crannie of my upper chamber unseeled, had beheld all this sad spectacle.[25]

Nashe is so often described as a writer with an 'exceptional sensitivity to the materiality of words'.[26] The way he draws attention to the material components of a book, including the (recyclable) paper from which its pages are made, as well as the clutter of objects and bodies we find in them, is part of this. But the materiality of his writing is also physiological, and it has an airy quality too. Reading is not simply immersive or absorbing. If we read his writing aloud, as so often he invites us to do, or even just imagine we are doing so, we embody what we read, and likely respond physically, emotionally to it. Just how involved our bodies are when reading Nashe is highlighted by Preedy in her study of reading as 'pneumatic process'.[27] Nashe creates some breathless experiences, Preedy notes, an idea illustrated nicely by Willie in Chapter 7. The words of *Mar-Martine*, Willie notes, 'are unleashed at a breathless pace: the words beg to be uttered aloud and the timbre and texture of the voice add further inflections to the satire'.[28] What is innovative about the self-consciousness of Nashe's breathy prose, Preedy helpfully reminds us, is the way he is able to negate criticisms of its lightness and airiness, making it meaningful by comparing it to the poisonous 'Heavie', 'gor-bellied Volume[s]' of his enemy, Gabriel Harvey.[29] I would add that it is when we breathe life into a narrator Jack Wilton that we are compromised.

All of this makes it sound as if Nashe is playing with us, creating entertaining and vicarious experiences. As I have argued elsewhere, much of his inspiration, and many of his techniques (like direct address) come from perhaps the most exciting entertainment industry of the decade: live theatre. But Nashe is not just seeking to entertain us, as contributors to this volume differently argue. Liapi starts to develop this thought in Chapter 4, looking at the way Nashe discriminates between educated and uneducated readers, and it is developed further by Douglas Clark and Kirsty Rolfe, Chapters 3 and 2. Nashe's style is important to how he thinks, and Clark recognises his anxiety about being read superficially as a result. He carefully explores the interplay between surface and depth in his writing, inviting us to think about where its 'substance' may actually lie.[30] Clark also reminds us of Nashe's motivation: the superficiality of an educational culture that equips its students to prioritise surface over depth. We only have to read Nashe's early work, the preface to *Menaphon,* to understand how his writing across his career is a response to what he sees as a schoolroom focus on 'facile eloquence'.[31]

Rolfe invites us to probe the surfaces of Nashe's writing in a different way, addressing his preoccupation with the bane of our lives today: fake news. In the late sixteenth and seventeenth centuries, Rolfe explains, news encompassed many different forms, spoken and printed, and genres, from (idle) gossip to ballads to (fanciful) news reports from Europe to prophetic and 'wonder' literature popular in the 1580s (to which Gabriel Harvey

174   THOMAS NASHE AND LITERARY PERFORMANCE

and his brothers contributed).[32] All of these forms and genres feature in Nashe's writing, and so too does his concern with their impact on credulous readers. Nashe's preoccupation with 'correct interpretation' runs through his writings, and this explains his attacks on 'ignorant soothsayers' in *Terrors of the Night*, and fake newsmongers, including the Harvey brothers.[33]

I may have started this 'Afterword' with a question: how did an influential writer from the age of Shakespeare – a collaborator *with* Shakespeare no less – become so unpopular in the present age? I now find myself formulating a new question: how could such an antagonistic writer ever be popular? This is no longer a question only for readers today. It is also one for those of us interested in his contemporary readers. Liapi reminds us that Nashe was not only *not* popular in his own time – her comparison of his output with that of Robert Greene clinches the case – but he did not want to be popular anyway (even if he employed the kind of populist techniques bequeathed by 'Martin Marprelate', described so compellingly by Willie in Chapter 7).[34] He made 'choices about the format of his texts', and the content of his title pages, that make clear he did not to want to have broad appeal.[35] If so-called 'popular' literature is in his sights, then so too are its readers; here we see Nashe at his most snobbish. Yet popularity is perhaps not the right term to apply to him. With an eye on his afterlife, what he really wanted, Liapi adds, was notoriety. On this I think we can all agree with this volume's contributors that he certainly succeeded.

Finally I move from unpopular Nashe to notorious Nashe, from material Nashe to ghostly Nashe, from readers to fellow writers, and to the comparison of the experience of reading Nashe to being 'haunted' by him. This is the focus of the final chapters in this volume. We are invited to think about the afterlife of Nashe via Chris Salamone in Chapter 5, which recognises the many ways in which Nashe was himself interested in spirits. 'Nashe', writes Salamone, 'was well read on the subject of spirits'.[36] Discussions of demonology appear in many of his works, and he is adept at resurrecting the ghosts of the past, such as the clown Will Summers in *Summer's Last Will and Testament*, or the figure of the great Roman orator Cicero by the necromancer Cornelius Agrippa in *The Unfortunate Traveller* in a nod to *Doctor Faustus*. All of this is part of Nashe's 'ludic performativity', Salamone argues, although Nashe is making a serious (but not entirely gratifying) point about a 'culture marked by imitation and literary resurrections'.[37] Nor should we forget Nashe's own spectral presence as he haunts readers – and enemies like the Harvey brothers – hinting at 'his textual afterlife'.[38]

The raising of Cicero also features in De Rycker's chapter as a reminder of Nashe's view of the deadening effects of humanist Ciceronianism; the ghost of Cicero is juxtaposed to Wilton's/Nashe's complaint about students who 'stealeth not whole phrases but whole pages out of Tully'.[39] So too does Nashe's far more successful raising of the spirit of Pietro Aretino. If Cicero is only partly revived (by slavish Ciceronians), then Aretino is fully revived and animated by the breath and pen of Nashe himself: he is the inspiration for the latter's lively, colloquial prose, and sharp pen, and, as Harvey surely understood all too well, the revenge he takes against his enemies. But the spirits of the dead are not only invoked by way of revenge; they can also have a connecting role to play, creating traditions and lines of transmission, *and* virtual (and loyal) communities, as De Rycker argues Robert Greene did for Nashe, and Nashe does – in the guise of his most successful persona 'Pierce Penilesse' – for precarious, freelance writers like himself, Thomas Dekker, and Thomas Middleton. Recalling the ghosts of the past creates a bond between writers who have no other stable connections – no guild to support and protect them – but much to say about the contemporary condition. The pen of the satirist is a baton that gets passed on for De Rycker, and also for Willie in Chapter 7, which traces a line of transmission from Martin Marprelate to John Taylor the Water Poet via the ghostly ventriloquised voice of Nashe in the religious debates of the 1640s. Oddly, for one who positioned himself so much at the edge, as a voice of challenge on the sidelines, Nashe is raised in Taylor's religious, polemical writing as 'the authority figure who offers commentary on religious and political discontents'.[40] How much Nashe has changed, from edgy polemist to the restorer of order, at least in Taylor's imagination. Yet some things remain unchanged too. What Nashe bequeaths is his emphasis on the 'physicality of writing and the capacity for it to be a messy and error-fuelled activity where words are deliberately scratched out or accidentally blotted out through ink spills'.[41]

    The spirit of Nashe that I have been describing, provocative, vengeful, but also loyal, sociable, even generous, lives on, not only in the imagination of the writers inspired by him – and here I include Charles Nicholl who is revising his biography of Thomas Nashe even as the editorial team of the Thomas Nashe Project are finishing their edition of his works[42] – but also of the literary scholars who contribute to this volume. Nashe is a challenging writer for all the reasons they explore, but he is also good to think with about the questions that still matter to us: about reading, not just texts but contexts, interpretation, knowledge (surface and depth), comfort and discomfort, fake news, enmity and friendship, social, religious, and political discontent. His restless spirit inspires this volume so attentive to the liveness (and challenge) of his poetry and prose. So too does his intellectual generosity to his and our 'present'. Nashe undoubtedly gifted his contemporaries and successors the opportunity to challenge platitudes in startlingly new ways, and so he does for us too. Cathy Shrank, one of the General Editors of the new edition, once described him as the 'gift that keeps on giving'. There are just so many different ways he continues to speak across time to us: and thus Shrank and Kate De Rycker are now reviving the spirit of 'Pierce Penilesse' again, this time to explore the precarity of our own moment.[43] Equally inspiring is Nashe's loyalty to fellow professional writers. It is easy to remember Nashe's quarrels, and the sharpness of his pen, and we might want to think more kindly of those who felt it most keenly. However, it is equally easy to forget that, as Andrew Hadfield (another of the General Editors) once reminded me, Nashe had good friendships too with fellow writers: he was no lone scholar. He remembered them when they were dead, unable to defend themselves, and he is remembered by the friends who outlived him, and also by the fine scholars contributing to this volume: 'When any wronged him living, they did feel / His spirit quick as powder, sharp as steel; / But to his friends his faculties were fair, / Pleasant, and mild as the most temperate air'.[44] Perhaps I no longer need to worry whether Nashe is popular or not: he is still haunting us.

NOTES

1 Marshall McLuhan, *The Gutenberg Galaxy: The Making of Typographic Man* (Toronto: University of Toronto Press, 1962, rpt 2011).
2 Jonathan Crewe, *Unredeemed Rhetoric: Thomas Nashe and the Scandal of Authorship* (Baltimore: Johns Hopkins University Press, 1982); Neil Rhodes, *Elizabethan Grotesque* (London: Routledge & Kegan Paul, 1980).
3 Andrew Hadfield, 'An Interview with Thomas Kilroy', The Thomas Nashe project blog, 2017. https://thomasnashe.wordpress.com/2017/07/13/an-interview-with-thomas-kilroy/ (accessed 17 January 2024).
4 Lorna Hutson, *Thomas Nashe in Context* (Oxford: Oxford University Press, 1989).
5 Reid Barbour, *Deciphering Elizabethan Fiction* (Newark: University of Delaware Press; London and Toronto: Associated University Presses, 1993), p. 64.
6 Ian Frederick Moulton, *Before Pornography: Erotic Writing in Early Modern England* (Oxford: Oxford University Press, 2000).
7 Chloe Kathleen Preedy and Rachel Willie, 'Introduction, above.
8 Preedy and Willie, Introduction, p. 3.
9 Charles Nicholl, *A Cup of News: The Life of Thomas Nashe* (London: Routledge & Kegan Paul, 1984), pp. 19–21.
10 Erasmus, *Collected Works of Erasmus: Literary and Educational Writings II: De Copia, Volume 24*, ed. Craig R. Thompson (Toronto: University of Toronto Press, 1978), p. 630.
11 Peter Mack, *Elizabethan Rhetoric: Theory and Practice* (Cambridge: Cambridge University Press, 2002), pp. 11–14.
12 Sarah Knight, 'Universities', in *Cambridge History of Rhetoric. Volume 3: Rhetoric in the Renaissance*, ed. Virginia Cox and Jennifer Richards (forthcoming).
13 Mack, *Elizabethan Rhetoric*, p. 73.

AFTERWORD

14 Lena Liapi, Chapter 4 above, p. 96.
15 Thomas Nashe, *The vnfortunate traueller* (London, 1594), sig. A2r.
16 H. R. Woudhuysen, 'The Foundations of Shakespeare's Text', *Proceedings of the British Academy*, 125 (2004), 69–100 (p. 82).
17 Rachel Willie, Chapter 7 above, p. 35.
18 See Chloe Kathleen Preedy, Chapter 1 above, quoting Jason Scott-Warren, 'Nashe's Stuff', in *The Oxford Handbook of English Prose 1500–1640*, ed. Andrew Hadfield (Oxford: Oxford University Press, 2013), pp. 204–18 (p. 218).
19 Liapi, Chapter 4 above, p. 24.
20 Kate De Rycker, Chapter 6 above.
21 De Rycker, Chapter 6 above, p. 128.
22 De Rycker, Chapter 6 above, p. 128.
23 Kirsty Rolfe, Chapter 2 above, p. 44.
24 Liapi, Chapter 4 above, p. 90.
25 Nashe, *Unfortunate Traveller*, sig. L2r.
26 Scott-Warren, 'Nashe's Stuff', p. 210; Hutson, *Thomas Nashe in Context*, p. 4.
27 Preedy, Chapter 1 above, p. 28.
28 Willie, Chapter 7 above, p. 152.
29 Preedy, Chapter 1 above, p. 29.
30 Douglas Clark, Chapter 3 above.
31 Clark, Chapter 3 above, p. 31.
32 Rolfe, Chapter 2 above.
33 Rolfe, Chaper 2 above, p. 54.
34 Willie, Chapter 7 above.
35 Liapi, Chapter 4 above, p. 91.
36 Chris Salamone, Chapter 5 above, p. 107.
37 Salamone, Chapter 5 above, p. 113.
38 Salamone, Chapter 5 above, p. 117.
39 De Rycker, Chapter 6 above, p. 175.
40 Willie, Chapter 7 above, p. 157.
41 Willie, Chapter 7 above, p. 162.
42 Nicholl, *A Cup of News*.
43 For details of Cathy Shrank, Kate De Rycker, and Archie Cornish's AHRC-funded project 'Penniless? Thomas Nashe and Precarity in Historical Perspective', see Cathy Shrank and Kate De Rycker, 'Penniless? Project', *The Thomas Nashe Project* (Newcastle: Newcastle University, 2020). https://research.ncl.ac.uk/thethomasnasheproject/pennilessproject/ (accessed 17 January 2024); and Archie Cornish, ed., 'Penniless?', *Medium* (2022).
44 'Elegy on Thomas Nashe, "Ad Carissimam Memoriam Thomae Nashi"', in *The Cambridge Works of Ben Jonson Online* (Cambridge: Cambridge University Press, 2014), https://universitypublishingonline.org/cambridge/benjonson/k/works/nashe/facing/# (accessed 17 January 2024).

BIBLIOGRAPHY

PRIMARY SOURCES

Allott, Robert. *Englands Parnassus: or the choysest flowers of our moderne poets*. London: N. L[ing,] C. B[urby] and T. H[ayes], 1600; STC [2nd edition] 378.

Amyot, Jacques. *Les Oevvres Morales & Meslees de Plutarque*. Paris: Michel de Vascosan, 1572.

Aristotle. *Poetics*, trans. Stephen Halliwell. Cambridge, MA: Harvard University Press, 1995.

Babrius [Aesop]. *Fables*, trans. Ben Edwin Perry. Loeb Classical Library 436. Cambridge, MA: Harvard University Press, 1965.

Bacon, Francis. *Sylua syluarum: or A naturall historie In ten centuries*. London: J[ohn] H[aviland and Augustine Mathewes] for William Lee, 1627; STC [2nd edition] 1168.

A breiffe of the Depositions allredy taken, touching the printing and publishing of Martins Libelles, and of the supposed Author thereof. Lambeth Palace Fairhurst Papers MS 3470, fols 105–6.

Bullein, William. *Bulleins bulwarke of defence*. London: Thomas Marshe, 1579; STC [2nd edition] 4034.

Burton, Robert. *The anatomy of melancholy*. Oxford: John Lichfield and James Short for Henry Cripps, 1621; STC [2nd edition] 4159.

Chettle, Henry. *Kind-Harts Dreame*. London: [J. Wolfe and J. Danter] for William Wright, 1593; STC [2nd edition] 5123.

Cope, Michael. *A godly and learned exposition vppon the Prouerbes of Solomon*. London: [Thomas Dawson] for George Bishop, 1580; STC [2nd edition] 5723.

Cotgrave, Randle. *A Dictionarie of the French and English Tongues*. London: Adam Islip, 1611; STC [2nd edition] 5830.

A countercuffe given to Martin Iunior. London: Martin Junior [i.e., John Charlewood], 1589; STC [2nd edition] 19456.5.

Curione, Celio. *Pasquine in a Traunce*, trans. William Page. London: Thomas Este, 1584; STC [2nd edition] 6131.

Darrel, John. *A detection of that sinnful, shamful, lying, and ridiculous discours, of Samuel Harshnet*. London: [English secret press], 1600; STC [2nd edition] 6283.

Dekker, Thomas. *A knights coniuring*. London: T[homas] C[reede] for William Barley, 1607; STC [2nd edition] 6508.

Dekker, Thomas. *Newes From Hell Brought by the Divells Carrier*. London: R. B[lower, S. Stafford, and Valentine Simmes] for W. Ferebrand, 1606; STC [2nd edition] 6514.

Dickenson, John. *Greene in Conceipt*. London: Richard Bradocke for William Jones, 1598; STC [2nd edition] 6819.

Doleta, John [?]. *Straunge Newes out of Calabria Prognosticated in the Yere 1586, Upon the Yere 87*. London: G. Robinson for G. Perin [?], 1587; STC [2nd edition] 6992.

Drayton, Michael. *The battaile of Agincourt Fought by Henry the fifth of that name*. London: Augustine Mathewes] for William Lee, 1627; STC [2nd edition] 7190.

Elizabethan and Jacobean Journals 1591–1610, ed. G. B. Harrison. Abingdon: Routledge, 1999, III.

Elyot, Thomas. *The dictionary of syr Thomas Eliot knight*. London: Thomas Bertheleti, 1538; STC [2nd edition] 7659.

Erasmus, Desiderius. *Collected Works of Erasmus: Adages: Ivi1 to Ix100, Volume 32*, trans. and ed. R. A. B. Mynors. Toronto: University of Toronto Press, 1989.

Erasmus, Desiderius. *Collected Works of Erasmus: Literary and Educational Writings II: De Copia, Volume 24*, ed. Craig R. Thompson. Toronto, Buffalo, London: University of Toronto Press, 1978.

Fletcher, John. *The Tamer Tamed*, ed. Lucy Munro. London: Methuen, 2010.

Freeman, Thomas. *Rubbe, and a great cast Epigrams*. London: [Nicholas Okes] for [L. Lisle], 1614; STC [2nd edition] 11370.

Fulke, William. *A goodly gallerye with a most pleasaunt prospect*. London: William Griffith, 1563; STC [2nd edition] 11435.

Fulwell, Ulpian. *The First Parte, of the Eyghth Liberall Science*. London: [William How] for Richard Jones, 1579; STC [2nd edition] 11472.

Galen. *On the Usefulness of the Parts of the Body*, trans. and ed. Margaret Tallmadge May. Ithaca: Cornell University Press, 1968.

Greene, Robert [?]. *Greenes groats-vvorth of witte, bought with a million of repentance*. London: [J. Wolfe and J. Danter] for William Wright, 1592; STC [2nd edition] 12245.

Greene, Robert. *Menaphon Camillas alarum to slumbering Euphues*. London: T[homas] O[rwin] for Sampson Clarke, 1589; STC [2nd edition] 12272.

Greene, Robert. *A quip for an vpstart courtier*. London: John Wolfe, 1592; STC [2nd edition] 13200.

Gosson, Stephen. *The schoole of abuse*. London: Thomas Woodcocke, 1579; STC [2nd edition] 12097.5.

Harington, John. *The most elegant and witty epigrams of Sir Iohn Harrington*. London: G[eorge] P[urslowe] for John Budge, 1618; STC [2nd edition] 12776.

Harvey, Gabriel. *Foure letters, and certaine sonnets*. London: John Wolfe, 1592; STC [2nd edition] 12900.5.

Harvey, Gabriel. *A nevv letter of notable contents*. London: John Wolfe, 1593; STC [2nd edition] 12902.
Harvey, Gabriel. *Pierces supererogation or A new prayse of the old asse*. London: John Wolfe, 1593; STC [2nd edition] 12903.
Harvey, Gabriel. 'To his very gentle and liberal frendes'. In Gabriel Harvey, *Pierces supererogation or A new prayse of the old asse*. London: John Wolfe, 1593; STC [2nd edition] 12903.
Harvey, John. *An Astrologicall Addition*. London: Richard Watkins, 1583; STC [2nd edition] 12907.
Harvey, John. *A Discoursive Probleme Concerning Prophesies*. London: John Jackson for Richard Warkins, 1588; STC [2nd edition] 12908.
Harvey, Richard. *An Astrological Discourse*. London: Henry Bynneman, 1583; STC [2nd edition] 12911.
Heylyn, Peter. *Antidotum Lincolniense· or An answer to a book entituled, The holy table, name, & thing*. London: [Miles Flesher, R. Bishop, and Thomas Harper] for John Clark, 1637; STC [2nd edition] 13267.
Heywood, Thomas. *An apology for actors*. London: Nicholas Okes, 1612; STC [2nd edition] 13309.
Heywood, John. *Two Hundred Epigrammes, Vpon Two Hundred Prouerbes*. London: T. Berthelet, 1555; STC [2nd edition] 13296.
Hoper, R. *The instruction of a Christian man*. London: H. Bynneman, 1580; STC [2nd edition] 13766.5.
Horace. *Art of Poetry*, trans. H. Rushton Fairclough. Cambridge, MA: Harvard University Press, 1926.
James, Thomas. *The Jesuits downefall threatned against them by the secular priests*. London: Joseph Barnes for John Barnes, 1612; STC [2nd edition] 14459.
Jonson, Ben. *'The Alchemist' and Other Plays*, ed. Gordon Campbell. Oxford: Oxford World Classics, 1995.
Jonson, Ben. *Bartholomew Fair*. In Ben Jonson, *'The Alchemist' and Other Plays*, ed. Gordon Campbell. Oxford: Oxford World Classics, 1995.
Jonson, Ben. 'Elegy on Thomas Nashe, "Ad Carissimam Memoriam Thomae Nashi"', in *The Cambridge Works of Ben Jonson Online* (Cambridge: Cambridge University Press, 2014), https://universitypublishingonline.org/cambridge/benjonson/k/works/nashe/facing/#.
Ker, George. *A Discoverie of the Vnnaturall and Traiterous Conspiracie of Scottisch Papists ... Wherevnto are Annexed, Certaine Intercepted Letters, written by Sundrie of that Factioun*. Edinburgh: Robert Waldegrave, 1593; STC [2nd edition] 14937.
King, Humphrey. *An halfe-penny-worth of vvit, in a penny-worth of paper. Or, The hermites tale*. London: Thomas Thorpe for Edward Blount, 1613; STC [2nd edition] 14973.
Laertius, Diogenes. *Lives of Eminent Philosophers*, trans. R. D. Hicks. Loeb Classical Library 184. Cambridge, MA: Harvard University Press, 1925, I.
Langbaine, Gerard. *An account of the English dramatick poets*. London: L.L. for George West and Henry Clements, 1691; Wing L373.

BIBLIOGRAPHY

Langbaine, Gerard. *The lives and characters of the English dramatick poets*. London: William Turner, 1699; Wing L376.
Laud, William. *The history of the troubles and tryal of the Most Reverend Father in God and blessed martyr, William Laud*. London: Ri[chard] Chiswell, 1695; Wing L586.
Lavater, Lewes. *Of Ghostes and Spirites Walking By Nyght* (1572), ed. J. Dover Wilson and May Yardley. Oxford: Oxford University Press, 1929.
Lavater, Ludwig. *Of ghostes and spirits walking by night ... translated into Englyshe by R.H.* London: Henry Benneyman for Richard Watkyns, 1572; STC [2nd edition] 15320.
Le Loyer, Pierre. *IIII Livres de Spectres* (Angers, 1586), trans. Z. Jones, *A Treatise of Specters or straunge Sights*. London: Val. S[immes] for Mathew Lownes, 1605; STC [2nd edition] 15448.
Letters conteyning sundry deuises touching the state of Flaunders and Portingall: Written by Card. Granuelle and others, and lately intercepted and published. London: Thomas Dawson for Thomas Charde, 1582; STC [2nd edition] 19768.
Lichfield, Richard [?]. *The trimming of Thomas Nashe Gentleman*. London: [E. Alldé] for Philip Scarlet, 1597; STC [2nd edition] 12906.
Lodge, Thomas. *A Treatise of the Plague*. London: Thomas Creede and Valentine Simmes] for Edward White and N[icholas] L[ing], 1603; STC [2nd edition] 16676.
Lyly, John. *Campaspe* (1584). In *The Works of John Lyly*, ed. R. Warwick Bond, 3 vols. Oxford: Clarendon Press, 1902, II.
Lyly, John. *Euphues and his England*. London: Gabriel Cawood, 1580; STC [2nd edition] 17069.
Lyly, John. *The Works of John Lyly*, ed. R. Warwick Bond, 3 vols. Oxford: Clarendon Press, 1902, I.
Lyly, John. *The Works of John Lyly*, ed. R. Warwick Bond, 3 vols. Oxford: Clarendon Press, 1902, II.
Mar-Martin. London: [s.n.], 1589; STC [2nd edition] 17461.5.
Mar-Martine. London: [s.n.], 1589; STC [2nd edition] 17461.
Mar-Martine, ed. T. G. Crippen. Transactions of the Congregational Historical Society. BL Shelfmark 11630.ee.20.
Marbeck, John. *A Booke of Notes and Common Places*. London: Thomas East, 1581; STC [2nd edition] 17299.
Marlowe, Christopher. *All Ovids Elegies*, ed. Roma Gill. In *The Complete Works of Christopher Marlowe*. Oxford: Oxford University Press, 1986; 2012, I.
Marlowe, Christopher. *Christopher Marlowe: The Complete Poems and Translations*, ed. Stephen Orgel. London: Penguin, 2007.
Marlowe, Christopher. *The Complete Works of Christopher Marlowe*. Oxford: Oxford University Press, 1986; 2012, I.
Marlowe, Christopher. *Doctor Faustus, B-Text (1616)*. In Christopher Marlowe, *'Doctor Faustus' and Other Plays*, ed. David Bevington and Eric Rasmussen. Oxford: Clarendon Press, 1995.

Marlowe, Christopher. *'Doctor Faustus' and Other Plays*, ed. David Bevington and Eric Rasmussen. Oxford: Clarendon Press, 1995.
Marlowe, Christopher, trans. *Lucan's First Book*, ed. Roma Gill. In *The Complete Works of Christopher Marlowe*, 5 vols. Oxford: Clarendon Press, 1986; 2012, I.
Marlowe, Christopher, trans. *Lucans first booke translated line for line, by Chr. Marlow*. London: P. Short for Walter Bure, 1600; STC [2nd edition] 16883.5.
Marprelate, Martin [pseud.]. *The iust censure and reproofe of Martin Iunior*. Wolston: John Hodgkins, 1589; STC [2nd edition] 17458.
Marprelate, Martin [pseud.]. *Oh Read Over D. John Bridges*. Molesey: Robert Waldegrave, 1588; STC [2nd edition] 17453.
Marprelate, Martin [pseud.: Job Throckmorton and John Penry?]. *Hay any worke for Cooper*. Coventry: [Robert Waldegrave], 1589; STC [2nd edition] 17456.
Marprelate, Martin [pseud.: T. Nash?]. *I know not why* [London?]; [1589]. BL Shelfmark 702.g.20.
The Martin Marprelate Press: A Documentary History, ed. Joseph Black. University of Massachusetts Amherst. https://people.umass.edu/marprelate/documentfifteen.html.
The Martin Marprelate Tracts, ed. Joseph L. Black. Cambridge: Cambridge University Press, 2008.
Martins months minde. London: Thomas Orwin, 1589; STC [2nd edition] 17452.
Meres, Francis. *Palladis tamia. Wits treasury being the second part of Wits common wealth*. London: P. Short, for Cuthbert Burbie, 1598; STC [2nd edition] 17834.
Middleton, Thomas. *The Black Book*, ed. G.B. Shand. In *Thomas Middleton: The Collected Works*, gen. eds Gary Taylor and John Lavagnino. Oxford: Oxford University Press, 2007, pp. 204–18.
Middleton, Thomas. *Thomas Middleton: The Collected Works*, gen. eds Gary Taylor and John Lavagnino. Oxford: Oxford University Press, 2007.
Montaigne, Michel de. *Essays*, trans. John Florio. London: Melch[ior] Bradwood for Edward Blount and William Barret, 1613; STC [2nd edition] 18042.
Nashe, Thomas. *An almond for a parrat*. London: [Eliot's Court Press?], 1589; STC [2nd edition] 534.
Nashe, Thomas. *The anatomie of absurditie*. London: J. Charlewood for Thomas Hacket, 1589; STC [2nd edition] 18364.
Nashe, Thomas. *Christs teares ouer Ierusalem*. London: James Roberts for Andrew Wise, 1594; STC [2nd edition] 18366.
Nashe, Thomas. *The Complete Works of Thomas Nashe*, ed. Alexander B. Grosart, 6 vols. N.p.: Huth Library, 1883.
Nashe, Thomas. 'The Epistle to the Reader'. In Thomas Nashe, *Strange newes, of the intercepting certaine letters*. London: John Danter, 1592; STC [2nd edition] 18377a.

BIBLIOGRAPHY

Nashe, Thomas. *Haue vvith you to Saffron-vvalden. Or, Gabriell Harueys hunt is vp*. London: John Danter, 1596; STC [2nd edition] 18369.

Nashe, Thomas. 'The Induction to the dapper Monsier Pages'. In *The vnfortunate traueller. Or, The life of Jacke Wilton*. London: T. Scarlet for C. Burby, 1594; STC [2nd edition] 18380.

Nashe, Thomas. *Nashes Lenten stuffe*. London: [Thomas Judson and Valentine Simmes] for N[icholas] L[ing] and C[uthbert] [Burby], 1599; STC [2nd edition] 18370.

Nashe, Thomas. *Nashe's Lenten Stuff*. In *'The Unfortunate Traveller' and Other Works*, ed. J. B. Steane. London: Penguin, 1971.

Nashe, Thomas. *Pierce Penilesse his supplication to the diuell*. London: Abell Jeffes, for J. B[usby], 1592; STC [2nd edition] 18373.

Nashe, Thomas. *A pleasant comedie, called Summers last will and testament*. London: Simon Stafford for Walter Burre, 1600; STC [2nd edition] 18376.

Nashe, Thomas. 'A private Epistle'. In Thomas Nashe, *Pierce Penilesse his supplication to the diuell*. London: Abell Jeffes, for J. B[usby], 1592; STC [2nd edition] 18373.

Nashe, Thomas. 'Somewhat to reade for them that list'. In Philip Sidney, *Syr P.S. His Astrophel and Stella*. London: John Charlewood] for Thomas Newman, 1591; STC [2nd edition] 22536.

Nashe, Thomas. *Strange newes, of the intercepting certaine letters*. London: John Danter, 1592; STC [2nd edition] 18377a.

Nashe, Thomas. *The terrors of the night*. London: John Danter, 1594; STC [2nd edition] 18379.

Nashe, Thomas. 'To all Christian Readers'. In Thomas Nashe, *Haue vvith you to Saffron-vvalden. Or, Gabriell Harueys hunt is vp*. London: John Danter, 1596; STC [2nd edition] 18369.

Nashe, Thomas. 'To the Gentlemen Students of both Universities'. In Robert Greene, *Menaphon Camillas alarum to slumbering Euphues*. London: T[homas] O[rwin] for Sampson Clarke, 1589; STC [2nd edition] 12272.

Nashe, Thomas. 'To his Readers'. In Thomas Nashe, *Nashes Lenten stuffe*. London: [Thomas Judson and Valentine Simmes] for N[icholas] L[ing] and C[uthbert] [Burby], 1599; STC [2nd edition] 18370.

Nashe, Thomas. 'To Master or Goodman Reader'. In Thomas Nashe, *Pierce Penilesse his supplication to the diuell*. London: Abell Jeffes, for J. B[usby], 1592; STC [2nd edition] 18373.

Nashe, Thomas. 'To the most Orthodoxall ... Corrector'. In Thomas Nashe, *Haue vvith you to Saffron-vvalden. Or, Gabriell Harueys hunt is vp*. London: John Danter, 1596; STC [2nd edition] 18369.

Nashe, Thomas. 'To the Reader'. In Thomas Nashe, *Christs teares ouer Ierusalem*. London: James Roberts for Andrew Wise, 1594; STC [2nd edition] 18366.

Nashe, Thomas. 'To the reader'. In Thomas Nashe, *Haue vvith you to Saffron-vvalden. Or, Gabriell Harueys hunt is vp*. London: John Danter, 1596. STC [2nd edition] 18369.

Nashe, Thomas. *The vnfortunate traueller. Or, The life of Jacke Wilton*. London: T. Scarlet for C. Burby, 1594; STC [2nd edition] 18380.
Nashe, Thomas. *The Vnfortunate Traueller*. In *The Works of Thomas Nashe*, ed. R. B. McKerrow. 2nd edn, rev. F. P. Wilson. 5 vols. Oxford: Blackwell, 1958. II.
Nashe, Thomas. *'The Unfortunate Traveller' and Other Works*, ed. J. B. Steane. London: Penguin, 1972.
Nashe, Thomas. *The Works of Thomas Nashe*, ed. R. B. McKerrow. 2nd edn, rev. F. P. Wilson. 5 vols. Oxford: Blackwell, 1958, I.
Nashe, Thomas. *The Works of Thomas Nashe*, ed. R. B. McKerrow. 2nd edn, rev. F. P. Wilson. 5 vols. Oxford: Blackwell, 1958, II.
Nashe, Thomas. *The Works of Thomas Nashe*, ed. R. B. McKerrow. 2nd edn, rev. F. P. Wilson. 5 vols. Oxford: Blackwell, 1958, IV.
Nashe, Thomas. *The Works of Thomas Nashe,* ed. R. B. McKerrow, 2nd edn, rev. F. P. Wilson. 5 vols. Oxford: Basil Blackwell, 1958, V.
Newes From Antwerp, the 10 Day of August 1580, Contayning, a Speciall View of the Present Affayres of the Lowe Countreyes: Reuealed and Brought to Lyght, by Sundrie Late Intercepted Letters. London: John Charlewood, 1580; STC [2nd edition] 692.
Ovid [Publius Ovidius Naso]. *Metamorphoses*, trans. A. D. Melville, ed. E. J. Kenney. Oxford: Oxford University Press, 2008.
Perkins, William. *A discourse of the damned art of witchcraft*. Cambridge: Cantrel Legge, 1608; STC [2nd edition] 19698.
Pico Della Mirandola, Gianfrancesco. *On the Imagination*, trans. Harry Caplan. New Haven: Yale University Press, 1930.
Phillips, Edward. *Theatrum poetarum, or, A compleat collection of the poets*. London: Charles Smith, 1675; Wing P2075.
Plat, Hugh. *A nevv, cheape and delicate fire of cole-balles*. London: Peter Short, 1603; STC [2nd edition] 19995.
Plato. *Phaedrus*, trans. Robert Hackforth. Cambridge: Cambridge University Press, 1972.
Plato. *Theaetetus, Sophist*, trans. Harold North Fowler. Loeb Classical Library 123. Cambridge, MA: Harvard University Press, 1921.
Pliny the Elder. *Natural History*, trans. H. Rackham. Loeb Classical Library 394. Cambridge, MA: Harvard University Press, 1952, IX.
Plutarch. *The philosophie, commonlie called, the morals*, trans. Philemon Holland. London: Arnold Hatfield, 1603; STC [2nd edition] 20063.
Puttenham, George. *The arte of English poesie*. London: Richard Field, 1589; STC [2nd edition] 20519.
R., T. *A Confutation of the Tenne Great Plagues, Prognosticated by John Doleta from the Country of Calabria*. London: Robert Waldegrave, 1587; STC [2nd edition] 20589.5.
Rankins, William. *The English Ape, the Italian Imitation, the Footesteppes of Fraunce*. London: Robert Robinson, 1588; STC [2nd edition] 20698.5.
Rankins, William. *A mirrour of monsters*. London: J[ohn] C[harlewood] for T[homas] H[acket], 1587; STC [2nd edition] 20699.

Rushworth, John. *Historical Collections From The Year 1628 to the Year 1638, Abridg'd and Improv'd*. vol. 2. London: D. Browne, 1706.

Scot, Reginald. *The discouerie of witchcraft*. London: [Henry Denham for] William Brome, 1584; STC [2nd edition] 21864.

Shakespeare, William. *Antony and Cleopatra*, ed. John Wilders. London: Arden Shakespeare, 1995.

Shakespeare, William. *King Henry VI, Part I*, ed. Edward Burns. London: Arden Shakespeare, 2001.

Sheppard, Samuel. *God and Mammon, or, No fellowship betwixt light and darknesse*. London [s.n.], 1646; Wing [2nd edition] S3165A.

Sidney, Philip. *The Defence of Poesie*. London: William Posonby, 1595; STC [2nd edition] 22535.

Sidney, Philip. *The Defence of Poesy*, in *'The Defence of Poesy' and Selected Renaissance Literary Criticism*, ed. Gavin Alexander. London: Penguin, 2004.

Sidney, Philip. *'The Defence of Poesy' and Selected Renaissance Literary Criticism*, ed. Gavin Alexander. London: Penguin, 2004.

Sidney, Philip. *Syr P.S. His Astrophel and Stella*. London: John Charlewood] for Thomas Newman, 1591; STC [2nd edition] 22536.

Smel-knave, Simon [Thomas Nashe?]. *Fearfull and Lamentable Effects of Two Dangerous Comets*. London: J. C[harlewood] for John Busbie, 1590; STC [2nd edition] 22645.

Spenser, Edmund. *The Faerie Queene*, ed. A. C. Hamilton. Abingdon: Routledge, 2006.

Spenser, Edmund. *The Faerie Queene*, ed. Thomas P. Roache Jr and C. Patrick O'Donnell, Jr. London: Penguin, 1987.

Spenser, Edmund. *The Ruines of Time*. In *The Yale Edition of the Shorter Poems of Edmund Spenser*, ed. William A. Oram, Einar Bjorvand, and Ronald Bond. New Haven and London: Yale University Press, 1989, pp. 225–61.

Spenser, Edmund. *The Yale Edition of the Shorter Poems of Edmund Spenser*, ed. William A. Oram, Einar Bjorvand, and Ronald Bond. New Haven and London: Yale University Press, 1989.

Taylor, John. *Crop-eare Curried*. Oxford: L. Lichfield, 1645; Wing [2nd edition] T446.

Taylor, John. *Differing worships*. London: [R. Bishop?] for William Ley, 1640; STC [2nd edition] 23746.

Taylor, John. *Tom Nash his ghost*. London: [s.n.], 1642; Wing [2nd edition] T518A.

Taylor, John. *A verry merry vvherry-ferry-voyage*. London: Edward Allde, 1622; STC [2nd edition] 23812.

Thorpe, Thomas. 'To the Kind and True Friend: Edmund Blunt'. In Christopher Marlowe, trans., *Lucan's First Book* (London, 1600), ed. Roma Gill. In *The Complete Works of Christopher Marlowe*, 5 vols. Oxford: Clarendon Press, 1986; 2012, I.

Thorpe, Thomas. 'To his Kind, and True Friend: Edmund Blunt'. In Christopher Marlowe, trans., *Lucans first booke translated line for line, by Chr. Marlow*. London: P. Short for Walter Bure, 1600; STC [2nd edition] 16883.5.

A True and Plaine Declaration of the Horrible Treasons, Practised by William Parry the Traitor ... *Together With the Copies of Sundry Letters of His and Others, Tending to Diuers Purposes, for the Proofes of His Treasons.* London: C. B[arker], 1585; STC [2nd edition] 19342.

Vaughan, William. *The Newlanders cure.* London: N[icholas] O[kes] for F. Constable, 1630; STC [2nd edition] 24619.

Whetstone, George. *The enemie to vnthryftinesse.* London: Richard Jones, 1586; STC [2nd edition] 25341.5.

Winstanley, William. *The lives of the most famous English poets.* London: H. Clark for Samuel Manship, 1687; Wing W3065.

Wood, Anthony. *Athenae Oxonienses.* London: Thomas Bennet, 1691; Wing W3382, vol. 1.

SECONDARY SOURCES

Ahmedzai, Sam H., and Martin F. Muers (eds). *Supportive Care in Respiratory Disease.* Oxford: Oxford University Press, 2011.

Ahnert, Ruth. 'Maps Versus Networks'. In *News Networks in Early Modern Europe*, ed. Joad Raymond and Noah Moxham. Leiden: Brill, 2016, pp. 130–57.

Alexander, Gavin. *Writing After Sidney: The Literary Response to Sir Philip Sidney, 1586–1640.* Oxford: Oxford University Press, 2006.

Allen, Don Cameron. *The Star-crossed Renaissance: The Quarrel about Astrology and Its Influence in England.* London: Frank Cass, 1966.

Anderson, Benedict. *Imagined Communities: Reflections on the Origin and Spread of Nationalism.* London and New York: Verso, 1991.

Appelbaum, Robert. *Aguecheek's Beef, Belch's Hiccup, and Other Gastronomic Interjections: Literature, Culture, and Food Among the Early Moderns.* Chicago: University of Chicago Press, 2006.

Arblaster, Paul. *From Ghent to Aix: How They Brought the News in the Habsburg Netherlands, 1550–1700.* Leiden: Brill, 2014.

Arblaster, Paul. 'Posts, Newsletters, Newspapers: England in a European System of Communications'. In *News Networks in Seventeenth-Century Britain and Europe*, ed. Joad Raymond. London: Routledge, 2006, pp. 19–34.

Aston, Margaret. 'The Fiery Trigon Conjunction: An Elizabethan Astrological Prediction'. *Isis*, 61 (1970), 159–87.

Badcoe, Tamsin Theresa. '"As Many Ciphers without an I": Self-Reflexive Violence in the Work of Thomas Nashe'. *Modern Philology*, 111 (2014), 384–407.

Bakhtin, Mikhail. *Rabelais and His World*, trans. Hélène Iswolsky. Bloomington: Indiana University Press, 1984.

Bamborough, J. B. *The Little World of Man.* London: Longmans, 1952.

Barbour, Reid. *Deciphering Elizabethan Fiction.* Newark: University of Delaware Press; London and Toronto: Associated University Presses, 1993.

Barkan, Leonard. 'Making Pictures Speak: Renaissance Art, Elizabethan Literature, Modern Scholarship'. *Renaissance Quarterly*, 48 (1995), 326–51.

Barker, S. K. '"Newes Lately Come": European News Books in English Translation'. In *Renaissance Cultural Crossroads: Translation, Print and Culture in Britain, 1473–1640*, ed. S. K. Barker and Brenda M. Hosington. Leiden: Brill, 2013, pp. 227–44.

Barker, S. K., and Brenda M. Hosington (eds). *Renaissance Cultural Crossroads: Translation, Print and Culture in Britain, 1473–1640*. Leiden: Brill, 2013.

Barnard, John, and D. F. McKenzie (eds). *The Cambridge History of the Book in Britain, vol. 4: 1557–1695*. Cambridge: Cambridge University Press, 2002.

Baron, Sabrina A. 'The Guises of Dissemination in Early Seventeenth-Century England: News in Manuscript and Print'. In *The Politics of Information in Early Modern Europe*, ed. Brendan Dooley and Sabrina A. Baron. London: Routledge, 2001, pp. 41–56.

Bartolovich, Crystal. 'Humanities of Scale: Marxism, Surface Reading – and Milton'. *PMLA*, 127 (2012), 115–21.

Bayman, Anna. 'Printing, Learning, and the Unlearned'. In *The Oxford History of Popular Print Culture*, ed. Joad Raymond. Oxford: Oxford University Press, 2011, pp. 76–87.

Bennett, Gillian. 'Ghost and Witch in the Sixteenth and Seventeenth Centuries'. *Folklore*, 97 (1986), 3–14.

Best, Stephen, and Sharon Marcus. 'Surface Reading: An Introduction'. *Representations*, 108 (2009), 1–21.

Black, Joseph. 'The Marprelate Controversy'. In *The Oxford Handbook of English Prose*, ed. Andrew Hadfield. Oxford: Oxford University Press, 2013, pp. 544–59.

Blayney, Peter W. M. 'The Alleged Popularity of Playbooks'. *Shakespeare Quarterly*, 56 (2005), 33–50.

Bloom, Gina. *Voice in Motion: Staging Gender, Shaping Sound in Early Modern England*. Philadelphia: University of Pennsylvania Press, 2007.

Botelho, Keith M. *Renaissance Earwitnesses: Rumor and Early Modern Masculinity*. Basingstoke: Palgrave Macmillan, 2009.

Bourne, Claire L. *Typographies of Performance in Early Modern England*. Oxford: Oxford University Press, 2020.

Bristol, Michael D., and Arthur F. Marotti (eds). *Print, Manuscript & Performance*. Columbus: Ohio State University Press, 2000.

Brooks, Douglas A. (ed.). *Printing and Parenting in Early Modern England*. Farnham: Ashgate, 2005.

Brown, Georgia. *Redefining Elizabethan Literature*. Cambridge: Cambridge University Press, 2004.

Brown, Georgia (ed.). *Thomas Nashe*. Farnham: Ashgate, 2011.

Brown, Georgia. 'Sex and the City: Nashe, Ovid, and the Problems of Urbanity'. In *The Age of Thomas Nashe: Text, Bodies and Trespasses of Authorship in Early Modern England*, ed. Stephen Guy-Bray and Joan Pong Linton. Farnham: Ashgate, 2013, pp. 11–26.

Brown, Theo. *The Fate of the Dead*. Ipswich: D. S. Brewer, 1979.

Bruster, Douglas. *Shakespeare and the Question of Culture: Early Modern Literature and the Cultural Turn*. Basingstoke: Palgrave Macmillan, 2003.
Bruster, Douglas. 'The Structural Transformation of Print in Late Elizabethan England'. In *Print, Manuscript & Performance*, ed. Michael D. Bristol and Arthur F. Marotti. Columbus: Ohio State University Press, 2000, pp. 49–89.
Butler, Martin. *Theatre and Crisis, 1632–1642*. Cambridge: Cambridge University Press, 1984.
Caldwell, Melissa. *Skepticism, Belief and the Reformation of Moral Value in Early Modern England*. Abingdon: Routledge, 2016.
Campana, Joseph. *The Pain of Reformation: Spenser, Vulnerability, and the Ethics of Masculinity*. New York: Fordham University Press, 2012.
Carlton, Charles. *Archbishop William Laud*. London: Routledge, 1987.
Carson, Leland H. *Martin Marprelate, Gentleman: Master Job Throkmorton Laid Open in His Colors*. San Marino: Huntingdon Library, 1981.
Cavanagh, Dermot. 'Modes of Satire'. In *The Oxford Handbook of English Prose, 1500–1640*, ed. Andrew Hadfield. Oxford: Oxford University Press, 2013, pp. 380–95.
Cavert, William M. *The Smoke of London: Energy and Environment in the Early Modern City*. Cambridge: Cambridge University Press, 2016.
Clark, Sandra. *Elizabethan Pamphleteers; Popular Moralistic Pamphlets 1580–1640*. Rutherford: Fairleigh Dickinson University Press, 1983.
Como, David R. 'Secret Printing, the Crisis of 1640, and the Origins of Civil War Radicalism'. *Past & Present*, 196 (2007), 37–82.
Craik, Katherine A. '"The Material Point of Poesy": Reading, Writing and Sensation in Puttenham's *The Arte of English Poesie*'. In *Environment and Embodiment in Early Modern England*, ed. Mary Floyd-Wilson and Garrett A. Sullivan. Basingstoke: Palgrave Macmillan, 2007, pp. 153–70.
Cressy, David. *Birth, Marriage and Death: Ritual, Religion, and the Life-Cycle in Tudor and Stuart England*. Oxford: Oxford University Press, 1997.
Crewe, Jonathan. *Unredeemed Rhetoric: Thomas Nashe and the Scandal of Authorship*. Baltimore: Johns Hopkins University Press, 1982.
Cust, Richard. 'News and Politics in Early Seventeenth-Century England'. *Past & Present*, 112 (1986), 60–90.
Davies, Owen. *The Haunted: A Social History of Ghosts*. Basingstoke: Palgrave, 2006.
Day, Matthew. 'Hakluyt, Harvey, Nashe: The Material Text and Early Modern Nationalism'. *Studies in Philology*, 104 (2007), 281–305.
De Rycker, Kate. 'Commodifying the Author: The Mediation of Aretino's Fame in the Harvey-Nashe Pamphlet War'. *English Literary Renaissance*, 49.2 (2019), 145–71.
De Rycker, Kate. 'Guide to Folger's *Have With You to Saffron Walden*'. *The Thomas Nashe Project*. https://research.ncl.ac.uk/thethomasnasheproject/resources/digitisednasheeditions/guidetofolgershavewithyoutosaffronwalden/#d.en.429655.
De Rycker, Kate. 'The Political Function of Elizabethan Literary Celebrity'. *Celebrity Studies*, 8 (2017), 157–61.

Degenhardt, Jane Hwang, and Elizabeth Williamson (eds). *Religion and Drama in Early Modern England: The Performance of Religion on the Renaissance Stage*. Aldershot: Ashgate, 2011.

Derrida, Jacques. *Limited Inc.*, trans. Samuel Webster and Jeffrey Mehlman. Evanston, IL: Northwestern University Press, 1988.

Derrida, Jacques. *Spectres of Marx: The State of the Debt, the Work of Mourning, & the New International*, trans. Peggy Kamuf. New York and London: Routledge, 1994.

Derrida, Jacques, and Bernard Stiegler. *Echographies of Television*, trans. Jennifer Bajorek. Cambridge: Polity Press, 2002.

Dimmock, Matthew, and Andrew Hadfield (eds). *Literature and Popular Culture in Early Modern England*. Farnham: Ashgate, 2009.

Dooley, Brendan. 'International News Flows in the Seventeenth Century: Problems and Prospects'. In *News Networks in Early Modern Europe*, ed. Joad Raymond and Noah Moxham. Leiden: Brill, 2016, pp. 158–77.

Dooley, Brendan. 'Preface', in *The Dissemination of News and the Emergence of Contemporaneity in Early Modern Europe*, ed. Dooley and Sabrina A. Baron. Farnham: Ashgate, 2010.

Dooley, Brendan, and Sabrina A. Baron (eds). *The Politics of Information in Early Modern Europe*. London: Routledge, 2001.

Duncan-Jones, Katherine. 'Thomas Nashe and William Cotton: Parallel Letters, Parallel Lives'. *Early Modern Literary Studies*, 19 (2016), 1–13.

During, Simon. *Modern Enchantments: The Cultural Power of Secular Magic*. Cambridge, MA: Harvard University Press, 2002.

Ellinghausen, Laurie. *Labor and Writing in Early Modern England, 1567–1667*. Aldershot: Ashgate, 2008.

Erll, Astrid. *Memory in Culture*, trans. Sara B. Young. Basingstoke: Palgrave, 2011.

Espejo, Carmen. 'European Communication Networks in the Early Modern Age: A New Framework of Interpretation for the Birth of Journalism'. *Media History*, 17.2 (2011), 189–202.

Fallon, Samuel. *Paper Monsters: Persona and Literary Culture in Elizabethan England*. Philadelphia: University of Pennsylvania Press, 2019.

Fallon, Samuel. 'Robert Greene's Ghosts'. *Modern Language Quarterly*, 77 (2016), 193–217.

Farmer, Alan B., and Zachary Lesser. 'The Popularity of Playbooks Revisited'. *Shakespeare Quarterly*, 56 (2005), 1–32.

Farmer, Alan B., and Zachary Lesser. 'What Is Print Popularity? A Map of the Elizabethan Book Trade'. In *The Elizabethan Top Ten*, ed. Andy Kesson and Emma Smith. Farnham: Ashgate, 2013, pp. 19–55.

Fincham, Kenneth (ed.). *The Early Stuart Church, 1603–1642*. Basingstoke: Macmillan, 1993.

Fincham, Kenneth. 'Episcopal Government, 1603–1640'. In *The Early Stuart Church, 1603–1642*, ed. Kenneth Fincham. Basingstoke: Macmillan, 1993, pp. 71–92.

Fitter, Chris. '"The quarrel is between our masters and us their men": *Romeo and Juliet*, Dearth, and the London Riots'. *English Literary Renaissance*, 30 (2000), 154–83.
Floyd-Wilson, Mary, and Garrett A. Sullivan (eds). *Environment and Embodiment in Early Modern England*. Basingstoke: Palgrave Macmillan, 2007.
Fludernik, Monica. 'Scene Shift, Metalepsis, and the Metaleptic Mode'. *Style*, 37 (2003), 382–400.
Folkerth, Wes. 'Pietro Aretino, Thomas Nashe, and Early Modern Rhetorics of Public Address'. In *Making Publics in Early Modern Europe: People, Things, Forms of Knowledge*, ed. Bronwen Wilson and Paul Yachnin. Oxford and New York: Routledge, 2010, pp. 68–78.
Friedenreich, Kenneth. 'Nashe's Strange Newes and the Case for Professional Writers'. *Studies in Philology*, 71 (1974), 451–72.
Gardner, William N., and Alex Lewis. 'Hyperventilation and Disproportionate Breathlessness'. In *Supportive Care in Respiratory Disease*, ed. Sam H. Ahmedzai and Martin F. Muers. Oxford: Oxford University Press, 2011, pp. 323–38.
Genette, Gerard. *Paratexts: Thresholds of Interpretation*, trans. Jane E. Lewin. Cambridge: Cambridge University Press, 1997.
Gordon, Andrew. 'The Ghost of Pasquill: The Comic Afterlife and the Afterlife of Comedy on the Elizabethan Stage'. In *The Arts of Remembrance in Early Modern England: Memorial Cultures of the Post Reformation*, ed. Andrew Gordon and Thomas Rist. Aldershot: Ashgate, 2013, pp. 229–46.
Gordon, Andrew, and Thomas Rist (eds). *The Arts of Remembrance in Early Modern England: Memorial Cultures of the Post Reformation*. Aldershot: Ashgate, 2013.
Green, Jonathan. *The Strange and Terrible Visions of Wilhelm Friess: The Paths of Prophecy in Reformation Europe*. Ann Arbor: University of Michigan Press, 2014.
Green, Jonathan. 'The Toledo Letter in Print'. *Research Fragments*, 16 May 2014. researchfragments.blogspot.com/2014/05/the-toledo-letter-in-print.
Green, Jonathan. 'Toledo, Toledo Letter, am Toledosten'. *Research Fragments*, 5 November 2010. researchfragments.blogspot.com/2010/11/toledo-toledo-letter-am-toledosten.
Griffin, Benjamin. 'Nashe's Dedicatees: William Beeston and Richard Lichfield'. *Notes & Queries*, 44 (1997), 47–9.
Grosart, Alexander B. 'Memorial-Introduction – Biographical'. In *The Complete Works of Thomas Nashe*, 6 vols. N.p.: Huth Library, 1883, I.xi–lxxi.
Groves, Beatrice. 'Laughter in the Time of Plague: A Context for the Unstable Style of Nashe's *Christ's Tears over Jerusalem*'. *Studies in Philology*, 108 (2011), 238–60.
Guy-Bray, Stephen, Joan Pong Linton, and Steve Mentz (eds). *The Age of Thomas Nashe: Text, Bodies and Trespasses of Authorship in Early Modern England*. London: Routledge, 2016.
Guy-Bray, Stephen, and Joan Pong Linton. 'Postscript – Nashe Untrimmed: The Way We Teach Him Today'. In *The Age of Thomas Nashe: Text,*

Bodies and Trespasses of Authorship in Early Modern England, ed. Stephen Guy-Bray, Joan Pong Linton, and Steve Mentz. London: Routledge, 2016, pp. 160–82.

Hackett, Helen. *Women and Romance Fiction in the English Renaissance*. Cambridge: Cambridge University Press, 2000.

Hadfield, Andrew. 'An Interview with Thomas Kilroy', The Thomas Nashe project blog, 2017. https://thomasnashe.wordpress.com/2017/07/13/an-interview-with-thomas-kilroy/.

Hadfield, Andrew. 'Lenten Stuffe: Thomas Nashe and the Fiction of Travel'. *Yearbook of English Studies*, 41 (2011), 68–83.

Hadfield, Andrew. *Literature and Class: From the Peasants' Revolt until the French Revolution*. Manchester: Manchester University Press, 2021.

Hadfield, Andrew. '"Not without Mustard": Self-publicity and Polemic in Early Modern Literary London'. In *Renaissance Transformations: The Making of English Writing, 1500–1650*, ed. Margaret Healy and Thomas Healy. Edinburgh: Edinburgh University Press, 2009, pp. 64–78.

Hadfield, Andrew (ed.). *The Oxford Handbook of English Prose, 1500–1640*. Oxford: Oxford University Press, 2013.

Hadfield, Andrew. 'Spenser, Raleigh, Harvey, and Nashe on Empire'. *English*, 68 (2019), 143–61.

Hadfield, Andrew, and Jennifer Richards. 'Thomas Nashe: A Dominant Literary Voice in Elizabethan England'. *Shakespeare and Beyond* blog, Folger Shakespeare Library. https://shakespeareandbeyond.folger.edu/2017/09/26/thomas-nashe-elizabethan-england/.

Halasz, Alexandra. *The Marketplace of Print: Pamphlets and the Public Sphere in Early Modern England*. Cambridge: Cambridge University Press, 1997.

Halasz, Alexandra. 'The Patrimony of Learning'. In *Thomas Nashe*, ed. Georgia Brown. Farnham: Ashgate, 2011.

Hale, J. R. *Renaissance War Studies*. London: Hambledon Press, 1983.

Hardie, Philip. *Rumour and Renown: Representations of Fama in Western Literature*. Cambridge: Cambridge University Press, 2011.

Harlow, C. G. 'A Source for Nashe's *Terrors of the Night*, and the Authorship of *I Henry VI*'. *Studies in English Literature 1500–1900*, 5 (1965), 31–47.

Hasler, Rebecca. '"Tossing and turning your booke upside downe": The *Trimming of Thomas Nashe*, Cambridge, and Scholarly Reading'. *Renaissance Studies*, 33 (2019), 375–96.

Healy, Margaret, and Thomas Healy (eds). *Renaissance Transformations: The Making of English Writing, 1500–1650*. Edinburgh: Edinburgh University Press, 2009.

Helmers, Helmer. *The Royalist Republic: Literature, Politics, and Religion in the Anglo-Dutch Public Sphere, 1639–1660*. Cambridge: Cambridge University Press, 2015.

Hibbard, G. R. *Thomas Nashe: A Critical Introduction*. London: Routledge and Kegan Paul, 1962.

Hilliard, Stephen S. *The Singularity of Thomas Nashe*. Lincoln: University of Nebraska Press, 1986.

Hoenselaars, Ton (ed.). *The Cambridge Companion to Shakespeare and Contemporary Dramatists*. Cambridge: Cambridge University Press, 2012.

Holbrook, Peter. *Literature and Degree in Renaissance England: Nashe, Bourgeois Tragedy, Shakespeare*. Newark: University of Delaware Press, 1994.

Hunt, Maurice. 'Thomas Nashe, *The Vnfortvnate Traveller*, and *Love's Labour's Lost*'. *Studies in English Literature 1500–1900*, 54 (2014), 297–315.

Hutson, Lorna. *Thomas Nashe in Context*. Oxford: Oxford University Press, 1989.

Hutton, Ronald. 'The English Reformation and the Evidence of Folklore'. *Past & Present*, 148 (1995), 89–116.

Hyde, Jenni. *Singing the News: Ballads in Mid-Tudor England*. London: Routledge, 2018.

Ingold, Tim. 'Surface Visions'. *Theory, Culture & Society*, 34 (2017), 99–108.

Jacobson, Miriam. *Barbarous Antiquity: Reorienting the Past in the Poetry of Early Modern England*. Philadelphia: University of Pennsylvania Press, 2014.

Johnson, Laurie, John Sutton, and Evelyn Tribble (eds). *Embodied Cognition and Shakespeare's Theatre*. London: Routledge, 2014.

Jowett, John. 'Johannes Factotum: Henry Chettle and Greene's *Groatsworth of Wit*'. *Bibliographical Society of America*, 87 (1993), 453–86.

Kalas, Rayna. *Frame, Glass, Verse: The Technology of Poetic Invention in the English Renaissance*. Ithaca: Cornell University Press, 2007.

Kastan, David Scott. 'The Body of the Text'. *ELH*, 81.2 (2014), 443–67.

Kesson, Andy, and Emma Smith (eds). *The Elizabethan Top Ten: Defining Print Popularity in Early Modern England*. Farnham: Ashgate, 2013.

Kesson, Andy, and Emma Smith. 'Introduction: Towards a Definition of Print Popularity'. In *The Elizabethan Top Ten*, ed. Andy Kesson and Emma Smith. Farnham: Ashgate, 2013, pp. 1–16.

Kettnich, Karen. 'Nashe's Extemporal Vein and His Tarltonizing Wit'. In *The Age of Thomas Nashe: Text, Bodies and Trespasses of Authorship in Early Modern England*, ed. Stephen Guy-Bray, Joan Pong Linton, and Steve Mentz. London: Routledge, 2016, pp. 99–114.

Kinney, Arthur F. 'John Lyly and the University Wits: George Peele, Robert Greene, Thomas Lodge and Thomas Nashe'. In *The Cambridge Companion to Shakespeare and Contemporary Dramatists*, ed. Ton Hoenselaars. Cambridge: Cambridge University Press, 2012, pp. 1–18.

Kirwan, Peter. '*Mucedorus*'. In *The Elizabethan Top Ten*, ed. Andy Kesson and Emma Smith. Farnham: Ashgate, 2013, pp. 223–34.

Knight, Sarah. 'Universities', in *Cambridge History of Rhetoric. Volume 3: Rhetoric in the Renaissance*, ed. Virginia Cox and Jennifer Richards. Forthcoming.

Knoppers, Laura Lunger. *Constructing Cromwell: Ceremony, Portrait and Print, 1645–1661*. Cambridge: Cambridge University Press, 2000.

Lake, Peter, with Michael Questier. *The Antichrist's Lewd Hat: Protestants, Papists and Players in Post-Reformation England*. New Haven: Yale University Press, 2002.

Landreth, David. 'Wit without Money in Nashe'. In *The Age of Thomas Nashe: Text, Bodies and Trespasses of Authorship in Early Modern England*, ed. Stephen Guy-Bray, Joan Pong Linton, and Steve Mentz. London: Routledge, 2016, pp. 135–52.

Lesser, Zachary. *Renaissance Drama and the Politics of Publication: Readings in the English Book Trade*. Cambridge: Cambridge University Press, 2004.

Levelt, Sjoerd, and Ad Putter. *North Sea Crossings: The Literary Heritage of Anglo-Dutch Relations 1066–1688*. Oxford: Bodleian Library, 2021.

Levy, Fritz. 'The Decorum of News'. In *News, Newspapers and Society in Early Modern Britain*, ed. Joad Raymond. London: Frank Cass, 1999, pp. 12–38.

Lewis, C. S. *English Literature in the Sixteenth Century, Excluding Drama*. Oxford: Oxford University Press, 1954.

Liapi, Lena. *Roguery in Print: Crime and Culture in Early Modern London*. Woodbridge: Boydell & Brewer, 2019.

Liebler, Naomi Conn (ed.). *Early Modern Prose Fiction: The Cultural Politics of Reading*. New York: Routledge, 2007.

Loewenstein, David, and Janel Mueller (eds). *The Cambridge History of Early Modern English Literature*. Cambridge: Cambridge University Press, 2002.

Mack, Peter. *Elizabethan Rhetoric: Theory and Practice*. Cambridge: Cambridge University Press, 2002.

Manley, Lawrence. *Literature and Culture in Early Modern London*. Cambridge: Cambridge University Press, 1995.

Marshall, Peter. 'Deceptive Appearances: Ghosts and Reformers in Elizabethan and Jacobean England'. In *Religion and Superstition in Reformation Europe*, ed. Helen Parish and William G. Naph. Manchester: Manchester University Press, 2002, pp. 188–208.

Martin, Randall. *Shakespeare and Ecology*. Oxford: Oxford University Press, 2015.

Mazzio, Carla. 'The History of Air: *Hamlet* and the Trouble with Instruments'. *South Central Review*, 26 (2009), 153–96.

McEleney, Corey. 'Nashe's Vain Vein: Poetic Pleasure and the Limits of Utility'. In *The Age of Thomas Nashe: Text, Bodies and Trespasses of Authorship in Early Modern England*, ed. Stephen Guy-Bray, Joan Pong Linton, and Steve Mentz. London: Routledge, 2016, pp. 153–69.

McGinn, Donald. 'Nashe's Share in the Marprelate Controversy'. *PMLA*, 59 (1944), 952–84.

McGinn, Donald J. *Thomas Nashe*. Boston: Twayne, 1981.

McIlvenna, Una. *Singing the News of Death: Execution Ballads in Europe 1500–1900*. Oxford: Oxford University Press, 2022.

McIlvenna, Una. 'When the News was Sung: Ballads as News Media in Early Modern Europe'. *Media History*, 22 (2016), 317–33.

McInnis, David, and Matthew Steggle. 'Introduction: Nothing Will Come of Nothing? Or, What Can We Learn from Plays That Don't Exist?'. In *Lost Plays in Shakespeare's England*, ed. David McInnis and Matthew Steggle. Basingstoke: Palgrave Macmillan, 2014, pp. 1–16.

McInnis, David, and Matthew Steggle (eds). *Lost Plays in Shakespeare's England*. Basingstoke: Palgrave Macmillan, 2014.
McLuhan, Marshall. *The Gutenberg Galaxy: The Making of Typographic Man*. Toronto, Buffalo, London: Toronto University Press, 1962, rpt 2011.
McRae, Andrew. *Literature, Satire and the Early Stuart State*. Cambridge: Cambridge University Press, 2009.
Melnikoff, Kirk, and Edward Gieskes (eds). *Writing Robert Greene: Essays on England's First Notorious Professional Writer*. Farnham: Ashgate, 2008.
Melnikoff, Kirk, and Roslyn L. Knutson (eds). *Christopher Marlowe, Theatrical Commerce and the Book Trade*. Cambridge: Cambridge University Press, 2018.
Mentz, Steve. 'Day Labor: Thomas Nashe and the Practice of Prose in Early Modern England'. In *Early Modern Prose Fiction: The Cultural Politics of Reading*, ed. Naomi Conn Liebler. New York: Routledge, 2007, pp. 18–32.
Mentz, Steve. 'Forming Greene: Theorizing the Early Modern Author in the *Groatsworth of Wit*'. In *Writing Robert Greene: Essays on England's First Notorious Professional Writer*, ed. Kirk Melnikoff and Edward Gieskes. Aldershot: Ashgate, 2008, pp. 115–32.
Mentz, Steve. 'Introduction: The Age of Thomas Nashe'. In *The Age of Thomas Nashe: Text, Bodies and Trespasses of Authorship in Early Modern England*, ed. Stephen Guy-Bray, Joan Pong Linton, and Steve Mentz. London: Routledge, 2016, pp. 1–8.
Mentz, Steve. 'Nashe's Fish: Misogyny, Romance, and the Ocean in *Lenten Stuffe*'. In *The Age of Thomas Nashe: Text, Bodies and Trespasses of Authorship in Early Modern England*, ed. Stephen Guy-Bray, Joan Pong Linton, and Steve Mentz. London: Routledge, 2016, pp. 63–73.
Mentz, Steve. *Romance for Sale in Early Modern England: The Rise of Prose Fiction*. Farnham: Ashgate, 2006.
Menut, Alfred D. 'Castiglione and the Nicomachean Ethics'. *PMLA*, 58 (1943), 209–21.
Micaela, Maria Teresa. 'Promiscuous Textualities: The Nashe-Harvey Controversy and the Unnatural Productions of Print'. In *Printing and Parenting in Early Modern England*, ed. Douglas A. Brooks. Farnham: Ashgate, 2005, pp. 173–96.
Milton, Anthony. 'The Church of England, Rome and the True Church: The Demise of a Jacobean Consensus'. In *The Early Stuart Church, 1603–1642*, ed. Kenneth Fincham. Basingstoke: Macmillan, 1993, pp. 187–210.
Milton, Anthony. 'Laud, William (1573–1645), Archbishop of Canterbury'. *Oxford Dictionary of National Biography*. Oxford: Oxford University Press, 2009. https://www.oxforddnb.com/view/10.1093/ref:odnb/9780198614128.001.0001/odnb-9780198614128-e-16112.
Mottram, Stewart. *Ruin and Reformation in Spenser, Shakespeare, and Marvell*. Oxford: Oxford University Press, 2019.
Moulton, Ian Frederick. *Before Pornography: Erotic Writing in Early Modern England*. Oxford: Oxford University Press, 2002.

Mullaney, Steven. 'Affective Technologies: Towards an Emotional Logic of the Elizabethan Stage'. In *Environment and Embodiment in Early Modern England*, ed. Mary Floyd-Wilson and Garrett A. Sullivan. Basingstoke: Palgrave Macmillan, 2007, pp. 71–89.
Mullaney, Steven. *The Reformation of Emotions in the Age of Shakespeare*. Chicago and London: University of Chicago Press, 2015.
Nance, John V. 'Gross Anatomies: Mapping Matter and Literary Form in Thomas Nashe and Andreas Vesalius'. In *The Age of Thomas Nashe: Text, Bodies and Trespasses of Authorship in Early Modern England*, ed. Stephen Guy-Bray, Joan Pong Linton, and Steve Mentz. London: Routledge, 2016, pp. 115–31.
Navitsky, Joseph. 'Disputing Good Bishop's English: Martin Marprelate and the Voice of Menippean Opposition'. *Texas Studies in Literature and Language*, 50 (2008), 177–200.
Nelson, Carolyn, and Matthew Seccombe. 'The Creation of the Periodical Press 1620–1695'. In *The Cambridge History of the Book in Britain, vol. 4: 1557–1695*, ed. John Barnard and D. F. McKenzie. Cambridge: Cambridge University Press, 2002.
Newcomb, Lori. '"Social Things": The Production of Popular Culture in the Reception of Robert Greene's *Pandosto*'. *ELH*, 61 (1994), 753–81.
Newcomb, Lori Humphrey. 'What Is a Chapbook?'. In *Literature and Popular Culture in Early Modern England*, ed. Matthew Dimmock and Andrew Hadfield. Farnham: Ashgate, 2009, pp. 57–72.
Nicholl, Charles. *A Cup of News: The Life of Thomas Nashe*. London: Routledge and Kegan Paul, 1984.
Nicholl, Charles. 'Thomas Nashe'. *Oxford Dictionary of National Biography*. Oxford: Oxford University Press, 2020. https://www.oxforddnb.com/view/10.1093/ref:odnb/9780198614128.001.0001/odnb-9780198614128-e-19790.
Nielson, James. *Unread Herring: Thomas Nashe and the Prosaics of the Real*. New York: Peter Lang Publishing, 1993.
North, Michael. *Novelty: A History of the New*. Chicago: University of Chicago Press, 2013.
O'Callaghan, Michelle. *Crafting Poetry Anthologies in Renaissance England: Early Modern Cultures of Recreation*. Cambridge: Cambridge University Press, 2020.
O'Callaghan, Michelle. '"Thomas the Scholer" versus "John the Sculler": Defining Popular Culture in the Early Seventeenth Century'. In *Literature and Popular Culture in Early Modern England*, ed. Matthew Dimmock and Andrew Hadfield. Farnham: Ashgate, 2009, pp. 45–56.
Parish, Helen, and William G. Naph (eds). *Religion and Superstition in Reformation Europe*. Manchester: Manchester University Press, 2002.
Parker, Patricia. '*The Merry Wives of Windsor* and Shakespearean Translation'. *Modern Language Quarterly*, 52 (1991), 225–61.
Parry, Graham. 'Literary Patronage'. In *The Cambridge History of Early Modern English Literature*, ed. David Loewenstein and Janel Mueller. Cambridge: Cambridge University Press, 2002, pp. 117–40.

Partner, Jane. *Poetry and Vision in Early Modern England*. London: Palgrave, 2018.
Paster, Gail Kern. 'Becoming the Landscape: The Ecology of the Passions in the Legend of Temperance'. In *Environment and Embodiment in Early Modern England*, ed. Mary Floyd-Wilson and Garrett A. Sullivan. Basingstoke: Palgrave Macmillan, 2007, pp. 137–52.
Paster, Gail Kern. *Humoring the Body: Emotions and the Shakespearean Stage*. Chicago and London: University of Chicago Press, 2004.
Penteado, Bruno. 'Against Surface Reading: Just Literality and the Politics of Reading'. *Mosaic*, 52 (2019), 85–100.
Pettegree, Andrew. *The Invention of News: How the World Came to Know About Itself*. New Haven: Yale University Press, 2014.
Pierce, Helen. 'Anti-Episcopacy and Graphic Satire in England, 1640–1645'. *The Historical Journal*, 4 (2004), 809–48.
Pollard, Tanya. *Drugs and Theater in Early Modern England*. Oxford: Oxford University Press, 2005.
Pollard, Tanya. 'Spelling the Body'. In *Environment and Embodiment in Early Modern England*, ed. Mary Floyd-Wilson and Garrett A. Sullivan. Basingstoke: Palgrave Macmillan, 2007, pp. 171–86.
Poole, Kristen. *Radical Religion from Shakespeare to Milton: Figures of Nonconformity in Early Modern England*. Cambridge: Cambridge University Press, 2000.
Porter, Joseph A. *Shakespeare's Mercutio: His History and Drama*. Chapel Hill and London: University of North Carolina Press, 1988.
Preedy, Chloe Kathleen. 'The Smoke of War: From *Tamburlaine* to *Henry V*', *Shakespeare*, 15 (2019), 152–75.
Prendergast, Maria Teresa Micaela. *Railing, Reviling, and Invective in English Literary Culture, 1588–1617: The Anti-Poetics of Theatre and Print*. Farnham: Ashgate, 2012.
Purnis, Jan. 'The Belly-Mind Relationship in Early Modern Culture'. In *Embodied Cognition and Shakespeare's Theatre*, ed. Laurie Johnson, John Sutton, and Evelyn Tribble. London: Routledge, 2014, pp. 235–52.
Raymond, Joad. 'Introduction'. In *The Oxford History of Popular Print Culture*, ed. Joad Raymond. Oxford: Oxford University Press, 2011, pp. 1–14.
Raymond, Joad (ed.). *News Networks in Seventeenth-Century Britain and Europe*. London: Routledge, 2006
Raymond, Joad. 'News Networks: Putting the "News" and "Networks" Back In'. In *News Networks in Early Modern Europe*, ed. Joad Raymond and Noah Moxham. Leiden: Brill, 2016, pp. 102–29.
Raymond, Joad (ed.). *News, Newspapers and Society in Early Modern Britain*. London: Frank Cass, 1999.
Raymond, Joad (ed.). *The Oxford History of Popular Print Culture*. Oxford: Oxford University Press, 2011.
Raymond, Joad. *Pamphlets and Pamphleteering in Early Modern Britain*. Cambridge: Cambridge University Press, 2003.

Raymond, Joad, and Noah Moxham. 'News Networks in Early Modern Europe'. In *News Networks in Early Modern Europe*, ed. Joad Raymond and Noah Moxham. Leiden: Brill, 2016, pp. 1–16.
Raymond, Joad, and Noah Moxham (eds). *News Networks in Early Modern Europe*. Leiden: Brill, 2016.
Reynolds, Bryan, and Henry S. Turner. 'From *Homo Academicus* to *Poeta Publicus*: Celebrity and Transversal Knowledge in Robert Greene's *Friar Bacon and Friar Bungay* (c.1589)'. In *Writing Robert Greene: Essays on England's First Notorious Professional Writer*, ed. Kirk Melnikoff and Edward Giesk. Farnham: Ashgate, 2008, pp. 73–94.
Rhodes, Neil. *Elizabethan Grotesque*. London: Routledge & Kegan Paul, 1980.
Rhodes, Neil. 'Shakespeare's Popularity and the Origins of the Canon'. In *The Elizabethan Top Ten*, ed. Andy Kesson and Emma Smith. Farnham: Ashgate, 2013, pp. 101–22.
Richards, Jennifer. *Voices and Books in the Renaissance: A New History of Reading*. Oxford: Oxford University Press, 2019.
Richards, Jennifer, and Andrew Hadfield. 'The Edition'. *The Thomas Nashe Project*. Newcastle: Newcastle University, 2020. https://research.ncl.ac.uk/thethomasnasheproject/theedition/.
Roberts, P. B. 'Underemployed Elizabethans: Gabriel Harvey and Thomas Nashe in the *Parnassus* Plays'. *Early Theatre*, 21 (2018), 49–70.
Rooney, Ellen. 'Live Free or Describe: The Reading Effect and the Persistence of Form'. *Differences*, 21 (2010), 112–39.
Roper, Hugh Trevor. *Archbishop Laud*. 3rd edn. Basingstoke: Palgrave Macmillan, 1988.
Ryan, Kiernan. 'The Extemporal Vein: Thomas Nashe and the Invention of Modern Narrative'. In *Thomas Nashe*, ed. Georgia Brown. Farnham: Ashgate, 2011, pp. 3–16.
Ryan, Yann Ciarán. '"More Difficult from Dublin than from Dieppe": Ireland and Britain in a European Network of Communication'. *Media History*, 24 (2018), 458–76.
Saengar, Michael. *The Commodification of Textual Engagements in the English Renaissance*. Aldershot: Ashgate, 2006.
Sale, Carolyn. 'Eating Air, Feeling Smells: *Hamlet*'s Theory of Performance'. *Renaissance Drama*, 35 (2006), 145–68.
Salamone, Chris. 'Nashe's Ghosts & the Seventeenth Century', in *The Oxford Handbook of Thomas Nashe*, ed. Andrew Hadfield, Jennifer Richards and Kate De Rycker. Oxford: Oxford University Press, forthcoming 2025.
Sauer, Elizabeth. *'Paper Contestations' and Textual Communities in England, 1640–1675*. Toronto: University of Toronto Press, 2005.
Schobesberger, Nikolaus, Paul Arblaster, Mario Infelise, André Belo, Noah Moxham, Carmen Espejo, and Joad Raymond. 'European Postal Networks'. In *News Networks in Early Modern Europe*, ed. Joad Raymond and Noah Moxham. Leiden: Brill, 2016, pp. 17–63.
Scott-Warren, Jason. 'Harvey, Gabriel (1552/3–1631), Scholar and Writer'. *Oxford Dictionary of National Biography*. Oxford: Oxford University Press,

2016. https://www.oxforddnb.com/view/10.1093/ref:odnb/9780198614128. 001.0001/odnb-9780198614128-e-12517.

Scott-Warren, Jason. 'Nashe's Stuff'. In *The Oxford Handbook of English Prose, 1500–1640*, ed. Andrew Hadfield. Oxford: Oxford University Press, 2013, pp. 204–18.

Shrank, Cathy, and Kate De Rycker. 'Penniless? Project'. *The Thomas Nashe Project*. Newcastle: Newcastle University, 2020. https://research.ncl.ac.uk/thethomasnasheproject/pennilessproject/.

Sivefors, Per. '"Maymd soldiours or poore schollers": Warfare and Self-Referentiality in the Works of Thomas Nashe'. *Cahiers Élisabéthains*, 95 (2018), 62–73.

Sivefors, Per. 'Prayer and Authorship in Thomas Nashe's *Christs Teares over Jerusalem*'. *English*, 65 (2016), 267–79.

Slater, Ann Pasternak. '*Macbeth* and the *Terrors of the Night*'. *Essays in Criticism*, 28 (1978), 112–28.

Smith, Helen. '"Imprinted by Simeon such a signe": Reading Early Modern Imprints'. In *Renaissance Paratexts*, ed. Helen Smith and Louise Wilson. Cambridge: Cambridge University Press, 2011, pp. 17–33.

Smith, Helen. '"Rare poemes ask rare friends": Popularity and Collecting in Elizabethan England'. In *The Elizabethan Top Ten*, ed. Andy Kesson and Emma Smith. Farnham: Ashgate, 2013, pp. 79–100.

Smith, Helen, and Louise Wilson (eds). *Renaissance Paratexts*. Cambridge: Cambridge University Press, 2011.

Smyth, Adam. 'Almanacs and Ideas of Popularity'. In *The Elizabethan Top Ten*, ed. Andy Kesson and Emma Smith. Farnham: Ashgate, 2013, pp. 125–34.

Sprunger, Keith L. *Trumpets from the Tower: English Purtian Printing in the Netherlands, 1600–1640*. Leiden, New York, and Cologne: E. J. Brill, 1994.

Steane, J. B. 'Introduction'. In Thomas Nashe, *'The Unfortunate Traveller' and Other Works*, ed. J. B. Steane. London: Penguin, 1972, pp. 13–44.

Steggle, Matthew. *Digital Humanities and the Lost Drama of Early Modern England: Ten Case Studies*. London: Routledge, 2016.

Steggle, Matthew. 'Gabriel Harvey, the Sidney Circle, and the Excellent Gentlewoman'. *Sidney Circle Journal*, 22 (2004), 115–29.

Steggle, Matthew. *Laughing and Weeping in Early Modern Theatres*. Aldershot: Ashgate, 2007.

Stone, Walter B. 'Shakespeare and the Sad Augurs'. *The Journal of English and Germanic Philology*, 52 (1953), 457–79.

Sutton, John. *Philosophy and Memory Traces: Descartes to Connectionism*. Cambridge: Cambridge University Press, 1998.

Taylor, Charles. *Modern Social Imaginaries*. Durham, NC: Duke University Press, 2004.

Taylor, Gary. 'Shakespeare and Others: The Authorship of *Henry the Sixth, Part One*'. *Medieval & Renaissance Drama in England*, 7 (1995), 145–205.

Thomas, Keith. *The Ends of Life: Roads to Fulfilment in Early Modern England*. Oxford: Oxford University Press, 2009.

Thomson, Leslie. 'The Meaning of *Thunder and Lightning*: Stage Directions and Audience Expectations'. *Early Theatre*, 2 (1999), 11–24.
Tsentourou, Naya. 'Untimely Breathings in *The Rape of Lucrece*'. *Shakespeare*, 18 (2022), 385–407.
Turner, Henry S. 'Nashe's Red Herring: Epistemologies of the Commodity in "Lenten Stuffe" (1599)'. *ELH*, 68 (2001), 529–61.
Van Es, Bart. *Spenser's Forms of History*. Oxford: Oxford University Press, 2002.
Van Raamsdonk, Esther. *Milton, Marvell, and the Dutch Republic*. London: Routledge, 2021.
Vanhaelen, Angela, and Joseph P. Ward (eds). *Making Space Public in Early Modern Europe: Performance, Geography, Privacy*. Oxford and New York: Routledge, 2013.
Vickers, Brian. 'Thomas Kyd, Secret Sharer'. *Times Literary Supplement*, 13 April 2008, pp. 13–15.
Vivier, Eric D. 'John Bridges, Martin Marprelate, and the Rhetoric of Satire'. *English Literary Renaissance*, 44 (2014), 3–35.
Wall-Randell, Sarah. 'Marlowe's Lucan: Winding-sheets and Scattered Leaves'. In *Christopher Marlowe, Theatrical Commerce and the Book Trade*, ed. Kirk Melnikoff and Roslyn L. Knutson. Cambridge: Cambridge University Press, 2018, pp. 11–25.
Walsh, Brian. "Unkind Division': The Double Absence of Performing History in *1 Henry VI*'. *Shakespeare Quarterly*, 55 (2004), 119–47.
Walsham, Alexandra. *Providence in Early Modern England*. Oxford: Oxford University Press, 1999.
Warner, Michael. *Publics & Counterpublics*. New York: Zone Books, 2002.
Weimann, Robert. *Authority and Representation in Early Modern Discourse*, ed. David Hillman. Baltimore and London: Johns Hopkins University Press, 1996.
West, Russell. *Spatial Representations and the Jacobean Stage: From Shakespeare to Webster*. Basingstoke: Palgrave Macmillan, 2002.
White, Paul Whitfield. 'Archbishop Whitgift and the Plague in Thomas Nashe's *Summer's Last Will and Testament*'. In *Religion and Drama in Early Modern England: The Performance of Religion on the Renaissance Stage*, ed. Jane Hwang Degenhardt and Elizabeth Williamson. Aldershot: Ashgate, 2011, pp. 139–52.
Wiggins, Martin, with Catherine Richardson (eds). *British Drama 1533–1642: A Catalogue*. Oxford: Oxford University Press, 2012, II.
Wiggins, Martin, with Catherine Richardson (eds). *British Drama 1533–1642: A Catalogue*. Oxford: Oxford University Press, 2013, III.
Williams, Wes. *Monsters and Their Meanings in Early Modern Culture: Mighty Magic*. Oxford: Oxford University Press, 2011.
Willie, Rachel. 'Sensing the Visual (Mis)representation of William Laud'. *SPELL: Swiss Papers in English Language and Literature*, 34 (2017), 183–210.
Willie, Rachel. *Staging the Revolution: Drama, Reinvention and History, 1647–72*. Manchester: Manchester University Press, 2015.

Willie, Rachel. 'Viewing the Paper Stage: Civil War, Print, Theatre and the Public Sphere'. In *Making Space Public in Early Modern Europe: Performance, Geography, Privacy*, ed. Angela Vanhaelen and Joseph P. Ward. Oxford and New York: Routledge, 2013, pp. 54–75.

Wilson, Bronwen, and Paul Yachnin (eds). *Making Publics in Early Modern Europe: People, Things, Forms of Knowledge*. Oxford and New York: Routledge, 2010.

Wilson, J. Dover, and May Yardley. 'Introduction'. In Lewes Lavater, *Of Ghostes and Spirites Walking By Nyght* (1572), ed. J. Dover Wilson and May Yardley. Oxford: Oxford University Press, 1929.

Wilson, Katharine. *Fictions of Authorship in Late Elizabethan Narratives: Euphues in Arcadia*. Oxford: Oxford University Press, 2006.

Wiseman, Susan. *Drama and Politics in the English Civil War*. Cambridge: Cambridge University Press, 1998.

Wolfe, Cary. *What Is Posthumanism?* London and Ann Arbor: University of Minnesota Press, 2010.

Woodcock, Matthew. *Thomas Churchyard: Pen, Sword and Ego*. Oxford: Oxford University Press, 2018.

Woudhuysen, H. R. 'The Foundations of the Shakespeare's Text', *Proceedings of the British Academy*, 125 (2004), 69–100.

Zlatar, Antoinina Bevan. *Reformation Fictions: Polemical Protestant Dialogues in Elizabethan England*. Oxford: Oxford University Press, 2011.

INDEX

Aesop 9
Achelley, Thomas 138
Agrippa, Cornelius 15, 110, 111, 114, 123n.23, 131, 132, 174
Alexander the Great 110
Alleyn, Edward (Ned Allen) 9, 135
Allott, Robert, *England's Parnassus* 99
Amyot, Jacques 71
Anabaptists 158, 162
Apelles 53, 54
Aretino, Pietro 1, 97, 98, 121, 127, 130, 136, 138, 105n.42, 175
Ariosto 72
Aristotle 72

Bacon, Francis, *Sylva Sylvarum* 40n.79
Baldwin, William, *The Mirror for Magistrates* 116, 130
Bancroft, Richard 6, 153
Barnes, Barnabe 34
Bentley, John 138
Bird, Christopher 46, 47, 48, 56, 58, 62
Bishops' Ban 8, 18n.10, 86n.100
Bishops' Wars 156
Blount, Charles 70, 71
Blount, Edmund 116
Book of Common Prayer 153, 162
Breton, Nicholas, *A Bower of Delights* 23, 36n.6, 36n.8

Bridge, John, *Defence of the Government* 155–56
Brownists 162
Bullein, William 50
  Bulleins Bulwarke of Defence 36n.7, 64n.33
Burre, Walter 10
Burton, Robert, *The Anatomy of Melancholy* 36n.7

Caesar 170
Caligula 120
Cardano, Girolamo 112, 124n.31
Carey, Elizabeth 4, 68
Carey, George 112, 128
Catholicism 112, 156, 157, 158, 159
Chaloner, Thomas 155
Chaucer, Geoffrey 137, 138
Chettle, Henry 129
  Kind-Hart's Dream 120, 121, 139, 140, 142
Children of Paul's 8
Churchyard, Thomas 116
Chute, Anthony 34
Cicero 72, 110, 114–115, 130, 131, 132, 170, 174, 175
Civil War(s) 4, 147, 156, 162
Cope, Michael 50, 51, 52, 53
  A Godly and Learned Exposition 64n.31, 64n.39, 64n.45
Coryate, Thomas 157
Cotton, William 8

Croft, James 57
Cromwell, Oliver 157

Danter, John 140
Darrell, John 101
Dekker, Thomas 98, 130, 138, 139, 141, 143, 175
  A Knight's Conjuring 122, 137, 139
  News from Hell 121, 135–136, 137, 143, 145n.50
Deloney, Thomas 119, 142
De Montaigne, Michel 26
De Vere, Edmund 57
Dickenson, John 125n.75, 130
Diocletian 118
Diogenes 82
Doleta, John (fictional) 14, 43, 44, 46, 47, 49, 52, 54, 55, 58, 61, 65n.63, 65n.64
Drayton, Michael, 'To my most dearely-loved friend Henry Reynolds' 99, 100
Dutch Revolt 57

Elderton, William 119, 141, 142
Elizabethan Church Settlement 6
Elyot, Thomas, *The dictionary of Syr Thomas Eliot Knyght* 40n.67
episcopacy 6, 115, 152–53, 156, 157
Erasmus, Desiderius 17n.2, 114, 132, 176n.10
  Adages 53
  Praise of Folly 2, 155

Fletcher, John, *The Tamer Tamed* 36n.8
Foxe, John, *Book of Martyrs* 128
Freeman, Thomas 101
  Rubbe, and A Great Cast Epigrams 104n.11
Fulke, William, *A Goodly Gallerye* 40n.63

Galataeon 78
Galen, *On the Usefulness of the Parts of the Body* 39n.49
Gosson, Stephen, *The School of Abuse* 25, 26, 29, 38n.26, 32, 41n.83, 155
Greene, Robert 8, 33, 90, 91, 92, 93, 97, 98, 99, 102, 119, 120, 121, 129, 130, 131, 138–39, 140, 141, 153, 174, 175
  A Disputation 94
  Greene's Groats-worth of Wit 20n.46, 120, 139
  Greene's Never Too Late 91, 92
  Gwydonius 92
  Mamillia 92
  Menaphon 6, 34, 72, 73, 74, 75, 76, 79, 91, 173
  Pandosto 94
  A Quip for an Upstart Courtier 91

Hakluyt, Richard 24
Harborne, William 24
Harington, John, *A Prophesy* 102
Harsnett, Samuel 101
Harvey circle 6, 94, 174
Harvey, Gabriel 14, 17, 24, 31, 32, 33, 34, 35, 38n.21, 44, 46, 47, 48, 54, 56, 58, 62, 69, 91, 100, 102, 115, 118, 119, 120, 132, 133, 140, 141, 142, 151, 153, 157, 160, 173, 175
  A New Letter of Notable Contents 6, 38n.20, 55
  Four Letters, and Certain Sonnets 6, 20n.34, 33, 46, 47, 56, 57, 58, 61, 83n.14, 119, 140
  Pierce's Supererogation 1–2, 6, 37n.12, 40n.68, 33, 34, 42n.106, 37n.11, 37n.12, 39n.46, 40n.68, 41n.86, 42n.106, 55, 59, 60, 61, 119, 133, 86n.92
  Three Proper, and Witty, Familiar Letters 57

INDEX

Harvey, John 46, 54, 91, 121
  A Discoursive Problem 46
Harvey, Richard, 6
  Astrological Discourse 46
  Lamb of God 6, 60, 121
Heylyn, Peter 101
Heywood, Thomas 133, 137
Hippocrates 34
Hodgkins, John 153
Holland, Philemon 71
Homer 52, 78, 97
Hooker, Richard 158
Horace 75, 170
Howard, Henry, *A Defensative* 107
humanism 1, 24, 114, 153, 154, 174

Inns of Court 8

James, Thomas, *The Jesuit's Downfall* 101
Jonson, Ben 26, 98
  Bartholomew Fair 141
  Every Man in His Humour 25
  Isle of Dogs 8
Judson, Thomas 29

King, Humphrey, *An Halfpennyworth of Wit* 98
Kyd, Thomas 138
  The Spanish Tragedy 130

Langbaine, Gerard, *An Account of the English Dramatic Poets* 100
Laud, William 16, 147, 154, 156, 159, 163
Lavater, Lewes, *Of Ghosts and Spirits* 107, 108, 111
Le Loyer, Pierre, *Discourse of Spectres* 107, 111, 112
Lichfield, Richard 49
  The Trimming of Thomas Nashe 6, 38n.21, 40n.69, 41n.86
Lodge, Thomas, *A Treatise of the Plague* 40n.79, 40n.82, 41n.96, 41n.97

Lucan, *Pharsalia* 116
Lucian, *Dialogues of the Dead* 121, 130
Lyly, John 6, 148, 153
  Campaspe 110
  Euphues and His England 50
  Euphues: The Anatomy of Wit 50, 51

Machiavelli, Niccolò 130
Marbeck, John, *A Book of Notes* 71
Marlowe, Christopher 133, 138–39
  Doctor Faustus 110, 111, 174
  First Book of Lucan 116, 135, 141
Marprelate controversy 6, 7, 15, 16, 88, 89, 90, 95, 97, 101, 115, 147, 148–150, 152, 154, 159, 162, 163, 175
Marshalsea 11
Meres, Francis, *Palladis Tamia* 99
Middleton, Thomas 98, 122, 130, 135, 143, 175
  Father Hubburd's Tales 121
  The Black Book 134, 145n.43
Mills, Richard 49
Munday, Anthony 153

Nabbes, Thomas 100
Nashe, Thomas (reputation) 2–3, 56, 98
  An Almond for a Parrot 92, 96, 115
  Christ's Tears Over Jerusalem 4, 6, 13, 25, 34, 74, 91, 92, 155
  Dido Queen of Carthage (likely author, with Christopher Marlowe) 8
  Doctor Faustus (likely author, with Christopher Marlowe) 8
  Fearful and Lamentable Effects of Two Dangerous Comets (possible author) 46, 54
  'Gentlemen Students' 34, 39n.53, 41n.102, 84n.36, 84n.37, 84n.38

INDEX

Have With You to Saffron Walden 2, 6, 24, 25, 27, 30, 31, 33, 34, 36, 37n.8, 39n.36, 40n.75, 40n.81, 41n.88, 41n.92, 41n.97, 41n.105, 42n.110, 47, 55, 58, 62, 91, 92, 93, 94, 104n.14, 117, 118, 121, 133
I Henry VI (likely author, with William Shakespeare & other[s]) 8, 9–10, 26, 113
Isle of Dogs (with Ben Jonson) 8, 11, 26, 86n.100, 128
Lenten Stuff 11, 12, 14, 37n.13, 26, 27, 28, 31, 37n.13, 38n.20, 39n.36, 41n.105, 68, 77, 78, 79, 80, 81, 82, 87n.126, 92, 98, 112, 119
'Letter to William Cotton' 20n.48
Pierce Penniless 4–5, 6, 7n.42, 7n.43, 8–9, 12, 13, 15, 18n.3, 22n.81, 25, 27, 30, 34, 39n.36, 39n.54, 40n.57, 40n.58, 40n.60, 40n.61, 41n.92, 41n.104, 51, 60, 76, 77, 78, 91, 92, 93, 94, 95, 96, 100, 106n.74, 107, 108, 111, 113, 114, 118, 119, 120, 130, 132, 133, 134, 137, 140, 142, 160
'Somewhat to Read' 22n.90, 22n.91, 42n.106, 36n.7, 37n.15, 38n.22, 39n.33, 42n.106, 42n.110
Strange News 6, 18n.5, 18n.8, 18n.13, 32, 33, 41n.93, 37n.8, 40n.78, 41n.93, 42n.109, 42n.110, 43, 44, 46, 47, 52, 53, 54, 57, 58, 60, 61, 62, 92, 115, 116, 118, 119, 128, 140, 141, 142
Summer's Last Will and Testament 7, 10, 11–13, 27, 38n.32, 49, 92, 109, 130, 134, 144n.20, 174
Terminus & Non Terminus (possible co-author) 7, 49

The Anatomy of Absurdity 14, 35, 43, 46, 47, 49, 50, 52, 53, 54, 58, 59, 61, 62, 63n.10, 63n.12, 68, 70, 71, 73, 74, 75, 76, 77, 79, 80, 85n.67, 92, 95, 105n.40, 121
The May-Game of Martinism (lost play) 8, 10
The Terrors of the Night 15, 27, 28, 31, 32, 41n.93, 46, 54, 67, 68, 92, 96, 104n.18, 107, 108, 111, 112, 113, 124n.32, 124n.33, 129, 174
The Unfortunate Traveller 1, 13, 15, 28, 40n.56, 37n.12, 40n.56, 42n.109, 51, 74, 92, 110, 114, 127, 128, 131, 136, 141, 155, 170, 171, 172
Newman, Thomas 14, 23

Overton, Richard 167n.47
Ovid 72, 114, 130, 132, 170
    Amores 32, 84n.40
    Metamorphoses 36n.4

Page, William, trans. *Celio Curione* 86n.78
Parnassus plays 16
Peele, George 138–39
Penry, John 88, 158, 165n.9
Perkins, William 108
Phillips, Edward 99
Pico Della Mirandola, Gianfrancesco, *On the Imagination* 40n.58
Pictorius, Georgius 92
    De Illorum Daemonum 107, 108, 118
Plato 114
    Phaedrus 76
Plautus 114, 132
Pliny the Elder 64n.46
Pliny the Younger 108
Plutarch, *Moralia* 70–1, 73, 84n.26
Pound, Ezra 76
Presbyterianism 152, 157

Privy Council 11
Prynne, William 161
　Histriomastix 159, 160
Puttenham, George 25, 26
　The Art of English Poesy 30, 75
Pythagoras 136

Rabelais, François, *Gargantua and Pantagruel* 2
Ramus, Petrus 53
Rankins, William 33, 51
　The English Ape 64n.36
Reformation 4, 156
regicide 4
Regiomontanus 46
Restoration 4, 154
Rich, Barnabe 129
Roper, H. 50
　The Instruction of a Christian Man 64n.32
Roscius 9, 130

Sallust 170
Sappho 118
Sarum Missal 153
Scot, Reginald, *Discovery of Witchcraft* 107
Scotto, Girolano 110
Seneca 118, 120, 130, 131
Shakespeare, William 26, 139, 169, 174
　Antony and Cleopatra 35, 41n.103
　Hamlet 130
　I Henry VI (likely with Thomas Nashe & other[s]) 8, 9–10, 26, 113
　Richard III 160
　Romeo and Juliet 128
　The Rape of Lucrece 39n.32
Sheppard, Samuel 101, 164
　God and Mammon 163
Sidney, Philip 5, 24, 26, 31, 99, 129
　Arcadia 23
　Astrophel and Stella 14, 23, 34, 38n.22, 72, 79
　Defence of Poesy 40n.66, 38n.27, 75
Simmes, Valentine 29
Socrates 76, 96
Spenser, Edmund 57, 99, 129, 137, 138
　Complaints 36n.4
　Faerie Queene 84n.35, 137
　The Ruines of Time 36n.4
St Paul's Churchyard 4, 67, 116, 133, 141, 142
Stuart, Charles I; King 156, 157, 158
Stuart, James VI and I; King 158
Stubbs, John 95

Talbot, John 9, 10, 15, 113–114, 132
Tarlton, Richard 7, 24, 93, 101, 150, 151, 152, 156, 164
Taylor, John 7, 16, 98, 115, 122, 147, 157, 158, 159, 160, 161, 162, 164, 175
　Crop-ear Curried 117, 157, 159
　Differing Worships 117, 157, 167n.49, 167n.50
　Tom Nash His Ghost: or The Currying of Crop-eare 168n.53
Terence 170
Thales of Miletus 53
Thorpe, Thomas 116, 135, 141
Toy 12, 109, 131, 134
Tudor, Elizabeth I; Queen 135, 158
Tudor, Henry VIII; King 13, 109, 131, 157

University of Cambridge 1, 16, 49, 60, 100, 128, 170
Urban VIII; Pope 156

Vaughan, William, *The Newlanders' Cure* 106n.73, 168n.64
Virgil 170

Waldegrave, Robert, *Hey Any Work for Cooper* 150
Watson, Thomas 138

Wentworth, Thomas 157
Winstanley, William, *Lives of the Most Famous English Poets* 99–100
Whetstone, George 54
  The Enemie to Unthryftinesse 65n.60

Whitgift, John 6, 7, 11, 13, 109, 128, 152, 153, 156, 158
Wolfe, John 6
Wood, Anthony 88

Zeuxis 71, 72, 75, 84n.35

Milton Keynes UK
Ingram Content Group UK Ltd.
UKHW031420111224
452151UK00004B/89